# THE POTTER'S HAND

A. N. Wilson

# THE
# POTTER'S
# HAND

ATLANTIC BOOKS
LONDON

First published in Great Britain in 2012 by Atlantic Books,
an imprint of Atlantic Books Ltd

Copyright © A. N. Wilson, 2012

1 3 5 7 9 10 8 6 4 2

A CIP catalogue record for this book is available
from the British Library.

Hardback ISBN: 978-1-84887-951-5
Trade Paperback ISBN: 978-1-84887-952-2
E-book ISBN: 978-0-85789-916-3

Printed in Great Britain by the MPG Books Group

Atlantic Books
An imprint of Atlantic Books Ltd
Ormond House
26–27 Boswell Street
London WC1N 3JZ

www.atlantic-books.co.uk

The Men that invent new Trades, Arts or Manufactures, or new Improvements in Husbandry, may be properly called Fathers of their Nation

~Benjamin Franklin

# PART ONE

## The Frog Service

# I

THE UNOILED HINGE JOINED ITS MELANCHOLY WHINE TO
the opium-dosed whimper of the patient who sat gagged in his chair,
and to the swift rasping of the saw. The door creaked ajar in the very
moment that the doctor sawed off the leg of Sukey's Pa.

—B-b-best done fast, Dr Darwin was saying, and whether Mr
Bent, who performed the operation, was following advice, or moving
fast by instinct, to get the whole cruel necessity over as quickly as
possible, who was to say? Certainly not a child aged two, who saw it
through the crack in the door: the saw going through flesh and bone,
the blood splashing.

No one had intended the child to be within earshot, or sight, of
the gruesome event. But the Brick House was not especially large.
When the child was born, her mother's screams could be heard not
only in every corner of the house, but in every house for yards
around in Burslem, that undulating little village. Indeed, all the thirty
hands in the adjoining works had heard her hollering. But today,
when the Master was to undergo his 'execution', as it had been
termed by Heffie Bowers, the hands were quiet, going about their
business in a subdued mood, speaking in hushed voices, as if a death
had occurred. As well it might. Most died from the pain and the
shock of amputation, which is why, both doctors said, it could not be
done fast enough. Heffie said that when one of her uncles, who went

for a soldier, had his arm off, he'd passed out just at the sight of the saw. Rusty. *It wunna clane, lahk*, and looked as if the blood of other executions still clung to it.

You'd hope better from Mr Bent, of course. He was the best surgeon in the district, and rode over from Newcastle-under-Lyme to administer potions to the hands. Bent had delivered all three of Mrs Wedgwood's children.

Richard, the baby, was scarcely a year old on the day of the execution, and himself sickly that day. John, almost always known as Jack, was a puling twenty months. It was the knowing little Sukey who was at large, in the next room. Sally, her mother, had assumed that Heffie was minding her. Baby Richard was screaming, it was only colic, Heffie was sure, and he had woken Jack, who was letting out his usual roars, and Annie the nursery maid was unable to quiet either of them. Such a commotion was the last thing that either Mr Bent or Mr Jos would want at that moment, and Heffie had gone upstairs to loll and lah and rock the little ones.

So Sukey was alone in the little panelled eating-room. In the adjoining parlour, with its pretty apple-green panels, the patient sat, without his breeches, in a chair covered with Turkish towels. His wife, Sally, held one of his hands, and Dr Darwin stood with a hand on one of his shoulders. Mr Bentley was there too, Josiah's friend and business partner.

—Oh, Jos, said his wife.

—Do you feel the effects of the laudanum, sir? Mr Bent had enquired. There was a quaver in his voice as he had produced the fret-saw from its case.

—What must be done, must be done, said Josiah Wedgwood. The evenness with which he spoke, the absence of slurring, demonstrated to his horrified hearers that he was still conscious.

—Perhaps w-w-we should wait a few more minutes, s-s-sir, for the narcotics to take effect, stammered Dr Darwin, whose large fleshy hand stopped kneading the patient's shoulder and reached out for Sal's hand.

It was then, with the whine of the unoiled hinge, that the door had swung open a few inches. It was easily wide enough for Sukey to view the spectacle. Afterwards, it became part of the family legend that she had spied on the execution. She 'remembered' the story, but whether she remembered the event was a matter about which she would change her mind in the course of the next forty-nine years. Was memory something which was carried about in one's brain, or did the brain, so to say, retain the capacity to repeat stories to itself, supplying images and incidents which fluctuated and altered with the perspective of time? Their friend Coleridge would write about images on the surface of a stream passing away when a stone was scattered, and then re-forming – though not in his mind.

Mr Bent had lifted the linen sheet in which he had wrapped his patient. When Dr Darwin, partly with an involuntary pleasantry, partly in deadly earnest, spoke, he did so for both the Wedgwoods.

—Remember to c-c-cut off the right leg, I entreat, he said.

Darwin wedged the gag into his patient's mouth. There reaches a point where the surgeon's task is inseparable from the torturer's, which is why the faint-hearted should never enter the medical profession. Her husband squeezed Sally's hand so tightly that she thought he would crunch her bones. The saw began its work. The first thing to happen was a fountain of blood, spattering all the towelling which had been laid in circles round the chair as well as the clothes of those who stood by. With each motion of the saw, with its dreadful butcher's-shop scrapings, Wedgwood flinched and shook his upper body.

—If you were able, sir, to remain stiller, said Mr Bent.

The scrunching changed to a slithering, as when the chump chops have been placed on the butcher's board, and he has turned to slice steaks. All the colour from Josiah Wedgwood's normally rosy face had vanished. He inhaled deeply through his nose, and then out through his mouth, several times, but no further whimper, no cry came from him.

—It is done, sir. And now I must dress the wound.

—It were clumsier than the way our Caleb ud darn a sock, not that ah'd let 'im loose wi' me needles!

So Heffie had declared, when she had helped to dress the wounds in after days. And, however clumsy the needlework, during all this, the stitching and the swabbing, Wedgwood was unable to remain silent. The first stabbing of the darning needle made him yelp. Darwin held out a small phial of laudanum to the patient's lips. When he had swallowed some more of the narcotic drops, Wedgwood let out the little yowl which a dog might emit while he thrashed, and then he slumped. This was the moment, as Mr Bent would later confess, when a patient often dies, either through loss of blood or through sheer pain.

Sukey, a thin little fairy with wavy mouse-blonde hair and a long face un-childlike in its attentive stare, its pallor, its obliquity, looked at the participants in the drama: Mr Bent, swabbing and dabbing; her mother being comforted by the gargantuan, stammering figure of Dr Darwin; and the remarkable person who sat in the chair minus his right leg, her father, Josiah Wedgwood, Master Potter.

One day, far in the future, when her father was dead, Sukey would marry the son of Dr Darwin. Her child, the grandchild of Josiah Wedgwood and Erasmus Darwin, would be Charles Darwin, whose theories about the Origin of Species by Natural Selection would revolutionize the world. From the loins of Josiah Wedgwood and Erasmus Darwin would spring a great intellectual dynasty. From thence came Tom Wedgwood, Josiah's son, who was the pioneer of photography; Ralph Vaughan Williams, whose music captured the English soul; Veronica Wedgwood, whose histories of the Civil Wars evoked the English past; Gwen Raverat the engraver; and dozens of others. But at present, as the little girl Sukey watched them patch up the stump of her father's leg, it was 1768. Across the seas, the Massachusetts Assembly was dissolved for refusing to assist in the collection of taxes. Louis XV had just completed the building of Le Petit Trianon at Versailles for his mistress Madame de Pompadour. The author of *Tristram Shandy* had just died in London. His body would be snatched from its grave and appear a few days later on a slab in the Cambridge dissecting room of Charles Collignon. One of the students standing by was a parishioner of Sterne's and passed out at viewing the corpse of 'Parson Yorick'. Such are the strange quirks which occur in real life, but which we dare not introduce into fiction. It was not Josiah Wedgwood who would die at this date. He had other works to do. It was Richard Wedgwood, the baby whose cries could be heard while his father's leg was removed, who died five days after the amputation.

# 2

AND NOW, SEVEN YEARS HAVE PASSED. AND WHAT SWISS goose supplied the feather which is now being clutched by a secretary in a wig, as he sits at a small table in the Château de Ferney hard by Lake Geneva?

Beyond the long window, overlooking the back of the château, is framed a view of formal gardens and, beyond the low box hedges, there are the Alps. And in obedience to his master's voice, the secretary scratches the words across the page. The wet ink shines on the quill's tip, as, hopping from one leg, at the other end of the bedchamber, a very old, very thin man gets dressed. He smells, the old man. He smells partly of urine, and partly of that decayed old-man smell which almost all ancient people have when they emerge from a night's sleep.

François-Marie Arouet skips gently, thrusting the withered hams into his breeks. François-Marie has been left behind in sleep. It is once again Voltaire who arises, Voltaire whose words echo across the world, threatening thrones and altars, but above all altars. From this Swiss château the famous playwright has become the voice of dissent everywhere. From this new-built famous spot, he has vowed to wipe out the Infamy – the Infamous Superstitions of the Roman Church, the Infamous Privilege of the Old Order – and to replace it with Reason, with Reasonableness, with Light.

His playful spaniel larks about as the great man balances on one leg and inserts one skinny calf into his breeches, his nightshirt rides up his scrawny shank, and his nightcap, a forlorn mitre, droops on his head. He is now over eighty. His cheeks are quite hollow. His nose and chin are sharp as a corpse's. His eyes luminesce, coruscate, with irrepressible glee, for he senses the world going his way.

As the philosopher-playwright paused, stocking in hand, his little dog grabbed the sock and nearly pulled him over. Voltaire shook the garment.

—Let go! Yeki, let go!

He named the spaniel bitch Yeki after Yekaterina, the great Empress of Russia, for they lived in times when the hierarchies of things were reversed. Though he could be a courtier with the best of them, and lard the enlightened despots – Frederick of Prussia and Catherine of Russia – with compliments to their learning, their foresight, their musicality, and in the case of the substantial German ruler of Russia, their sexual allure, both sides in these courtly friendship-games knew who was the master. Frederick and Catherine, perhaps alone among the European potentates, were intelligent enough to understand the inexorable march of change.

—Yeki, I say, let go!

The dog pulled vigorously on the well-made stockings, but the old man's grip was tighter than a spaniel's jaw, and he pulled the sock, moist with dribble, out of the animal's mouth. He sat down again on his bed to pull on the stockings.

—Should we write to Mr Franklin? he mused aloud to the secretary. He is in Paris, and wrote to us yesterday. It would be good to hear at first hand.

Voltaire shrugged, smiling to himself. Franklin was a coarse fellow, but a brilliant one. Not only was he tapping, with his experiments in Natural Philosophy, the very forces of Nature itself – tapping the electrical power of lightning, even – but he also, this Boston tallow-chandler, was alive to the no less explosive convulsions which prepared themselves to ignite the world. His 'Edict of the King of Prussia' a few years back had been enjoyed by Frederick himself as well as by Voltaire. In the Edict, Frederick had imposed taxes on the inhabitants of England because they were a colony, so to say, settled long ago by Angles, Saxons and Jutes from old Germany. All the arguments deployed by the King in Franklin's satirical pamphlet were the ones used by Lord North's ludicrous Ministry in London to impose taxes upon their colonists in America. And now Franklin had himself been in London, and in Paris, arguing the colonists' case. It would have been good to discuss these matters with him. Voltaire was an Anglophile and the dispute between the thirteen colonies and the old country was a distress to him. But there could be no doubts about where justice lay. The English would win the battles in the short term. It was said that the Virginians had sent a ship to France to buy ammunition, but what could untrained farmers from America do against the thousands of German mercenaries at King George's disposal? The English would send their redcoats to put down any insurrection which the Americans might offer. The colonists would, Voltaire had little doubt, submit. But it was ideas, the idea of Liberty, the idea of an independent republic without kings, that would ultimately prevail.

So, to whom should the next letter of the morning be written? Letters had been flooding in to express sympathy upon the illness of his beloved niece Madame Denis. The ancient cynical face creased with contempt as he read them. These bloodhounds wanted him, by one hint or phrase, to admit in writing what everyone knew, that this woman, his niece, was also his lover. Since 'everyone' knew it, why should he bother either to confess to it, or to deny? God knew the truth.

With his breeks, breeches and stockings on, Voltaire now padded
to the window. It was a beautiful March day in this year of 1775. He
could see the new church which he had recently had built – with its
Latin inscription in its porch: DEO EREXIT VOLTAIRE. 'Voltaire
built this for God'. Was it an act of piety, or was it like his letters to
King Frederick and the Empress Catherine – a polite reminder to an
old potentate that they both knew now who truly was the Master?
His correspondence, and all his sycophantically expressed courtship
of Frederick and Catherine, were elegantly disguised instructions:
that if monarchy was to survive, it could do so only on Voltaire's
enlightened terms. God too had been served notice. If He were a
mere hypothesis, and explanation for how things be – well and
good. If He were the First Cause of Mr Franklin's electricity, then the
First Cause could rest secure, with Voltaire's blessing, untroubled by
His creation. He could sit back, having set in motion the intricate
machine of the universe, and allow the more intelligent men and
women of Europe and America to set it into some kind of reasonable order. But if God thought He could come back with all the
mummery of the Middle Ages and all the power over human minds
of the Inquisition, then He must think again!

Unable to think, for the moment, of anything further he had to
say to his Creator, Voltaire said to the secretary,

—Let us write to the Empress of Russia.

*Madame, vous avez posé une question à l'ancien malade de Ferney
au sujet des Anglais, toujours un sujet—*

*Madam, you have put a question about the English to the old sick
man of Ferney—*

—Let me see her last letter, said Voltaire to the secretary.
Fumbling in the bureau, the secretary found the last effusion of the
Empress, written in French, in her large-bottomed German hand.

The Empress kept up a regular correspondence with the old

gentleman and each of her letters made clear her fervent admiration. His *Lettres Philosophiques*, of which she was especially fond, described his visit to England in 1726 and his belief that, with all its faults and foibles, England was freer and more enlightened than his own benighted France. He was always too ironically subtle and yet too sycophantic to spell out the fact that England was, and always would be, a good deal more enlightened than Catherine's benighted Russia!

The old sage, who had visited London nearly fifty years before, had in fact, as a young man, been dazzled by the extent of toleration, political enlightenment, freedom of expression and thought. It puzzled him all the more, this quarrel with America. Was George III trying to behave like a Russian tyrant? He could hardly ask the question in a letter to Catherine. For a while, having cleared his throat, he dictated generalities. By the time a prolific and opinionated man has reached Voltaire's age, he can scarcely hold back the flow of self-parodying generalization.

*—and taken all in all, Madame, the English are a reasonable Nation. But it would be a mistake ever to take this Reasonableness for granted. In the matter of Shakespeare, for example, there is an incomprehensible national madness. I told their most celebrated actor, M. Garrick, that I could see no merit whatsoever in* Romeo and Juliet. *A young man meets a thirteen-year-old girl and decides that his whole happiness depends upon marrying her sur le coup. With no canonical precedent or justification, a member of the Franciscan order not only consents to this, but administers narcotics to the young woman which will render her totally insensible – giving her the appearance of death itself. And this is the stuff of realism! This is their great love drama! Garrick is a reasonable man, and by his acting he tries to make natural, and reasonable, passions which Shakespeare has only disfigured and exaggerated in the most ridiculous manner! Garrick merely chided me for being 'an amiable barbarian'!*

*But, Madame, you ask of M. Wedgwood. Naturally, I have heard of his prodigious invention of an English pottery to rival even the finest productions of Sèvres. Indeed, he has flattered me by producing a portrait bust of this ancient invalid of Ferney, which the old man is vain enough to have in his library alongside Houdon's portrait-bust and another of the Emperor Marcus Aurelius. I also possess a portrait medallion of myself in M. Wedgwood's exquisite white biscuit ware. (Where does he find such white clay outside China?)*

*He has arisen to prominence in England long since my own departure from that mysterious land. As well as being a distinguished ceramicist he is also a Natural Philosopher, who has made many experiments into geology. He belongs to a philosophical circle who discuss such developments of human knowledge as Electricity, and the properties of Matter. His friends are M. Priestley, Dr Darwin, M. Watt, a pioneer of industrial engineering and whose invention of a steam-powered engine I should love to import into my small manufactory at Ferney. So, all in all, a group of philosophes likeminded with Your Imperial Majesty and myself. It was a happy chance that Lord Cathcart had been the British Minister at St Petersburg. Lady C., as Your Imperial Highness knows, is the sister of Sir William Hamilton, whose discoveries of Italian and Etruscan antiquities have done so much to inspire M. Wedgwood, and it was a happy fortune that M. Baxter in London was able to facilitate your order and to put you in touch with M. Wedgwood.*

*The dinner service which M. Wedgwood has already made for Your Imperial Highness sounds exquisite. Twenty-four pieces of the most formidable ceramic work — not china, I note, but M. Wedgwood's own invention of 'Creamware' — a new word to add to my English vocabulary! I myself possess a tea set and a dinner service made by M. Wedgwood and I can only echo Your Majesty's delight, not only in their beauty, but in their practicality: the jugs truly pour, the lids of the bowls and tureens actually fit. When piled up, the plates fit together as neatly as if they are made of paper.*

*And now, Your Imperial Majesty has decided on a truly Imperial commission for M. Wedgwood – nearly a thousand pieces for your palace of the Finnish Frogs, the Kekerekeksinen. Our English friends would find a drollerie, perhaps, in Your Majesty asking the advice of a famous 'Frog' Philosopher for your 'Frog' Palace.*

*But, I pray you, do not listen to Sir William when he requests a dinner service of a design which he deems to be 'classical'. True, M. Wedgwood makes exquisite copies of Etruscan and Roman originals. And if Your Imperial Majesty wanted to eat soup from a dish of gambolling Dryads, and sturgeon from a plate depicting Poseidon or Aphrodite, M. Wedgwood would be the best man in Europe to gratify your Imperial desire. But would it not be in every way more original, more amusing and more comme il faut to ask that honest son of English clay to celebrate his own country – to decorate Your Imperial Highness's service with Topographick and Architectural Scenes of the Island of Britain? Here you could view a great Duke's house, as it were Chatsworth or Blenheim. Here you could see the poor huts of Hebridean fisher-folk. Here a park, and there a mountain. And so through the hundreds of views which M. Wedgwood could supply Your Majesty you would begin to build up a picture of this strange kingdom. We watch – we enlightened ones of the world! – with wonder as the Ministry in London quarrels with the coarse but honest colonists of America! Come what may, England, that land of paradox, will always hold a special place in the heart of the sickening, and ageing, Methuselah of Lake Geneva.*

# 3

—THEY DON'T SEEM TO COMPREHEND, THOSE MERCENARY fools they sent over here – we're all trained fighters! Trained to shoot. Trained to use a gun. More than any Englishman is likely to be.

—Yes, sir, but we are trained to shoot the wolf and the bear. To defend our homes against the Indian savage. Not to fight fellow Englishmen.

—It won't come to that.

—Didn't you just hear what Bowood said? The fighting has started.

—It was a skirmish that got out of hand. A skirmish is not a battle. Still less a war.

—I tell you, my boy came down from Concord last night. That was no fuckin' skirmish. If Paul Revere hadn't ridden out and warned 'em to reach for their muskets, those boys in Lexington would have been slaughtered. As it is, there were boys killed up there.

—Hal, no one doubts there's been some shooting. But a shooting don't make no war. Don't you remember what John Adams keeps a-sayin' – we're part of the British Dominions!

—And what do we get for it? Sausage-eating mercenary soldiers shootin' our little boys. By Christ, Bowood, one of them lads up at Lexington was sixteen, fuck it.

While this conversation took place in Strong's, the good new coffee-house lately opened in Pell Street, New York City, a young man of twenty-four sat in a neighbouring booth reading his correspondence from England. Tom Byerley was well made, and well dressed. His angular, bony face was divided by a pronounced Roman nose. His chin was sharp. His eyes, which were of so dark a blue that many, when they remembered him, thought of them as brown, were deep set, and shone with an intelligent knowledge of the effect which he produced upon his company. He knew himself to be highly attractive to women, and it was a knowledge which had led to his present predicament – love affairs with two women at once, and the near certainty that he was about to conquer a third.

Time was when Tom Byerley would have been highly contented with this state of things. But the affair with Mrs Aylmer, the wife of the theatre proprietor, was quite out of control. Mrs Aylmer, a handsome woman some fifteen years Tom's senior, had professed herself so inflamed with love that she was going to inform her husband. This course of action would not only have cost Tom his employment in the theatre company, but it would also have thrown him back, penniless, on the sole company of the lady herself. And the truth of the matter was that, however happy he was when they were alone together in the lady's bedchamber, her conversation was so tedious that he could scarcely endure the hours of dinner with her after their lovemaking. The prospect which she held out to him – of their eloping with her small savings and fleeing to some other city, perhaps to the capital, Philadelphia – was the stuff of which nightmares are made.

There was also the disagreeable fact that, were his intrigue with Mrs Aylmer to become public, he would be constrained to own the affair to Polly Dwyer, an actress of his own age with whom he sometimes supposed himself in love. Whenever the occasion permitted, and when Mrs Aylmer was required by her husband to attend to costumes or props or other aspects of theatre management, Tom and Polly would repair to her dressing-room. Polly Dwyer's white skin was paler even than Cherokee kaolin clay, baked into the snowiest jasperware. Her hair was raven black and her Irish eyes were sea-green. Tom had enjoyed love affairs with numerous women, but there had never been anyone to match Polly for sheer insatiability, for the gusto with which she went to it, for the almost literal hunger with which her rosy lips curled on the object of their passion. Nor, when Polly was naked, had any painter or sculptor, not Rubens himself, envisaged so great a wonder.

But, in the works of Shakespeare, there was indeed a phrase for every situation, and 'appetite increased by what it fed on'. The more Mrs Aylmer offered Tom her all but unwanted devotion, and the more Polly accepted his amorous attentions, the more Tom found himself in a haze of lust which felt as if it could never be satisfied. And he had of late become preoccupied by a young married woman who was staying in the inn off King Street which served as Tom's temporary lodgings.

She was a redhead, tall and unscrupulous-looking, as, with one gloved hand on her husband's arm, she shot shy glances at Tom across the breakfast-room. Her name was Mrs Sternfeld, her husband being German. Her nationality was hard to guess. He fancied she might have been German also, but perhaps she came from the Low Countries. They had not advanced their affair very far on an emotional level. A week since, however, as they passed one another in the lobby of the inn, she had asked his help with a portmanteau which needed to be taken to her room. The inn was well supplied with slaves, and there was absolutely no need for one of the guests to lift luggage on his own account. Indeed, it was a place of sufficient gentility that for one of the guests to lift so much as a pocket hand-kerchief would excite notice, for the slaves were there to attend your every bidding. But Tom did not need Mrs Sternfeld's intentions spelling out, and he had carried the case – light as it turned out – to her chamber on the first floor. Once they were alone together in the room, her hand had reached, not for his hand, but for his breeches.

Seated as he now was in the Coffee-Room of Strong's, one of the more fashionable establishments in this new part of town, Tom Byerley surveyed the same nankeen breeches with a mixture of self-congratulation, amusement and wistfulness. The escapades into which he was constantly being led by the most overpowering of passions were, after all, not merely exciting. They were also a little sad.

Over the nankeen breeches, Tom wore an elegant, pale green top coat and a yellow vest, double-breasted and much adorned with brass buttons. His ruffle of white cravat beneath his chin could have been a spoonful of the purest whipped cream. His chin was freshly shaven. His brow was framed by a brown tie-wig. This alone marked him out to any intelligent observer to be an Englishman, since, even in fashion-conscious New York, the defiant mood of the political moment somehow decreed with an urgency that could not logically be explained that the colonists should cast off not merely the political shackles and ecclesiastical restraints of the Old World, but also its wigs.

*Dear Tom,*

he read as he sipped his coffee – and damned good coffee it was. The proximity of Jamaica meant that you could drink coffee in America which was fresher and stronger than anything you ever tasted in London. As for Burslem! Tom smiled as he recollected his mother sniffing the beans which his Uncle Jos gave her.

—Sister, I've made you these elegant coffee-cans. Surely you will at least try the drink?

—I don't think coffee-housing would be quite my line, Mother had said with one of her satirical snorts of laughter. And the little coffee-mill which Uncle John had once brought from London and the costly bag of beans imported from Ceylon were left unused, unground and untasted.

—I should conjecture it were very rich, had been her final dismissive judgement of the matter.

When it came to people, Mrs Byerley did not mind how rich they were: the richer the better. When it came to comestibles, 'rich' was a term of disapprobation.

Tom sipped eagerly from the crude Delftware coffee-can in front of him – where did the Americans find these things? – and read on.

*It is now nearly a year since we heard from you directly, though your good mother keeps us informed of your welfare. She keeps up the shop and is, I believe, doing pretty brisk business. Believe me, my Boy, I love you as a son and would never have wished to stand in your way of success either in the literary line or on the stage. A part of me hopes that you will be the American Garrick!*

*But another part of me wishes you home. Your brave mother has never indicated that she resents your going, but I know how much she misses you – as we all do. And now, Tom, I renew a request for you. When I asked you last year you said that my request was impossible, and that it came at an inopportune moment. If once again, you refuse me, well and good, but please, my dear Boy, I should be in your debt were you to reply instanter, either direct or via Mr Griffiths the agent.*

*May I repeat what I wrote last year. As you will recollect, 'tis eight years since – when you, dear Nephew, were still working as my boy clerk – that we persuaded an unwilling Mr Griffiths to sail the Atlantick Ocean and, having dock't at Boston, to make the laborious journey southwards to the country of the Cherokee. There, by supreme good fortune, good sense and industry, he managed to acquire five tons of this* exquisite white kaolin. As you know, Tom, there are spies abroad, and I dare not communicate to you my reasons, my desperate reasons, for requiring more of this precious commodity! If it were injudicious, in the Extreme, to communicate the exact Formulae of my experimental Ventures, however, it is equally no secret that I need white china clay for two of my most distinctive Inventions: the Creamware which has made my name, not only in England but in Europe, not only in Europe, but in the world; and the Jasperware which has become my hallmark.

Tom, an opportunity has arisen which is without parallel not only in my life, but in the history of European pottery manufacture. I cannot tell you what it is, but I need white china clay in enormous quantities. If I were able to acquire it from Cornwall, I should do so, without putting myself to the expense, and you, dear Boy, to the danger and worry, of travelling into the country of a strange people. But, dear Tom, the dispute over the rights of ownership and purchase of Cornish china clay goes on and on. My old enemy Cookworthy (worthy to be roasted alive more than to be cooked, in your old uncle's opinion!) continues to hold on to the patent for china clay and the exclusive right to purchase Cornish clay.

I need white clay and I need it in great quantities. If you were able, my dear Tom, to journey to the Cherokee country, you would place your-self everlastingly in the debt of your loving old Uncle. Ever since your father died, I have looked upon you as a son. Your dear mother, my sister, depends upon me as a protector, but she depends upon you for her emo-tional sustenance. I need not labour these points to you, since you know them.

The Cherokee are not a race of Savages, despite what some of the Americans will tell you. You will perhaps recollect that when thou wast a lad, three noble Cherokee tribesmen visited London and had the honour to be presented to His Majesty the King. I had been going to write that the Chief of them, Ostenaco, was their equivalent of my Lord North or His Grace the Duke of Grafton. But this would be to mislead you, since, in so far as I have been able to establish the truth of the matter, the Cherokee would appear to have no kings, dukes or princes. Ostenaco, if he has an English counterpart, would appear to be a theocratic personage, perhaps the equivalent of the Archbishop of Canterbury. (I am no more a judge of Church matters than you are and rejoice in my ignorance!) These people do not have politicks, but they have warriors, and their craftsmanship is not to be despised. The pots they make are not unlike – in shape – the old Greek vases lately excavated by Sir William Hamilton in Italy. But they are not of your Italian terracotta. Rather, they are of the most exquisitely delicate white clay. Tom, this clay of the Cherokees is whiter than anything in Europe – it is as white as the Chinese kaolin itself!

They were assured by His Majesty that the British Crown would protect Cherokee lands from the colonial settlers and that there would be an everlasting alliance between the English and the Cherokee peoples. So if you penetrate Indian country, Tom, you will be among friends – so long as you are able to persuade them that you are not an American!

The American colonists have Justice on their side in their quarrel with the Crown. All decent men and women at home support the American cause, certainly all my friends the Lunar men do so, but in Parliament even Mr Pitt and Mr Burke take the colonists' side against the intemperate Toryism of Lord North. In their quarrel with the Cherokee, we can be less certain of the righteousness of the American cause. But I am sure that you are as able as I am to keep the two matters separate in your mind. Whatever the rights and wrongs of individual colonists' disputes with the Indians, it is impossible to doubt the overall rightness of the American position. They have no representation in our Parliament. All decent folks must sympathize with the Americans in their grievance against the various taxes and Stamp Duties &c. imposed upon 'em by the Ministry. As for the punishments and embargoes meted out to the *good people of Massachusetts since that unfortunate incident in Boston Harbour with the consignment of Indian tea, we can only hang our heads in shame, as Englishmen, that such pettiness and lack of generosity could be exercised by a sovereign Government against the courageous and independent-minded colonists. None of us here supposes for one moment that the hostility at present erupting between the Americans and the Ministry could possibly result in violence.*

*I should be most grateful of a reply, my dear Boy, as soon as at all possible, and not least should I be grateful for your American news. Some here say that the colonists desire a complete liberation from their dependent status. My own judgement coincides with that of my closest friends Mr Bentley and Dr Darwin: the inflated rumours of American Independence are nothing but wild talk. I remain trustful and confident that the Americans have no intention whatsoever of breaking away from Great Britain, still less of fighting a war against us. I am sure that the dispute will be settled peaceably, and without loss of blood. Indeed, it is unthinkable that good English soldiers should fight their colonist brothers to the death over Townsend's Stamp Duty. In this, all my ingenious friends in the Lunar Society – Dr Darwin, Mr Edgeworth, Mr Boulton and the rest – are in entire concurrence and agreement. My partner Mr Bentley, however, is of the view that the longer the dispute goes on, the worse it will be for trade – not only in pots but in all branches of Commerce. So any Intelligence which you were able to supply would be received with the utmost gratitude by your ever-loving uncle, Jos.Wedgwood.*

*p.s. Whatever fine feelings I might have expressed for our friends the Cherokee, this is not to say that I wish to offer them one penny more per ton for their excellent china clay. It would, indeed, set a very unhappy precedent if we paid them more than Five Pounds per ton. Do not permit them to haggle, Tom! Were you to do so, it would not merely excite greed on their part, it would, even more dangerously, arouse the suspicions of my trading rivals were it to be known that I am intending to buy more Indian clay in great quantities.*

Upon the completion of reading his uncle's letter, Tom nodded, for an attentive slave was at his elbow with a coffee pot, offering to refill his cup. Instinctively, Tom looked at the cup. It was a crude blue and white thing – Dutch, Tom should not have been surprised to hear. One of the things about the New World which excited his Uncle Josiah was not merely its progressive political outlook and its freedom of thought and expression in matters of religion, but the fact that none of the thirteen colonies had, as yet, a pottery manufactory of their own; and in consequence, all crocks, even ones as debased as this heavy Delft cup and saucer, must be imported from Europe. Even though Josiah did not believe that the colonies would ever opt for full independence, he could see, as could anyone with eyes in their head, that America was achieving, year by year, an independence of a general kind. It was only a matter of time before there were American potteries, and old Jos wanted to cut in on the deal. There had even been the idea, expressed in more than one of his letters over the last four years, that Tom Byerley himself might like to preside over a Wedgwood manufactory in New York or Philadelphia.

But the immediate question now was how to answer Uncle Jos's strange request:

*p.p.s. Eight years ago, I paid Tom Griffiths Fifty Pounds to fetch home the Cherokee clay. This involved him in crossing the Ocean and returning. If you undertake this work for me, my Boy, I will pay you the same sum, even though it be that you are already in America and would only have to make one Ocean crossing compared with Griffiths's two! JW*

This was a consideration: fifty pounds was more than he would make in eighteen months on the stage. Last year, he had earned so little as an actor that he had been obliged to supplement his income by school-teaching and by taking pupils. And he had more than once, while so employed, asked himself in the manner of the Prodigal Nephew of the Parable whether he would not be better off to arise and go unto his uncle and beg him to kill the fatted calf.

In boyhood, Tom Byerley had possessed no ambition to be a potter, so he had not been apprenticed to the trade. From an early age, his way had been with words, not clay, and it had seemed, as he entered his teens, that he would merely have to choose between the profession of Letters or that of the Stage. Perhaps, like Mr Garrick, he would excel in both fields. He was young enough, and held a high enough opinion of his own accomplishments, not to have heeded Johnson's warning that the writer's life was attended by *Toil, envy, want, the Garret and the Jail.*

His mother's pleading, and the sheer necessity of life, led to him accepting work at his uncle's Burslem manufactory. He laboured there for five years as a clerk, serving at the end as his uncle's personal assistant and secretary.

In all that time, the impression formed during early childhood of his uncle's genius and benevolence was confirmed. Jos set himself high standards and he expected others to do likewise. He could seem harsh as an employer, but never cruel, and never unjust. Were it not for the overwhelming tedium of the work, Tom Byerley might well have settled to it. In time, Jos would probably have allowed him to go to join Uncle John, who, together with Mr Bentley, ran the London end of the business, and in London he might have combined the duties of his work with the dissipations at which he had already become adept. There might even have been time left over for Letters and the Theatre.

In the end, however, he had decided to cut loose before his uncle made any such offer. Tom Byerley left Staffordshire behind him when he was aged twenty. He went first to Dublin, where he enjoyed a modest success, followed by a period of failure on the stage. The chance to join a travelling theatre company which was sailing to New York was leapt at. He had been in America nearly five years. And now he sat in a coffee-house, many plays, many periods of worklessness, many spells of sorrow and self-doubt, many cheap lodgings and un-healthy garrets, many enjoyable amours later – and some acutely painful.

His Uncle Jos was a man of power. There was something com-pelling about the energy of the man. Also, Tom felt a deep reserve of affection and gratitude to the uncle who had quietly helped Mother set up the draper's shop in Newcastle-under-Lyme, and continued to allow her the – illusory? – sense of independence. In those years that he had worked for Jos, he had been awestruck by the amount the man had achieved, not merely in his two – and at one stage three – manufactories, but also in his public works, his campaign for canals to be built, his supervision of turnpike roads, his many scientific dis-cussions with his friends in the Lunar Society, all remarkable figures in their own right but also – you could sense it when you were with them – all sharing some of Tom's awe for his uncle.

Indeed, at that stage it would seem to Tom that the only person who was not aware of Jos Wedgwood's genius was his wife, Sally. Nothing he did seemed to please her and Tom became increasingly embarrassed both by her impatience with her husband and by the tenderness which she displayed towards himself. Indeed, one of the delicacies of Jos's character, in his nephew's eyes, was that Tom was unable to ascertain whether Jos was aware of the 'situation'. They were miles away from the danger an affair, but nephew Tom knew that Sally's love for him was disproportionate, intense and physical. Was it for that reason that Jos had been prepared not only to allow Tom to go to Dublin, but also to be generous in financing the escapade – for an escapade was all, five years later, it had been. Of that Tom was quite well aware. He was no Garrick. He was never going to make a distinguished career out of acting, and he now knew that he did not possess the stamina for this profession: the emotional stamina, that is to say, to live with the long periods of rejection and waiting for work.

It would be inevitable – he had known this for a very long time – that one day an opportunity would arise for him to leave the theatre, and he should seize it. The only question in his mind was whether this bizarre opportunity – the chance to ride south to the Cherokee country in quest of china clay – was the moment to leave the theatrical world and its ladies. Ah! Its ladies! Should he not string things out a little longer with Mrs Aylmer, and the divine Polly? Should he not continue his run as Macheath in *The Beggar's Opera* at Mr Aylmer's theatre? It was a leading role, but not a well-paid one. But it was some money, which was better than no money and it enabled him to put up at the same inn as the very distinctive red-headed Mrs Sternfeld. (The vision when, in her bedroom, she had lifted her petticoat and revealed that dark, moist red thatch was not to be forgotten.)

Or had he reached one of those staging-posts in life when some inner voice makes it plain that it is time to move on? Should he return at once to Griffiths, the agent, where he had collected his mail hard by Trinity Church on Broadway? Griffiths, already a pot-bellied, middle-aged successful man of commerce, had made his own purchase of the first consignment of clay into an epic, and it was with a memory of the man's stories that Tom now felt a tingling of excitement. He knew what would be involved. A ride by the stagecoach to Philadelphia would be followed by meeting an Indian agent. There were always a number of Indians who travelled, either for reasons of trade or politics, up and down the roads south of the capital. Griffiths would either know where to meet them, or, quite possibly, their names. From there, the adventures would begin.

But for one last time, to hold Polly in his arms! And for one last time, to make an attempt on the highly questionable virtue of Mrs Sternfeld. And did he not owe it to the accommodating wife of his employer to give one last bed-shaking rogering to poor Mrs Aylmer? For one last time – ah! He smiled, the conceited smile of the young and amorously successful, and summoned the slave-waiter so as to pay his bill.

# 4

THE FINE ROMAN CHARACTERS READING *M. BYERLEY* MIGHT have signalled, to the coarser-grained inhabitants of Newcastle-under-Lyme, no more than the name of a draper's shop. The proprietor, however, was of the opinion that they were of such classical elegance that they would not have disgraced a triumphal arch in the Forum at Rome in the days before its lamentable decline. The fact that she had not had the opportunity to visit that former centre of useful commerce did not in her view diminish the justice of the comparison.

Beneath the sign was a clean shop window, displaying four or five rolls of the best Macclesfield silk, in different colours, suitable for upholstery or clothing. Some customers had the temerity to suggest that the sign would have been improved by the addition of the word DRAPER after the surname, but in Mrs Byerley's view the rolls of silk in the window provided a sufficiently clear signal of the nature of her business. Besides, as far as the local population were concerned, Mrs Byerley felt she could, without immodesty, have applied to herself the Miltonic line *Not to know me argues yourself unknown.*

Any person with the discernment to press further into Mrs Byerley's establishment would not be disappointed. The little bell, dancing upon a spring at the top of the door, made a welcoming jingle-jangle. The clean, oft-swept boards of the well-ordered

interior, the tasteful pale blue paint of the panelled doors of cup-
boards which ran round the whole of the shop interior, concealing
the wares of cloth, of lace, of sewing materials and various items of
haberdashery as well as of drapery; the gleaming polished elmwood
of the counter, all set the visitor at ease, and the atmosphere of
civilized calm was enhanced by the faithful ticking of the eight-day
clock on the chimney piece at the end of the shop, a clock on either
side of which stood two elegant vases. All these things attested to the
fact, never once doubted or controverted by anyone of discernment
in Newcastle-under-Lyme, that Mrs Byerley ran a tidy shop, and an
efficient one. She was, after all, a Wedgwood. The circumstances
which had led her to open the establishment in the first instance
had been sad, even humiliating. She had been left a widow young,
and she had no means of support. Her younger brother gave what
assistance he could, but she did not expect him to keep her and
her boy, and she believed in the virtue of standing on one's own
feet.

How they'd laughed, incidentally, when, a few days after her
brother's leg had been sawn off, Heffie had said,

—See, Josiah, it'll only be a wick or two afore they's back, standin'
on they oon two feet. Oh there I go! Ah's put mah foot in it when
they asna but the wun.

When circumstances decreed that Meg Byerley should open a
shop, she determined to make it the best draper's establishment
in the district. Fifteen years on, and there were few people in
Newcastle-under-Lyme, or as far afield as Hanley, Stoke or Longton,
if requiring yards of black crepe for a funeral, or ticking for their
mattresses, or ribbons for their summer bonnets, who would not
have the sheer common sense to place such requirements in her
capable hands.

In consequence, Mrs Byerley seldom left her neat, well-appointed premises, unless it were to repair to her apartments above the shop itself, which she did twice a day. The purpose of the first of these rit-ualized withdrawals from the world of commerce, which took place in the middle of each morning as the clock struck ten, was, as she invariably explained to Everett, her assistant, 'to make herself tidy'. Since Mrs Byerley had been born tidy, and had remained a model of tidiness in the elapsing fifty-seven years, there was no discernible difference in her appearance before and after her first withdrawal. The second withdrawal, which occurred as the clock noisily, slowly and portentously announced the coming of noonday to Newcastle, was the opportunity for something a little more radical than tidying. Each day, Everett would be informed that Mrs Byerley thought the time had come 'to nip up and change'.

Unlike her younger brother, who positively revelled in the alter-ations coming, not only upon Staffordshire, but upon the world, Mrs Byerley was a Tory of the old school, who deplored change itself as a concept. While young Josiah hollered with enthusiasm for Wilkes and Liberty, bought – though Mrs Byerley saw small evidence of his actually reading – stories by Mr Voltaire, an old gentleman in Mrs Byerley's estimation who should keep his thoughts to himself, and revelled in the philosophical discoveries of his friends Messrs Priestley, Watt, Boulton and Darwin, Mrs Byerley would have been perfectly content if change could be stopped, like a clock. She heard one and all praise her brother's part in the building of turnpike roads, and she was prepared to concede that it was now possible for a cart in winter, bearing the precious cargo of Wedgwood creamware, to make its way from Burslem to Stafford without falling into a mud-hole and smashing into pieces. But no change in Mrs Byerley's estimation was ever more than a mixed blessing, and did it, she asked, advance the general good to permit any Dick or Harry to gad about the country? And though it might be of profit to her brother to speed the journey from Burslem to London, should they really rejoice at the prospect of Londoners – she slightly shuddered at the notion – having ease of access to Burslem?

No, when Mrs Byerley said she was going up to change, all that was connoted by this daily explanation to Everett was that she was climbing the narrow stairs to her apartments to change her clothes. It was only proper for a lady, and Mrs Byerley aspired to that status in her imagination, even if birth had not bestowed the privilege, to change her clothes at midday. The change was mitigated by the oxymoronic trick of always taking the same form. She would remove the mob cap with which she had covered her head in the morning, and replace it with one all but identical. She would in a similar fashion take off the starched pinafore she had been wearing in the morning, and replace it with a newly laundered specimen of the same garment. Then, having spent a few meditative minutes at her dressing table, prodding hairpins, applying powder to her cheeks, and looking closely into her own eyes, she would arise, and descend the small narrow staircase into the shop once more and announce,

—There! That's better.

If Mrs Byerley deplored her younger brother's political outlook, she was prouder of Josiah's success in life than words could properly express. It was something, to have altered, in the space of a decade, the domestic habits of an entire nation. Before Josiah Wedgwood, your English family ate off pewter or wooden platters, or from salt-glazed lumpen affairs that scarcely merited the name of crockery. What passed for Delftware on the tables of the middling sort of people was crude and easily chipped. Since he had completed his apprenticeship and set up his works in Burslem, all that had changed, and within a decade of his production of creamware, there was hardly a respectable household in the kingdom which did not eat its dinner off well-glazed, delicate plates, and pour its milk from jugs manufactured as like as not in Staffordshire, and drink its tea from pots imitated from her brother's catalogues.

She loved Josiah best of all her — alas too few! — surviving siblings, perhaps especially because he had so narrowly avoided the fate of so many brothers and sisters, death of smallpox. She loved him for his childhood vulnerability, and for his courage, and for his having triumphed over these adversities and built up so great a business. Jos had been the last child in a family of twelve. Meg, with whom destiny would one day reward Mr Byerley as his bride, had looked on the little boy as her child. Their father had died when Jos was nine years old, and the pox had swept through the fatherless family like a plague in Scripture, taking eight of them. It had returned when he was eleven, and he had contracted the disease, and very nearly died of it. He'd survived, but the disease had permanently weakened his leg.

The survivors had felt instinctively that they owed it to the vanquished dead, as to the unborn future, to make a success of things. None of the siblings had made so stupendous a success as Josiah. He had been apprenticed to his elder brother Thomas, but though many in Staffordshire had thrown fine pots, there was no one who had ever matched the genius of Josiah Wedgwood.

Where did such genius come from? The Wedgwoods were a clever tribe. It was an observation of simple fact to say that, and Mrs Byerley thought none could accuse her of vainglory for so believing. But whereas her other surviving brothers, and her cousins, with their small pot banks spread over the fields surrounding Burslem's small village, had been good jobbing craftsmen, in Josiah a spark of genius had always been alight. Even as a child with virtually no schooling, he had collected minerals and fossils. His skill at the potter's wheel was matched by an intellectual curiosity which made of their ancestral craft a branch of Natural Philosophy. How to improve, how to blend clays, mix different varieties of what was, after all, no better than dirt, and transform them into the gleaming glories of the dinner table – that had been Josiah's fought-for, struggled-for and yet somehow instinctive skill.

As success transformed him from being a good local craftsman into being a man in the great world, Mrs Byerley believed that she owed it to Jos to behave with due decorum. No one in the family could remember a time when Margaret did not speak like a grand lady. There was no suggestion that she had adopted the voice out of affectation. Yet anyone meeting her for the first time outside the shop premises might have supposed, from her perfect diction, not that she was an aristocrat, most of whom spoke in those days with the accents of their locality, but a member of her son's chosen profession; her tones could have been those of the great Siddons. She had always used southern vowels. She had always been a reader. Family parties and Christmas dinners would often end with Aunt Byerley reciting from Milton or Shakespeare, authors she had seldom or never been seen to read through, but great passages from which she could commit to memory. 'Cromwell, I charge thee, fling away ambition!' 'So let it be with Caesar!' Jos could remember his sister uttering these phrases to him in her full contralto when he was but a lad. In maturity, he would affectionately laugh and say you could see why Meg's son had wanted to run away and go on the stage.

In her theatricality, she was very different from Josiah himself, who was in too much of a hurry to care for airs and graces. Though he spoke grammatically, he always retained his local accent. Mrs Byerley's voice alluded to the world of crowned heads and coroneted wigs, of royal saloons and ducal drawing-rooms into which her brother's ware and sometimes her brother's very foot found its way. The fact that none of these august personages had as yet had the privilege of meeting Mrs Byerley did not prevent her from alluding to them, obliquely but definitely, to customers who came in for lace and ribbons.

She was perfectly aware that some of the humbler sort who came with their shillings and pence must on occasion have permitted themselves to wonder whether Mrs Byerley was entering the kingdoms of fantasy when she allowed their modest purchases to prompt thoughts of the royalties and nobilities. This was because she combined, in a manner which she considered the very embodiment of discretion, an irresistible urge to allude to her brother's more glorious clients with an unwillingness to divulge their specific identities.

If a coal-hauler's wife from Newcastle bought a length of calico, she might be surprised to hear that it was of that very stuff, if she did but know it, that a certain nobleman, not twenty miles down the road, lined the curtains of his carriage windows.

—A better choice I could not have made myself, Mrs Dutton, and though I am sure you would not want me to name names, His Lordship's fingers were touching cloth from that very bale only a fortnight yesterday.

There was scarcely a button, a ribbon, a length of silk or cotton fabric which was not imbued with some aristocratic or royal connection in Mrs Byerley's well-stocked, but very discreet head.

—Now, I declare, she is saying to a customer at the moment when we join her (it was a doctor's wife from Leek who had come in for a length of muslin for her daughter's dress), if sprig muslin were not the very stuff which Her Grace – though which particular Grace I leave it to your imagination to conceive – had chosen a sample only this week!

—I thought it would be a pleasant birthday surprise for my daughter to have a new dress run up, said the doctor's wife. And this sprig muslin is so very pretty!

—The very sentiments – Mrs Byerley allowed herself a rakish wink – expressed by Her Grace.

—And I was thinking of some pink ribbon.

—We have this, at ninepence ha'penny a yard.

—That's expensive.

—Everett, said Mrs Byerley.

This obedient creature was a sallow, freckled woman of about Mrs Byerley's age – and what that age was, though I have revealed it to the reader, was always somewhat uncertain in the minds of the customers. If Mrs Byerley seemed to have stepped from a canvas by Hogarth, Everett had stepped from the subdued grey of an interior by Chardin. There was next to no colour in Everett. Her hair, which was actually mouse-grey, was covered by a mob cap. The rest of her person was concealed by a floor-length pale grey dress and a white apron. The only colour was found in the two glistening smudges of red on either side of her nose where an ill-fitting pince-nez had over the years left its indelible impression.

—Everett, said Mrs Byerley with some condescension, not only to her assistant but to a customer sufficiently ill-guided as to think she could get away with cheaper stuff and not know the difference, show Mrs Sawyer the good pink ribbon and the cheaper one which came in the other day. I think she will see why Her Grace, when looking for ribbon to hold on her bonnet during the last meeting at Epsom, elected to purchase good Macclesfield silk, rather than the Indian imports. But, as Her Grace implied – not that the subject of money as such would have crossed Her Grace's lips – people get what they pay for.

—I confess, said the doctor's wife, who spoke with some firmness and unwillingness to be impressed by the range of Mrs Byerley's acquaintance, that I do not see much difference between the two ribbons. And after all, for a child . . .

The good general knows when to sound a retreat as well as when to make sorties into the enemy lines.

—Everett, sniffed Mrs Byerley, Mrs Sawyer will take three yards of the cheap Indian ribbon.

—I should think two would be amply sufficient.

—Well, said Mrs Byerley with another sniff, that is Mrs Sawyer's decision. I am not saying that the Indian ribbon is not pretty but whether it lasts the whole season is a question on which I should not care to be drawn.

—It'll fray, said Everett, thinking of the cheap ribbon, only she pronounced the word 'free'.

—It was just a little bit of a display, said Mrs Byerley. She wanted to show who was paying the piper. Well, we know who was paying Everett, but the piper is entitled to opinions of her own.

—And rightly – though she said 'raightly' – so.

At this point the bell on the door jangled and Jos opened the glass-panelled door.

—Mr Wedgwood, sir!

—Good day, Mrs Everett.

There is Jos stomping energetically into the shop with his walking stick and his wooden leg. There is that large, honest face, pink with the morning air, its expression eager, amused and happy, in the company of his friends. Sir Joshua, when he painted it, disguised the fact that it was heavily scarred with the pox which had afflicted him as a child of eleven years. Sir Joshua once referred to Josiah's 'capacious countenance'. Sir Joshua said that he had never known a face so to *fill* a canvas; not, said he, that Jos's head was abnormally large in proportion to his body, but that the face was large in proportion to the skull. It was as if all Jos's energy, all his enthusiasms, all his zest for inquiry and living, and all his good-heartedness, all his eagerness, could not be expressed in eyes, nose, cheeks and chin of a regular size, and needed the accommodation of a larger than average mirror of emotion and intelligence. So in that Reynolds portrait, you see not only the personal modesty and the good humour, but also this overpowering strength of will behind the bright blue eyes. You see such firm determination in the almost-opened lips, as if he is about to say, *What do you mean, you must wait until next week? Let's start on this enterprise now! This moment! Let us go back and dig this canal, build this road, expand this manufactory! This instant! And while we are about it, let us reframe society, abolish superstition, extend trade and in so far as it in us lies, make the lot of our fellow mortals more bearable, more rational, less dangerous.*

There is no wonder that his workers were frightened of him, and that not all of them liked him. No wonder, the cry of 'Ere coom Owd Wooden Leg!' excited an immediate frenzy and a theatre of artificial activity, when they heard his artificial limb clip-clopping on the wooden stairs from his office, and as he made his brisk and unpredictable tours of inspection of the works.

He'd speak to the workers in their own dialect on such occasions, as his peg leg clicked and clocked on the floorboards or the stone paving, and as he darted in and out of the various rooms, the modelling room, the throwing rooms, the painting rooms.

Sometimes impatience would get the better of him – Ee, Abner Barlowe, they disna throw a pot lahk that, lad! – and, shoving poor Abner to one side, he would occupy the potter's stool and call to the boy to start in motion the great wheel which Jos himself had invented, the size of an enormous cartwheel which, by an ingenious system of pulleys and straps, enabled him to get up a good speed on the throwing-wheel without the nuisance of kicking the trestle of the throwing-wheel with his peg leg.

When Jos sat at the throwing-wheel, the men would stop work and gather round. For, skilled as many of these men were in the noble art of potting, none could throw a vase with the delicacy or expedition of this greatest of all Master Potters. It was the work of seconds. At one moment a wet, grey lump of clay would be slapped on to the fast rotation of the wheel. As his left hand kept it centrally poised, the right hand, a large, strong hand with thick yet nimble fingers, would make a hole in the wet clay with the thumb, and then, with a few sure pinches, coax and pinch it into such a shape as Sir William Hamilton might have exhibited in his Etruscan collection at Naples. It was all so skilful that it felt like a completion of some celestial purpose; as if this lump of earth, from the moment of its first geological formation, had been but half-finished until re-crafted by the hand of Josiah. Some Roman Emperor was supposed to have found Rome built of brick and left it marble. Josiah found the earth's clay unformed mud, and left it fashioned, shapely, and, in the fullness of the great ceramic process of firing, glazed and shining.

—Theer, lad! – and with the lordliness of an Emperor holding out his hands for ablutions, he would extend those grey wet fingers for a boy to wash and wipe and rub. Then he'd rise to his one foot and his wooden stump, and continue his tour of inspection, praising where due, and instructing: for the Wedgwood works was, as well as a manufactory, a school for everyone who worked there under the great craftsman. At the time of which we write, they spoke of 'Vase Madness' having gripped England.

His sister had looked up in alarm, as if the appearance of Josiah in her shop, at midday on a working day, was suggestive of disaster. And a day never passed in which she did not worry about her son in New York.

—Has there been news, Jos?

In the mother's vocabulary, the word 'news' always primarily carried the association of intelligence about her absent boy. And with the worsening situation in the colonies, her yearning for him to return to England intensified.

—Good day, my dearest, and Josiah stomped across the shop, came behind the counter and leaned over to embrace her. He was a good six inches taller than she was.

—It's not good, is it, Jos?

—There's no news, said her brother. Not of our Tom.

—I am bound to say that the American atrocities try anyone's patience beyond endurance. Ten thousand pounds' worth of tea, brother, of the best Indian tea, thrown into the harbour at Boston!

—If you thrash a dog it will snarl, said Jos simply.

—Everett, said Josiah's sister.

—Mrs Byerley, ma'am?

—Be so kind as to find me the *Advertiser* which was in the back shop only yesterday.

The news-sheet was within easy reach, but, even if the American colonists were throwing off hierarchies, it was evident that such radical notions had not reached the premises of M. BYERLEY, Newcastle-under-Lyme; and if a piece of paper were to be fetched, the task should fall to an underling.

When Everett had waddled the few paces necessary for the retrieval of the paper, Mrs Byerley held the document at arm's length and muttered,

—Where is it now? Yes, here . . . Two hundred and ninety-eight chests of tea, worth an estimated sum of £10,994 . . . the property of the East India Company . . . several hundred citizens of Boston, painted and disguised as savages . . . attacking the ships . . . pouring the tea into the harbour . . . Where is it, yes. It says that, although order was restored by the Governor of Massachusetts . . .

—General Gage, said Josiah.

—An excellent gentleman, said Mrs Byerley. The air of authority with which she pronounced the judgement could not have been firmer had she known him all her life, though as a matter of fact she would not have recognized a picture of the General if she had been shewn it.

—The citizens of Boston are fortunate to have him. But see here, brother, as she brandished the paper, insults to His Majesty, a jeering crowd, a speech by Mr John Adams that Americans would not submit to the dictation of a crowned potentate . . . liberty? Liberty, brother? What sort of nonsense is that supposed to be, I should like to enquire?

—The Americans are good people, honest people. They were caught up in a war between ourselves and the French. It was not of their making. Now the Ministry in London expects them to foot the bill for the war with taxation. But they are not represented in our Parliament.

—Nor are we represented in our Parliament, said Mrs Byerley with one of her sniffs.

—If by representation you mean – she paused, as if about to utter a word not used in polite society – Votes. It does not mean that we steal other people's property and throw it in the Trent.

—They, or their ancestors, sailed the ocean to escape the tyrannies and superstitions of the Old World, said Jos affectionately. They are a freedom-loving people, sister.

—Freedom-loving fiddlesticks. If it goes on like this they'll be asking for their independence and become a separate nation. Then see how they enjoy their freedom without the soldiers of the Crown to protect them from the savages they like to impersonate. It is beyond my imagination, brother, how you can sympathize with such rogues who have openly insulted your most illustrious client. Where would we be without Her Majesty having bought your tea sets?

—I can distinguish, sister, between my politeness to a customer, and indeed, my reverence for our Royal House at home, and a belief in the essential justice of the American cause.

—I hope that Her Majesty will appreciate the distinction when she next orders a dinner service. She has done? She has placed another order? A bigger order? Brother, I can see something in your face. There is something afoot! Oh, I declare!

—Meg, I can't tell you. When it is definite, when it is really and truly definite, you will be the first to hear. But at present, my lips are sealed.

—Well, I can hardly imagine you have found a client more illustrious than the Queen of England, said Mrs Byerley, with some satisfaction.

—My lips are sealed, repeated Jos, but they were not, because he always had the habit of allowing his mouth to hang very loosely and lightly open, a trick of the facial muscles which was in accordance with the openness of his personal dealings.

—Meg, he began again, something very big has come up. It's all coming together at once and . . .

—What is coming together?

—It is not only sorrows, sister, which come not single spies but in battalions. Happy events also come in clusters. The lawyers in London believe that we are within an inch of defeating my old enemy Cookworthy.

—Oh, but that is wonderful news.

—You remember Cookworthy, sister . . .

For many years, Cornish clay – the whitest in our island – was denied to the greatest Master Potter of the times. A Quaker from Plymouth, a Mr Cookworthy, had patented Cornish china clay – taken God's earth and put a Government patent upon it! *Cookworthy!* Josiah pronounced the name lingering on the last two syllables with heavy irony, and with a strong Staffordshire burr in the first syllable of 'worthy'. Cookworthy the Chymical inquirer. Back in the forties, Cookworthy had been visited by a Huguenot colonist from Virginia. He had been told that in the country of the Cherokee Indians there was a white mineral, kaolin, which was similar if not identical to the mineral used by the Chinese in the manufacture of porcelain. If the worthy Cookworthy could but perfect the formula, by mixing kaolin with petuntse, he would be in a position to manufacture porcelain. The untold wealth which came to the importers of Chinese porcelain for the tables of the European rich could pour into the old Quaker's pockets. No more would the merchants of Shang Hai crate their blue and white vitrified china tableware in straw and pack it off to Europe. No more would the shining blue and white dinner plates and soup tureens of old Peking grace the tables of your English milord, no, nor the translucent imitations of Herr Böttger and Herr von Tschirnhaus of Meissen glimmer in the candlelight of my lady Marchioness's banqueting hall! No, by your leave, my lady's Ragouts and Fricassees and exquisite made dishes would be glooped and dolloped on to a Cookworthy trencher, and His Grace's Mock Turtle would gurgle into Cookworthy's Mock Porcelain. For, canting Quaker rogue, he did manage a concoction which was near enough to true porcelain. He found good white china clay in Cornwall which was fit for his purpose, and he bought up the Bristol pottery manufactory. He then had the hard-nosed Quaker humbuggical effrontery to patent the invention and to set an embargo upon any other potter in England purchasing Cornish china clay. It would require an Act of Parliament to undo his work. Jos Wedgwood, hyper-energetic and straining in every fibre to make advance – in knowledge, in commerce, in life – needed white clay from somewhere, even if he never attempted to make porcelain. He wanted ever-whiter faces on his jasper medallions, ever-whiter sheen in the creamware.

Thereafter, not to be thwarted by Cookworthy, or by anyone else in the world for the matter of that, old Jos had been prepared to cross oceans to find clay white enough for his jasper medallions and for the manufacture of what was perhaps his greatest invention: the fine glazed earthenware known variously as creamware or – because he had the honour of selling it to no less a worthy than Queen Charlotte herself – as Queen's ware.

—We have more or less trounced Cookworthy in the courts, Meg, said Jos, leaning against the counter and rubbing his hands. I've persuaded the Neales, the Wilsons, the Fenwicks, the Adamses – he named some of the minor potters of the district – to unite with me in petitioning Parliament to change the law and deprive Cookworthy of his patent. But until we can buy china clay from Cornwall, sister, we must get it from somewhere.

Meg Byerley began to laugh as she remembered her brother's desperation for white clay at the time his quarrel with Cookworthy began, some ten years since.

—Do you recollect sending poor Mr Griffiths? she chuckled.

—That is what I came to talk to you about, sister.

—You gave Mr Griffiths fifty pounds to cross the Atlantic Ocean, traipse his way half across America to buy china clay from a pack of wild savages! And he did it! Five tons of white clay.

—Five tons of the best white clay in the world outside China itself. Griffiths is the best agent I ever had. And now he is settled as my American agent, with business booming in New York and Philadelphia. They have no pottery manufactories in the colonies, sister. Think of that! One day, perhaps, we can think of setting up an American branch of the firm, but in the meanwhile, our exports depend upon the goodwill of the Americans. But we will have no good white clay if we do not revisit the Cherokee.

—I knew there was a name for them. Cherry-picker, Cherry ripe. She laughed once again. Three of the rogues even came up to

London, all dressed in feathers to visit His Majesty. What was the name of those curious markings?

—Tattoos.

—It's enough to shock any good Christian.

—They are an honourable old people, the Cherokee.

—I see nothing honourable in making crude splodges on your face and wearing clothes made of feathers. In fact, I consider it disrespectful to array yourself in such a manner when being presented at Court. Remember the trouble you took when first presented to Her Majesty. You even . . .

More pause for laughter.

—you even had to fit yourself out with a sword, which you hired for the occasion. If you could take the trouble, I am sure I do not see why these Cherry-picking merchants could not display the same consideration.

—Meg, Griffiths got me the best white clay in the world. He buried it in America, and dried it, and preserved it in straw and transported it back to England. With quantities of that white clay I have managed to make the jasper medallions which have helped to create the Wedgwood fortune. I've used it for mixing with the English white clay we bought from Dorset and it has made the creamware so much whiter than I was able to make it a decade ago. Meg, I need that clay. There is something. I cannot tell you what it is, but it is an order so great that the mind boggles at what I am going to be asked to do.

—Well, brother, she teased, it would seem as if you have come to the wrong shop. Here you will only find ribbons and silks.

—Sister. Meg. I've written to our Tom.

A silence descended and they listened to the ticking of the old eight-day clock.

There was perhaps the telepathic sense, which always exists

between two people who love one another, that she knew what he was about to say before he had said it.

—You've asked Tom to get more white clay?

—I should like him to do so, Meg.

—You've asked our Tom to leave New York, which is far enough away in all conscience. You've asked my boy to go through forests and swamps and rivers to meet with a tribe of savages who scalp the colonists and do I don't know what to the American women. You've asked our Tom to go there? To buy more white clay? Because you have a very important client and you need—

—Our Meg, lass, it would make our fortunes.

—Josiah Wedgwood, you have already made a fortune.

—But this is different. This is something quite extraordinary. And, do you know something? I think this will be the best way of persuading Tom to come home.

—I fail to see the logic, I must own.

—There's our Tom in New York, trying to be an actor and by all accounts not being very successful.

Mrs Byerley drew herself up defensively.

—He was in *She Stoops to Conquer*. And there was the hope of his playing Macheath in a revival of *The Beggar's Opera* at one of the most distinguished houses in New York.

—If I wrote to him imploring him to come home, said Jos with a dogged cunning which refused to respond to the near-grief of his robust, small sister, he would resist such a plea. But if I write asking him to do something difficult for us, something for the whole family, Meg, not just for me . . . if I ask him to go and re-negotiate a contract with the Cherokee, then he'll feel that we cherish him. And I'd offer him good money, not only to buy the clay but to come home, Meg. If he accepts my offer, why we'd see him in six months!

She looked at her brother and was unable to prevent the ecstatic vulnerable flickering of hope that she would see her son again.

—Assuming we don't have a war with America, she said brusquely, to hide her emotions.

—Meg, darling, if the British Ministry and the King declared war on the American colonists, I'd eat not only my best felt tricorn hat, I'd eat my wooden leg as well, said Josiah Wedgwood, and the two of them fell, as they usually did when they were alone together, without the rest of the family, into childish laughter.

# 5

SALLY WEDGWOOD WAITED IN THE CHILLY DRAWING-ROOM of Etruria Hall. The family had been resident in the new-built palace for nigh on five years, but it still felt spanking new, and a day did not pass when she did not miss the Brick House, her first marital home. The Brick House was a compact, sensible dwelling, with small, easily heated rooms of elegant and human proportion. The apple-green panelling of her drawing-room there had set off to advantage her own watercolours, and the silhouette-portraits of siblings and cousins which she so skilfully cut out. Etruria looked, to her husband, like a mansion, and to his wife, like a large saleroom. Indeed, if she had taken a little too much laudanum, or if she were half-asleep, there were moments when she could suppose herself in the Wedgwood salerooms in West Buildings, Bath, where the glacial classical busts and vases stood in rows on the blue-grey shelves for the general admiration of the purchasing public.

Some years later than the moment when we first, in the mid-1770s, meet Sally, she would be painted by Reynolds, but it was a face which would have better suited the genius of Gainsborough. Long, raw-boned, with a hint of ginger in her light, springy hair, Sally was pale, oblique, understated. The passions were hidden beneath opium-induced pallor. Gainsborough would have conveyed what was going on within by depicting her against wind-swept, almost grey elms. But we find her indoors, incarcerated in arctic good taste. Her quietness was mistaken by her husband for sulks, by strangers for snootiness, by her children as 'mother's humours'. Cleverness was in one sense a disadvantage. True, it enabled her to retreat, from an early age, into the narcotic of bookishness. (At present, she was reading Pope's *Odyssey*. It was a book to which she returned again and again for comfort.) In other ways, it did not help, being a woman of intellect. Since childhood, she had been better at mathematics than her boy cousins or brothers. She had taught herself Greek. The sharper her wits became, the less marriageable, in her father's eyes, the tall girl became. She possessed, or was possessed by, 'those thoughts that wander through eternity'. This enabled her to penetrate dark places of the soul which a simpler person would have avoided. The truth is, she was one of those people born with low spirits, but life in a dull province of England in the early years of King George III had done little to improve them.

—Don't mope, child!, had been her mother's and her father's repeated injunction, easier to speak than to obey.

At Brick House, which directly adjoined the old Brick House Works in Burslem, there was less danger of moping. She had seldom been alone. The works, and her family, were near at hand. Friendly faces, above all that of her beloved Heffie, her best friend, her confidante, were always about her, and when the children began to arrive, although the small panelled rooms felt crowded, well, that was what Wedgwood houses always felt like, for they were a tribal people, and a large tribe at that, and they were used to swarming in and out of one another's living spaces.

At the new house, built with such expense and ostentation, things were otherwise. Dr Darwin, fat, merry, cleverer than Josiah ever quite noticed, clever in human as well as philosophical terms, had nicknamed it Etruria, and the soubriquet had stuck. Sally was condemned

to live in a palace of beauty to rival the pre-Roman Italian world, and
the newly discovered wonders of Pompeii, unearthed by Sir William
Hamilton.

Etruria – and not Etruria House, of course, oh no, but the Hall.
It was a house far out of their class, larger even than the pretentious
Barlaston Hall which Thomas Mills, a Leek attorney, had built ten
years before. Two hundred yards down the hill, Jos had built the
Etruria Works, and it was here that he set about making the ornamental ware which fed the 'Vase Madness' currently gripping
England. At the old Brick House Works, they continued to make
'useful ware' – plates of various measurements, cups, saucers,
teapots, *vases de nuit*, eggcups and tureens. Then, after a restless year
or two, Jos had closed down the Brick House Works and moved the
whole operation to Etruria. The men and women who worked in the
Brick House Works had protested. Some had implored him, others
had remonstrated against a move which forced them to walk a mile
or more to work each day and the same weary distance back, up the
hill, in the evening. Some had actually left and gone to work for other
pottery manufactories in Burslem or Hanley, or even as far afield as
Fenton. He'd contemptuously told them they were cutting off their
nose to spite their face. Some brave souls had even written a letter
to Jos to say that if he were prepared to treat his workers in this
manner they would leave *en masse* and go to live in America.

He had responded in his robust, unsympathetic way. Whereas
with wealthy customers his manners were always of the best, to the
men who threw his pots or fired them, or to the men and women
who modelled and painted them, he would often behave as if
they were fools, lazy, incompetent, unworthy of the high tasks he set
them.

This vein of cruelty in Jos reminded Sally of her father, Richard
Wedgwood. Unlike the drawing-room at the Brick House which gave

an immediate sensation of intimacy and comfort as you entered it, the saloon at Etruria was icy: not merely in temperature, but in its spiritual mood. The ceiling, with its multiplicity of plasterwork by Mr Adam, was a variety of cold pale blues and whites. No one who saw its delicate working of swags and fans and shells and leaves could fail to admire its ingenuity, which was replicated in all the decorations around the frames of doors and windows. The chimney piece from a design by Mr Adam was inlaid with blue and white jasper medallions designed by Jos. Nymphs gambolled. When Sally thought of nymphs, as she might read about them in ancient Greek, she thought of girls with eager, moist faces, girls whose complexions shone with desire and sport, hands sticky with fun, running naked through grass on some Achaean hill, or chased for love through wooded glades. But the nymphs you ordered from Mr Adam's catalogue were frigid nymphs, and the nymphs in Jos's medallions and reliefs were colder still. Frozen in white clay, they had never laughed, never held another human being, never excited, and still less gratified, desire.

Everything in the bare, soulless room was new – not merely the mouldings and the paintwork, but the furniture and the silver. As for the antique vases on the classical chimney piece, they were the newest thing in the place.

When Sally was a child, her father Richard had deplored the very idea of her playing with her 'poor relations' the Wedgwoods at the works in Burslem, the more so, understandably enough, when small-pox had attacked. When Jos had been apprenticed to his brother Tom, likewise, Richard Wedgwood had disliked the idea of Sally's friendship with a man who got his hands dirty with clay, who had no education, and who spoke so coarsely. But, little by little, it emerged that Jos was, after all, a man rather different from his lowly siblings, and Richard's attitude had begun to change. By 1759, when Jos, nearly thirty, had finished his apprenticeship and become a Master

Potter, the lad had, as the saying went, begun to make his intentions clear in relation to Sally.

Sally had never been in love with Jos, but she had grown by then to like him, and she felt protective of him – partly because of his limp, partly because she felt her father's loftiness towards the 'poor relations' was intolerable. Who were they – the Richard Wedgwoods – mere Cheshire cheese merchants!

'Richard' was another of the Wedgwood names overused by that parsimonious tribe, like hand-me-down clothes redistributed among the innumerable children. How many Tom Wedgwoods were there? How many Johns? Half a dozen of each, she thought, and as she produced offspring herself, Sally had not fought the convention, but come forth with her own Tom, her own Josiah, her own John. They could have called her father Ebenezer or Robinson, or Athanasius or Tristram, but, just as when in doubt Wedgwoods marry a cousin, so, if stuck for a name, they use one which half a dozen members of the family already confusingly carry. Jos's brother was Richard, their lost baby was Richard, her father was Richard.

Richard Wedgwood of Spen Green, Cheshire. He became a dealer in Cheshire cheeses, and made enough money to establish a small private bank and to comport himself as a gentleman. He it was who bankrolled Josiah's firm. He knew to the last half-guinea what the young man was worth, and Richard's estimation of the boy's suitability as a son-in-law grew in incremental proportion to the guineas his genius amassed.

If everything in nephew Jos's face suggested a surprised innocence, everything in Uncle Richard's countenance suggested that he had seen through everyone and everything. His was a long face, an unyielding mouth, and dark deep-set eyes. The eyes seemed not so much to see people as to see through them, and the sneer of the lips seemed to say, 'You can't fool me'. Yet, perhaps 'sneer' is too strong a word. Richard Wedgwood was not, intentionally, an unkind man; he was merely a heartless one. In his vocabulary, 'soft' was a term of abuse.

As soon as he had discovered the possibility of Jos marrying his gangling daughter Sally, Richard Wedgwood saw the alliance as a potential business proposition. There was nothing unusual in the marriage between cousins in those parts. All the Potteries families were intermarried, many times over. And the Wedgwoods, when it came to matrimony, made a useful habit of 'keeping it in the family'. Richard made no pretence of 'soft' feelings towards his tall, spirited daughter. As far as he was concerned, she was just a little too sharp-witted for a woman. Many of the Wedgwood women were brighter than was altogether convenient for members of their sex. Sally never had her nose out of a book. She'd spoil her eyes, reading – and not just women's books, novels and such like. Why, he had even caught her reading Mr Hume – the cheeky hussy!

She was quick in retort, and, when in spirits, she could be hilarious. But those spirits could swoop, and then! Richard could not be 'doing' with such fluctuations of humour. But she'd settle, as all women had to; and the best way of settling a woman was to marry her off. It was safer to keep her in the family. But if young Jos had any notion in his innocent-looking noddle that he could use her dowry to set himself up in the way of business, he could think again. Richard, who had a keener eye than the boy himself for exactly how much money he had already made, stipulated that Jos could not have Sally until he had matched her dowry penny for penny, pound for pound. When Richard made that clear to his nephew, the corners of his mouth had drawn back in something like glee.

Jos had accepted the proposition, as he accepted all declarations of authority by older members of the family. Radical he might turn out to be in his notions – especially after he met Dr Darwin, and Mr

Boulton and Mr Edgeworth and the rest of the Lunar men. As a young man, however, Jos had no trace of rebellion in his nature: he pined after new heights of knowledge and of wealth, he thirsted after innovatory power, his great desire was for new and exciting inventions in his manufactory, in his laboratory, in society at large: but he would no more have questioned the authority of his elders in the family than he would have questioned Sir Isaac Newton's Laws of Gravity.

So it was that the energetic young potter was in business for some years before he could afford his Sally. She was a luxury for whom he must wait. He was thirty-four when they were married, and she was thirty.

Sally, like many of the Wedgwoods, accepted the idea that marriage was kept, in so far as was possible, within the family. She had no notion, when she had first befriended the poor, limping, pockmarked dolt, that he would turn out to be the man who made her family name famous throughout the world. At some stage, what had begun as an act of almost-rebellion on her part was turned to serve her father's purpose.

She had inferred since infancy that she would probably, when the time came, marry one cousin or another. In Jos she had at least found a cousin of whom she was fond, and one of whose industriousness and ingenuity any wife could justly have been proud. From the moment that his wooing had begun – when she was perhaps seventeen years old – she had accepted the arrangement without question or protest. It was only at a late stage of the negotiations, and several years after her father had stipulated that Jos must match the dowry penny for penny, that Richard, in his thin, rather sneery voice, had asked,

—And we are assuming that the young woman in the case is happy? Contented with the arrangement?

—I am honoured, Papa.

Her father was exact enough in his usage to observe that she had not answered his question. He had smirked in reply, as if, perhaps, some element of feminine unhappiness added zest to the humdrum family marriage contract. Hitherto, the only excitement from the proceedings had been to screw an exacting bargain from young Jos. Now Richard could have the pleasure of suspecting that his daughter nursed some secret sorrow.

Sally had no intention of providing her father with the satisfaction of revealing whatever that sorrow might be. Nor did she intend to occasion her honest cousin Jos the anguish of disappointing him. The negotiations between the two men had advanced so far at the moment her father asked her the question that it would have been quite unthinkable to break off the engagement. And there was, after all, no reason to do so, except for one somewhat uncompromising negative: she did not love Jos. She admired him. She was determined, given their circumstances, to be loyal to him, and to support him in all his multifarious works. She would never, except in moments of extreme distress when she confided in Heffie, ever reveal the limitless depths of sorrow which he sometimes induced in her. She would always be his loyal friend. But her heart was not engaged to him. She had never felt for him so much as a flicker of those emotions which she had read about in poems and novels.

This had pained her, in the early weeks of their marriage, much more than she had supposed. Their first coming-together in the bedchamber had been rough and tumble more than affection. She had been left sore. She was too shy to discuss the matter with anyone else. Besides, there was no one whom she could ask. Her mother was dead by the time she married. Dr Darwin, the brilliant Lichfield physician who tended her husband in his various ailments, was not a man with whom a woman might easily discuss such matters,

without the fear of ribaldry, or worse. She took care not to be alone
with Dr Darwin. His large hands, so obviously more experienced in
every way than those of poor Jos, were all too ready to fumble, feel,
caress and explore the person of any female who was near, be she
housemaid or marchioness, guest or family.

No satisfaction, none, had ever come to Sally from her husband.
And yet, the regularity of the occurrence, his heavy neediness,
the frequency of his writhings and fumblings, his pushing and
sweating, made her conscious for much longer, she suspected, than
he was of the predominance of this side of existence. For him, she
suspected, it was a need, easily satisfied, like eating. For her, he had
merely awoken in her an aching lack. Her absence of satisfaction was
deeper than the purely physical. There were times when she could
thrust him away, or simply hide from him and sleep in different
rooms. He had never forced himself, though his approaches were
always clumsy. Yet she now knew that it would be possible to find
some type of satisfaction, though never with him. There were
moments when she was submitting to examination by Dr Darwin,
with his fleshy fingers, when she thought that, although he was a
man-Mountain, and fat and by no means conventionally handsome,
she could imagine his knowing how to satisfy her – almost in a
medical way. In another sphere of imagination, she was flattered
by the obvious attraction she held for bald, energetic Mr Bentley,
Jos's business partner, whose eyes played around any room containing women, lighting on this and that like a boy surveying a fully
stocked cake shop. And there was always Caleb Bowers, Heffie's
brother.

She felt a kind of inner certainty that Caleb looked upon her to
lust after her. She accepted this in a matter-of-fact way, with half of
herself believing that she would be open to the opportunity, and with
the other believing fiercely that she could never betray all the trust

and friendship which existed between her and Heffie. Caleb had always loved Sally. She knew that as surely as she knew that the scornful cheesemonger would never have countenanced a union between the great Wedgwoods and the poverty-stricken Bowerses. Even to indulge Caleb's affections as a flirtation (and they were something, she knew, much deeper than this) would have involved her in humiliating Heffie, by drawing attention to the great gulf fixed between them by the cheese-chandler's money.

It was only after the birth of her firstborn, Sukey, when she was in particularly low spirits and unable to control her weeping fits, that she had first confided the bedroom aspect of her unhappiness to Heffie Bowers. It was a helpful conversation. The other woman was dispassionate, sympathetic but humorous. Sally could hardly believe that cold-cream was being recommended.

—Tha' nadest cowd crame, poo-er lamb! Jus' rub theesel afore 'e coom inter thee and mac it smoother fer theysel! They disna ken ow we fale whahl they do it! Ah reckon not one man in a thahsand ever stops and asks issel ow t' lass fale while ah's abaht is bus'ness! Ee!, and she stroked Sally's brow and chuckled, not with satire but with sympathy, as she asserted, Tha 'aster laff!

So, Hephzibah Bowers. Her claim that laughter was obligatory provoked an explosion of sobbing from Sal.

—Oh, Heffie! Heffie! I am so unhappy!

She had hugged Heffie. How comforting the other woman was, the acrid smell of her armpits as she clasped Sally. The wetness of her kisses which she implanted on Sally's neck made her feel like a child again. As she sobbed on Heffie, Sally wondered how it had been possible, even for a minute, to dream of upsetting her friendship by beginning an intrigue with Caleb. It was unthinkable, no? Yet, when Heffie hugged her, Sally thought – this is what bodies are for. Heffie knew what a body was for, and Caleb must do so too. Whereas Jos and Sally felt like two galumphing dance partners treading on one another's toes and unable to move to the same rhythm.

And yet it was so clear to Sally's mind, to her rational self, that she had not the smallest reason to be unhappy. She was married to an upright man, who, every year that passed, achieved ever-greater success, in commerce and in society, was held in ever-higher esteem, not only in the nation, but in the world. But his wife was not his passion in life, and she longed to be somebody's passion. Caleb's? Her nephew Tom Byerley's on whom she nursed a more than aunty crush? Anyone's. To be loved, to be the object of lust, was it so much to want?

It was not self-pity, but simple accuracy, which made her say to herself that Jos loved Mr Bentley more than he loved her. She did not intend by this phrase to suggest – indeed, she did not even begin to think – that her Jos, her big, honest Jos, with his half-open mouth and his clay pipes and his limp, nursed an unnatural passion for Mr Bentley. It was simply that his passionate nature – as fiercely passionate as her own – was entirely directed towards the running of the business, towards ever more ingenious and beautiful vases, tea sets, medallions; towards his inventions; towards his schemes for improving trade; and towards the circle of men who stimulated these interests. He was dutiful to his wife, and in matters of taste he deferred to her, not merely in the decoration of their ever-grander houses, but in designs for ware. But Sally and the family were like chattels to him, or like domestic animals, figures whom he affection-ately took for granted.

There was a time, not long ago in years, but an infinity of distance covered in their emotional journey, when they lay together talking in bed. It was these colloquies in the darkness which made the husband's physical clumsiness almost bearable. She would lie there while he grunted on top of her, and she could think, Soon it will be over, and after a little quietness, we can talk. They talked of their childhoods, and of how she had befriended him long, long ago, in the Churchyard Works in Burslem, the poor little lame cousin. They talked of the books she had been reading, and she told him the stories in *Gulliver's Travels*, and the jokes from *Tristram Shandy*. Sometimes they talked of Heffie and Caleb, and Jos would remember his own schooldays – the two years he had been sent to school, with Caleb, in Newcastle, and been taught by Mr Blunt.

But it was never long, as Josiah and Sally lay together in the darkness of their bedroom in the Brick House, before he would revert to Mr Bentley. They had met, the two men, fortuitously, two years before Jos and Sally were married. The year had been 1762. Jos had been travelling for the firm to Liverpool, to arrange for the export of a cartload of tea sets and dinner services to the American colonies.

—Not one of the thirteen colonies possesses a pot bank. It's a huge market, love. Huge.

She would feel his great rough hand clasping hers as he spoke, and she would half-listen, and half-imagine America, its mountains and swamps, its vast emptiness, its rivers and its lakes. She would think of its native peoples, and how like they perhaps were to the primitive and courtly men of the heroic age met in the pages of the *Odyssey*, with their patriarchal tribes, and their welcoming halls where old tales were told and old courtesies respected.

—A huge market, Jos would be saying, as she lay in the dark, imagining an American Indian Nestor or an Alcinous in a feathered headdress.

—Those colonists took all with 'em, love, from the Old World – pots, pans, the lot!

He let out a contemptuous laugh.

—Eee! They canna make owt, can the Americans. All waiting for us to sell 'em stuff.

And he would tell then of that trip to Liverpool, and how he had been on the point of inspecting the warehouses, when his old leg trouble had started up again.

—Old Turner! Old Dr Turner! Again, his laugh.

—The doctors I've had, eh, Sally? He's a man of parts, is Turner. We fell to talking of Natural Philosophy, as he tried to get my knee to function. He told me about Mr Franklin's experiments with electricity in the thunder-clouds. Why, we could harness the power of the clouds themselves. And I said to him—

What had Jos said to the doctor, while she, so relieved that their intimacies were over for the night, snuggled against his shoulder, and half-thought of the aegis-bearing Jove with his Thunderbolts, and Neptune, the sea god who sent storms to drive Ulysses off course. And Jos would be saying,

—I said, Why sir, if you can harness the power of electricity through a lightning-rod, imagine harnessing it to machinery – in a manufactory, let us say! And the doctor – Turner – he said to me, You would harness the power of the clouds, sir? I said to him, I would harness any power you care to find. We are the lords of the earth, sir. We? asked the Doctor. We? Who are We, sir? Are you saying the Wedgwoods are the lords of the earth?

There was always a harrumph at the end of Josiah's anecdotes, the equivalent, perhaps, of Homer strumming his lyre and announcing a pause in the wanderings of Ulysses. Then Jos would fall into a meditative vein, and, stroking her hand or arm, he would say,

—But, lass, I meant the human beast. That's who is the lord of this earth. What was that line you were saying to me?

—*Presume not God to scan*, she quoted. *The proper study of mankind is man.*

—That's the one! he said with innocent triumph, as if, for the nonce, the words explained everything.

The meeting with Dr Turner, the philosophically inclined doctor, was a short anecdote in itself, but in the nights when she was able to stay awake to hear it, the conversation about electricity and the powers of the universe was only the prelude to Jos describing what happened next: how Dr Turner had introduced his young patient to his philosophical friends in Liverpool, chief of whom was a merchant named Mr Thomas Bentley.

—I thought when I first met him. Well, you know me, Sally. I stand on ceremony to no man, but I thought, here is a gentleman. He's out of your class, Josiah!

Quietly, he chuckled.

—They're of very good family, are the Bentleys, with land in Derbyshire. But the minute we met, Sally, it was as if I were Mr Franklin harnessing the electric currents in the clouds. We were made for one another. I harnessed Mr Bentley's electricity. We saw the same truth.

—What truth is that, then?

—You know he started his own Chapel in Liverpool, the Octagon Chapel? He's hoping to build another in London, nall. Small temples of Reason, Sal. Reason. The religion of the reasonable man.

—What about the reasonable woman?

His prodding finger suggested she had put the question in a coquettish spirit.

—He sent his liturgy, the form of service they use in the Octagon Chapel, to Mr Voltaire himself! Good old Bentley! Go to the top of the class! He wrote back, too, the old boy, hoping that Mr Bentley would spread reason and light among the citizens of Liverpool. Not just in Liverpool, Mr Bentley wrote back, but throughout the world! But it's something, isn't it? To have old Voltaire as your correspondent? That's why we had that bust made of the old gentleman.

—Good night, Jos.

When these nocturnal conversations took place, it did not trouble her, as it had come to trouble her since, that all his emotional as well as intellectual energy was channelled into the business. She thought of Jos as the same clumsy boy she had known since childhood. Obviously, to him, that visit to Liverpool two years before he married was more important to him than women and babies. His health had improved, and he had walked the streets of that noble city discussing with an equal fervour the possibilities of trade and the starlit universe of ideas which was bursting upon European humanity. As a result of that visit to Liverpool, Josiah's universe was a larger place. In the course of their conversation, it became clear to both men that they could become business partners. But they had also discussed, over their veal chops and their half-pints of sherry wine, the prodigious phenomenon lately engineered by Mr Watts: steam-driven engines! Not merely did it suggest a future infinite with mechanic change. It became so clear, once they had meditated upon the phenomenon, that Nature, which in all previous areas of humanity had been a mystery which could only be revered by Superstition, was now a set of usable and useful tools which could advance a resourceful people and make them rich.

Never had Sally come closest to loving her husband than when he called to mind one such walk, and conversation, with Bentley, as they went down to Liverpool Docks, the younger man still hobbling on his bad knee, but able to walk again on the newly cobbled streets. Wedgwood had been to London, but only for fleeting visits. It was in Liverpool that he first tasted the idea of a city, felt its largeness, its power, its pitilessness on the edge of the murmuring metallic sea. Bentley had warehouses on the very quayside, stocked high with bales and crates for export to America. And it was as they made their way towards this storehouse of Bentley's prosperity that they had passed the quay, and seen, enchained by shackles on ankles and wrists, a fresh consignment of slaves, disembarked from one of the huge, merciless ships specially designed for that godless purpose.

—Oh, Sal. He sounded close to tears, in the darkness, as he recollected it.

—That scandalous trade! Some of the men and women had steel collars and chains around their necks. Mr Bentley said how fervently he wished the trade could be abolished. We must do it, Sal. We shall do it.

She feared to kiss him then, lest he took this as an invitation for a repeat performance of the clumsiness. But nevertheless, she had taken that chance and kissed his ear, and when he held her tight once more, murmured,

—Not tonight, dear Jos. Not again.

So, this was the completion of the transformation, from limping, clever cousin Jos whom she had known as an awkward little child, to Josiah Wedgwood, the man of the world. He had gone to Liverpool a lonely, clever potter. He had returned from Liverpool as a man with a circle, a life woven into a larger tapestry. He had gone as a man of Burslem and returned as a man of the world.

Yet this very fact, as its implications slowly became clear to her, led to disgust in her mind, and the end of those post-coital conversations in the dark. Ever since girlhood, her own thoughts about love, Eros, the men and boys she dreamed of, had been part of a floating, continuous story inside her, awoken whenever she read novels or poems. Sometimes the element of fantasy would come to the surface and she would actually suppose herself to be Clarissa Harlowe, or wonder what it would be like to be loved by Tom Jones. More, however, there had been a flowing river of hidden and often inarticulate thoughts and memories, in which the sexual element was never absent, but never made coarse by isolation.

It became clear to her, during one of her pillow conversations with Jos, the great booby, that he had allowed Bentley and his friends to inflame him by ribaldry.

—Eee!

A harrumph signalled the beginning of a new anecdote, and, oaf that he was, she recognized, when she looked back on it, that he intended it as some kind of compliment that he should be repeating the words. Bentley and his friends had been discussing John Wilkes, the radical Member of Parliament who was then mounting his attack on the Ministry of Bute.

—They all supported Mr Wilkes, of course, and . . .

—What is it, Jos?

He was laughing, but it was not his normal laugh. Hindsight made her feel that he had, in those moments in the darkness, turned into a monster, a different person, not the essentially innocent Jos she had known.

—Well, you've heard of a poem called 'An Essay on Man'?

—I've quoted it to you, she said.

—Of course you have.

—Well – more of the coarse laughter – Mr Wilkes wrote a poem called 'An Essay on Woman'. They all had passages of it by heart.

—They all?

—Mr Bentley and his friends. It said in the news-sheet that the Earl of Sandwich had used Parliamentary privilege to recite the whole poem in the House of Lords, allegedly to prove that Wilkes was guilty of an obscene blasphemy. The bishops must have half-died of shock to hear it.

—Not again, Jos, not again.

There had been a silence in the dark, and then he had recited the remembered lines.

O blindness of the future! Kindly given
That each may enjoy what fucks are mark'd in Heaven!
Who sees, with equal eye, as God of all,
The man just mounting, and the Virgin's fall,
Pricks, cunt and bullocks in convulsions hurl'd
And now a hymen bursts and now a world . . .

His laughter had fallen into her appalled silence. Almost worse than the words themselves was the fact that he had not noticed her silence, had not felt her disgust.

—I can tell you, Sally, I kept myself pure for thirty year. I was apprenticed to brother Tom, and the terms of the indenture were quite clear. I was forbidden from 'swearing, drinking, gaming and marrying'.

—And you put the four things into the same bracket?

—You can't imagine what I went through, holding myself back all those years, Josiah told the darkness. He was no longer talking to her, he was talking to himself. And as he blurted out his own crude needs and bodily urges, he thought nothing of her emotions, nothing of her wants, nothing of what might have given her satisfaction!

—I've seen other men go to the bad over women . . . My poor brother John! You know, he lived with Griffiths at Turnham Green – the brother of my American agent? He published this book, Griffiths. It's said to be pretty strong.

Unlike the dolt who lay beside her with these thoughts, Sally had read *Fanny Hill*, and had turned its pages with a sort of amused won-derment, a bewildered, if half-horrified sense of how some of her fellow mortals derived pleasure from the bodily expressions of love. She knew that John Wedgwood was a rake. She knew that there was 'that side' to some of the men in her family. There had been storms of anxiety when Meg Byerley, Josiah's sister, had somehow found out that her son Tom had 'disgraced himself', aged fifteen, with an eighteen-year-old factory girl at the Billington Works, the somewhat roughneck pot bank up the hill in Hanley. Tom Byerley had subsequently gone in the direction feared – on to the stage, with its actresses and their painted faces. John Wedgwood was known to be addicted to night-prowls in London's pleasure gardens, the Vauxhall and the Ranelagh. It was on one such occasion that he met his death. The body was found in the pleasure gardens, but no one knew how he had died.

—They're not just bad for the character, they're bad for trade, Josiah had artlessly told her.

—But when Bentley recited those lines to me, *Pricks, cunt and bullocks in convulsions hurl'd* . . . Oh, Sal, girl, I heard the words and I so much needed . . . I needed . . . I couldna waste my life, not like our Tom's wasting his life in America, not like brother John in London. I'd work to do, and I couldna think of nowt else but pricks, cunt and bullocks . . .

His big potter's fingers held her thigh and she froze with contempt.

—I needed you, lass. I needed you so much. The firm needed you. Without all this, I'd er, I'd er, I'd have gone mad, I'm telling you now.

And what was so horrible was that this speech had in some convoluted way been intended as a compliment to her. Stiff with disgust and with an anger which was beyond disappointment, beyond grief, she had lain in his rough arms and smelt the stale pipe-smoke on his breath and thought that almost the worst of the whole matter was that there was no one in the world with whom she could share her revulsion and distress.

So, Jos had returned from Liverpool befriended, and determined to marry. And the marriage had caused rejoicing in the family.

Greedy, cynical old Richard had got a return for the money he laid out as a dowry. The purchase by the monarch of a creamware tea set, and the exquisite quality of Wedgwood Queen's ware would alone ensure their fortune. But there was another fortune (and more) to be made by the manufacture and sale of all the decorative ware, such classical vases as gleamed in their newness from the mantel-shelf over the chimney piece.

Everyone in the family was pleased with them. How could they not be? The Wedgwoods had been bigwigs in Burslem for generations. But Jos, with his prodigious energy, was destined to make them bigwigs on a larger stage. Anyone could see that, by the time he had married, and certainly by the time they had taken possession of their sparklingly new cold Etruscan palace. Obedient to that law of Nature which decreed that it should not be in Jos alone, but in his whole tribe that the families of the earth should be blessed, Sally had given birth to children.

The four came tumbling into the room now, to interrupt her reading: Sukey so much taller than her brother John, though she was only a year older, Jos a clumsy seven, who set a little wine table wobbling as he crashed his entry. The whey-faced, clever Tom, as always, seemed elsewhere, slightly staring, and yet amused.

Heffie took up the rear.

—Coom on, Jos, watch weer yer goin'.

—Jos did nearly knock over the table, Tom informed the company from his authority of five years old.

—Don't be a tell-tale tit, snapped Sukey, causing the little boy's lower lip to tremble.

—Mama, it's the greatest possible fun, said John, they say the Americans will fight a full-scale war. I can't wait to join the Navy and get at 'em.

—I'm sure, said Sukey, with a laugh, that this will scare Mr Adams and Mr Franklin to bits. A little squit of ten staring at them from the quarter-deck of a sloop.

Although irritated to be interrupted, Sally laughed. She approved of her eldest child's having so completely mastered, aged eleven, the female duty to put down, and to satirize, male pretension at every opportunity.

—Mama, look, Tom was saying.

—Boot, our Tom, ah told they, not in t' house. E found a hedge-hog, blessim! Heffie told her.

—It'll have fleas! Sukey screeched, more in amusement than reprimand.

—Oh, Heffie! Sally sighed.

This was supposed to be what women were born into the world to do, to listen to the jabber of children, to attend to their needs, to find humour in all their quarrels, and to impose order on their instincts. Heffie held up the last result of Jos Wedgwood's unwanted bedtime fumbles, a sickly two year old, blotched with appalling teething trouble and dribble-lipped, called Kitty.

—If it wasn't for you, Heff, I'd lose my wits.

Heffie did not reply directly. She spoke to the red-faced two year old who had just awoken from a nap.

—That'd be a heck of a lot of wits to lose, eh, our Kitty, if yer mother lost 'er wits. I'd be better off losin' mahn – no one ud knoo t' difference.

And Heffie laughed.

—I'm cutting out the map from the *Advertiser*, John was continuing to say to no one in particular. Admiral Howe has sailed into New York harbour! He'll show them!

—Who'll show whom what? asked Jos, who had appeared at the door of the saloon. Sally could see what was passing through his lump of a head. He was looking on the scene, and thinking it was his

dynasty, he was thinking it was the future of England, he was thinking it was a happy family scene. She hated the gormless glee lighting
up his countenance at the prospect of his tribe's increase. And Sally
was thinking, I want to be alone, I wish I was dead, I will never let
him do it to me again, never, never. I will never have another of these
brats.

—You see, said John in his high, piping, gentlemanly tones, it will
be quite a dilemma for poor Papa. On the one hand he has to think
of his clients, the King and Queen, and on the other, there are his
political convictions which tug him quite in the opposing direction.

—What's all this nonsense? asked his father, in his broad
Staffordshire voice.

—Pa. Sukey took command above the noise. John is being impertinent.

—But, I say, continued Jos to his wife, we're getting there, our Sal,
we're winning.

She knew that he referred neither to the war with America nor to
the progress of family happiness, but to the dinner service for the
Empress.

—Jus' been oop at works! – he lapsed entirely into North Staffs
in his excitement – and we've another hundred pieces ready to send
off.

He turned to Heffie to make ironical reference to her carrier
brother.

—When Caleb can manage to tear hissel away from t' bosom of
his family.

—Oh 'e's easy, said Caleb's sister untruthfully.

With his right hand firmly gripping his walking cane, Jos stomped
on his peg leg across the polished wooden floor. Did he notice the
glances Sally shot to the silhouette of Tom Byerley which she had cut
the year he left for America and which now stood on a stand beside

her sofa-table? Did he notice anything as, klonk klonk klonk, the peg leg paced towards her languid form? Only one person in the room noticed her wince – and that was her daughter – as, with his tobacco breath, her husband stooped to kiss her on the cheek.

# 6

SOON, SAID SWAN'S WING, THEY WOULD MEET A SQUAW.

The horses, good Spanish horses, never seemed in a hurry, but they made determined progress. They were both splendid, strong animals, as were, indeed, the pack horses who followed them, whose two grooms were from time to time addressed by Swan's Wing in their own language. At first, Tom had been inclined to accept the offer to saddle up his horse in the European manner. But he was glad he had been bold enough to sit on the blanketed arrangement used by the Cherokees themselves. He was a good horseman, and riding Indian style, though it made him sore for the first week, was easy when you got used to it.

Tom Byerley reflected on the squaws he was about to meet, and on the women he had left behind. There was a certain peacefulness in all-male society. The scene in New York had been, as it turned out, of the most painful kind. With the blindness of youth to other people's feelings, it had not crossed Byerley's mind that Mr Aylmer would object to finding his production of *The Beggar's Opera* without a Macheath. And it had been during the theatre manager's loud remonstrations on this account that Mrs Aylmer had entered, and Tom's imminent departure from New York had been confessed.

Quite how many indiscretions, conversational, marital, professional, had occurred during the ensuing ten minutes, Tom could not, even at the distance of four weeks, reconstruct in his memory. All he knew was that Mrs Aylmer had joined with her husband in upbraiding him. Tears had accompanied her suggestion that to leave now was out of the question – he must not think of it. Then he had returned to his dressing-room with the whole matter unresolved, thinking that the best plan would be to slip away, to leave the Aylmers a letter, since they would not accept his leave-taking when he had stumblingly attempted to give it by word of mouth. And in the dressing-room there had been Polly. More tears had followed, and with the tears embraces, and with the embraces unlacing and unbuttonings, expressions of everlasting affection had been interspersed with earthier exclamations of desire. In the midst of it, the door had been opened by Mrs Aylmer, the loudness of whose screams, and the tearfulness of whose exclamations of grief, had not merely summoned her husband but made clear to him the nature of the deceptions practised upon him so long.

A month had elapsed since that scene but something told Tom Byerley that it would never be erased from his memory: not the half-buttoning-up of his breeches, and the seizing of his coat as he ran from the dressing-room, nor the shrill passions of three voices which yelled at him down the corridor as he took the brick steps three at a time and skedaddled through the alley – Mrs Aylmer calling him a wretch, a monster and a breaker of hearts, and Mr Aylmer vowing to remove his limbs and – as he would never be able to forget – make them into sausages – and as Polly, poor Polly, let out such ear-piercing cries that he feared she might already have put into effect her threats to kill herself if he tried to live without her. Such scenes as this, when enacted upon the stage in the Italian comedies which were part of the repertory, invariably had the audience in convulsions of mirth. And yet all he could remember of the actual incident was distressing. His own sensations – genuine fear of Mr Aylmer's newly discovered sausage-making ambitions, dread combined with something like scorn and hatred of Mrs Aylmer for her lack of dignity, pity combined with the twisted thought that perhaps after all he was in love with Polly, whatever 'love' in this set of circumstances quite meant – all these feelings were intensely disagreeable and sad. And yet, night after night, women who would be as sad as Polly if deserted by their actual lovers would rock with laughter at the sight of others so depicted on the stage, and married couples whose happiness would be shattered by the knowledge of their partner's infidelity roared out their merriment at the thing artificially drawn. Was this what Aristotle meant by the purifying efficacy of drama?

And when they met a squaw, Swan's Wing was telling him as they lolloped along on their horses, it would be a sign that they had nearly reached Old Kowes, the Cherokee township where they were heading. Women guarded the gates and doors of every settlement. That made sense to Tom. Whether his mind summoned up his widowed mother, keeping the draper's shop in Newcastle-under-Lyme, or whether his thoughts called forth the other formidable Wedgwood women, it seemed that Cherokees ordered things much as they did in the Potteries. The squaws kept the gates.

Swan's Wing was a languid, long-faced man aged, by Tom's estimation, about thirty. During the three weeks Tom had now spent in his society, he was yet to see the man's heavily tattooed face crease into a smile. Swan's Wing wore a calico shirt, white leggings, which never seemed to become dirty with the ride, and beaded moccasins on his thin feet. Though Tom stank like a pole cat, having journeyed now from New York for a month in the same heavy blue-grey coat, and with few changes of shirt, Swan's Wing appeared to be odourless, unless you counted the scent of aromatic tobacco which clung to the thick black hair that grew in a crest from the otherwise shaved skull, and his shirt-sleeves and his perfect, long fingers. You could see that from his neck downwards, he was heavily tattooed on his throat and chest with serpentine patterns. For many extended hours of the journey, Swan's Wing did not speak.

After the tragi-farce at the theatre, there had been no difficulty in making up his mind. Tom had gone back to Griffiths in Wall Street, and been given directions about how to meet the agent in Philadelphia. That had been the first American town where Tom had dwelt, when he arrived five years earlier, and he had enjoyed his few days there, pacing its familiar neat brick streets, or walking beside the banks of the gigantic Delaware, the greatest river he had ever seen.

It was only after he arrived in America that Tom had begun to see why, in classical antiquity, the River Gods were depicted so distinctly one from another. In England, he had been acutely aware of the differences in character between, let us say, the tranquil Trent and the tempestuous, troubled Severn. But nothing had quite prepared him for the extremes of character in American rivers. In Philadelphia alone, the placid waters of the Schuylkill sang a gentle pastoral which was quite at variance with the rushing power of the Delaware. Not until, much later in life, he had seen the waters of the Danube washing its vast barges at speed through southern Germany did Tom feel he had ever encountered a river with more godlike energy.

Of course, Philadelphia had buzzed with talk of the Situation. Most people he spoke to felt that the hotheads of Massachusetts were pushing things too far in their quarrel with the Crown. What sense was there in talking of independence?

But Tom had bought a pamphlet while he was in the city: *Common Sense*, by Thomas Paine.

Although so many in Philadelphia, including the agent for Wedgwood's, believed that everything would settle down and that the military engagements would be seen as an unfortunate, indeed tragic, episode in the history of America, Tom knew, after he had read the pamphlet, that this was not so.

> The cause of America is in a great measure the cause of all mankind. Many circumstances have and will arise, which are not local, but universal, and through which the principles of all Lovers of Mankind are affected, and in the event of which, their Affections are interested. The laying of a Country desolate with Fire and Sword, declaring War against the natural rights of all Mankind, and extirpating the Defenders thereof from the face of the Earth, is the Concern of every Man to whom Nature hath given the Power of feeling . . .

These were words which, once read, were difficult to remove from the mind. The Wedgwood agent who had given Tom the introductions to Swan's Wing said that the author of the pamphlet, Tom Paine, was a drunken ne'er-do-well of lowly origins who had only just arrived in America. What did he know, the agent had asked, about the colonies? He'd only come here to escape criminal charges. But Tom Byerley had known as soon as he read the opening words of *Common Sense; Addressed to the Inhabitants of America* that the author had not merely intuited the future but harnessed it. Byerley felt changed, and could sense the change in the world as he read it.

It's only a matter of time, one of the friends had told him. General Clinton had captured Charleston in the South for the King. New York was in Loyalist hands, and if General Gage was having some difficulties in Boston, well, everyone knew that Massachusetts was the hotbed of the revolutionary idea. It would take little to scotch it. Bunker Hill had been a clumsy victory, but a victory it was. The Rebels had failed to take Canada. You could not set amateur soldiers such as Washington against the might of the British army and expect anything else but an American humiliation.

Yet even as they had spoken, the Philadelphia friends, Tom had known them to be wrong, not by any superior military knowledge – of that he possessed not the smallest jot or inkling – but by the sense which is given to intuitive men and women when history is on the verge of change, to know, and to feel part of such a transformation. It was as palpable as the changing of a season.

The American friends had continued to speak optimistically of the colonies coming to their loyal senses. Tom knew that it was never going to happen. Though the Loyalists spoke confidently about the conflict being resolved, his reading of the pamphlet convinced him that something had happened from which there could be no retreat or reversal.

There had been several letters from England since the first, more than a year ago, suggesting this expedition to the Cherokees. It was clear from Tom's correspondence with his mother that Mrs Byerley considered the Americans to be perpetrating the most unpardonable breach of manners. Had the colonists no conception of all that His Majesty had done for them when they might have been conquered by Frenchies? But her brother, Uncle Jos, in his letters took a different view. As Tom would have expected, the old boy was very much on the side of the Rebels, and hoped that all their demands would be met. It took such an age for any missive to reach its destination that Josiah's sunny prediction that the disagreement would never reach the point of actual fighting arrived several months after Bunker Hill. Even the Royal Governor of Massachusetts, General Gage, Jos assured his nephew, in words written long since in Etruria and read over breakfast on the banks of the Delaware, was said to be uneasy about a policy which could compel him to open fire upon those who were, after all, his own countrymen.

As it happened, William Revere had ridden to Lexington long before Tom had left New York. By the time the British had won their Pyrrhic victory at Bunker Hill, Tom had begun his expedition in search of the white china clay in Cherokee lands.

It was after a few restorative days in Philadelphia, and the chance to visit a few friends, that Tom had become acquainted with what was required of him. The two men had ridden together from a small township south of Philadelphia, to which Tom had been escorted by some sympathetic redcoats. These soldiers – Germans, though they wore the English uniform – had warned him that it was never safe to enter Indian territory at the best of times: and these were decidedly not the best of times, with colonists openly at war with their sovereign, and slaves being on the point of rebellion against the colonists, and Indians wanting to see the back of colonists, who'd settled illegally on their land; and altogether, one of the soldiers had said, it 'voss ein how-you-say a blotty kettle off feesh', and Tom was a madman to be 'making such a journey'. Tom felt he did not need a Kraut mercenary to tell him that and he allowed himself some republican thoughts – which would probably have been too strong for Uncle Jos, though not for some of Jos's Lunar Society friends – that in a battle between a Kraut king's Kraut mercenaries and the honest Americans of good British stock, he knew which side he would be on!

And then the Krauts had told him he would find the journey too hot, and he had said, Why, man, it is still spring, and the air is light and balmy. The sausage-eating mercenary had told him that the further they rode south, the more it would become a sodden, sticky cloud of insects and disease – worse than trying to ride, the sausage-eating mercenary had opined, through 'ze blotty laundry with damp hot sheets hanging up and swinging in your blotty face all ze blotty day'.

So far, luckily, this prophecy had been unfulfilled. With luck it was still early enough in the year to escape the worst of the Southern humidity and oppressive heats – at least for the duration of the journey.

He still blushed to recall the discourteous manner in which the mercenaries, when they had reached the small trading post twenty miles south of Philadelphia, had introduced him to his Indian guides and new friend, and he wondered whether Swan's Wing still, after three weeks, supposed that all Europeans secretly thought of the native Americans in this uncompromisingly stupid light.

—Ere's ze English gent, yer bloody savage, had been his form of introduction.

—You are from Wooden Leg? Swan's Wing had solemnly asked.

And, upon Tom confirming this pronouncement, even going so far as to say he was Owd Wooden Leg's nephew, the Cherokee brave had become positively friendly, by his own somewhat sombre standards.

—Wooden Leg is a friend to the Cherokee, he had announced. As is King George.

So the two men had set out together, first down a track which was as rutted and primitive as any in Staffordshire before Owd Wooden Leg had the turnpikes built, and then on to an open plain where there was no road at all. They had traversed forests, and negotiated swamps, and ridden over hill country not unlike the heath beyond Leek and going towards the Derbyshire peaks and, when not silent for long spaces, they had spoken together. Tom Byerley sang during these intervals. His clear baritone rang through a grove, and echoed through the crystalline rocks of the Appalachian highlands.

> —Were I laid on Greenland's coast,
> And in my arms embrac'd my lass,

> Warm amidst eternal Frost,
> Too soon the Half Year's night would pass.

Swan's Wing did not have small talk. Several hours of silence passed after Tom sang this snatch from *The Beggar's Opera*.

—Then, you have been as far north as Greenland? Wooden Leg has found clay there also?

—No, I haven't been to Greenland.

—You sing of it, with some authority, said Swan's Wing.

The silence which followed gave to Byerley the disconcerting sense that a man should, perhaps, not sing about places he had not visited. After about an hour of silent riding, he burst forth, involuntarily, with more of the song:

> —Were I sold on Indian soil,
> Soon as the Burning Day was clos'd
> I could mock the sultry Toil
> When on my Charmer's breast repos'd.

These words took ten minutes or so for Swan's Wing to absorb into that long shaven head, with its plume of shining black hair.

—So it is a love song, said Swan's Wing.

—Yes, said Byerley with a smile, and he gave Swan's Wing another verse.

> —And I would love you all the Day,
> Every Night would kiss and play,
> If with me you'd fondly stray
> Over the Hills and far away!

—This is a beautiful song, said Swan's Wing meditatively. Did you make it yourself?

—It was a popular song fifty years ago. A man called Gay made it even more popular because he put it into a play called *The Beggar's Opera*. It is about a highwayman, a man who robs travellers on the road.

—An American?

—No, we have robbers in England.

—But you make them heroes?

—In Gay's play, it is satire. The robber is supposed to make you think of the Prime Minister.

—Lord North?

—An earlier Prime Minister. Sir Robert Walpole.

—He was a robber? asked Swan's Wing with evident surprise. Then how could King George honour him?

—He was not a robber as such, began Tom. How could one explain a joke?

—It seems strange, said Swan's Wing, to say that Sir Robert Walpole was a highway robber if he was not.

There was a long uncomprehending silence between the two men. Then, as if speaking to himself, the brave said,

—In England, robbers steal your purse. In Cherokee Nation, the Americans steal our land.

—I reckon that is why the King sends the German redcoats, said Byerley, to make sure that the colonists do not settle on territories which have been agreed to remain yours. And in turn, you attack the colonists.

—The Cherokees are a warrior people, said Swan's Wing. They do not attack the colonists if the Americans stay in their own towns, near the great sea. But when they push further and further west, and when they build on Cherokee land, where your King has said they may not build, then we attack.

—And then, the Americans want the redcoats to protect them, said Tom good-humouredly. And then the King says, well, if you want me to pay the soldiers to protect you, you must pay me some tax, and the colonists do not think that is such a good idea after all.

—Things would be very bad for the Cherokee people if the Americans drive out the redcoats.

—There seems little danger of that just at present? asked Tom.

—There is every danger. Do you not talk to the Americans in New York? What can you have been doing there which allowed you to form such a judgement?

It was the first time in two days that Swan's Wing seemed to smile.

—I've been busy in New York. I have been singing that song in New York.

—You have been singing a song for months? Singing it so much you could not read a newspaper? Do you not hear of Mr Adams in Massachusetts? Do you not know of the Virginians, Mr Washington and Mr Jefferson, who want to make Cherokee people, Mohawk people, Iroquois people and other peoples of this land into slaves – like the African slaves they buy from the English?

—I am an actor, said Tom Byerley, then, with a little hesitancy, I tried to be an actor.

It was shaming to admit to this highly intelligent interrogator that he had spent so much time acting and fornicating in the previous twelve months that the political situation had very largely passed him by.

—An actor?

—I tried to pretend to be someone else.

—I know what the word means. Why would you want to do that?

—To please the audiences. The people who paid to come to hear me.

—You pretended to be a thief, you pretended to be a man who robbed road passengers? And this pleased other people in New York?

And instead, you could have been at home in – is it Etruria? Working for Wooden Leg?

Tom Byerley conceded that this was the case.

He looked at his companion. It was impossible to guess, from the composure of his long face, whether he was mocking him. Tom suspected that there was at least an element of satire in Swan's Wing's apparently simple questioning.

—Yes, my acting pleased other people – but not enough. I was not a successful actor. That is why I must go back and work for my uncle, for Wooden Leg.

He wanted to talk about the tragi-farce with the women, but he was not sure that the subject would be agreeable to so serious a man. They were silent for another hour or so.

Then at length Swan's Wing said,

—Wooden Leg a great man, no?

—Indubitably.

—He does not need to pretend to be somebody else?

—Certainly not.

—He thought you a fool for wishing to do this?

—Indeed. When I told him it was my ambition, he thought it was a monstrous idea. He wanted me to work for him, to help make vases and cups, to make crocks from the clay of the earth.

—That is better, no? To be a potter is a noble calling. A better thing for a man to do than to pretend to be somebody else.

After another interminable silence, Swan's Wing for the first time smiled.

—But Wooden Leg was a wise man. He knew you would want to pretend to be someone else because you were a pretty man who needed many women. When you would finish with the women, you could stop, what do you say? Fucking about? Then you would go home and do useful work.

It was such an accurate assessment of the way in which Tom had spent the previous five years, and so vividly accurate an account of his own feelings, and those of his Uncle Josiah, that Tom felt that Swan's Wing was a magician.

Tom did not ask Swan's Wing what he 'did'. He assumed the question answered itself: Swan's Wing had been north to trade, to sell the woven baskets and beaded shoes which his people so exquisitely made, and even to sell a few pots, for the Cherokee were the only people this continent possessed, as far as Owd Wooden Leg could discern, who were able to produce china worthy of the name.

If Swan's Wing did not talk of himself, he was happy for the younger man to speak of his own life. Tom Byerley had been unable, as they rode along, in long hours of trance-like silence, not to meditate upon his changing circumstances. While he sank into mental abstraction, lines from plays drifted into his head. The company Tom had joined gave the New Yorkers *She Stoops to Conquer* and *The Rivals*, some Goldoni farces, and even one of these new revolutionary comedies by that Beaumarchais fellow. Tom, as the self-confident twenty-four year old that he was, had taken the role of Figaro.

> How happy would I be with either
> Were t'other dear charmer away

had too accurately summed up his sentimental predicament when torn between Mrs Aylmer and Polly Dwyer. He had begun to tell Swan's Wing a little about it, but the other man either did not listen or had no interest in the subject. He failed to reply. He certainly volunteered no information about his own relations with women. Tom could not guess whether Swan's Wing was a married man. He smiled a little and sang once more. In fact, it suited him very well to be 'over the hills and far away', and to have left the complexities of love behind him in New York. Some presentiment, however, of riding towards a new destiny undoubtedly had begun to take possession of Tom Byerley, before they reached the township guarded by squaws. At first, however, it was the land itself which overpowered Tom by its beauty. The woods which they had now approached were such woods as he had never seen in Staffordshire: an abundance of different shrubs, rhododendron and azalea, and behind them the towering American chestnuts, and the richly foliated varieties of oak – red oak, white oak, rock chestnut, umbrella trees. Tom had discovered the excellence of Swan's Wing's English. He nevertheless held back from comments which implied a set of unfamiliar references. Was Swan's Wing, for example, familiar with the Scriptures? Tom, though no Bible-thumper, or even Bible-reader, tried to think of a way of saying that he felt he had stepped into a new Garden of Eden. Their horses, the two they rode, and the two pack horses which followed behind, had just ridden through a clearing, and they had their first sight of the mountains.

—God brought the Cherokee people here because we are the Principal People, said Swan's Wing.

—I see why you feel you have a lot in common with Owd Wooden Leg. I rather fancy he thinks his family are pretty damned principal!

—The Almighty Lord brought us here, just as he brought Wooden Leg to your valleys and hills. He taught them skills, how to cultivate wheat and rye, how to hunt, how to fish, how to build towns. Yes, and how to make pots. The Americans do not know how to make pots.

—So I have heard.

—They have few skills.

—Is that so?

—In the Beginning, this world was all water. Living things lived above, in the sky – the animals, the fish, the insects and the birds – and men and women, of course.

—I have often wondered how we got here, said Tom in an accommodating manner. Owd Wooden Leg has a friend called Dr Darwin. He has some idea of our all having evolved into life on earth – one species changing into another!

—That was not the story told to Cherokee people, said Swan's Wing. We began, all of us, in our story, the animals, the birds, the fish, the insects, in the sky. The earth was all covered in water, so we had to be in the sky. But at length, it became, shall we say, a little crowded up there, and some of the animals began to complain. So they agreed that one of them should be sent down to the earth to see if there was a way – any way – of sustaining life down here. They sent the Dayunsi.

—And he is?

—He is what you call the Water Beetle. And the Dayunsi came down from Heaven, and he swam about in the waters which covered every part of the earth's surface, and he could find no rest. And then Dayunsi thought to himself, maybe if I dive yet deeper. So he dived and he dived and he came to the bottom of the waters, where he found soft white clay – just such white clay as Wooden Leg wants to buy from the Cherokee people. And so the Water Beetle flew back up to Heaven and he told the other animals, if only we could find a way of driving back the waters, we should be able to live on this earth, and there would be more room in Heaven, in what we call Galunati. And God heard the desire of the Water Beetle, and the soft clay spread out, and spread out until it became an island, the island which we now call Our Mother the Earth. But it was still too wet to walk upon. So they sent birds to fly around it, promising that they would come back and tell the other animals when the Island was fit for habitation. At first, they say, it is much too wet, like the pot which has just been fashioned and before it is fired. But eventually it dries out, like what Wooden Leg calls biscuit ware. And so the animals send out the Great Buzzard, the father of all the Buzzards you see now. Maybe your Dr Darwin is right that all Buzzards come from this father Buzzard.

—I'm not completely sure that this was Dr Darwin's theory.

—The Great Buzzard, who is the father of all Buzzards, flew over all the earth when it was still wet clay, waiting to be moulded, and sometimes he nearly landed, and sometimes he swooped again into the sky. And at length he came to Cherokee Country. He was very tired, and his wings drooped and flapped. And as he thumped the wet ground, his wings made what we call the valleys, and when the wings came up, they drew with them skeins of wet clay. And so he formed the mountains which you see yonder. And as they watched him from Galunati, they called out to him: Do not drum the earth with your wings or it will all be mountains, and it will be hard for us to live there! And so he flew home, but to this day the Cherokee People they live in the mountains and in the plains.

—That is a charming story.

—Stories tell us how we came here, how the earth came here. Yes, but he wanted to say, the story is not true?

—Not long now, said Swan's Wing, and then we meet the squaws.

They had come to a clearing, where evidence of human habitation was visible. Tom had not formed specific predictions about the nature of an Indian settlement. The journey itself, the abundance of new impressions and fresh landscapes, the mysterious company of Swan's Wing and the almost totally silent pair of braves who looked after the pack horses, had occupied him for more than a month, and it was impossible to know, before he saw it, what an Indian 'township' would be like. But as he had grown to respect Swan's Wing, so too he had perhaps deliberately not envisaged the primitive, and perhaps squalid, nature of what he was riding towards.

It only took a very few minutes, as they approached the settlement, for Tom to feel a mixture of disgust and embarrassment. For this was worse than anything he could have predicted.

Into the dusty expanse between a few mean huts, various ragged, sunburnt children were running. One was naked, another wore a torn shirt and no shoes. From the doorway of one of the makeshift huts, and a doorway was all it was, because their architectural accomplishments did not rise to the making of doors and hinges, stood a woman with bare breasts gazing drunkenly and sullenly at the horsemen who came into her yard.

Tom looked again. He could not believe his eyes. This 'squaw' was no squaw. It was a woman of evidently European extraction. His first horrified conjecture was that this was a woman who had been seized by the Indians and made their slave, but then, from the entrance of the hut, there emerged a long-haired, bedraggled man, also evidently European in appearance. He was as drunk as the woman, and as he staggered in front of Swan's Wing's horse, he seemed in danger of being trampled.

—Christ! called this man. You come to scalp us? We ain't got nothin' ter steal, friend . . . and his words trailed off into incoherence.

—They're redskins, shouted the semi-naked woman from the hut.

Then, catching the eye of Tom on his piebald, she shouted,

—What you fucking doing with a lot of fucking redskins? Don't you know they're fucking murderers?

—Shut your cunting face, bitch, shouted back her paramour.

Swan's Wing had dismounted. With perfect courtesy, he said to the oaf,

—With your permission, we should like to water our horses.

The colonist stared red-eyed at Swan's Wing. Other figures were now beginning to cluster round Tom and Swan's Wing. Some were visibly frightened. Children were laughing.

They had come upon a poor colonists' village. The half-hour they spent there, watering their horses, and preparing for the last hour's ride to the Cherokee township, was horrible to Tom. Everyone to whom he spoke asked for money. At first, they assumed that Tom, using an Indian horseman as his guide, was recruiting for the Rebel army, and they called out simple-minded insults to King George. Then, when it was established that Tom was an Englishman, they reversed their opinions of the King, and wished to assure him, in so far as they were capable of any finished sentence, of their detestation of sedition, and their abject loyalty to the Crown. It appeared that this little scrub of land had been occupied by this group for about five years. So Swan's Wing guessed, when they were remounted and had ridden with great relief upon their way.

—Many poor white families live like that, all through these regions, he said. They come to farm here but they possess no farming skills. No rich people come with them. Some of them are runaway servants from the bigger estates in Virginia, some are criminals. As you see, they live like beasts. The fathers sleep with their daughters and even their granddaughters. They produce as many as a dozen children, born of sisters, granddaughters, nieces. They possess no skills as farmers or hunters. It is sad, this place.

Tom felt burning shame that he had mistaken this uncivilized and horrible community for a Cherokee town: it was closer to the Yahoos in Dean Swift's darkest fantasy than to anything he had ever experienced in real life.

—Let us put it out of our minds, said Swan's Wing. Soon, we see the squaws, and we shall know we are at home.

## 7

—THE WORLD HAS GONE MAD WITH ANTI-AMERICAN fever, quite mad, said Matthew Boulton.

His thick eyebrows seemed arched in perpetual surprise at the irrationality of his fellow mortals. There was something almost aristocratic about the fine-boned face of this Birmingham manufacturer. He looked more like Josiah's idea of a Duke than the actual Dukes who had begun to purchase Wedgwood ware.

—They say, said Boulton, shaking his head, which was adorned with a full, slightly ill-kempt tie-wig, they *say*, there are riots in London.

—Not just in London, said Mr Watt.

Josiah was not part of the inner circle who called themselves the Lunar Society. He lived too far from the neat, clean little town of Birmingham, their usual meeting place, and he was too busy with his other affairs. But their interests were so various, their intellectual accomplishments so impressive, that he could not rejoice in their company.

They met at the time of the full moon – hence their soubriquet – usually at the house of Matthew Boulton, though sometimes at Dr Darwin's house in Lichfield.

—Yet every reasonable man is a friend of America! You're a friend of America, Mr Wedgwood, I take it?

—Indeed, sir. Have I not had the honour of meeting Mr Franklin at this very table?

—He told us then that we could resolve our differences amicably. Now it looks much less certain, said Watt.

—We have done such good trade with them! lamented Josiah. If only this tedious business of a Stamp Duty were done away with, we could trade again. Why, even old Lord Chatham has urged the unreasonableness of it.

At the mere mention of Pitt there was general laughter. Wedgwood did not completely understand the mirth, which rose to a roar. Then Mr Watt added,

—And Mr Burke. These are hardly revolutionaries!

—P-p-perhaps not so tactful to mention M-Mr Burke, said Dr Darwin humorously, in front of our f-f-friend.

He jerked his thumb sideways in the direction of Josiah.

Jos, uneasy at ribbing, especially by his intellectual peers, tried to look the good sport.

—I have no doubt Mr Burke has good reason to support Mr Cookworthy in his claim to patent all the china clay in Cornwall!

But it was no good, he could not get the tone of conviviality required for such a gathering; he could not keep the seriousness out of his voice, as he added,

—Quite how you can persuade Parliament to patent clay, English clay, is beyond me.

He jutted out his lower lip, which trembled slightly, and for a split second he looked like a child on the verge of tears.

—We knew that Mr Burke had lent his voice to support the Americans, but no one is perfect, my dear sir, and I had no idea he had been so foolish as to take arms against the great Josiah! said Watt.

Wedgwood smiled weakly. His boyhood and young manhood had

contained no social life outside his family. He had scarcely ever eaten among strangers until Dr Darwin introduced him to the Lunar men and, though there was plenty of robust jest and teasing in the Wedgwood family circle, he was unused to the peculiar badinage in which men indulge when they gather together around tables.

When the meal was over and the cloth removed and the wine set down, there was no formality as there might have been at a domestic dinner, or in the Common Room of an Oxford college. The men moved about happily, drawing up their chairs sideways to one another, while they held their glasses, and talked, nearly always, of technicalities, inventions, physics, chemistry. If Mr Watt wished to discuss the workings of a steam engine with Mr Edgeworth, or Mr Priestley wanted to discuss electricity with Mr Boulton, they walked round and did so, with perfect ease and informality. Dr Darwin held forth on no less a theme than botanic life itself, its singular origin, all plant forms stemming from one genus.

The table broke up at about four that winter afternoon. There was about an hour of light left in the sharp January sky. Jos walked into Mr Boulton's Soho Manufactory yard with Dr Darwin.

Between both men there existed a close fondness. Erasmus had been Josiah's physician for over a decade, but he had developed into a deep family friend upon whom all the Wedgwoods depended, seeing it as his duty not only to tend their ever-recurrent sicknesses but also to laugh them out of their glooms.

Six inches taller than Josiah, and weighing a third as much again, Darwin was a man of huge appetites: greedy at table, ever-hungry for women, devoted to the bottle, though not its slave. His face was a great ham of shining cheeks, double chins and smiles. Even when the stammer did not actually prevent the outpouring of words, there was a slight hesitancy of speech so that much of the sound produced by his larynx was a wordless vocalization – oohh, err, um. His smiling manners made everything he said seem complimentary, although much of what he said was sharp.

—I was sorry, sir, not to sit beside you. I was n-n-next to Priestley, and since he st-st-stammers w-w-w-w—

'W's were always the hardest with him.

—Worse than you? Josiah supplied.

Angered at having the words supplied for him, Darwin continued,

—He thinks there will be all-out war with America now.

—Surely he's wrong? I know we've sent troops but . . .

—You're fearful for young Byerley? He's yet in N-N-New York? The Garrick of the American stage?

—I've asked him to see if he can supply me with Cherokee clay. If this wretched conflict escalates, there is no knowing where my supplies will come from.

—It will probably b-b-blow over. But I can tell you have a scheme afoot. You have that preoccupied air. The l-l-*look*, my dear. I know the *look*!

—You know what it is?

There was real anxiety in Josiah's tone. Two things could wrench his guts and reduce his nerves to terror: his wife's ill humours, and industrial espionage.

—Your new ploy? It was advertised in the l-latest n-newspapers in L-london and Brummagem.

—Don't play such tricks with me, Dr Darwin, sir!

—Y-your face, Jos!

—You'll be passing through Etruria this week? Good, good. I was going to tell you this week, but I could not tell you here. Boulton is an excellent fellow, but, well, if he hears of a scheme, he has a tendency to muscle in on the act. In this particular case, that would not do at all.

—A royal commission would be m-m-my guess.

—You *do* know?

—My dear Jos, be calm. Your face is as a book where m-m-men may r-read strange matters. Apart from the birth of your sons, and the building of the Trent and M-M-Mersey Canal, I never knew anything to excite you so much as a royal commission.

Jos's voice sank to a whisper as he told Darwin the gist of the task before him. The Empress of Russia . . . a dinner service . . . nigh on a thousand pieces, each different, each hand-painted.

Before he heaved himself into his phaeton, the doctor asked in a low voice,

—And Mrs Wedgwood?

—She is of course delighted, as delighted as I by the possibility of this great increase in our name and reputation. Why, with – his voice sank to a whisper – with the Empress of Russia as my client, the world is at my feet.

—I meant, how is Sal in her spirits?

Dr Darwin chuckled.

—She is well.

Wedgwood could dissemble in his words but not in his tone.

—I'll look in this week. Laudanum, my dear sir, plenty of laudanum! Drown her sorrows with the p-p-poppy until I come.

—We are so grateful to you, my dear Doctor. And remember, you are always welcome to dine, or if you come too late to dine, to have tea and supper and to spend the night.

—Oh, that would be c-capital! Oh! To s-stay, oh, I say!

He spoke as if everything were a treat set before him.

The bright yellow carriage creaked as he squeezed his bulk into the seat. An incessant traveller, the doctor was in perpetual quest of faster and faster wheels. He had recently invented a new steering device. He had even discussed with Mr Watt the possibility of a steam conveyance, but they could not work out how such a vehicle could carry sufficient fuel, while outstripping that well-designed speed-machine, the horse. All Darwin's carriages were of his own design. They were intended for one man, but contained enough space for a writing desk, books, papers, food and drink.

—Who's meeting you at Stone?

—The usual.

—The f-f-faithful Caleb! I don't know why you continue to tolerate that man, Jos. You are very loyal.

The two men laughed, a little mirthlessly, as at some inexplicable shared joke. Jos closed the door of the carriage upon his friend. The corners of his mouth drew back in a smile but his grey-blue eyes were sad. He was aware that there was something about his relations with Sally which were, if not shaming, then at least visible to others but not to himself. Was there something the matter with Mrs Wedgwood or were all women so constituted? Josiah assumed that her sulks and ill humours and long spells in bed were as normal as her constant scoldings of her husband. But what if these things were not normal? His own mother had died when he was a child. He only saw women at work, or women on their best behaviour, and had no way of judging how they behaved when alone with their husbands. Was the doctor afraid that Sally was on the verge of insanity (a fear Josiah sometimes nursed himself)? Had Erasmus seen the hand of death upon her? Should they be ceasing marital relations and remaining content with the children who had been given to them? If there was an answer to these questions, it was hidden with the occupant of the yellow carriage which had swept down the Birmingham street with spatterings of dirt.

Josiah travelled post from the coaching inn in Birmingham. The postilion started the horses. The lead horse strained forward at his collar. The springs of the carriage creaked and swayed and they were away down the turnpike road, northwards on the Stafford road. There were two gentlemen passengers 'outside', but Jos had the inside to himself and, leaning back on the leather seat, he could give himself to reverie.

His entire being tingled with excitement at the Russian order. Ever since Lord Cathcart had conveyed that the Empress would want the stupendous, the truly enormous, dinner service, Josiah's mind had played with the design of the thing. He must look out his Tooke and refresh his memory of the various Roman divinities. One possibility would be to have Mars for the soup plates, Poseidon for the fish, Juno for the twelve-inch plates, and so on. Borders might be acanthus leaves. Jos had a mind to draw and design these himself, though he might consult his young cousin Stringer, a budding designer and watercolourist, and see whether for the greater items — for example, the large oval compotiers — he might not include noble ruins of classical antiquity.

Together with these creative imaginings, his brain allowed technical questions to mingle. He weighed in his mind whether to stick to the tried and trusted formulae for baking creamware or whether to experiment with yet further refinements. If only there was more white clay in the world.

And this thought led on to a tender consciousness of how much he had asked of his nephew Tom Byerley in America. He missed the boy. When Meg, his elder sister, became a widow, Jos and his brothers had befriended young Byerley. For a while, the boy had worked for him at the Brick House Works in Burslem, for a while with Jos's brother John, the firm's London agent. It was before Jos had married. Many of the instincts which had subsequently made him a loving, if insensitive, father were as yet latent in him. He had poured these feelings of love into the boy. Indeed, there was a sense in which he loved Byerley more than anyone else in the family.

It was to John, Jos's worldly, London brother, to whom Tom had revealed all his true ambitions – the desire for literary fame and success on the stage. Clearly, the lad had been afraid of confiding these deeply held aspirations to Josiah, for fear of hurting his feelings. Far from angering Jos, this made him love the lad more. Perhaps if his Uncle John had lived, Byerley would have remained in England? But Josiah's brother had been found dead in the Ranelagh pleasure gardens. It was one of those appalling, arbitrary visitations of misfortune to which, over the years, Josiah had become accustomed.

He had lost not merely a brother (in all but scandalous circumstances, for what would a respectable man have been doing in the pleasure gardens at such an hour of night, when whores and pickpockets were abroad?). He had also lost the one figure who held his nephew Byerley to the firm. Saying goodbye to Byerley at Liverpool Docks five years since had been one of the most painful wrenches of Josiah's life, more painful than John's mysterious death. The stoical manner in which Meg had clapped her hands and moved into the routine of reciting 'Farewell, a long farewell to all my greatness' as the boy went up the gangplank had only added to the pathos it was intended to dissolve.

Jos knew that there would have been other means of getting possession of more Cherokee clay than by employing his nephew. What he had asked was an arduous and dangerous assignment. He had done it, in part, of that there was no doubt, because he wanted that clay. But he had also done it in the fervent hope that, with the clay, Tom would come home again and be welcomed as the Prodigal Nephew. Get the boy interested in the works again. Drive all this literature nonsense out of his noddle, and get him doing summat useful!

The kaleidoscope of disconnected thoughts – about Tom, about the Empress of Russia and her service – jangled in his head, as the coach rumbled along, as the shades lengthened, and the still wintry sun went finally to rest. The violent orange of the setting sun caught the frozen puddles in the fields and was reflected with a series of dazzling colour splashes against the dun clods.

Into Wedgwood's thoughts came vacancies, during which he half-dozed, waking with the jolts and shaking of the mail coach to other recollections and reflections. Now he would see in his mind's eye Erasmus Darwin and Joseph Priestley, stammering to one another at Mr Boulton's table about the origins of the universe. Now, again, he would be visited by a feeling of oppressive heaviness, and would be unable to account for it. Into his energetic and usually sunny disposition, there drifted these clouds of sorrow. Sometimes they were without cause, but this evening, he knew that the sorrows had identifiable origins.

He pulled back the leather flap which covered the window of the coach and saw the full moon shining upon trees and hedgerows. They were north of Lichfield by now and – the moonlight allowed him to consult the repeater from his fob-pocket – in two hours they would be in Stafford. Some shadowy forms beneath dark blue-black trees were discernible as sheep whose fleece caught the silver of the moonshine.

His sorrows had a double origin. On the one hand, he was returning to a wife who did not love him. Although a man who found the emotional life puzzling, and the range, depth and ardour of his wife's passions as unreadable as Greek script, he was not such a fool as not to know that whatever should exist between a man and his wife did not exist between them. And this he found truly incomprehensible. When the idea of marrying his cousin Sally had first been mooted, he had been so thoroughly excited. An iron discipline had kept in check, through all his years of apprenticeship, those animal and amorous appetites which had always been strong in him. Beside these considerations, he was fond of his cousin. They had always liked one another, and both – or so he had supposed – enjoyed the companionable idea of a marriage which was a family affair. So many marriages in the initial stages must be difficult as the various tastes and assumptions of the parties shake down together. There was a Wedgwood way of looking at the world. In this, Sally and he were already united, before they had even been so much as conceived, let alone betrothed.

Tall, shy, angular, clever Sally was in so many ways his superior: this he readily conceded. At family weddings, or Sunday dinners, whenever he had seen her, during their growing up (she was nearly four years his junior), Jos had found her an agreeable, amusing com-panion. Her accomplishments, whether at the keyboard or with the colour box and the sketchbook, were easily the equal of any lady in the land, and indeed, she was, by his standards, a lady, more refined in her manners, more quietly composed in her bearing, than his immediate family, who had grown up in a somewhat harum-scarum manner at the old Churchyard Works, all living next door to the pot banks and taking their turn to work together and to play and fight. Anyone meeting Sally's parents and Jos's simple brother Tom, to whom he was apprenticed, might suppose them to have come from different classes of society, not so much because of the way they spoke as because of Sally's whole bearing, and by the sharpness of her mind and the intellectual acuity with which she followed public events, reading news-sheets as well as popular novels, and literature in several tongues.

As their private married life together had begun, however, a shadow had descended, and they had never been happy companions. Even when the children began to come along – Sukey, John, Richard, Jos Junior, Tom, Kitty, Sarah – Sally's spirits had not notably improved. There had hardly been a period of more than three days' duration, in the previous eleven years, when Sally had been in a good humour with her husband. Oh, she kept up appearances before strangers and was polite with him. As if politeness was all that a husband desired or deserved. But she resolutely withheld friendship from him. Or so it felt to him. And his heart was heavy as the coach heaved and rattled along.

At times, the new turnpike road was almost smooth, and they made a good speed. At other bends in the road, they were compelled to follow older roads, pitted with holes and puddles. Sometimes, in the cold night air, Jos could hear the gentlemen on top call out to the driver,

—Have a care, sir! We were nearly turned over!

And once, as the horses dragged the reluctant carriage over Cannock Chase, the driver stopped, and asked everyone to get out to walk for half a mile, because the dirt was so deep that the wheels were in danger of sinking.

—We'd hoped ter be in Stafford afore midnate! said one of the outside gentlemen, peevishly, Jos thought, for it was only nine o'clock and the coachman was doing his best.

It did Jos's heart good, however, to hear a North Staffordshire voice. Soon enough, he'd be hearing another of those: the voice of Caleb Bowers. If Jos had had no domestic or marital reason for the heaviness which lay upon his soul as he made his way homeward, there was always Caleb to puncture or diminish the merriment of things.

# 8

WHEN THEY RODE THROUGH THE NEXT CLEARING, THEY
entered cultivated territory. The wildness of the woods, the domain
of the turkey, the bear and the humming bird, was left behind for
farmland. Tom Byerley had never seen such enormous fields of
wheat. It was all the more remarkable, having left behind, by only a
few miles, the miserable hutments and squalid mud-patches of the
colonialist Yahoos.

Here, acre upon acre of golden wheat and barley swayed in the
light summer breeze. The immense undulating ocean of corn was
unlike anything he had ever seen in England. Even on the great
estates of the Duke of Bridgewater, or of Lord Gower at Trentham,
which he had sometimes visited with his Uncle Jos, there had never
been cultivation on such scale, or with such a degree of agricultural
sophistication. Next to the vast cornfields were smaller fields growing
potatoes, squash, melons and cabbage. And then, beyond the fields,
and beside a wide, calmly flowing river, in which the blue of the
firmament was sparklingly reflected, Tom could see a neatly planned
township, a few timber-built and apparently windowless houses near
the entrance to the settlement, and beyond, huge conical structures
which could accommodate easily thirty or forty people. Smaller
dwellings were also dotted around, beside which were carefully cultivated gardens. With admiration, and some envy – for he and his

mother at home were keen gardeners – Tom noted neatly constructed frames over which flowering beans healthily rampaged.

As they approached what was evidently the entrance to the town, Swan's Wing turned to him and repeated what he had said on their journey.

—Remember, it is the squaws who keep the entrance to our dwellings. They will decide whether or not you come in peace.

—Is that not something which I decide? I have assured you that I come in peace. My friend, Swan's Wing, you can vouch for me that.

—They decide. When we arrive, you must explain to them the nature of your journey. Tell them you come in peace to the Cherokee people. Bring them news of Wooden Leg, for they revere him. Tell them, if you know news of him, of King George also.

Tom dismounted, and led his horse towards the first wooden structure: this he took to be the equivalent of a European customs house. Two women, at his approach, came out of the building. It was obvious from their demeanour that they had been watching his approach from afar. One, perhaps forty years of age, was tall, with her blue-black hair braided with beads. The other, a slightly shorter, younger woman, appeared to be little more than twenty years old. She wore her hair loose over her shoulders. Tom noted her long nose, her heavy sensual lips, and the high cheekbones which were similar to those of the older woman. But what struck him chiefly about this younger squaw were the eyes: they shone with brightness from their dark globes, and it was a brightness which seemed deeply wise. Her eyebrows made a suggestion of irony, rising as they did at a sharp angle above her smooth brow. Crude American-speakers spoke of 'redskins', but the skin of these women was a light brown, paler than many an English rustic or English sailor. No flicker of a smile appeared on either of the women's faces.

—O *si yo*, said the older woman.

Attempting to be polite, Tom, an accomplished mimic and lin-
guist, repeated the words. Here the women almost smiled, and the
younger one replied,

—*Ho wa!*

Tom looked to Swan's Wing for help, but none came. This was no
game.

The women bowed to Tom, and he bowed in return. He felt
clumsy in doing so, and hoped he was doing the right thing.

Uncle Jos's first taste of life at Court, some ten years earlier, had
passed into family legend. The creamware which Jos had pioneered
at the Brick House Works had enjoyed phenomenal success. At last,
it was no longer necessary for an English family to go to Meissen
or to Sèvres if they wanted elegant glazed pottery. Moreover, the
creamware being produced by Wedgwood at Burslem was not
merely as elegant as anything you could buy in France or Germany:
it was by no means expensive. He had several aristocratic customers
who had begun to buy in great quantities. This popularity among the
higher sort of folks had made Wedgwood popular with the aspirant
middlings. And then had come the moment when a Miss Chetwynd,
daughter of the Master of the Mint, and Seamstress to the Queen,
had given it to be understood that Her Majesty would like to sample
Mr Wedgwood's wares. The initial negotiations had been handled
by Uncle John, who lived in the capital and acted as his brother's
London agent. The Queen, it was understood, wanted 'a complete set
of tea things, with a gold ground and raised flowers upon it in green
in the same manner of the green flowers that are raised upon the
*mehons*, so it is wrote, but I suppose it should be melons'.

And the day had come when Jos had been obliged to discard his
plain old buff coat and breeches, and to array himself as a courtier,
in a blue surcoat, a scarlet waistcoat trimmed with lace, and a 'lite

Brown dress bob wig'. He had even called at the 'Sign of the Flaming Sword' in Great Newport Street, near the London showrooms, to buy himself a sword. And thus arrayed, the Master Potter of Burslem had presented himself at Buckingham House with some samples. The sun was streaming through the drawing-room windows as the Queen tried to look at the pattern upon the vase which Mr Wedgwood presented to Her Majesty for inspection. Miss Chetwynd and another lady-in-waiting should have called for a footman to adjust the light, but Uncle Jos, oblivious of protocol, strode to the window on his peg leg and pulled down the blind.

The Queen had smiled and said, in her heavy German accent,

—Ladies, Mr Wedgwood is, as you see, already an accomplished courtier.

There was always laughter at the family table when Uncle Jos told this story, but from an early age, Tom had wondered whether the Queen's words had in truth been intended as a compliment or as a rebuke. Some social antennae which Tom possessed, and his uncle apparently did not, had made him ask himself, even as a lad, whether or not a true gentleman would have waited for the footman to pull down the blind. Such was his uncle's innocence, or directness of attack, or simple common sense – Jos always told the story as if the royal words meant what they seemed to mean.

'Mr Wedgwood, is, as you see, already an accomplished courtier.'

Dear old Jos! No one was ever less like a courtier! A courtier must be a flatterer. A courtier must always have something of Byerley's chosen profession in the theatre. There must be artifice of manners. Jos was able to be a salesman, no one more accomplished at that. He could be testy, but he was naturally good-humoured, so there was no need for him to pretend. He liked human beings, and he had an ease of manner with them, whether they were the German-born Queen of England, or a noble lord, or a little boy or girl whom he was training up as a painter or a modeller. But the dissembling skills of a courtier? Fiddlesticks!

Something of embarrassment on his behalf, an embarrassment which Byerley suspected Jos was not capable of, now came over the young man as he approached the Cherokee squaws. They seemed, in their graceful poise, as completely intimidating as Queen Charlotte or Miss Chetwynd. Byerley had no difficulty in attracting the women-folk. The swagger of Macheath had not been very hard for him to adopt when he had played *The Beggar's Opera*. And as he looked into those dark, deep eyes, he said inwardly,

—Surely you could give me a smile?

But even as, silently and inwardly, his self-conceit formed the words in his brain, they nervously died. His heart began to beat.

It was the younger woman who spoke first. Her voice was a perfect contralto.

Swan's Wing translated her words.

—Has the stranger come with Mr Daniel Boone and Mr Bird?

Swan's Wing explained that Daniel Boone was a colonist who was attempting to acquire Cherokee land for European settlers. Tom was able to answer that he had come alone, on behalf of Wooden Leg. Some years ago, Wooden Leg had sent his representative, a Mr Griffiths, to buy white clay or kaolin from the Cherokee Nation.

At this point, Tom unstrapped his satchel. The action produced an immediate reaction. The young woman spoke rapidly to Swan's Wing, and the warrior said,

—The Beloved Gatekeeper thinks you look for a gun in your sack. Tom Byerley is not to produce his weapon while he is in the town. The Beloved Gatekeepers will believe his story of Wooden Leg but if he produces a gun—

But he was not fishing in his bag for a gun.

—On the other horse, he said, there are more pots made by

Wooden Leg, which he sends with affectionate regard for the Cherokee Nation. But I thought you would also like to see this.

With what he afterwards realized was rashness amounting to lunacy, he defied their injunction and rummaged in the satchel.

—Here.

And he produced a small packet. With a bow, he held it out to the younger woman, but it was the older squaw who took it.

Some debate between the two women ensued. Tom was unable to decide whether they were discussing the etiquette or the safety of the next procedure. That is to say, when presented with a gift, was it their custom only to open the present later that day, or were they afraid that the little paper-wrapped parcel contained something of danger?

Clearly, the earlier speculation was closer to the truth, for Swan's Wing told him,

—Later, when you meet the Beloved Assembly, will be a time to smoke a pipe, and to exchange gifts. The women believe you have come with Mr Boone and Mr Bird.

—Be assured, Tom replied, I know of neither Boone nor Bird.

He bowed and there followed a silence.

Then the older woman asked a further question.

Swan's Wing replied, and then, as if to confirm the accuracy of what he had said, the brave enquired,

—I am right? You have travelled from far and would like to stay here in the town?

—If I am offered hospitality, he said with a smile.

This time the younger woman spoke, and Swan's Wing translated.

—Ka Ma Ma says that you are welcome for as long as you stay with us. I am to show you to your quarters. Later, they would like you to attend the palaver in the Hall of Meeting. The Old Priest has summoned the meeting to still our fears about Mr Boone's proposal. Ka Ma Ma believes it is very strange that three white men should come to the town in one day with such similar requests, Mr Boone and Mr Bird to buy our land and you to take our clay.

Byerley wished to explain that he had no intention of taking the clay; he, that is to say his Uncle Josiah, wanted to pay a fair price for it.

—If you open the package, you will see what he has done with the last Cherokee kaolin which he bought – the clay which Mr Griffiths brought away from here years ago.

The package contained an exquisite Wedgwood teapot, fashioned in the shape of a cauliflower, with the richest green and yellowish glaze to colour the leaves and the creamiest cream for the white floweret. All the way from Philadelphia, he thought to himself with some exasperation, all the way from blasted Philadelphia, I have brought that teapot undamaged, and you still will not open it!

While Swan's Wing translated his words and explained that the object had been made with an admixture of clay from England and Cherokee kaolin, the women apparently ignored the words. He might as well have been whistling, or silent, for all the response he was able to elicit.

Frustrating as this was, Tom could not restrain a feeling of intense excitement at spending his first night as a guest in the Cherokee township. Swan's Wing took him to a small wooden hut. It was one of the cottages beside which the bean-poles were in abundant flower. The air was filled with the scent of the bean plants, mingled now and again with that of wood smoke, though he could not see any fires alight.

—You will be looked after by a brave called Running Deer.

—I hoped we were going to see more of one another. Thank you, Swan's Wing, for guiding me on my journey.

—It was a pleasure to travel with you, over the hills and far away. Swan's Wing now smiled quite normally, adding,

—I must go to my wife.

It was the first time this woman had been mentioned. Byerley, a naturally gossiping, chattering young man who lived on the surfaces of life, had wondered whether Swan's Wing was married, but such was the brave's taciturn manner on the journey, no moment had occurred when such an inquiry would have come without seeming forced.

Before he left Tom in the cottage set apart for hospitality, Swan's Wing pointed to the flagpole which stood in the middle of the settlement, outside the large conical building which Tom rightly took to be the village hall.

—You see that it flies the white flag, said Swan's Wing. For the Cherokee, the white flag means peace and when we fly a red flag or array ourselves in red garments, it means war. But for you men of Europe, the white flag means surrender, no?

—That is so.

—For many of us younger Cherokee, it also seems a surrender when the old priests of our people signed away the Cherokee land to Mr Boone and his men. That is what they will be discussing in the Hall of Meeting later. Still Waters fears that you have come to support Mr Bird and Mr Boone. Blue Squirrel believes you come in peace.

—But surely they could tell I was not American?

—How could they?

—My clothes? My speech? Damn it, man, do I sound like an American?

—To Cherokee, white men all sound and look alike.

—Thank you very much.

—But Blue Squirrel says that there is a yearning in your heart, that you did not come to make war but to find salve for that yearning.

He wondered which of the two women was which – was it the beautiful younger woman who had looked into his heart?

Later, refreshed by a wash and a change of clothes, and by a bowl of vegetable broth which was brought to his cottage by Running Deer, a pleasant young brave, tattooed from neck to ankles and who appeared to have no English, Byerley presented himself at the Hall of Meeting.

There were nearly a hundred people present. The men and women sat separately. On a raised dais in the centre of the hall, several old men, robed and decked with feather headdresses, sat. Beside them, on two leather chairs, sat two white men, Mr Boone and a gangling, whiskered buffoon who was introduced as Mr Bird. Tom could not tell whether Bird had been brought along as a business partner or as a servant. Bird spoke with a nasal whinnying voice which was instantly unsympathetic.

Swan's Wing eventually came on to the stage to join them, acting as interpreter.

Mr Boone, in an awkward speech which was plainly intended to insinuate the white men into the good graces of their hosts, said that the colonists and the Indians (as he called them) had mutual interests. It could only be to the shared benefit of both the Indian and the American people, he said, for the colonists to expand further into territories which at present were, as far as they could tell, entirely devoid of habitation.

Tom was drowsy from his journey but Mr Boone's manner of speech would have been soporific to the ears of the most alert hearer. He spoke with many hesitations, and, if not exactly repetitions, circumlocutions and pauses which were almost intolerably tedious.

—I, we, the representatives of the People of the States, we have nothing, that is to say, there is absolutely no feeling of hostility, that is, we nurse no feelings of enmity whatsoever . . .

And here the buffoon Mr Bird would nod his head in agreement.

—And we are pleased, gratified, it is with the utmost feeling . . . of . . . er . . . friendship and . . . amity . . . that we have drawn up this agreement between . . . I thank you.

Ill-constructed as Mr Boone's sentences had been, there could be no mistaking their sense. Nor could there be the smallest doubt that they were having a divisive effect upon their audience. Tom gauged that about a third of those present understood the drift of Boone's words. But it was when Swan's Wing began to interpret that the murmurings in the audience grew to a roar.

One of the men on the platform was a proud old man of about sixty. His head was shaved, save for four or five plaited tresses near the crown and neck. His brow was tattooed with four parallel blue lines, not unlike a musical score, and his cheeks were tattooed with large X-shaped crosses. He wore a multiplicity of copper rings in both ears.

He rose to his feet, and to Tom's surprise, he spoke excellent English. This was, as he later found out, none other than the famous Ostenaco, who, with two other Cherokee braves, had visited London some years before.

—Gentlemen, Mr Boone, Mr Bird, Mr Byerley, nephew of Wooden Leg, I give you greeting from the Cherokee people. We know that there have been times when the English colonists and the Cherokee people have not been friends. Why do men and women fight wars? Is it not hunger which drives the spear? Is it not fear of the empty belly which fires the cannon ball? More and more European men come to America. Many cross the ocean. But even in the time that the thirteen colonists have had their late quarrels with King George, many thousand new Americans have arrived, not by sea, but by the passage of their mothers' wombs.

At this mention of female anatomy, Mr Bird, who sat with his legs crossed and his hands behind his head, laughed as if a ribald tavern joke had been made.

—We must all find a way of living together in peace, said the old mage. And the best way is for Cherokee to accept Mr Boone's offer: not to conquer land by much fighting, but to buy land.

There was uproar in the Hall of Meeting at this. The younger squaw, who had greeted Tom's arrival, the beauty with the long hair, was on her feet and speaking furiously. It was as much as Swan's Wing could do to keep up with her and translate her words into English.

—What use was money when they lost land? The spirits of her grandmothers inhabited this place. The Cherokee knew how to cultivate the land and to cherish it. Compare our well-run farms with the mess made by the . . . colonists (Tom suspected a less polite word had been used) down the road. Even if all the gold in the world had been offered, it would still not be worth it.

Uproarious applause at these words.

Another voice now, that of a young brave named Dragging Canoe. Who knew what the so-called money of the white men was worth? Who knew that they were not counterfeit coins? The white men brought coins emblazoned with the head of their King, but they were not loyal to their King! They were fighting their King, lying to the Cherokee. Their words were worth nothing, their money was worth nothing.

Ostenaco rose, and tried to calm the tumult which these words provoked, but the cheering was infectious. All the younger members of the audience had their arms raised. Tom's gaze was fixed on that of the young squaw who had been the first to speak out against the proposed land purchase. As she cheered, her face was lit with radiant joy. She held a fist clenched and waved it aloft. The armpit of her light grey shift was dark. Tom's gaze became a fixed stare; it was as if a spell had been cast over his heart, such rapture, and such lust did he feel.

—————⌣—————

—You oughta . . . mm . . . er . . .

The tall gangling American, the man whom Tom had initially taken to be Mr Boone's idiot servant, was beginning one of his long, unfinished sentences. Indeed, so unfinished were these clusters of words that blurted through his whiskery lips, that they really did not aspire to the condition of any clause or sentence framed in the civilized world. It was as if language itself had been torn up, and the words thrown into the air like a pile of leaves being kicked by a careless urchin.

The two men, Tom Byerley and Mr Bird, were standing near the entrance of the Hall of Meeting. The conference about the future of the Cherokee lands was over. Tom had understood those parts of the discussion which had been conducted in English, but much had not been – even though the responses of the various Cherokee viewpoints had been translated for the benefit of the visitors. Boone was clearly the senior partner, and Bird, if not the servant, had clearly been brought along as his supporter. Because of the tall, whiskery American's uncouth clothes, the clumsy cut of his coat which did not fit his bony shoulders, and the crudity of the leggings which hung from his greyhound-thin haunches, Tom had taken Bird for an attendant, and it was a surprise to realize that, among his many gaucheries, the man clearly had pretensions to gentility.

As far as Tom could tell, the meeting had ended with a victory for Boone. The old magus or visionary, Ostenaco, had made a speech which had been translated into English by the interpreter. He thanked Mr Boone for his offer and said that he hoped to live in peace with the settlers. The Cherokee would accept the payment he offered and move out of a part of their territories; but at present, the colonists were asking too much, and they must meet again, with maps, to determine just how much acreage of the Beloved western plains, rich in horses, the white man would claim.

At first it seemed as if there could be no resolution to the debate. Then, at a certain point, Ostenaco had risen, like an Archbishop at the State opening of Parliament, surrounded by his robed heralds and acolytes, and the old priest had intoned what Tom took to be a prayer. The meeting was over, and the two visitors, Mr Boone and Mr Bird, were escorted to the door of the huge conical hall. Mr Boone was exchanging some words with the old priests, who had rudimentary English, while his companion, Mr Bird, that skinny, foolish-looking fellow, had buttonholed Tom. The two would-be purchasers of Indian land were about to be escorted to the entrance to the township and sent on their way in the company of their Mohawk guides.

—You oughta get . . . that is to say, by Christ, these people!

Mr Bird blinked and looked about him at the Cherokees, who milled around.

—By Christ, these people, they are savages, Mr Byerley, sir. By God, holy shit, they'd take the scalp off you while you slept. That is, er, to say, slept in your . . . I really would urge you, if you have any . . .

Byerley did not know which of the man's conversational quirks he found the more vexing: the imperious bossiness, which implied that he was entitled to tell another man whether he should stay at Old Kowes or move on; the grotesque blend of lordly grandeur, for the man spoke always *de haut en bas*, and coarse bar-parlour oaths and earthiness; or the simply infuriating device of never finishing his sentences.

—I think, sir, said Byerley, that I can be the judge of whether I stay or leave.

He certainly had no desire to take to the road with Boone and Bird. He even allowed himself the thought that these men, who were so plainly intent upon doing the Cherokee out of their ancestral lands, were provoking the younger warriors; that it would be no surprise at all if they found themselves being attacked as they rode back in the direction of North Carolina through the mountain passes. Far from offering him safety, Boone and Bird, and their Mohawk guides, would be if anything a liability, and he would be much safer on his own or in the company of Swan's Wing.

—I do not know, sir, if, er, shit. If . . . you have access. Jesus!

He laughed contentedly to himself as at some private joke, and as if he had all the time in the world to hurl the words together, and if necessary form a sentence; if necessary leave the words ungrammatically floating in the air.

—If you have access in this highly civilized shithole to a newssheet. But General Washington . . . er . . . er, my family, sir, are, as you may or may not be aware, are among the . . . better type of folks, in Virginia, sir, we, er, that is to say, there are few people unknown to the . . . Birds, sir, and General Washington is among them. He is amassing his armies, sir, in Virginia, and . . .

—I had heard, lied Tom, who had not, as a matter of fact, learnt any public intelligence in the previous three weeks.

—I understood, said Tom, that General Washington had lost New York, that the colonists in Massachusetts had been defeated by General Gage, that . . .

—You, my friend, are, Mr Bird shook his head, are . . . some weeks out of . . . if I say out of date it is because . . . Jesus, don't these savages tell you *anything*? Believe me, Mr Byerley, you have just got to come out with us.

To Tom's dismay, he found that Swan's Wing had joined him and the tall American.

—Bird's Feather is right, said Swan's Wing. The fighting between the white men is worse. At first the fight was between redcoats and the hotheads of Massachusetts—

—Now see here, redskin, who're you calling a hothead? interposed Mr Bird in one of the few finished sentences he had uttered that afternoon.

—And the redcoats would find it hard, in the Carolinas or in Virginia, to resist if they found a large enough body of colonists against them. General Gage and General Burgoyne have offered their freedom to any negro slaves if they join the King's Army. In some parts – for example, in Savannah and in Charleston – thousands have left their plantations, risen against their—

—Holy shit! This from Byerley's eloquent fellow European.

—But this is extraordinary news, said Tom.

—Today, we fly the white flag from the pole, said Swan's Wing. Tomorrow, the red. These lands are at war. Ostenaco saw a vision. He saw hawks and kites flying, hovering. That was what he was saying back there in the Hall of Meeting.

—I thought he was bringing the proceedings to an end with a prayer, said Tom.

—In a sense, yes. He said that he saw Our Mother (this, Tom was to learn, was the Cherokee way of speaking of the earth) moist with blood. The kite tore at the gizzard of the chipmunk, the eagle tore the throat of the deer. Men were at war with men—

—Shite, you do not need to be a fucking magician to see that!

—At present, said Swan's Wing, ignoring the interjection, we have no way of knowing who will be victorious, but a war is coming. War between the white men, the redcoats and the colonists. Friend Tom Byerley—

Swan's Wing laid a hand on Tom's shoulder and looked deep into his eyes.

—Ostenaco has asked me to speak to you. He thinks you are not safe here with the Cherokee. He asks you to go with the Chattering Bird—

—Now see here, you redskin varmint, who you start calling names?

—and Mr Boone, said the tall, dignified young man. Some in the village here, some in the Beloved Assembly, believe that you are a secret friend of Boone and the Chattering Bird.

—I told you to cut that out, savage!

—Others believe me: that you are here solely from Wooden Leg, that you came as a simpleton with almost no knowledge of the war between the white men. That you came as our friend, as Wooden Leg is our friend. But these others say no, you are a spy.

—But that is preposterous! Tom began.

—So, said Bird, you'd rather be taken as a friend of these cutthroats, these mumbo-jumbo painted savages, than admit to being friends with me and Boone.

—The law of hospitality decrees that if you wish to stay with the Cherokee, you will be welcome as our friend, said Swan's Wing. But you would be safer if you go with Boone and the Chatterer. Their Mohawk guide will give you all safe passage to Ramsour's Mill. Thereafter you will be able to find protection from the American army. When they discover that you are an Englishman, you will be able to find another safe passage and go back to England, to leave this sad land, to return with the blessings of the Cherokee to Wooden Leg. Come back to us if we ever enjoy peace again.

—And if I go with Chattering Bird, said Tom, taking great satisfaction in repeating the soubriquet in the man's presence, then this will confirm what those mistaken Cherokee believed, that I came here as their friend and as their spy. I came from Wooden Leg, only to buy clay, and to pay good money for it. No tricks, no subterfuge, no—

—We weren't offering no subterfuge! said Bird. Didn't you hear what was going on in that place?

—I heard you offering them money, yes, said Tom. And I know that if some foreigner came to us in Burslem and offered us a hundred pounds, or a thousand pounds or a million pounds to clear out of Staffordshire and give it to the French or the Scotch or the Americans, I know how that scoundrel would be answered!

There was a silence. While no one spoke, Tom thought of Hamlet's line – *Sir, in my heart there was a kind of fighting.* He knew that common sense dictated that he should leave the township with Bird and Boone, however repellent they might be to him. He knew that by staying, he was endangering not only himself, but also Swan's Wing, and any other Cherokee who believed in him, for he threatened to divide these noble people at a vital turning point in their lives. He was a stranger there. He had no business with them. He had no business, even, with the Americans and their quarrel with the British Crown. Into his heart, where there was a kind of fighting, there came the image of his mother, so strong that it was the equal of any of Ostenaco's visions. He could see the bustling, and in many ways comical, little woman in her draper's shop in Newcastle. He could, even in this moment of mental agony, smile at the thought of her, and at the recollection of why so many in the family found her an object of affectionate mockery. It was at home that Byerley belonged. He thought of his Uncle Jos, his kind, sensible, moon-shaped face, the smell of pipe tobacco on his mouth, the sharp intelligence of his blue eyes. It was almost as if he had summoned them up as the Witch of Endor summoned the dead Samuel.

But even as Byerley's mother and uncle tugged at his heart, he looked across the crowded tent and felt the excitement of the moment, he also felt himself in the middle of a crisis which was not merely dangerous but of the deepest interest. He had surprised

himself by his fanciful speech about Staffordshire being sold to the
French or other strangers. Only when he himself had articulated in
words what had happened during that meeting did he feel the full
intensity of the moment. And as he felt it, and looked across the sea
of excited faces, he saw the squaw with the damp armpits, who had
greeted him at the gate, and who had made the first of the patriotic
speeches. She was in a group of women. She now turned, as if she
could feel the rays of his glance. They were too far away from one
another to speak or to be audible to one another. She looked at him
with an intense stare.

—If the offer of hospitality has been made, then I know, on behalf
of Wooden Leg, that I should stay, said Byerley.

—Fucking Jesus!

—I should like to see the pots you have been making, he went on,
and maybe take some home to show to Wooden Leg. I am prepared
to take the risk that fighting will have broken out in other parts of
America while I am here.

—The risk! Man, did you not . . . holy mackerel, er, they were saying . . . it is no risk, they are already . . . Washington amassing armies,
sir, Bunker Hill by no means, er . . . end of the matter. Jesus, he's so
stubborn!

—If you would allow me to stay one more week? Tom asked.

Swan's Wing merely touched his shoulder with a long, bony hand.

—I must show Mr Boone and Mr Bird to the gate, he said.

—Well, goodbye, Mr Bird.

Tom extended a hand to the lanky American.

Mr Bird looked at the hand as if it might in some way be con-
taminated. He failed to extend his own hand in return.

—I, er, wish it were. The sheer god-damned stubbornness. Mr
Boone and I . . . safe passage but if that's what you . . . Jesus! And,
as he had done once or twice before during their strange conversa-

tion, he broke into a laugh which seemed entirely private and added, I wish you well, sir.

Mr Bird and Mr Boone were escorted from the Hall of Meeting by two elderly priests in feathered robes. They were followed in turn by their Mohawk guides who wore linen shirts of a design similar to Swan's Wing, but their leather chaps were brown and less elegant in their cut than Swan's Wing's white trousers. Tom supposed that it would be in order for him to return to the guest hut where he had stored his belongings. It occurred to him for the first time since the origin of the political crisis in America that it would be a good idea to write down his experiences. Yes. He would go back to his quarters and pen a letter to his mother. But as he watched the two Americans go, he became aware that all was not well. Whether it was the heat of the tent, or whether he had eaten something to which his body was unaccustomed, or for whatever other reason, his head was possessed by a great dizziness, and he knew that he was on the verge of throwing up. He ran across the field towards some bushes and, having vomited up not merely his previous meal, but what felt like his innards themselves, he felt a cold sweat breaking out all over him, and, as he looked into the bright blue sky and saw Mrs Byerley, leaning on the counter of her draper's shop in Newcastle, he passed into unconsciousness.

# 9

VISIONS OF ENGLAND ALSO CROWDED INTO THE FUMED brain of Tom Byerley as he lay upon his truckle bed in a scrupulously clean wooden house. He was semi-conscious. The young woman named Blue Squirrel sat on her haunches at his head and sometimes stroked his brow. As she did so, he was sometimes four years old again, and his mother was stroking his brow to soothe away a nightmare. And sometimes he was fishing for chub or dace in the Trent, and the dank smell of river-water and the rich moist sensation of England filled him with a calm joy. And sometimes Polly Dwyer, naked, and with legs wide open, laughingly advanced upon his face, while at other times the old tower of Burslem church stood out against a silvery mist of winter sky, as the smoke rose from the Churchyard Works, and Uncle Jos came towards him, walking stick in hand, a smile upon his lips.

—Let's be having you, our Tom, let's be having you! Weer shull we start today, lad? Letters to clients? Noa? A letter to Bentley. We'll pen a letter to friend Bentley . . .

And the smell of the works, the almost sweet smell of clay, and the greyish dust it made everywhere, and the old pot banks, warm in the winter air.

—Sit by me, Tom, sit by me, read Homer with me, Tom, let's read Pope's Homer.

—*What sounds are these that gather from the shores*, Aunty Sal?
—Yes, that bit, Tom.

> —The voice of nymphs that haunt the sylvan bowers,
> The fair-haired Dryads of the shady wood;
> Or azure daughters of the silver flood;
> Or human voice?—

—Hold my hand, our Tom.
*And she is kissing his hand and bathing it with tears.* —What's the matter, Aunty Sal?
—Oh, Tom, never mind, pet, never mind.
London. The streets of London. Uncle John in Ranelagh Gardens. Women of the night with their painted faces, and their breasts which showed above their dresses. And the lights which hung in the bunchy lime trees as the music of Handel played, and Uncle John saying, 'If it is money you need, young Tom, I can see you right with one of the painted hussies.' And his coy refusal, and his uncle's tolerant laugh, not knowing that he and Tilly Weekes from Billington's, though he was but fifteen years old, had already done that thing, and he was repelled by the painted women. And the passing macaronis, yet more grotesque than the whores, with their huge wigs, and their walking canes, and their powdered, painted faces – *Trick'd out like dolls, to pace in Rotten-row* – and the moon on the Thames as they walked back to Chiswick, and the hooting through dark leaves of an invisible owl.

Mrs Byerley has never left his side, and strokes his brow. She kisses him gently and says,
—*Jigililli.*
—What is that? What is Jigililli?
—It is Tom, the Cherokee word for Tomtit.

He smiles with a wonder of enchantment as if he and she had been playing a children's game.

—Then you speak English after all.

Dark, dark hair, blue-black hair, falling in curtains on either side of her intense face, brushes his own cheek as he awakes. He sees the young squaw who had been the first to welcome him to the town.

—You have been sick. But now you are well.

She smiled at him. For the first time, he felt the strength to heave himself on to one elbow and to lift his head. Her voice had a musical lilt.

—Jigililli, a Tomtit. And what bird are you?

—I am not a bird, she said.

He had never seen her smile before, but when she smiled he felt that he had never seen any smile before. This was Plato's Idea of a smile, from which all other smiles were mere forms; this was the radiance of joy, and the freedom of Eros, and the peace of God which passeth all understanding.

—If you are not a bird, what is your name?

—Sadloli, but for you in English it is, another smile, Blue Squirrel.

—Sadloli.

—Jigililli. Tomtit. You have been very sick.

—And Blue Squirrel, you nursed me?

—You are our guest.

—I have been . . .

—You have been in England, dreaming. You have been in strange lands.

—Did I speak while I slept?

—No.

Tom required no explanation of how she knew what had passed through his mind. Blue Squirrel had always been there, always part of his consciousness. She was not exactly Another Person, she was the other half of his soul from whom he had always mysteriously been detached.

—Here, she said.

She had put a pipe between her lips and lit it. Now she held it to his mouth.

—Breathe deeply, she said. Breathe the tobacco into your lungs. This will bring Tomtit peace.

He had not heard of tobacco smoking as a panacea for such ills as had tormented him, but this pipe did indeed bring a preternatural calm as his lips, eager to enclose Blue Squirrel's spittle on the stem of the pipe, took the carved bone. He did not cough. Whether it was pure tobacco, or whether there was an admixture of some other herbs, he did not pause to enquire. He remained awake, but a dream of peace possessed his soul.

—*Gha, Sadloli galvadi . . . gisaghi adi-haaaa . . .*

—What are you singing?

—Shh, shhh, Tom must be quiet. Jigililli, calm, calm. Blue Squirrel drives the bad air from your intestines, and the bad thoughts from your heart.

He lay back on his bed, and she took the pipe from him as she continued to sing in a low, quiet contralto. With her long fingers, she stroked his moist brow, as the incantation continued.

—It sounds like a prayer.

—Shh, shh . . . I sing to the Blue Crow

Blue Crow!
The Crow is not to ask me.
'You have been put to sleep in the ground'. You and I are
    to say
Now – Bluebird!

Now, perhaps, the Crow has us all in this condition, this
    frenzy!
Blue Crow! Blue Crow! You are a wizard!
May an Evil Mind climb over her!
May she eat Black Earth for ever!
May she be tormented till she dies!


—What do the words mean?
She was singing an incantation to destroy a rival in love, but she
said quietly,
—Blue Squirrel sings to make Jigililli calm.

# IO

—PLEASE LET ME, MR BOWERS! PLEASE LET ME CHANGE the next lock by myself!

—You can help, John.

—But I want to do it alone.

—It's not as easy as it looks.

The first voice was a high, piping treble of supreme self-confidence, the second a gruff *basso profundo*.

The two speakers were a swarthy man of some forty-five years old and Josiah Wedgwood's ten-year-old son. Caleb Bowers, like his sister Heffie, had a Mediterranean appearance. (Josiah always said their mother had been a gypsy.) Whereas Heffie was fleshy, bosomy, expansive and smiling, Caleb was sinewy, muscular. His angular features looked scornful and tortuous. He could very easily have modelled Milton's Satan for a line illustration to the poem which was his constant reading. There was scorn and pride in his expression. He had thick, dark, curly hair, abundant whiskers at his ears, and tufts of chest hair showing at the top of his shirt. He had a prominent brow, very bright blue eyes, an aquiline nose and a dimpled chin which was considered one of his finest features by his many female admirers. Not one of these female admirers had ever, with one exception, attracted him, even faintly. The one who more than attracted him, and indeed possessed his unhappy heart, was not his. He was too proud to own his unhappiness on her behalf (though of course she knew it) and too honourable to make an attempt upon her virtue.

Beside John Wedgwood and Caleb Bowers on the barge stood Sukey Wedgwood, aged eleven. On the towpath, leading the shire horse which pulled the barge, was Caleb's nephew Ted Bowers (Heffie's younger son), a handsome lad of fifteen, curly-headed like his uncle.

—I still want to try, announced John.

—And I'm telling you, John, it's not a job for one little fella.

Sukey savoured every moment of the canal voyage. Her face was as amiable as her father's and as acute as her mother's. Her very dark blue eyes were never still, everlastingly taking in impressions. Her mouth, like her father's, would hang open very slightly when she was distracted. It was a smiling mouth. Her cheeks were much fuller than those of her mother, but she had the same long bone structure. It was a face which radiated observational intelligence and, for a child of that age, a somewhat alarming capacity to take in and understand what it saw. She loved the differences between the squeaking tones of her brother's voice, already that of the would-be gentleman, and Caleb's voice. Caleb spoke like Papa. He did not speak with the dialect, or at least not when he was speaking with them. (He spoke Staffordcher to Heffie.) Indeed, Caleb was a clever man. Although Mama treated Heffie almost as if she were a lady's maid, they were notionally friends, not servants. They held themselves aloof, the Bowerses, and made it clear that they were not exactly to be treated as if they were subordinates. Caleb and Papa had been boyhood friends. All this Sukey, half-comprehendingly, absorbed, noted, savoured. She also luxuriated in the sight of Ted on the canal bank, his beautiful shoulder blades which were visible through his shirt, the curly dark hair in the nape of his neck, his brown strong arms, and his tight backside in brown worsted breeches. She rejoiced in the

morning, and the moisture of the canal bank. The grasses, the flowers
in the hedgerows — meadow-sweet, bramble, rest-harrow and kidney
vetch, campion and groundsel — all dripped with the recent shower;
and the tufts of grass were a green so vivid that if you had painted
them straight from the colour box, Papa, who was a good drawing-
master, would have said you had made them too bright.

Through all the moisture of that day, Sukey sensed life. Through
the dripping verdure of the hedge she caught a glimpse of a kingfisher, which swooped low out of the foliage, over the water. In the
water itself, as well as the gentle circles caused by the softly falling
rain, there were the pops and bubbles of jumping roach and chub.
They passed a handsome house, Meaford Hall, the seat of the local
naval hero Jervis.

—Do you think they'll send the Captain back to America, Mr
Bowers? asked Sukey.

—I wouldn't know, replied Bowers with a sardonic smile. The
Admiralty don't often ask my advice about their appointments.

—Only, Mama says he did so prodigiously there during the last
war.

—Please let me change the lock on my own, Mr Bowers.

And when Caleb refused to be drawn by the nagging, John puppy-
ishly added, so as to make his sister wince,

—After all, it was my Papa who built this canal, and you are just
a bargee.

The smile of Caleb Bowers, which was all the response which he
deigned to give this piece of pert cheek, was not a happy one. It
would have been difficult to imagine two men more temperamentally
opposed to one another than Caleb Bowers and Jos Wedgwood.
Whereas Jos, with all his fervour and energy and bright optimism,
saw existence as an extension of almost limitless possibilities, Caleb
saw the life of conscious beings, animal or human, as a dark ordeal

through which they must make a tortured progress. He saw Nature itself as a battleground. Earthworms were harmlessly devouring the earth only themselves to be seized and pecked by the beaks of small birds. Those birds in their turn were wrenched and torn apart by carrion crows, and by sharp-toothed mammals. The smaller mammals provided meat for the larger. Each belly in the universe, larger than an earthworm's, was filled with the meat of sacrifice, with the blood and entrails ripped from some other creature. And Man, who in turn tore the flesh off muttons and beeves to fill his belly, was cursed with the knowledge and consciousness that he inhabited this world of Pain. He was conscious of his own inescapable end, which was Death: a death which, as Caleb had been able to observe from his earliest infancy, was seldom pleasant or easy.

It was true, what young John had said. Jos Wedgwood had been one of the principal advocates of building the Trent and Mersey Canal. With his grand friends the Duke of Bridgewater and Lord Gower, and Dr Darwin of Lichfield, he had put up money – Jos had paid a thousand pounds for the survey – more money than Caleb and Heffie Bowers could put together in a decade. Jos had written letters, petitioned Parliament, eaten dinners, hobbled in and out of stagecoaches and phaetons, written more letters, solicited engineers, befriended the canal genius Mr Brindley, bought shares, made another fortune as if the fortunes he had already made were not enough for him, and naturally, when the day came for the first sod to be cut of the new canal project, it had been Jos who ceremonially dug it to the loud rejoicing of the crowds. There had been bonfires at Burslem on the muddy slope that day, and Jos had provided three sheep to be roasted for the general merriment and rejoicing, and the good people of Burslem, as he had called them, and plenty of the bad people and all, drank the taverns dry of their ale and porter. They had all come to accept the peg-legged potter as their king, while

Caleb, if not, like Cassius, a wretched creature, had stood in the shadows beside his sister and her children, very much the underlings. And an underling, he recognized that, was what he was, or had become.

In those days before the turnpike road was built between Hanley and Newcastle, and before the coming of the Trent and Mersey Canal, the only way out of Burslem had been by a dirt track which sloped and slithered up the slow incline towards the church. To transport the coal which was mined in small quantities in the village, or the pots which were manufactured in the numerous small pot banks scattered about the place, it had been necessary, in most cases, to carry crates on human backs and shoulders. Caleb Bowers, from young manhood, had the best carts in the town, and he ran a carrying service which was much in demand, but there were many seasons of the year when the depth of the puddles, and the mud and dirt, even in the more salubrious of the tracks, made movement out of the place all but impracticable. After the canal was built, Caleb had gone to Jos and asked him for a loan. It was not in Caleb's nature to be any man's employee and he did not wish to work for the new Trent and Mersey Canal Company as a mere bargee. But, he saw no reason why there should not be Number Ones as there had been on the River Trent ever since anyone could remember. A Number One was a man who owned his own barge, took charge of his own destiny, and was beholden to nobody.

Jos had forthwith told Caleb, when he had heard this proposition, that he would buy Caleb a barge outright for the sum of sixty-three pounds. If he were to do so, and his nephews were to keep the carts as a going proposition, there might be a time in the future when Caleb could pay him back the money.

The generosity which had been offered was accepted. Caleb was not grudging when he quietly nodded and thanked Jos for the purchase and construction of his first barge. The words which came from his lips, quiet and few as they were, included 'gratitude', 'Heffie and the lads', 'our Ted', 'buy our own horses, naturally' and 'ever so grateful, Jos Wedgwood'. Caleb called his boyhood friend 'Jos Wedgwood'. He could not call him 'sir', still less the deferential 'Mr Jos' which was what the men at the works called him (to his face — Owd Wooden Leg behind his back). But nor could he always bring himself to call him simply 'Jos', though Jos sometimes called him 'Caleb'. Between both men there was, as always, a terrible constraint. Caleb was a proud man and he had not liked Jos paying for the first barge — a handsome, seventy-foot vessel, six feet wide, with the capacity to carry twenty tons' burthen.

As Burslem boys, Jos and Caleb had played together; Jos was nine years old when his father died and the Bowerses had in some measure taken him under their wing while old Mrs Wedgwood sank under her grief. Not long after this it had been decided by their respective families that a little schooling would not come amiss, and Caleb and Jos had both been sent together to school in Newcastle-under-Lyme. Of the two boys, Caleb was the more linguistically adept and the more imaginative. For the first half, they had done little with Mr Blunt the schoolmaster except read Tooke's *Pantheon*. It was still a book which Caleb studied with pleasure. His boyhood imagination, battered by the repetition of illness and calamity, had been unable to absorb the Gospel: God who supposedly grieved over the death of every sparrow. Caleb found it easy, by contrast, to believe in, or at least to imagine, the capricious Gods of pagan antiquity, who played with humanity as a child might pull the wings off a fly, and whose own anger, lust, jealousy and whimsicality were magnified versions of identical propensities in human beings.

He often remembered the page of Tooke on which as lads they read of Aeneas being made a God by his mother Venus. The book contained short extracts from the Latin poets, rendered into English, sometimes in a well-known published version, such as Dryden's Virgil, and sometimes done into English by Tooke himself.

*Lustratum genetrix divino corpus odore*
*Unxit . . .*

Mr Blunt would intone.

They had the translation there in front of them on the page. It was not difficult, as it might have been had they attended the grammar school and been compelled to read Latin without the aid of a crib. But Mr Blunt liked them to unpick, as he called it, the Ovid. Caleb found this exercise interesting, and well within his capabilities. Jos, who was of a more mechanical and practical bent, found it much harder.

—So, who's going to unpick for us this morning? Wedgwood? Where's Mother hiding? Come on, boy.

Jos's heavy potter's hands would pore over the page, his finger straying here and there in search of the Latin word for mother. *Mater*, was it not? But, search as he would, the word *Mater* did not jump off the page.

—No, Bowers, don't help him. Mother, Wedgwood? Mother? Where is she, boy?

You could see that Jos could not take in the words, but that his eyes were feasting upon the illustrations in Tooke, upon the engraving of Mercury in his beautiful winged helmet; and beneath the God, there were three magnificent medallions depicting MERCUTIO PACIFERO, Mercury the Peacemaker.

—This is beyond endurance! We can't wait for you all day, Wedgwood! Bowers, come to our aid! *Ad adjutorium nos intende!*

—*Genetrix*, sir.

—Well done, sir, *Genetrix*, sir! *Lustratum genetrix divino corpus odore*, 'His mother then his Body purify'd/Anoints with sacred odours, and his Lips/In Nectar'. I dare say all Mothers worship their male offspring. Is that so, Wedgwood?

—I wouldn't raightly knaw, sir.

—You wouldn't raightly knaw? Rightly, sir, not raightly, and know, not knaw.

But as Caleb knew, harsh Old Mrs Wedgwood was not like the Goddess Venus in her dealing with her sons and had no wish to deify Jos. Mrs Bowers, by contrast, did lave her son with affection and worship

> *So deify'd, whom Indiges Rome calls*
> *Honour'd with Altars, Shrines and Festivals.*

It was when Jos was eleven that he was visited by the pox. Smallpox ravaged nigh half the population of Burslem at that time, like one of the plagues of Egypt. Five of Jos's siblings had already died of the disease and there were several months, in that bleak year 1741 which saw so many in Burslem perish, when it seemed certain that Jos would be the sixth. After much pain and delirium, however, he recovered.

Caleb's mother had nursed Jos as if he were her own son. The physicians despaired, but she stayed beside his fetid truckle bed day and night, mopping his brow, emptying his chamber pot, changing his sweated bedding, feeding those lips, swollen with pus and pustules, with milky gruel. Throughout this period, she told Caleb he must keep well away from the house. Caleb had gone to live next door with the Wedgwoods, and Jos had slept in his bed. Sometimes, though, Caleb had defied his mother and come into the house and had heard her singing quietly to his friend, or praying while she held his hand, praying to a merciful God to whom Caleb already found it impossible to pay homage. Although the pox afflicted his right leg, leaving Jos permanently lame, and although his face was for ever marred by the pits and welts of that merciless disease, Jos did indeed survive. When he recovered, Jos had been apprenticed to his brother Tom, and his friend Caleb was apprenticed too. It was Mrs Bowers, Caleb's mother, who, having contracted the illness from her patient, died of it.

This inescapable and terrible misfortune had coloured the whole of Caleb Bowers's existence. Everything which had happened to him since – all his professional life, all his loneliness as a man who, somehow, could not marry, all his anxiety on behalf of his sister Heffie with her ups and downs, all the hard tedium of his work skills as a haulier, and all his relations with the Wedgwood family – had been lived in view of this fact: the limitless and pointless malice of Zeus had decreed that Jos Wedgwood should live and Caleb's mother should die, that Jos, with his undoubted accomplishments, should become a rich man, and Caleb should be his inferior.

Jos treated him now as a servant. Indeed, Caleb's sister Heffie, a simple woman who in appearance was even more of a gypsy than he was himself, was taken for granted most of the time by Sally Wedgwood who relied on Heffie for companionship, advice but also much manual work and help with the children. And when Heffie was on terms with Caleb, which was not always – for they were both possessed of 'temperaments' – she had some tales to tell, particularly since Jos had developed *folie de grandeur*, and left the old Churchyard Works in Burslem and built himself a ruddy great stately home in the old Ridge House estate. It had been renamed Etruria. Heffie said it made you blush to watch Jos and Sal lording it in this palace of a place. But while Sal could convincingly pass herself off as a lady, and mooned languidly about the enormous rooms like a depressive

Dowager, Jos could not refrain from outbursts of common laughter.

—Eee, luke ut oos, eh? Jos had exclaimed one evening when Heffie had brought tea into the drawing-room for them all and Mr Wedgwood sat there with his fine clothes, amid the fine furniture sent up from London and beneath the glittering crystal of his chandeliers.

Well, friend, thought Caleb, we shall, friend. We'll look at you. And bloody daft you look, some of t' time.

It would entirely confuse the reader if it were hinted that Caleb disliked Jos Wedgwood. Quite to the contrary, he regarded his friend, in some ways, as he had always done, as a brilliant, though in some respects clumsy, fellow who needed protecting from himself.

Caleb had once said that Jos Wedgwood was the bull in his own china shop. At the same time, Caleb regarded Jos's shameless desire for social advancement and personal enrichment with as much contempt as he despised Jos's optimism and sunniness. Troubles would come, and Caleb would be ready for them, whereas Jos would always look at them with that mouth of his half-open, and his bright grey-blue eyes slightly filling with surprised tears. Jos – perhaps this was the nub of it – wanted to think of himself as a nice person. Caleb could see in all Jos's benevolence only a denial of Nature. In his thrusting of himself forward, in his driving of his workers to make him ever more crocks and ever more money, Jos was as voracious as any stoat tearing the innards out of a mouse, or any buzzard feasting on the entrails of the stoat. But he wanted to believe that trade was of its essence a benignant activity, quite detached from the brutally competitive world of Nature to which the human race, just as much as the stoats and the buzzards, so patently and obviously belonged.

This was, in large part, the reason for Caleb's reservations about Jos Wedgwood. There was, however, another, everlasting fact which gnawed at Caleb, and was of such painfulness that it overshadowed even the memory of his mother's death, and Jos's subsequent remarkable successes. As if the Immortals on Mount Olympus had not derived enough satisfaction from sending a mortal plague to kill his mother, they had also contrived to visit Caleb with a frenzy of love-madness for Josiah's wife.

Day after day, Caleb would quiz Heffie about Sally. He wanted to know everything: her moody humours, her explosions of petulance, her inability to eat, followed by bursts of appetite, her rages against the children, her collapses into exhaustion. Heffie, in her innocence, supposed that Caleb found comedy in her narratives of the Wedgwoods' domestic story. Heffie was a woman of unstoppably affectionate temperament, who loved Sally Wedgwood in the way some people love a difficult, overbred pet dog. She indulged all the humours, and the tantrums, and the clouds which suddenly darkened Sally's sunshine. But she found her ways comical.

For Caleb, however, this tall, white, bony Sally, with her springy light ginger hair, was an embodiment of everything he had most yearned for in a woman. In his youth, before Jos made his intentions plain, Caleb had sometimes made free in his conversations with Sally. Seeing her one day when she was fifteen, with her nose stuck into Pope's Homer, he had opened a conversation with her, and offered to show her Tooke, and to teach her Latin. She had replied that her Papa, the cheesemonger, had already allowed her to learn Latin and Greek from the local Unitarian minister, who was some kind of cousin, like all the men and women in her life – all, that is, except for the Bowerses.

Once, during one of these conversations – leaning on a stile and overlooking the meadows between Burslem and Hanley one calm evening in May 1750, when she was not quite sixteen – she had kissed him. It was she who had initiated the kiss, and it was done with great boldness and simplicity, with one hand round his waist and the other stroking his chest, and with her lips pressed to his, and her tongue inside his mouth. At the time, it had excited lust, and they had met, and kissed, a few times after that. Later, she had discontinued the kissing, saying that it would displease her father, and, later still, she had admitted to Caleb that she had been 'promised' as a wife to her cousin Jos.

—Can't you make your own mind up? he had asked her, or do you pass women round like goods and chattels in your family?

—I have made up my mind, Caleb. I am to marry Cousin Josiah.

What tormented Caleb now, some quarter of a century later, was to ask himself what would have happened if he had spoken out then; if he had declared himself then; if he had prevented her from becoming Mrs Josiah Wedgwood. Oh, he knew that that mean old cheeseparing cheesemonger would never have allowed his daughter to marry poor Caleb Bowers. But in his wilder flights of fancy, he saw this as having been no obstacle. They could have run away together. They could have lived in a cottage by the canal, as he now lived with his sister. And would he have been able to live with her sulks and changeable humours? Or were these everlasting squalls the symptom of her being unhappy with the husband who had been chosen for her?

Whatever the truth of the matter, he was now, in his forties, as much in love with Sally Wedgwood as he had ever been as a lad. Her long, white face, and her unhappy eyes, and her hair, and her bony fingers, and her voice, and her difficult, difficult temper all churned for him into the heartache which was his almost perpetual psychological condition. He was cursed with wisdom. He knew that none of the conventional remedies against heartache would be of any avail. He could not womanize, because, ever since that first kiss, there had been only one woman. Drinking too much made men into idiots. So did religion. No, there had been nothing for it but to work hard and to throw himself into an avuncular role with Heffie's children. With Sally's children now, it seemed, 'Mr Bowers' could be a kind of uncle, and there were moments when he knowingly added to the pain, when the children were very little, and he was able to go right up to her, if she was holding an infant and wanting to hand it over to 'Uncle Caleb'. And then he could feel her shoulders, or, removing the wet, sticky hands from their mother's hands, touch those white fingers.

The latest idea, since John and Sukey were surely old enough to travel without nursemaids or chaperones, was that the two eldest should accompany Caleb with the newest consignment of creamware to London. Sally's illnesses and pregnancies, and shifts of humour between high and low spirits, made it impossible for her to endure the company of the children on a permanent basis, even though she pined for them when they were away. All the elder children had been sent to school, but the establishment they found for Sukey – a boarding school in Derby which she attended with Maria Edgeworth, the daughter of one of her Papa's Lunar cronies – had not been satisfactory. The girl had taken ill, developed boils, become fretful. Then had arisen the suggestion that she should go to live for a while in London with Jos's business partner Mr Bentley and his wife, who had lately taken a new house near the works in Chelsea.

Josiah, Sally and Heffie went ahead to London by coach. Of course, Caleb Bowers had been only too delighted to take the children. It would be an adventure for them all. And, that very morning, as they had loaded the barge with Sukey and John's trunks and portmanteaus, he had been rewarded with what he had yearned for these past four months – a touch of Sally's gloved hand on his upper arm, as she thanked him for his kindness. Somehow, they had stood close enough for their chests to touch. With his large hand, as he stood at the tiller of the barge now in the late morning, he felt that upper arm where her hand had been.

—We must stop at Henshaw's yard, he said, when we get back to Stone, difficult bugger though he be.

—What is a bugger? asked Sukey.

—Henshaw is a bugger, was the circular and unenlightening reply.

No one liked Henshaw, who was a difficult man who had somehow been privy to the plans for the new canal from its inception. Henshaw had a large boat-building yard at Stone and four dry docks, and had built the barge of which Bowers was now the owner and commander. He had been in cahoots from the beginning with Brindley, the canal engineer, and it was because of Henshaw's stubbornness that Jos had built the Etruria Works on its present site. Henshaw had resolutely refused to emend the line of the canal to suit Wedgwood's, so they were obliged, if they were to make the most efficacious use of the canal, to fall in with Henshaw – the 'inflexible rascal', as Jos called him.

The barge, whose owner had adorned it with the name *Atalanta* (his secret name for Sally Wedgwood, never disclosed to a soul), had arrived at the elegant little market town of Stone. Henshaw had his shipyard bang in the middle of the town, not five minutes from the Crown Inn, and the five travellers – Caleb, John and Sukey Wedgwood, Ted Bowers and Dandelion, the slow, tolerant horse – were now confronted with that man's disagreeable face and temperament. His features were not especially ugly. It was his expression which gave to the jutting lower lip, the sly grin, the swagger of his stocky figure their nastiness.

—Thought yer'd never mac 't, but I dessay yer canner mester t' locks yet, Caleb Bowers!

Caleb disdained to answer, but Ted could not forbear to say,

—We isna leat, Mr Henshaw.

—Oh, we isna? And since when hast yo become timekeeper, young Ezra Bowers?

—Ted, Mr Henshaw, Ezra's me brother. And we are on tarm, even though we had twelve crates o' ware to load up at Etruria.

—Ted, Ezra, what care I what bloody silly names your mother give yer? If ye weren'tner so slaw and busy licking t' arse of Wedgwoods – Mrs Wedgwood's arse, Mr Wedgwood's arse – yer might appear on tarm for lesser folks like us.

Caleb was now stung to speak.

—Watch your tongue, Henshaw, there's children aboard.

—I don't care if there's Infant bloody Jesus aboard, if yo's bin licking arse, yo's bin licking arse. What's in t' crates, any road?

—It's creamware, explained Ted artlessly, for t' Empress of Rooshia. They meek it and model it and gleeze it up at Etruria Works and tek it dine ter London for decoration.

—And leave precious little space on t' barge for the cargo of lesser folks, added Henshaw.

—You've booked space for ten bushels of corn to go as far as Oxford, Mr Henshaw, said Caleb, and two cases of books, ditto, and two larger cases, containing furniture, which are being sent care of Williamson, to be delivered at Berkhamsted. Now, sooner we load, t' sooner we'll be gone.

Caleb and Ted, having long worked in their haulage business by land, were expert packers, and Henshaw, in spite of his protestations, had the crates and sacks all ready for them as agreed. It was work for strong men, but both Caleb and his nephew were strong. Sukey noted with admiration the way that Ted could heave a sack of corn over one shoulder, and she saw the muscles tauten and the veins stand out in his lightly hairy forearms as he lowered the sacks on to the decks. The crates of furniture and books were lowered on to the barge by means of a system of pulley and winch. Henshaw had a man who helped them, and the operation took no more than twenty minutes. Mr Henshaw himself did not offer to help, and all the time they worked, he kept up his unpleasant commentary. Much of what he said had to do with the Wedgwoods, and when Caleb remonstrated, and pointed out to him that two of Josiah's children were within earshot, it only seemed to goad the man into further rudenesses.

—Dost still keep pigeons, Caleb?

Upon being asked this question two or three times, Caleb admitted that he did so, as did most men in Stone.

—So do I nall, said Henshaw. And we select and breed fro 'em, biggest wings, sharpest beaks, bes' fliers! We make choice of which bird breed wi' what! Boot Wedgwoods, they breed with bloody oomans, breed with izzels! Keep it in t' family, that's their motto — sem uz when I kep bes' pigeons in cages together! No riff raff that way, preservation o' the species lahk. Cousin marrying bloody cousin.

—That's enough, thundered Caleb. Do you hear, Henshaw, that's enough, in front of the bairns?

And they continued their loading silently. Henshaw had to be asked to offer them water to drink, and they were on their way as soon as they could.

Stone, where the Bowerses had their canalside cottage, was a pleasant little place, and in spite of the repellent impression left on their minds by the barge-builder, the group had a happy half-hour there, sitting beside the lock, eating bread and cheese, drinking some good cider, and pretending to allow John to change the lock.

—You'll need to close the bottom gates first, said Caleb, and, winking at his nephew, No need to help him, Ted but jes' stand by, that's right, in case. Well done, lad. And now you open the ground paddle.

All this while, Sukey sat in a daze on the greensward beside the lock. The coarse words of Mr Henshaw had been upsetting. Was that really how other Staffordshire people regarded the Wedgwoods, a lot of overbred pigeons, who had been trying to select stronger and stronger species? And why should anyone hate them as much as Mr Henshaw seemed to do? Was it because Pa had a wooden leg? Or because he had made so much more money than they had? Was life a competition?

For a while, she numbed the pain of his words by reading *Gulliver's Travels*. She sat on the grass, half-watching as the three males fussed over the lock business. She had already lost her fascination with the exact technicalities of canal travel, clever as it was, to make the water in the lock rise to the new level, to allow them to open the top gates and go on their way towards Aston, Sandon Lock and Stafford.

And so, for the next week, the four of them journeyed through England in a wet summer month, whose rain was interrupted by a few hours, most days, of the most delightful sunshine. Sukey decided that this was the type of weather she liked the best, when the landscape was a mixture of intense blue, opalescent greys and bright greens.

Ten miles north of Birmingham they joined the Coventry Canal, and then at Hakesbury Junction they joined the Oxford Canal, whence they crossed over to Norton Junction and entered the Grand Union Canal.

On two nights they slept on the barge, but on the others they broke their journey at inns, and enjoyed the adventure of different types of food – pigeon pie at the Boat Inn, Stoke Bruern, and a magnificent mutton broth at the inn at Weedon, where the barracks was, and they saw what seemed like hundreds of soldiers in their red coats, drilling and marching. There was the dark thrill of Blisworth tunnel, which Sukey felt would never end. In the Chilterns, the sun came out, and they were in paradise, up among the beeches, and looking across three counties, clear and still as far as the Downs and the Vale of the White Horse. And then, by the ingenuity of engineering, but with so many locks for the menfolk to trouble themselves withal, the Watford staircase, which allowed the canal to sink down, down, down, hundreds of feet from the heights of the Chilterns towards their destination. There could be no more delightful way of travelling. There was none of the noise or the turbulent movement, which so often made her feel sick, of a carriage on the road. They simply followed Dandelion and Ted, who pulled them at walking pace down the towpath, and watched damp, fertile, mysterious England pass by them. Through wet reeds and eye-high meadow-grasses, they saw manor houses, village greens, farms, towns, spires. They saw men in smocks at work in fields and farmyards. Women in pattens and aprons, during rare moments of dry weather, were to be seen in back yards, shelling peas, hanging out clothes, dandling babies. They saw small towns, brick-built streets, medieval guildhalls, Elizabethan grammar schools, soaking in the silver light beside bright elms. They saw John Wesley, an old man now, astride his shambling nag, with his writing desk strapped to the horse, his Bible and his ancient, turkey throat open as he sang hymns to the hedge-sparrows. They saw one great house – none of them could put a name to it, maybe Papa would depict it on one of the plates or dishes for the Empress of Russia – with three carriages trotting through its elaborately gilded gates, and making a progress up a straight avenue lined with newly planted limes. They saw cows chomping, shin-deep in wet meadow. They saw sodden sheep, indifferent to the downpours. Behind the tower and the large, flint-built church of Berkhamsted on market day they saw a rainbow. There they stopped and left the consignment of furniture at the boatyard – with a much pleasanter fellow than Mr Henshaw of Stone. On, on they went through an England that knew no big industrial cities, no sulphurous pollutants, no railways. None of the consequences of Jos Wedgwood and friends' Industrial Revolution could yet blight the calm, the grey, the green of that sublime England which they saw. And then the new-built brick of Brentford church came into view and the medieval Kentish ragstone tower, and Mr and Mrs Bentley waving eagerly in the boatyard as Dandelion walked solemnly towards them.

## II

—OH, GO AWAY, CAN'T YOU?

—I were only trying to help thee, pet!

The long-suffering Heffie murmured into the tousled, pale ginger head which snarled from its tangled pillow.

—Oh, oh, tearfully now, where are you going?

—You said go away, my pet.

—Oh, don't be cruel, Heffie, don't provoke me! Oh, did a woman ever suffer such an ague? Oh, Heffie, we should never have come to London.

—You'll have ever such an 'appy tahm once yow're better.

—Oh, my head! Oh, Heffie, I think I might be about to puke!

—Mr and Mrs Bentley have taken t' littluns t' Vauxhall, and Mr Wedgwood's gone round t' works, and Caleb's gone back to Brentwood, so all is well.

Heffie made a point, sometimes, of replying to questions which had not been put to her, but which she felt that politeness had decreed.

—Oh, Heffie, just leave me, will you?

When she had done so, Heffie Bowers could let off steam with,

—Sal Wedgwood's so bound up in her own humours, the rest of the world don't exist – not sometimes!

She spoke to no one in particular, though the Bentleys' maid was standing by. The two women, one a servant, one treated as such, crept from the overcharged atmosphere of the guest bedroom in Mrs Bentley's house in Chelsea, and left Sally in tears.

The Bentleys had taken a tall terraced house, built in the reign of Queen Anne, in Little Cheyne Row. Bentley and Jos had recently bought the Chelsea china works, which were adjacent in Cheyne Row, and it was here that they were to accomplish the great work of decorating the Frog Service. Heffie had been offered a bed next to this maid, in the servants' quarter of the house, and neither Jos nor Sal had uttered a word of protest. Caleb would have none of that, and took Heff and Ted to spend overnight in a nearby inn.

By day, however, Jos, troubled, but by now cruelly hardened to Sally's shifts of temper, had left his wife in Heffie's capable hands, and gone down to the little manufactory. Ever since Lord Cathcart had confirmed the Empress's order, and the truly stupendous nature of his task had become clear, Jos had realized that it would require him to assemble as many as possible of the finest English painters and ceramic decorators in one place.

The decision to make the Empress's dinner service from creamware, rather than attempt to make it in fine china, had been made early. Ever since the coinage of the term Queen's ware for the shapes and glazes, this range of pottery had proved itself to be relatively easy to manufacture in large quantities and of consistently high quality. It had been clear from the outset, however, that skilled as some of his painters in Burslem were, there were simply not enough of them at the Staffordshire manufactory to bring the work to fruition. In Chelsea, the two best enamellers were Catherine and Ralph Willcox, a married pair who worked with prodigious application and skill, except during those regrettable phases when Ralph hit the bottle. As for the others in the team – Miss Isaacs, Thomas Simpcock, James Bakewell – some had been in London already, while others had to be lured away from the works at Crown Derby or Royal Worcester. Miss Glisson and Miss Parrs were as accomplished copiers of a landscape as Jos had ever met, and they could also be relied upon to paint borders when Ralph was too blotto to hold a brush.

But it was exacting work, and even with so skilled a team as Josiah and Bentley had assembled, they were asking for a very great deal. Each decorator had to be able to reckon on turning out several finished pieces a week, painting the borders in enamelled 'mulberry' monochrome, emblazoning each item with the frog, as an emblem of La Grenouillère, the frog marsh, where the Chesmenski Palace was built, and, above all, adorning each piece with a different British scene – a landscape, a park, a town, a village, a geological or prehistoric phenomenon such as Fingal's Cave or a Cornish menhir or a cascade in the Lake District, a ruined abbey or a new-built Palladian villa for a newly gentrified man.

And all this was being accomplished before Josiah's eyes as he entered the enamelling and painting room of the Chelsea Works that morning. The room where they worked was small, as small as the old modelling room at the Brick House Works in Burslem had been. Jos immediately remarked upon the difference of atmosphere between this and the great big workspace at Etruria. In Staffordshire, he felt the constant need to cajole or threaten his workforce. They always seemed to have a grievance, and what drove him half to distraction was the fact that very often they were right to have a grievance. He did work them hard, and he did watch the pennies and try to keep their remittance as low as feasible, and he was testy with them, and, yes, he did for the most part utterly despise them.

With these men and women assembled in Chelsea, it was a different matter altogether. He almost felt as if he were intruding to walk in upon them while they were engaged upon their labours. With the finest of brushes, Catherine Willcox, an exceptionally plain woman with two large whiskery moles on her right cheek, was reproducing Edward Stringer's watercolour of the rotunda at Ingestre. She painted the lid of a dish, and, around the leaf-framed scene, in the foreground of which two tiny deer stood in the shadows, she painted acorns and oak leaves. Beside Mrs Willcox, Miss Isaacs, a pretty little woman in a mob cap, whose sleeves were rolled up to reveal pin-thin forearms, reproduced another Stringer sketch, this of the ruins of Worksop Abbey, while, on the other side of the table, with a folio of Boydell's prints open on a stand, Mr Bakewell painted the park at Blenheim on a square compotier.

The calm scene was especially soothing, given the marital tempest Josiah had just, uncomprehendingly, left. (He had, as a self-protective device which had become necessary to his sanity, ceased even to ask whether his wife's rages had a cause.) They were a little more than halfway along with the Frog Service and they were, perhaps, a little behind schedule; but there was nothing to worry about. With workmanship of this quality on display, it was safe to be confident.

—Why, Mr Wedgwood, said Mrs Willcox, who continued to stare at Edward Stringer's watercolour and to add, here and there, tiny strokes with a brush so fine it had barely ten bristles. You came in so quietly, sir, that we barely noticed you. We welcome you, sir, and the more so, since you bring us good news.

—I hope so, said Jos.

—From Dorset, sir, said the well-informed Mrs Willcox. You have found white china clay in Dorset, so we need no longer go to the Cornish nor to the American savage.

—The strange fact is, Mrs Willcox, that in the very week I found this new vein of clay in Dorset, we all won our case against

Cookworthy. Parliament has agreed that it is not legal for Bristol to hog the patent on Cornish clay.

—And did we hear that you had sent your agent in America in pursuit of yet more white clay from the savages?

Mrs Willcox laid down her brush and turned to Jos with a smile. When she smiled, her plainness dissipated. The curls of brown hair sticking from her cap, the animation of her eyes and the straightness of her teeth conveyed pleasantness and intelligence.

—It's my dear nephew Mr Byerley, said Jos awkwardly. As soon as I heard from Dorset that white clay was available in England, I sent off a letter as fast as I could to New York. If it has arrived in time, he will not have set out, but in these times, the posts are slow. It is months since his mother – my dear sister – has heard from the boy.

—It must be very worrying for you, said Mrs Willcox. The more so, as I imagine, sir, with your radical principles, and she smiled, as though to indulge a roguish whim, you will be on the side of the thirteen colonies. The 'United States', as they invite us to regard them.

—I am, madam. I am, as you term it, on their side.

—We guessed as much, said Mrs Willcox. Miss Isaacs stopped painting Worksop Abbey for a little while and smiled complicitly.

Where these women, or any of the Chelsea workforce, stood on the most urgent political issue of the hour, they were all too diplomatic to divulge. But it was a subject which was on every lip, all over London: in the Soho salerooms, in coffee-houses, at dinner tables, and from the lips of hackney drivers, the talk was of America.

Although she was excited by London, and although she found Mrs Bentley an agreeable young woman, who was manifestly going out of her way to please, Sukey reacted powerfully to the shifts in her mother's temper. The child, or no longer quite a child, carried within her a consciousness of her mother's unhappiness which felt as strong as a physical weight. She knew her mother and father were not happy. She felt that Papa was too cowardly 'to have it out' with Mama: the girl could tease no more sense out of the situation than this. She knew there was something amiss, and that it was made worse by Papa's attempts to gloss it all over.

—Sign a letter to your grandfather, missy! he had said that very morning. A letter to stern old Grandfather Richard Wedgwood in Cheshire, written, as was transparent to Sukey, to cover their tracks, to throw dust in the old man's eyes. It was a merry letter, speaking of how happy they all were, how cheerful in particular was Richard's daughter Mama, and how jocund were the 'brats', Sukey and John. The other brats had been left behind, and that was further occasion for facetious expressions of thankfulness. And the work went cheerfully on with the Empress's service, and the London showroom was splendid and the Bentleys were happy, and if it was not exactly a lie, it was an attempt to pretend that everything was well.

The Bentleys were intent upon a programme of amusements. John asked if they could be taken to see a man hanged, and Mr Bentley laughed and said if you had to see entertainments involving a rope, it would be more diverting to watch Madame Saqui walking on one, and surrounded by fireworks in the public gardens.

—I declare, you'd like that, wouldn't you, Sukey?

—Thank you, so much, Mrs Bentley.

Later that day, she heard Mrs Bentley say,

—She is almost too polite, that child. Oh no, no trouble, quite the reverse, I assure you, my dear Mrs Wedgwood, but it is as if she has to half-apologize for her existence.

It was a good example of how they all, the grown-ups, had not quite adjusted to her being more than a child, that they still spoke about her, in her hearing, as if she could not possibly understand what they were saying.

Not that Mrs Bentley, who was a recent acquisition by her much-older merchant husband, the second woman to enjoy the privilege of being married to Josiah's business partner, was anything but solicitous to Sukey. In those first few days, she treated her very nearly like a grown-up. She took her to Cox's Museum where they saw an array of exceptional, jewelled mechanical devices. Another day, she took Sukey and John to Mrs Salmon's 'Court' to see the waxworks – an astonishing display, in which were represented Queen Elizabeth I and Henry VIII and Dick Turpin the Highwayman, and a bald man with spectacles who Mrs Bentley said was supposed to be a representative of one of the American Rebels – though whether it was Mr Franklin or Mr Washington or Mr Adams she could not remember because she thought they were all as bad as one another whatever her husband and Mr Wedgwood might say. And Mrs Bentley took her, *à deux*, saying, For we ladies do not always want to be in company, to drive beside the river, while Mr Bentley and Papa took John to coffee at Don Saltero's in Cheyne Walk, and afterwards they joined the boy in the adjoining museum; then they looked in at the decorating room in the works and saw the men and women painting the Frog Service, and eventually Mama surfaced, and Sukey felt half-guilty about thinking life really was much easier when Mama was in bed than when she arose and you did not know from one moment to the next what her temper would be like. And then, she felt even more guilty at having had such a feeling, because Mama, when well, was such very good company, the best, and insisted that they should all visit the Tower of London and see the menagerie and John had turned white as a sheet at the sight of the lions.

On the last day, when her mother and father were to go back to Staffordshire with John and Heffie, leaving Sukey behind with the

Bentleys, there was an air of constraint between them. Ma and Pa, having been at odds for the previous week, now seemed to be friends once more, and Ma was much caught up with John, and kept wondering whether they should have spent the week having the boy fitted by London tailors, and Papa kept making visits to the enamelling room, to check on the work they were doing to the Frog Service, but was also enraptured by his new wooden leg and foot which he had had specially turned by a Mr Addison, a figure-maker of Hanover Street, Long Acre. They were indeed magnificent: a full calf, upon which Papa could draw up a stocking, and a foot which could be swathed in a buckle shoe.

All would have been as happy as sunshine, were it not for the misfortune, in the very last hours of Mama and Papa's visit, of Mrs Bentley happening to remark upon the great good fortune.

—And what is that? asked Sally.

—Why, Mrs Wedgwood, said Mrs Bentley, for they had not advanced into the intimacy of first names, about Mr Cookworthy having lost the patent for the white clay, and of Mr Wedgwood having found yet more white clay near Blandford in Dorset. It means we have white china clay enough and to spare in spite of the American crisis.

—But you will have told Cousin Byerley, Jos, said Mrs Wedgwood at once. You will have had the time to be able to warn Tom not to go off into the swamps and forests in search of India clay.

—Which Tom is that? Mrs Bentley's vague puzzlement was caused by the abundance of Toms in the Wedgwood tribe. Jos and Sally had a son Tom and Jos had a brother Tom and there was yet another cousin, Useful Tom, so called because he presided over the useful ware manufacture.

—Why, Tom Byerley, Mrs Byerley's lad, said Bentley who overheard all this. And if he manages to get the clay in the present circumstances it will be a miracle, because all roads north and south between Carolina and Philadelphia have been closed by the war.

Bentley, a genial, clever man, was alive to the wasp's nest which his wife was unconsciously kicking out into the open, and he hastened to reassure Sally.

—You mustn't allow yourself any disquiet, Mrs Wedgwood. He is a good boy, and we ought, in reality, to be pleased that the situation in America will mean that he will be coming back to us.

—If alive, Mr Bentley! flashed back Sally Wedgwood. If not killed by his uncle's desire to make yet more money! So, from what you are saying, there was no necessity whatsoever to send our nephew on this wild goose chase?

Sukey thought afterwards that it would have been better to have the eruption of the volcano, rather than to see it fuming ominously as Mama got into the carriage with Papa. She sensed immediately that Jos must have withheld from his wife the knowledge that Tom Byerley had gone down to see the Indians. (How Sukey envied her cousin! She would have done anything to meet them!) She never saw her father look shiftier than when he climbed, on his convincing new leg, into the carriage.

# 12

UNCLE JOS HAD GIVEN BYERLEY HIS WATCH, A BEAUTIFUL
silver repeater which he had bought at Cox's in London.

—Remember, our Tom, the world divides unequally between
those very few who make something of life, and those whom life just
passes by. And do you know what distinguishes them?

—The smaller group have luck, Uncle?

—Happen. But happen, too, the lucky ones have watches. It's
time, laddie, it's the use you make of time, which determines whether
you will be a success in life. The Turkish tyrants of the Porte forbid
clocks throughout their Empire. And what have the Turks ever done
since they conquered Constantinople in 1453?

—They very nearly conquered the rest of Europe a century later,
they have made some mighty impressive ceramic tiles at Smyrna,
they've built mosques grander than St Paul's Cathedral, had been
Tom's pert reply, but his uncle was not persuaded.

—Keep your watch wound up, and keep your eye on the time, and
you won't go far wrong, had been his advice to the sixteen-year-old
lad, when he had been working as a clerk at the Etruria Works.

And now, as Tom wound up the watch, which was suspended
from its silver chain on a little peg, he thought of his uncle. Since
Tom met Blue Squirrel, he had continued to wind the silver repeater
day by day, but Time itself had changed, so that the old method of

dividing it, and his former method of taking note of the Newtonian mechanical movements of the sun and the moon, no longer had any meaning.

Blue Squirrel and he had now entered into a sunlit sexual mysticism. Tom had always keenly appreciated the beauty of women, but this was something quite other. Together their bodies had become beautiful in a new way. She was not a 'fetching' or 'beguiling' beauty in the sense that he might have used such words of actresses in New York, or young women in his life in Staffordshire. The intensity of pleasure was a shared intensity; the sense of being all but overpowered, not so much by physical gratification as by ecstatic joy, this too was shared. Her face, as they lay together, changed its contours. The solemnity with which she had at first greeted him was laid aside like a mask, and he saw what felt to be her soul itself. He seemed to be looking at a child in her facial happiness, and he knew that he too, laid bare in every sense, was showing her himself, vulnerable, yet never stronger in their united joy. There was no apparent end to the yearning they felt for one another's bodies. Even a finger's touch was enough to arouse the most extraordinary concentration of feeling. Yet never for one moment did this sexual need feel as ordinary lust had felt in the past. It was as if this most powerful of bodily appetites had been washed of egotism; and that what both of them needed, when this electric excitement and unconquerable yearning visited them both, was to bathe in something outside one another. So, although their long lovemaking – by day, by night, in the simplicity of his truckle bed, in the darkness of the woodlands near the village – was the source of their deepest pleasure, and although in this sense it was a shared gratification of the most profound self-centredness, there was a paradoxical experience for both of them of the self being forgotten. Tom knew, partly from their murmured conversations about it, and partly merely from the expression on Blue Squirrel's face, that she not only felt the same, but felt the same simultaneously. They had left self behind, left lust behind, left behind all that was least important, and, as their bodies entwined and re-entwined, they had both seen into the life of things. His true self met her true self. They both knew this was very rare, and, while being drunk with the happiness which they were able to give to one another, they were both awe-struck, unable completely to comprehend what had happened.

As he wound his watch, it was five o'clock in the morning, and he had already spent half an hour awake, watching the silver dawn-light glimmer in his room, and then rise to a refreshing cold sunlight which filled the room with light.

—What are you doing?

—Winding my watch.

—Why do you do it?

—Habit.

—Come back to bed, Tomtit.

Once again, her strong, slender arms around his shoulders, her thick hair falling down his back and cloaking his arms, her legs holding his legs, her mouth pressed to his lips, and her soul blended with his.

Afterwards, in the silence, she murmured,

—Maybe our bodies take us somewhere else when this happens. Maybe we go to another place, where there is no sadness, no fighting.

—I think we do so. Oh, darling Blue Squirrel.

—Darling Tomtit.

—I can't leave this place without you.

She sighed. One finger gently stroked him, starting at his lower lip, and following a line slowly and caressingly down his chin, his throat, his chest. He in turn rested a hand upon her breast.

—Maybe you can't leave this place at all.

—And poor Wooden Leg waits for his clay!

—He must wait. The roads north and south are blocked by the war. The Americans are losing this war, Tomtit. In a very short time, very short, the redcoats will defeat them. Swan's Wing says that it is only a matter of time before they lose New York. Then General Clinton or General Howe, they will follow them down, take Philadelphia, destroy their Congress . . . Why do you sigh, Tomtit?

—Because it is sad; because the Americans are not all bad men; because maybe they should be allowed to run their own affairs.

—And steal land from the Cherokee, from the Mohawk.

—No, but maybe they could learn to stay in their own land.

—There will never be peace, she said fiercely. The settlers agree not to move into our land. Then they move. They build their little huts, their dirty farms. They do not know how to farm the land, they live like pigs.

—But they are not all like that, Blue Squirrel.

Suddenly, she was angry, and sitting up, shaking off his caressing fingers.

—So, maybe Lark Song and Running Deer are right. They say that I sleep with the enemy, that you are a spy.

—What? But that's an absurdity.

—They say you came on the same day as Boone and the Chattering Bird.

—That was a coincidence. Besides, Swan's Wing brought me.

—They say that there is no coincidence.

—In this particular, or ever?

—I don't understand you. But you don't understand either, Jigililli. Sometimes, I ask myself, can anyone stop being the person that they are? You are an Englishman. I am Cherokee. The Americans are the Americans.

—Doesn't love cross all those barriers and boundaries?

—Some of the braves say you are an honest man. Old Ostenaco

says that it is not a trick, that you really and truly come from Wooden Leg to buy our clay and that Wooden Leg is a good man.

—He is a good man.

—King George loves Ostenaco. He received Ostenaco in his Court at London.

—I know.

—And Wooden Leg loves King George? He is on our side, King George's side against the Americans?

—Darling, everything is different in England. All intelligent people can see that the Americans have justice on their side, but only in—

—The clever people think the Americans can steal our land?

—They don't know about that. They just know that the King is asking them to pay taxes to him but he gives them nothing in return.

—But he does! He sends many redcoats to make sure they come to no harm from the French soldiers, and from our people. The red-coats make sure our people come to no harm from the American people. This is fair. King George is fair. Wooden Leg, he is a friend of King George, isn't he, he is on King George's side?

—Wooden Leg is friends with the Queen. He sells his china to the Queen. He names it after her – Queen's ware. That teapot I gave you when I arrived. That was Queen's ware.

There was a long silence, and he felt Blue Squirrel's anger evaporating a little. She hugged her knees. He tried to flatten them, tried to lay her out, spread her legs once more for lovemaking, but she remained taut and hunched.

—King George is a good man, but he is weak.

—Why do you say that?

—Why does he not cut off Wooden Leg's other leg as well? Why not cut off his head?

—Why would he do that?

—Wooden Leg jigs the Queen of England, and boasts about it to you – gives you pots to show he has jigged Queen Charlotte? Maybe Running Deer was right.

—What did Running Deer say?

—He said that Wooden Leg loved the Queen. Wanted to kill the King and so he could become King of England. He said that Wooden Leg is friends with the Americans, with Mr Franklin.

—Wooden Leg has *met* Mr Franklin.

—What if you are a spy?

—Are you insane?

—They say that you and the Chattering Bird and Mr Boone want to take Cherokee land – Wooden Leg takes the clay, and they build their pigsty huts for the white folks all over our land. That is what they say.

—But it is all nonsense, Blue Squirrel. You know it is nonsense. How can you believe that, that I . . .

—That you what, my Tomtit?

She was not looking at him, and her shoulders were still taut, the neck muscles in the depths and folds of her thick hair were tight as leather.

—I dream of marrying you, of our having children together. Your people shall be my people, and your Gods my Gods. How can you suppose that I am in league with two rattlesnakes like Boone and Bird?

After a long silence, Blue Squirrel said,

—These are hard times, Tomtit. I do not know what I believe any more.

Later, the silver repeater said about an hour later, they left the hut. He was utterly shocked by the doubts which she had revealed.

After they had eaten, Blue Squirrel went to work in the small pottery at the edge of the village. Blue Squirrel was skilled in the craft. Although a Wedgwood on his mother's side, Tom had always

been a clumsy potter. He had none of his Uncle Jos's almost preternatural skill, nor those of this most dexterous of women. He watched
her long fingers work. They did not use the wheel in the workshop
here, but the hand-built pots crafted by Blue Squirrel were as delicate as any European ware, and the vase which rose up in obedience
to her thumb and index finger bore classical resemblances to the
Etruscan ware being produced by his uncle.

They had not properly conversed since the disturbing conversation in bed. Silence had been punctuated by mere exchanges – about
whether they needed to eat, and whether she would allow him to
accompany her to the pottery. But now the cloud had passed, and
Blue Squirrel moved the conversation on.

Because the vase was now done, he could come forward and
massage her shoulders as she spoke. With a piece of cheese wire, she
delicately sliced the vase from the wheel and put it to dry with the
others she had made the previous afternoon.

Partly in English, and partly in her own language, which he was
beginning to pick up fast, she said,

—You are thinking that I could come to Etruria, and make pots
with Wooden Leg. And you were thinking that this would never
work, because it would make me unhappy and that I would miss
my own people, and the Cherokee customs. You were thinking that
marriage between your people and my people was not unknown.
That old Ostenaco gave his daughter in marriage to an Englishman, Lieutenant Timberlake. That Ostenaco's grandson, Richard
Timberlake, is half an Englishman and half a Cherokee.

Some of the other women who worked in the pottery looked up.

One of the other women, who was also making vases at the other
end of the modelling room, made a comment. She spoke too rapidly
for Tom to catch her drift, although he caught the words 'Timberlake'
and he thought he also understood 'Williamsburg'.

—Pouting Pigeon says that the Timberlakes do not know what to do. As the Americans retreat from the redcoats in Philadelphia, Charleston, they will attack weaker people, attack us. Just for revenge sake. Mrs Timberlake, Ostenaco, she fears for her baby. The Americans do not like white men to breed with savages.

—Squirrel, darling!

—No, Tomtit, that is what they call us. That is how they describe us in their great Declaration of Independence. They would like to kill us all.

Later, when they were alone again, Blue Squirrel said,

—You are still thinking of Lieutenant Timberlake, married to Ostenaco's daughter.

—Yes, yes, I am.

—Tom?

—Yes, darling?

—I want to carry your baby.

# 13

*YOUR IMPERIAL MAJESTY SEES ENGLAND AS A LAND OF THE Picturesque, and you are going to ask Lord Cathcart to single out Gothick ruins, sublime Landskips, and do we hear interesting things of the new professor of logic and metaphysics at Königsberg? We find Nature beautiful when we can shape it, when we can make it into Art? Is this what he says? That the Pleasure=principle is what touches us in a landskip or a waterfall or a mountain? That we can in this sense re-invent Nature, translate it into art? And Your Imperial Majesty and Mr Wedgwood between you will bring about a double-miracle? The trans-lation of a Scotch waterfall or a Welsh island into a picture; and the transformation of the picture into the decoration for Mr Wedgwood's plates, jugs, dishes and platters!*

*Incidentally, Your Majesty will be amused by the gossip which reaches me from England. The good Wedgwood, whose fortune as the greatest Master Potter of Europe Your Majesty has now guaranteed, is thrown, not only into an ecstasy of joy and industry, but also into an agony of choice. All the peerage of England, and all the great land-owners, await with eagerness to see how he will portray their palaces and their estates. If my lord, the Duke of Marlborough merits his Blenheim being depicted on a large serving dish, then the same privilege must be afforded to the Duke of Bedford's Woburn and the Duke of Northumberland's Syon House! Oh, the ignominy of having one's*

*Baroque palace depicted on a mere side plate. My English correspondent told me that my Lady ****** passed into Hystericks upon being informed that her husband's ancestral manor house in Lincolnshire was to be consigned to an Egg-cup. Honest Wedgwood, for fear of losing her custom, has been obliged to quell the malicious tongue of Rumour and promote this comparatively modest dwelling to become the decoration for a dinner plate. But the promotion of Squire Mutton entails the demotion of somewhere else: and the Dean of Peterborough will not look kindly upon seeing his Cathedral placed beneath a mill or a grammar school; and the Marchionesses and Countesses of England will be measuring their side plates to determine whether their country seats have been awarded more ceramic inches than the noble piles of mere Baronesses and Baronetesses. Thus has Your Imperial Majesty not merely given useful employ to all the most skilful painters and designers in the English potteries. You have also, with what a Sportsman would call a triumphant Left and a Right, managed to upset the entire nobility of England: you have, as they put it in their sublime phrase, put the cat among the pigeons.*

*But, Madame, you are also in a sense a Prophetess, and honest Wedgwood, as well as being a skilful Craftsman, is a harbinger of the coming Future. The frogs on the plates and soup tureens and creamware ladles croak a message. The stillness of the scenes which Wedgwood is depicting for Your Majesty is an illusory Stillness. The future croaks and rumbles like a Frog. America bursts out of its British straitjacket. But it could not have done so if it had not been British in the first place. Its concepts of Liberty all derive from Mr Locke. Its free and rational Worship of the Supreme Designer of the Universe, detached from the ragged superstitious vestments of the medieval Church – these American virtues it owes to English Oliver Cromwell and English George Fox. Its new-found political voice, proclaiming Revolution, what is it but the voice of Mr Wilkes of Middlesex, and Mr Paine, lately arrived from Southampton?*

# The Potter's Hand

*So, Your Majesty, though you have commissioned a dinner service which details a sublime Island of Vues and Ruines and Parks and Gardens and artificial Lakes, you have also created a political Souvenir of a Tinderbox before it explodes. This was the Island which gave the world its Revolution.*

She held the letter in her plump hands and smiled at its mannered attempts to amuse. He prided himself, the old *philosophe*, on his independence of mind, but in all his attempts to please her – and no doubt it was the same when he wheedled and joked with King Frederick of Prussia – there was a sense of his reverence for absolute power. She shared his distaste for the superstitions of the past and to that degree she saluted herself as part of *Die Aufklärung*. But it amused her to watch these enlightened gentlemen fawn and dance. Mr Wedgwood the radical, old pantaloon Methuselah of Ferney! She had power, and they fawned. Power was all that mattered. Might was right. Nature was the story of strength winning over weakness.

She picked up her pen.

*Dearest Methuselah, It is no secret that the King of England offered me money to send Russian soldiers to the American fiasco. The funds provided by this mercenary endeavour would have been of use to me in paying M. Wedgwood for his dinner service! I felt, however, that there would be humiliation involved if Russian troops were seen to retreat before a rabble of untrained bumpkins, yeoman farmers and religious crackpots.*

*I yield to no one in my admiration for the Russian soldier.*

She laid down her pen, and cupped one plump, moist hand into another. The Empress of Russia, a fleshy German woman of forty-seven years old, looked at the guardsman who had been sent to look after her for the afternoon. She savoured the sight of him, and allowed her eyes to play upon his glistening jackboots, his shapely white tights, his blue uniform-coat with its golden frogging and epaulettes, the strong hands clenched against his thighs, the pale, almost Asiatic face with its flattish nose and high cheekbones.

—You are Boris Ivanovich.

—Dolgopolov, Your Imperial Highness.

—Boris Ivanovich Dolgopolov. I yield to no one in my admiration for the Russian soldier, she said aloud, and then she returned to writing.

*And would detest it, were he to be made a fool of by the American bumpkins . . . My mentor the King of Prussia felt the same hesitancy. But now, I slightly regret it! The English generals, after a few false starts, have triumphed! General Howe, with the eight thousand sent by the Landgraf of Hesse-Cassel, has subdued New York, and it looks as if it is only a matter of time before General Clinton does the same in South Carolina. It would have been agreeable if these triumphs could have been attributed to my beautiful Russians. Still, as a proud German, I suppose I must be pleased that the honour of defeating, not merely the American soldiers, but also the idea of their impertinent Republic, has been granted to Colonel Carl Emilius Ulrich von Donop, whose rigorous drilling of his troops and whose relentless German discipline among the Jaegerkorps in America have paid their very decided dividends . . .*

She rang a bell. The dignified scholarly figure of Andrei Shuvalov, her secretarial and intellectual adviser, entered.

—Andrei Mikailovich, I have scribbled a few thoughts for the Master of Ferney. Be so good as to put them into better shape. Craft witticisms, make the French classical.

—And Your Majesty, when he had read her scrawl, is happy with the indiscretion? To admit that there had been that fleeting thought of sending the troops to America?

—It is well known. *Le monde* gossips of it wherever *le monde* foregathers. Besides, the American war is all but over. General Howe and

Admiral Howe have taken New York. The story is ended. Thank you, Andrei Mikailovich. I now want to be alone.

When she was left with the guardsman, he said,

—Your Majesty has said she wishes to be alone. She wishes for me to withdraw?

—She wishes, said the Empress, with a look which horrified him, you to do the opposite of withdraw. Come.

That evening, the dead body of Boris Ivanovich Dolgopolov was found floating in the Neva.

# 14

BYERLEY WAS LYING IN BLUE SQUIRREL'S ARMS WHEN THE attack came. When he woke, he knew that she too was awake. He felt her breath on his face, chest, throat. She had a way of holding him, and yet somehow not putting her full weight upon him, so that she could be on top of him, or half on top, and he would be aware of her breasts against his own, her face near his face, her hair mingling with his, and yet she would keep her distance from him. As he opened his eyes, he could see her eyes in the dark. In the suddenness of the emergency, he knew that what he was looking at was the most painful imaginable thing – more painful than the fear that followed. She only said his name – her special name for him, Jigililli. She whispered it, slowly, caressingly, between kisses, as an everlasting lament, as a low moaning farewell.

—*Jigililli, Jigililli* . . .

—Darling, Blue Squirrel, you're weeping . . .

—Oh, there is no time, there is no time.

This she said in English. And then, in her own language, she asked him to hold her.

As he did so, and he clasped her so tight that both of them could have suffocated, they could hear the commotion outside the huts: screams of children, war-cries of the braves, the thud of horses' hooves – and now and again terrible whoops of savagery from the colonial invaders, though it was they who shouted of the Cherokees as savages.

*Fire the filthy savages! Get some of the squaws. Fuck 'em!*

The next events must all have happened with great rapidity, perhaps in seconds rather than minutes. Byerley had fully awoken out of sleep and realized that the township was being invaded by the American colonists. Blue Squirrel had heard the men outside, not merely threatening murder and destruction throughout the town, but also intent upon rape.

—That will not happen to me, never, she said in her own language.

Somehow in the seconds which passed, they had both arisen. Byerley had pulled on his breeches and a shirt, and she likewise had put on a beaded shirt and the trousers she wore in the pottery. He also put on his vest, to which his silver repeater was still attached by its chain. In the darkness, he saw a knife glint. He had never before noticed that she carried a knife. He felt under the bedding for his pistol.

Everything in those seconds, or minutes, happened so fast, and yet they were the most dramatic of his existence. In one second, he had been lying asleep, with the breath of the woman he loved upon him. Their love, which was a perfect love, held them together in a union of sex, spiritual kinship, and a need and bliss which transcended happiness. But he knew without any question that as she woke him with his pet name, she was not merely alerting him to danger outside the wooden house. With a shock of terror and grief he sensed that she was saying goodbye to him. Were they about to die together? There was no way of asking her to explain. Nor was he, in those particular seconds, thinking. It was during the rest of his life – not all the time, for much of the time it was too painful to think about and he pushed it to the borders of his mind and, even, into total oblivion – but it was during the rest of his life that he asked himself the questions – why? Why had she not suggested that they should stay together as they ran to fight the men who were destroying the town? Why could they not have been together after the raid? What was it about the raid which made Blue Squirrel so certain, even before she knew precisely what was happening outside their hut, that they must part? And part of the pain, even in the split second as they dressed and seized their weapons, was the thought – suspicion, sometimes certainty – that Blue Squirrel had held the conception that he, Tom Byerley, her lover, the companion, surely, whom the Great Buzzard, or whoever controls our destinies on this muddled planet, had selected for her as the Life Companion, that she suspected him of being a traitor, of being secretly on the side of Bird and Boone.

But these were thoughts which would recur to torture him for decades to come, stabbing him to the heart not merely with their inherent painfulness, but also because there was no possibility of communicating them to Blue Squirrel herself, no way of finding her, no way of assuring her how wrong she had been and how completely he loved her.

They ran out together into the dark. He was wearing some moccasins which she had given him. He had the fleeting sense that she was barefoot. He saw in a flash of firelight her wonderful ankles. Then he looked up and saw her hair streaming behind her as she ran off into the fray with a loud scream, not a scream of terror but of rage, of bloodlust, of revenge. Boadicea, he thought, with admiration. Or the swift-footed Atalanta.

A scene of absolute devastation met Byerley's eyes. The huge Hall of Meeting in its great conical majesty was ablaze, like one of the vast beacons he had seen lit on the Wrekin to celebrate the end of the last war in 'sixty-three. There were people running to and fro with their clothes on fire. Animals which had been hit by botched gun-fire, or clobbered with axes or other instruments, horses and dogs, staggered to and fro, bleeding and whimpering. There were dead children. Against a tree – it was his first moment of pause, as he ran aimlessly – Tom saw a man, his trousers roughly torn open at the front, one arm round the neck of a child, violently raping her from behind. It was with great satisfaction that Byerley used his first bullet on that man. But the child? What could he do with the child, who now, weeping and timorous, shrank from him as if he too might be a predator? But the decision was not his. She ran away into the darkness.

Byerley blundered on through smoke and flame. It was impossible to guess how many Americans had come on the raid but the immediate impression was of a sizeable army – hundreds of mounted figures with guns, who were systematically mowing down the population, killing and firing and burning and destroying.

There was a terrible smell, not merely of burning wood but of what must be burning flesh, as whole houses were set alight, and as the colonists shot the inhabitants if they tried to leave.

*Burn the bastards! Burn the bloody bastards!*

Byerley found himself outside the pottery. Ten or twelve men were in there smashing crockery. As they did so they let out wild cries of *Yee-hi!* And there were coarse outbursts of laughter. Just beside the pottery, two other men were dragging an old man.

—Cut it off! Let's be seeing him. Cut it off, Clifford!

Byerley found the use of the raider's name made the disgusting act all the more horrific. He fired his pistol at the man who was trying to mutilate the old Cherokee, but this time the weapon failed. He shook it, and pulled back the safety catch a number of times, but in the darkness it was impossible to see what was wrong.

A horse came towards him, riderless, but with a saddle, so it had belonged to one of the Americans. Byerley, without thinking what he was doing, put his foot into the stirrup and mounted. The horse reared up, but Tom kept his seat in the saddle, and the frightened animal put all four feet on the ground and pranced into a canter. Was it this one impulsive action of his which made him seem to be on the side of the attackers? He would torment himself with that question for the rest of his life.

With a pistol which no longer worked, and with no other weapon to hand, he was useless. He was barely in control of the horse, which rode beyond the dwellings into the woodlands to the south of Old Kowes. Eventually, the animal calmed down, and Byerley was able to wheel her about, and from the seclusion of the woods, he could take in what was happening, as the dawn, a violent scarlet, rose above the Appalachian mountains. He saw the town ablaze. Not one building had been spared. All were on fire. Beyond it, he saw the great fields of wheat which had so impressed him upon his arrival. This too had been put to the flame, and the southerly wind was spreading the fire across all the crops. As daylight came, he could see that many human beings lay dead, others staggered or ran about, now in this direction, now in that, without any discernible purpose, as the mounted raiders, with whips, guns and captured Cherokee spears, drove the towns-people like so many vermin.

Somewhere in that mayhem was Blue Squirrel, dead or alive. The thought spurred him to ride back into the burning, into the fighting and the murder. He must find her. There must be the possibility that they could escape together. Or so he hoped.

As he came back to the fray on the horse, he could see that the raiders had not gone entirely unpunished. There were a number of Americans lying dead, as the morning light revealed. And beside one bonfire, he found a scene of horrifying torture. A group of women – for a moment he thought one of them to be Blue Squirrel, but it was another young woman with streaming black hair – had one of the raiders in their grip. He was screaming like a stuck pig, and the rays of morning sunshine, cruelly bright and cheerful, showed the piss drenching the legs of his breeches. One of the women held a burning brand which she was applying indiscriminately to different parts of the man's person, now to his feet, now to his arms and legs. Only the piss, it would seem, had prevented him from catching light, that and the sweat of funk which poured from every part of him. The light made it possible to see the man's face: Mr Bird. The impulse to save a fellow human being who, however odious, was known to him, made Byerley cry out to the women,

—No!

But the oldest of them held up her knife, and in one deft slice, and to the sound of excruciating cries, Mr Bird had been scalped. Bird's pale face was open, his mouth, surrounded by its snatches of whisker, was agape with primal horror. In the very second that it happened, the scalping, the man had caught Byerley's eye, and was looking directly at him with an expression of complete desolation as he died. Byerley, who was unaware that any of the old superstitions clung to him, felt he was watching a human soul being snatched to hell, and that no one deserved it more.

Byerley's horse trotted on. On every side, the burning, the knifing, the raping, the screaming, continued. What the dawn made abundantly clear was that this town was now uninhabitable. Every dwelling had been burnt, and most of the citizens had been either killed or put to flight. Horses lay dead. There were not dozens but hundreds of dead horses. Nevertheless, it would seem as if not every horse and not every Cherokee warrior had been slain there. Byerley was later to learn that this was the case, and that some had escaped; but the numbers were very small. After the war, this Cherokee stronghold was surrendered into the hands of the white man, and for hundreds of miles westward what would become the states of Mississippi and Kentucky passed, as a result of this genocide, into the possession of the colonists.

At that moment, however, Byerley's only thought was for Blue Squirrel. Though he had understood well enough her unspoken farewell at his moment of waking, he had not accepted it. He must find her, he must. He rode aimlessly, peering at the few surviving women. Far more had not survived. Corpses were on every side.

It was overwhelmingly probable that one of these dead bodies was that of the woman he loved. Of that he had no doubt at the time, and little reason to doubt in the months which followed. Why, then, had he not dismounted and begun the gruesome task of moving among the slaughtered victims, turning their heads and searching for his Blue Squirrel? He had been – or afterwards he believed himself to have been – on the verge of doing so. The truth is, however, that everything was so confused, everything was happening so fast, that there was no sequence to his thoughts or actions. Things simply happened, in those disorderly moments. He was the patient of events and not the agent. The next thing occurred to him in seconds, and he was unaware, at first, of what it meant.

—Come on, friend. There's nothin' more to do here, said a voice, and Byerley's horse was turning to follow the speaker. Afterwards he told himself that someone had actually taken the bridle and led him to join the group of raiders. This could not possibly have been the case, since he continued to hold the reins, but he felt quite as passive as if he had been led away. He was in a posse of about thirty horsemen, rather as if riding to hounds.

—Come on, said another.

And Byerley's horse, feeling himself, perhaps, among familiar company, trotted, and then galloped away from the destroyed town.

## The Potter's Hand

—That'll show the redskins, one voice was saying as they moved into the gallop.

—And it will show King George and his fucking redcoats.

While a third, to general whoops of laughter called out,

—God bless America!

# 15

SUKEY WAS TWELVE, ABOUT TO BE THIRTEEN. SHE WAS AT the age when grown-ups still considered her a child; or, if that was not quite the case, they had not yet adjusted themselves to dealing with her as if she was no longer exactly a child. For much of the time, therefore, she was left to herself, even when she was in company. Her perceptions flooded upon her with terrifying clarity. She was aware of everything. She saw London, in all its extraordinary energy: the scaffolding and dirt everywhere, for they seemed to be putting up new buildings all over town. From Mrs Bentley's chaise, she saw here a half-built square, there the river, and in the foreground a building – Somerset House, Mrs Bentley said – which was more a half-built palace, its court and arcades and some of its arches already completed in new-hewn stone. She saw the dark faces of Africans. So many of them! Mrs Bentley said they were not all slaves, that many of the slaves had either escaped their masters or that they had found freedom in some other way. It was an inequity, Mrs Bentley said, a terrible inequity, to buy and sell our fellow creatures as if they were cattle. But they saw not only the brown faces of Africans. They saw Italians, especially near the Wedgwood showrooms in Soho. They saw carriages on which stood two powdered footmen in livery on the outside, with outriders and, on the door of the carriage, coats of arms – some Duke or Duchess, Mrs Bentley said. They saw poor people.

There were none in Burslem with African faces, none with Italian voices, none with such ducal grandeur as in the coach with coats of arms unless you counted Dr Darwin, sweatily heaving himself out of his bright yellow phaeton; and none so poor as the London poor.

Sukey clutched Mrs Bentley's hand as they trotted past them in a region that she said was the Seven Dials. The faces were fallen in. The filth and rags in which they were clothed were far worse than the gypsies encamped on the Downs Banks near Caleb and Heffie's cottage at Stone. These poor people were like another species. Out of their sunken sockets, eyes of infinite desolation met Sukey's. The sorrow of one woman in particular, a grey-faced, scrawny thing whose face she glimpsed through the chaise window, three or four blackened teeth, cut cheeks, straggles of hair, no cap, no gloves, made an impression so strong that it penetrated the miasma of gloom which had been hanging over Sukey all morning, throughout the sightseeing tour. The spectacle of this miserable woman was a tremendous shock. They spoke, in these days of medical advancement, of cure by inoculation. The surgeon took a little of the pox and rubbed it into a cut in otherwise healthy skin. By giving a little of the disease, the patient was prevented from developing full-scale pox, such as had blighted poor Pa's boyhood. And the sight of this poor woman had been like that – for the first time Sukey had seen a sorrow which made her recognize her own sorrows as something she could live with, rise above. The abject physical degradation of this poor woman, the filth in which she must live all the time, the certainty that her life would be short, were all borne into Sukey's consciousness in an instant. And she realized that the comforts in which she and her family resided, their changes of clothes, their plentiful meals, their music, their diversions, and above all their books, gave her advantages which this woman, and swarming multitudes like her, would never possess.

Removed from sibling rivalries, the noises and illnesses of Etruria, and her mother's ever-fluctuating humours, Sukey found great contentment at the Chelsea house of Mr and Mrs Bentley. The Struggle for Existence could, for a while, be laid to one side. Books, chat, London walks and rides in the park made a very acceptable substitute to the screams of the younger children and the squabbles of the older ones. Chelsea made a happy change from Burslem.

There was the great Hospital, where she watched the old pensioner soldiers parading in their red coats. Mr Bentley said some of them were so old as to have fought in Marlborough's wars. She was fascinated by the faces of the most aged, their toothless mouths, the skeins of rheum which came from their nostrils; their sunken cheeks and bony brows beneath tricorn hats. And next to it was Ranelagh Gardens where Uncle John had met his sad fate, and where, on one of Pa's visits, they had been to a ridotto, though they had left early – Pa said the music and dancing at such affairs went on until all hours. And there was the Physic garden where she could walk with Mrs Bentley.

Mrs Bentley was younger than Mama – or seemed so. Sukey guessed she might be thirty. She had dark brown hair, and dark brown eyes, and she appeared to find almost everything funny. Her high spirits were in such contrast to those of Sally Wedgwood that, at first, Sukey became high on them herself. There was something almost exhausting about whole days in which there was nothing but chatter and laughter. So much was this the case that she became caught up in Mrs Bentley's unstoppable chatter and felt herself betrayed into disloyalty, recounting Mama's outbursts of bad temper, her rages against Pa, her tearful fits in Heffie's arms. Sukey found herself chattering as Mrs Bentley chattered, and making them all into a story: Caleb's dogged devotion to Ma and his surliness; Heffie's kindnesses, and her 'racy' past, for there had been no husband that anyone knew of to father the boys. The uppishness of John Wedgwood and the scientific melancholy of young Jos. She had poured it all out to Mrs Bentley, who had laughed, as she laughed at the antics of her own friends in London. But afterwards, Sukey felt she had been disloyal.

It was a comfort, when she became conscious of having said too much, blurted matters which, if not secret, were personal, to resume the role of sightseer. Almost the most impressive of London's sights was the Wedgwood and Bentley enamelling room, in the neighbouring field to the famous Chelsea Porcelain Works. And there were walks beside the river, and views to the open fields and trees of Battersea on the Surrey side, and when you turned back towards London, you could see the two towers of the Abbey against the sky, and not much between, except the sails of river barges and the smoke of a few houses.

At first, family loyalty had made Sukey suppose that the sensations of comfort and relief brought by every waking hour were occasioned by the contrast between Mrs Bentley's gentle, well-ordered household and the boarding school in Derby, with its uncongenial pupils (excepting Miss Edgeworth), its pappy, gruelly mealtimes, its pinched, half-informed teachers. But the passage of only a few weeks had, alas, confirmed what Reason could have told her from the first, that she had needed a holiday from her family. She had needed to be away from the endless warfare, sometimes manifested in fisticuffs, more often in conversational carping, between John and Jos. It went without saying that Sukey adored little Tom; he was quite stupendously the best member of the family, but his neediness, and his constant questionings about the origins of things, for he was already at five years old quite the natural philosopher. And no doubt Kitty would be adorable too, one day, but not yet, not at two. And poor mother, in Sukey's absence, had had another, Sarah.

But to be removed from the everlasting organic struggle of family life, the clamour for attention and precedence, was a luxury indeed. Mrs Bentley, young enough to be almost an elder sister, and much younger than Mr Bentley, had possessed the good sense to settle early into a blissful routine. Whereas, in her first week in London with Mama and Papa, Sukey had been surfeited with pleasures, the theatre, the waxworks, the Vauxhall Gardens, Sukey had discovered, once the Wedgwoods were all gone and it was simply herself and the Bentleys, that quotidian pleasures are greater than 'special occasions'. Mrs Bentley taught her needlework. Mr Bentley praised her sketching. She moved from simple airs of Thomas Arne on her flageolet to some lovely Albinoni pieces for oboe, which Mr Bentley said 'worked just as well with a penny whistle'. And then Mr Bentley had bought her an oboe of her own, and she had begun to take lessons with a Mr Ellis.

Sukey loved Mr Bentley, and could see why Pa did so also. Pa was always in a rush. Mr Bentley was very likely in a rush too, but he concealed it. He never passed Sukey in the hall without wanting to see her latest watercolour sketch, or without enquiring after Blanche, the Bentleys' little terrier whom they had permitted Sukey to 'adopt' for the time she was in London, or to make some comment about her music. Mr Bentley played the cello, and had promised to teach her one day, or at the least to arrange for lessons.

Sukey could see so many things about Papa and the Bentleys which only truly came into focus many years later; but the data, so to say, was gathered in these crucial months. She saw how Papa had modelled his household on that of the Bentleys. Though Sukey was too young to remember much of the Brick House – it was just a haze of impressions in her half-memory, it was Heffie holding and squeezing her, it was the smell of pies cooking on the range in the kitchen, it was the frayed damask of an old cushion, then at eye height, on a window seat in the parlour; it was not a whole. By contrast, she could watch her father trying to make Etruria Hall into a house where they could avoid putting feet wrong. The Bentleys dined at four, so the Wedgwoods must do the same, though it was an inconvenient hour and it would have been so much better to dine, as everyone else did, at two. The Bentleys called the upstairs drawing-room of their large house in Cheyne Row a saloon, and so the drawing-room at Etruria had to be a saloon. Mr Bentley bought quantities of books, so Papa bought books by the crate, though Sukey never saw him read one.

She saw – though she only saw it after she had grown up, but it was as a child that she saw – all the components of the thing which allowed her to form her judgement that Mr Bentley was a gentleman, and that Pa, who could never quite be a gentleman, could nevertheless make his children gentlefolk.

That, in part, was the reason for her quiet year in Chelsea, was it not? The needlework, the sketches, the outings were not simply forms of pleasure, they were ways of instruction. There was nothing so formal as an introduction of Sukey to 'society'. But in the friends selected for her amusement, her sensitive antennae noted certain graces lacking in the children of manufacturers. The Allens were one such family, a merry little gaggle of girls about her age, visiting an aunt in the capital, but located at Cresselly Place, their father's seat in Pembrokeshire. Splendid as Etruria had been made, Sukey knew, even at her young age, that one could not refer to it as a seat.

—If Etruria isn't a seat, what should we call it? Would you say a house?

—You could say 'our place in Staffordshire', suggested Mrs Bentley.

—Place, not seat?

But Mrs Bentley had only laughed, not explained.

Quiet for Sukey that year was, but into the Bentleys' saloon came allusions to strange convulsions – the American war won; then lost again. Vesuvius erupting once more in the Bay of Naples. Dr Darwin, who visited more than once, chuckled as he told them of one of his patients in Derby, Mr Wright, a painter, representing the volcano over and over again, though he had not set foot in the Bay of Naples.

—I know w-w-what physic to p-p-provide from the state of the latest v-v-volcano on the easel. If there are f-f-flames coming into the sky, I d-double the dose of l-laudanum, sir! If it s-smoulders. But ah, poor Wright, it is usually smouldering.

—Sir William is in London, said Mrs Bentley, who, while not knowing 'everyone', spoke as if she knew 'everyone's' comings and goings.

—We await another catalogue of Sir William Hamilton's Antiquities, said her husband, but I should rather see one of Lady Hamilton's attitudes.

—Mr Bentley, I declare!

His wife laughed, but blushed at mention of Lady Hamilton's 'attitudes'. Sukey asked her why, and it was hastily explained that the wife of the Minister in Naples pretended, for the amusement of his guests, to be a statue on his table.

—You know, said Dr Darwin, a strange throatiness coming into his tone, what Greek statues of young ladies are like.

—They are bare, said Sukey with astonishment.

To cover the embarrassment of the moment, Mr Bentley spoke hastily,

—When he passed through Paris, on his way home, Sir William told me, he saw the return of Voltaire. They carried the old rogue through the streets.

—It c-c-can't be long.

—What's 'it', Doctor? asked Sukey.

—W-w-why! Another eruption, another v-v-volcano!

# 16

THE YOUNG MAN WHO SAT IN THE MAKESHIFT BARRACKS
in Philadelphia, during that very cold December, was physically recognizable as the same Tom Byerley whom we first met sipping coffee
in New York, and smiling to himself about his feminine conquests.
Perhaps, if we had seen the New York Byerley in August and the
Philadelphia Byerley in December we should have noticed a few
changes in his face. He had lost weight, his clothes hung loose, his
aquiline nose and chin now seemed sharper than before, and his
high cheekbones were more prominent. But we should also have
noticed, if we had compared the two, that the Philadelphia Byerley
was tired, distrustful, scared. The New York Byerley had been, for all
his philandering, an essentially innocent person who merely took in
experience as it was offered, like a child gobbling sweetmeats. The
taste had turned sour. He was now afraid of what life might produce.
Nature, or some trick of the mind, had coated him almost instantaneously in a thick carapace, which concealed, even from himself, his
innermost fears and feelings, and which guarded him against the
intrusions of the outer world.

When he looked back in later years on this period, Byerley
remembered very little about it. He remembered the journey down
to the Cherokees, the love affair with Blue Squirrel, and the raid.
Quite how he remembered them varied with the passage of time, for

these passages in his life eventually became a secret story which he told to himself, and which altered in the telling. In the immediate aftermath of the raid, however, the wounds, both of lost love and of the appalling violence which he had witnessed, caused a numbness to descend upon his imagination.

The colonists who had sacked the Cherokee town and massacred most of its inhabitants had believed themselves to be protecting their own interests, rather than performing an invasive act of mass murder. It had not occurred to them, as they led away a white man from the scene, that Byerley could be anything other than sympathetic to their aims, even if he had displayed an understandable revulsion at the bloodshed. Some of the posse had been local smallholders, frightened of the Indians, as they called the Cherokee people. They had believed that it was a simple choice between their children's lives and that of the 'savages', who had shown themselves capable of devastating violence. Others in the raiding party had been members of one part or another of the American army. They shared the aims of the local smallholders, and wished to protect the colonial interest. But they were also conscious of the wider picture, and knew that King George's generals, cynically in the American estimation, had offered comradeship to the Indians in exchange for their willingness to fight the Rebels.

Edmund Burke had said in the House of Commons in Westminster that this policy was tantamount to murder, since it was an open incitement to the native Americans to kill the settlers. It was an obviously desperate attempt to intimidate the Rebels. American fortunes were low at that time. Boston was in the hands of the Tories. General Washington and his tatterdemalion army had been driven out of New York by the combined might of the British Navy and a huge mercenary army of Germans. Charleston to the south was in the hands of Loyalists. The future destiny of the fledgling Republic

now hung upon two slender chances: first, upon the Americans
surviving without further invasion or conquest by the British forces
in the territory between the conquered lands, in Maryland, Delaware
and Pennsylvania; and, second, the future of the revolution depended, if possible, on thrusting back once more across the river into New
Jersey. Any such revival in American fortunes would be undermined
or destroyed if the British army were to arm or incite the native
Americans against the colonists.

So it was, extraordinary as Byerley found it in retrospect to
believe, that after he had spent three or four weeks in the company
of the men who took him away from that scene of devastation in
Old Kowes that his perspective of it changed. He knew that he had
been, and that he still remained, in love with Blue Squirrel – though
this feeling of love was frozen, and the necessary grief for the end of
his affair would burst from him much, much later. His present state
of mind was one of numbed confusion, about love, about America,
and about his own future. He would always be the same Tom Byerley
that he had been since youth – sensual, quick, essentially a kind and
decent person. But he was also a changed Tom Byerley, a wounded
figure, more complex and nuanced, less capable of easy decisions,
either in matters of thought or action.

In fact, after they had ridden away from the destroyed Cherokee
town, Byerley found it impossible to separate in his mind the violence on one side or the other. The sight of Mr Bird's head ripped
open at the top, with blood and brains spurting from it, never left
him, and was quite as terrible in retrospect as the sight of the
American colonist sodomizing an Indian child under the tree, or the
smell of human flesh roasting as the raiders set fire to the wooden
houses. It had all been of a horror too impossible to absorb. Yet it
did not make him believe that the American question would be
solved by the redcoats reducing the colonists to submission.

After he had spent a night or two in one of the colonists' mean townships, he had been escorted by the military wing of the raiding party on the northern road back towards Philadelphia. They had ridden at speed along the same roads which he had traversed in such leisure with Swan's Wing in the summer. Now, the roads were pitted with puddles and potholes. The trees were bare of leaf. Much of the time, cold, sleety rain half-blinded the travellers, so that the stupendous expanses of landscape, of mountain range and forest, passed almost unnoticed.

Byerley was silent, all but totally silent, for the first ten days of their journey. The violence at Old Kowes had shocked him to speechlessness. He was frightened that they might encounter more, or worse, examples of human bloodlust. He yearned to be away from the whole scene. He yearned for home. At the same time, as they rode, rested, ate and slept, rode, rested, ate and slept, the men of the convoy impressed him. He had now, somehow, he knew not how, been separated from the smallholders and landowners whom they left behind to the south. The party which pressed onwards did so for a military purpose.

—How do we know?

—We can't know. But short of killing him on the spot, we have no reason to suppose he is actually in their pay.

—What was he doing in that village? He wasn't part of Boone's enterprise?

—If he was, he's a criminal. It's no wonder the savages hate us with sharks like that in the sea.

—Have you tried asking him what he was doing in the village?

—He seems more or less speechless.

Byerley had overheard this conversation about himself when they had been on the road for some ten days. It made him wonder whether he was not, in a sort, their prisoner. Some of the American military clearly believed him to be a British spy, or some kind of agent working with the Indians. Others thought he was a harmless, dumb idiot who had simply had the bad luck to get caught up in the fighting. Byerley preferred this latter notion, believing it to be nearer to the truth.

In retrospect, when he looked back upon this time from a perspective of months and years, he felt, if not gratitude to the American soldiers who had taken him in their posse to Philadelphia, then at least something very like it. Had they not taken him away from that scene of mayhem and murder, what would have become of him? It was highly improbable, given the dangerous nature of the times and his lack of any other guide, that he would have been able to find his way back to the roads. Indeed, it was all the most extraordinary set of chances which had led him back northwards, and now found him in a military bivouac, in freezing cold weather, just outside the city of Philadelphia, just before Christmas 1776.

He had been in Philadelphia about a month. By the time he had reached the city, he had recovered some of his old conversational capacities and he had responded to the friendliness of two American soldiers, the captain of the platoon with whom he was travelling, whose name was Peter Lyne, and a private soldier named Michael Yelton. When they heard Byerley's story, they agreed that they should escort him as far as the city, where it should be possible for him to meet up with the Wedgwood agent and decide what to do about finding his passage home to England. Yelton was an attractive young man, quietly spoken, slight in build, and with brown-blond hair which flopped across his brow. He was a reader, and had in the pocket of his old-fashioned buff-coloured coat a volume of *Tristram Shandy*, which he would read by the light of a candle before they went to sleep in their wayside camps. Sometimes, in the darkness, Yelton would burst into harrumphs of laughter, and when Tom asked him what had been so amusing, Yelton would relate the latest bizarre exchanges between the narrator's father and Uncle Toby.

Yelton's people ran a small stationer's shop in the middle of Philadelphia. Michael's father, Jim Yelton, came from the small Essex town of Witham, and had emigrated back in the fifties. He had married a Quaker woman called Elizabeth Rice, a neat, intense woman, whose hair was drawn tightly back to expose a shining pale forehead. Neither Michael nor his father shared the mother's faith, as Michael explained to Byerley. The mother was shocked at Michael's readiness to take up arms in the struggle against Britain, believing as she did that all human conflicts should be resolved peaceably and with talk, silence and prayer. In this optimistic and placid view she was joined by her three daughters, who equally deplored Michael's career in arms.

The Yeltons, however, who all squeezed into the living rooms of the orderly, brick-built terraced house above the stationer's shop in Chestnut Street, were advanced radicals in politics, even if they differed about the legitimate means to attain their ends. On the counter of the shop was a pile of Thomas Paine's *Common Sense*.

—Sells so fast you could say it walks out of the shop, said old Jim Yelton.

—I read it some months ago, said Tom. It is . . . persuasive, certainly.

—Read it again! urged Yelton.

Byerley liked his new friend's father. Together, they spoke of England. The Wedgwood connection was a good starting point, as was Uncle Jos's friendship with Joseph Priestley, a man whom Jim Yelton hugely admired. This talk, and the re-reading of Paine, had a transformative influence upon Byerley's whole outlook on life.

I challenge the warmest advocate for reconciliation, to shew a single advantage that this continent can reap, by being connected with Great Britain. I repeat the challenge, not a single advantage is derived. Our corn will fetch its price in any market in Europe, and our imported goods must be paid for, buy them where we will . . . Everything that is right and reasonable pleads for separation. The blood of the slain, the weeping voice of nature, cries 'TIS TIME TO PART . . .

Moreover, when Byerley had read, and been converted, by the pamphlet, the Yeltons took him to hear Paine speaking in person at the Philosophical Hall. Paine's gifts as a speaker were enhanced, rather than diminished, by the fact that he was drunk. Byerley, indeed, wondered whether the Yeltons, all of whom were curiously innocent, noticed that their hero's slightly slurred utterance, histrionic gestures, sweating face and willingness to shout had been evidently stimulated by alcoholic application. Paine's speech electrified a packed hall, and had any member of the audience entered that hall as a Loyalist or a Tory, the sheer power of Paine's voice, and the collective enthusiasm of those around him, would have made her or him walk out of the place a republican and an American.

Tom Byerley's mother was a Tory of Tories. But he took this as one of her foibles, like going upstairs at ten every morning to tidy herself, or expecting Everett to pass objects easily within reach. Byerley patronizingly supposed that his mother's political opinions were not thought out, because they were entertained not only beneath the mob cap of a woman, but of a woman who had given him birth. Mrs Byerley was to be 'indulged'. He loved her, and he was pleased, now that he had returned to Philadelphia, to be able to send her letters assuring her of his safety and wellbeing. But when it came to an idea of the world, he wanted to be at one with his Uncle Jos, and with the radicals.

His conversion to a belief in the American cause was easily effected within weeks. The Yeltons were obviously pleased by his warm fellow-feeling, but equally, they were a solicitous and amiable family who felt it was irresponsible to encourage Byerley's zeal to the point of his actually enlisting as a soldier on the American side. True, much to the horror of his mother and sisters, Michael had done so, but they deplored this and did everything they could to dissuade him from going to military training sessions in a camp on the banks of the Schuylkill, and in another base further out of town in the Wissahickon Valley.

But at least they could recognize that Michael was an American, fighting for his own country and for a cause which they themselves held dear. In Byerley's case, everything was different. He was an Englishman.

—*The only son of his mother and she was a widow*, quoted Mrs Yelton.

—I have had that phrase so often applied to me and my mother, ma'am, laughed Byerley.

—It does not prevent it from being true, said Elizabeth. Your plain duty as a son is to go home.

—And my duty as a human being. Is it not to history?

—Your duty as a human being is to go home too. Your uncle will be disappointed not to have his white china clay but he would be even more disappointed not to have his nephew.

It was in part because he saw the logic of Mrs Yelton's point of view that Byerley instinctively, and rather childishly, wished to defy it. And it was while they were exercising and practising in the frozen forest glades of the Wissahickon Valley that Byerley realized that he faced a decision.

Captain Peter Lyne called him out of the ranks where they were drilling.

—Byerley, a word, if you please.

—Yes, sir?

—I am afraid that I have hard words to speak.

—How so, sir?

—We have grown fond of you since we met you on the road, and I know that you have made friends with young Yelton.

—Yes, sir.

—An excellent soldier, Yelton.

—Yes, sir.

—And you would, I am sure, Byerley, have the makings of an excellent soldier.

—I am more than willing to—

—Byerley, you are an Englishman. This is a war between England and America. For you to fight on our side is an act of treason against the Crown, for which you could very well be hanged. I could not reconcile your death in such a cause with my conscience.

Byerley began to stammer out phrases from Paine's *Common Sense*, about the nobility of the American cause, about his wish to fight for liberty, about the numbers in England, including his uncle, who supported American independence.

—There is another thing, Byerley. We are about to go into action. The action which is about to be undertaken is of the utmost secrecy and the utmost importance. We cannot, we simply cannot, afford for this to go wrong. General Washington has made it clear that if we do not succeed in this endeavour, then our cause is lost. He is very much afraid that there are British spies among us.

—But surely, you could not suppose that—

Captain Lyne raised a hand to silence the young enthusiast.

—Tom, he said quietly, and smiled. Just let me tell you what are the orders from above.

—From General Washington?

—From His Excellency, yes. Anyone who is suspected of being a spy is to be shot, without court martial, trial or question.

There was a silence. Byerley could feel himself shaking, but it was not exactly with fear. He was visited by a feeling of tremendous excitement.

—Anyone who speaks during the engagement will be shot dead. Anyone who fires a gun before he is ordered to do so will himself be shot. This operation is to be conducted in total silence and with absolute secrecy and discretion.

—I can assure you, sir, that I would never—

—Young man, I am not allowing you to remain with us. I am sorry, but you must go home to London another way. Pray God, if the engagement is successful, we will be able to offer you safe conduct to New York in only a few weeks' time. Now, be a good boy. Go back to your lodgings in the town. Eat your Christmas dinner, if Quakers will give you one.

—Sir, I implore you, and now Byerley felt his gifts as a ham actor were coming into play. You have no reason to doubt my word or my honour. I do not pretend that when the next phase of the conflict is over, I will not go home to England. But I should not wish to go as a mere visitor to America, or one who was too scared, when he saw a noble cause, not to embrace it and fight for it. If I were to die in this endeavour I could imagine no nobler cause than this to which to give my life. And if I were to be dismissed from the service because you, sir, were unable to trust me or my word, if that were the case, then maybe I have been mistaken. Perhaps this great new nation is not, after all, worth the blood of its allies and comrades.

It worked.

—Don't say you were not warned, said Captain Lyne. It's going to be a hard, bitter campaign.

# 17

BY THE END OF 1776, GEORGE WASHINGTON HAD BEEN routed in New York. His enemies within the Congress were almost exultant, and saw it as an excuse to rid themselves of the Virginian landowner, even if his military blunders cost them the independence for which they had all been struggling.

Washington himself was aware that, had General Howe and the Hessian mercenaries followed up their victory in New York and pursued the Rebels, not only through New Jersey, but south across the Delaware, his tattered army of tired and defeated amateur soldiers would have been unable to put up a fight. It would have been the end. Philadelphia might have been the seat of the Congress, until they decamped, for safety's sake, to Baltimore. But the city as a whole was more Loyalist than revolutionary. The forces of George III would not have had to fight for Philadelphia in the way they had fought for Boston and New York. They would have taken it with ease. It would have been simply a matter of time before they took Washington himself prisoner, and shot him. They would then have been able to make their way to Baltimore, round up the Congressmen who had not fled into hiding, and thereby bring to an end the revolution which had been declared six months earlier, but which had so far been little more than a form of words.

The gigantic, inscrutable figure of Washington was perhaps never more taciturn than when he hatched his plans in the two weeks before Christmas. Once, when Dr Benjamin Rush was in his company, he noted that Washington nervously scribbled on small pieces of paper throughout their conversation, and screwed the papers into balls. Unwrapping one of these when it fell on the floor, Rush read the words, VICTORY OR DEATH.

Rush, one of Washington's closest companions at this time, was on record as believing that 'Washington has so much martial dignity in his deportment that you would distinguish him to be a general and a soldier from among ten thousand people. There is not a king in Europe that would not look like a *valet de chambre* by his side.'

On some of those days before Christmas Washington was in Philadelphia, and on others he rode out into the gelid winter air along the banks of the great river. Even those in his immediate entourage could not know with any exactitude what was passing through his mind while, hawk-beaked and silent, he stared across the waters of the Delaware, as though communing with its spirit and asking its counsel.

The rumour flew about – and Washington had in fact heard this from the more reliable source of his military intelligence – that the British, having retired to New York for the Christmas holiday, intended to cross the river as soon as it had frozen over. Already, in mid-December, it was bitterly cold, and as another week passed, chunks of ice had begun to form on the fast-moving surface of the water. Some of those who watched the turbid flow were in the strange position of being aware that they were in the very centre of a series of events of immeasurable historic magnitude. The outcome would depend upon so many things: the feasibility of Washington's plans, the health and strength of his army, many of whom were now barefoot and bleeding, hungry and blistered, upon the extent to which his plans remained a secret, and the extent to which the forces of the Crown might overpower them, when the next engagement occurred. These were only some of the contingencies of the august moment. But at the centre of it all flowed this river, this mighty water upon which Washington gazed with his hooded eyes. For if it, or its tutelary Deity, chose to freeze hard, and to freeze with load-bearing ice, then it would be possible for the paid armies of King George to gallop across the floes to achieve an almost certain conquest. If, however, the waters remained navigable, then it might, it just might, be possible for Washington to reassemble his forces on the Pennsylvanian shore, to cross in large Durham boats by night, and spring a surprise attack on the New Jersey town of Trenton. And if this were successful, and if his troops gained in morale, and if this encouragement spread from town to town and from state to state, then it might once again be possible to rekindle the American idea and save the future of the United States. Upon so many imponderable factors did the outcome hang, but chiefly it depended upon that near-freezing river, and that silent man.

Tom Byerley felt as if his face was being lashed with cold wires. The wind, bringing snow and ice, stung the face and blinded the vision. Standing in silence with forty other infantrymen in the low-lying Durham boat, which swayed and heaved with the storm, he cursed his arrogant folly in having remained with the American army. A lad of sixteen might be stubborn for stubbornness's sake, but what strange trick of the brain had made him, a grown man, resist Captain Lyne's sensible advice? Self-doubt and self-hatred shook his spirit, as the heaving of the boat shook his legs. Whatever the justice of the American cause, he had no desire to kill for it: once again, he questioned how he could ever have sided with Michael Yelton in the arguments at the back of the stationer's shop with Michael's sensible Quaker mother. If this was a cause with so much right on its side, it could surely be won by argument, and not by force of arms. And he thought, as he so often did, of his own mother, and of the sheer cruelty, the unnecessary cruelty to her, of risking his life upon this reckless adventure.

No one spoke. It was very dark. Although there was meant to be a full moon, the darkness was complete, because the storm clouds hid the lights of heaven. The only sounds, apart from the howling wind, were the echoing thumps caused by huge plates of ice which buffeted the sides of the boats.

But there was no going back. Two thousand four hundred men had been assembled in the base camp on the Schuylkill shore. There, when they were divided into companies, the orders of the generals had been repeated. From now onwards, any talking in the ranks and any attempt at desertion would be punished by instant death. The men were to stay within hearing distance of their officers. They were to be conveyed across the Delaware in companies of forty. They had been warned that the river was freezing fast and that there were many parts of the New Jersey banks which would be inaccessible to the boats. If they achieved their aim, and managed to cross the great river, they were to disembark swiftly and silently and await further commands.

They were now about halfway across. It was impossible to see, in the dark, how many other boats were crossing with them, but you could sense the presence of others. Every now and again, the howling storm would be interrupted by the stentorian tones of General Knox, whom Washington had placed in charge of this most difficult of operations. Above the roar of the nor'easter, they could sometimes hear Knox's bass tones: 'Ice ahead, steer to starboard. STARBOARD!' Sometimes you could hear the whinnying of frightened horses. Tom's heart had been wrung to see these poor animals being whipped and driven on to the boats. Almost as unwillingly, it would seem, the artillerymen had loaded the heavy field guns on to the boats at the ferry.

The actual crossing took little more than half an hour, but while it lasted, time stood still. Tom, and he was sure this was true of his fellow passengers, was simply fixed in a resolution to endure: to endure the cold and biting wind, to endure the coming conflict and, if necessary, to die. The full nature of the operation was hidden to all but a small handful of initiates surrounding Washington. There were to have been three principal crossings. Washington had gone ahead of his men, through the chunks of swiftly flowing ice, on the eight-hundred-foot journey, to the Jersey shore, where he sat, shrouded in a thick cloak and sitting on an upended beehive, awaiting developments. Colonel Cadwalader's contingent of troops was scheduled to cross from the Neshaminy Ferry, where the river was a quarter of a mile wide. The wind was so strong, the dark so impenetrable, the ice on the water so thick, that he called off the crossing. Colonel Daniel Hitchcock's New England Continentals had orders to cross near Bristol, Pennsylvania to Burlington, New Jersey and likewise found conditions impossible. Tom and his companions were literally in the dark about these disasters as they made their crossing, and assembled on the New Jersey side.

It had been intended that they should all cross at midnight, march on Trenton by the light of the moon, and stage a surprise attack upon the town before dawn. Because of the extreme weather conditions, and a series of minor mistakes repeated, and delays, the soldiers who eventually managed the crossing did so at three o'clock in the morning. The storm was so terrible, the snows so deep, the icy surfaces of the dirt tracks so treacherous that many found it difficult to stand upright. They lost a handful of men who fell into snowdrifts and died of hypothermia, but this was not discovered until they had marched back once more.

It was six in the morning, and dawn was beginning to glimmer when they approached Trenton. It was in those days a small village of some one hundred houses, which had been entirely deserted by its civilian population. The Hessian redcoats occupied it as a garrison. With them, they had gathered a force of armed Loyalist supporters. Threatened with death at the hands of their own sergeants if they spoke or stepped out of line, Tom and his platoon quick-marched in formation through the freezing darkness towards the blue-black silhouette of Trenton's roofline.

# 18

IN THE EIGHTEENTH CENTURY, WHICH WE HAVE COME TO inhabit for the duration of this story, they were very interested in how we perceive things, and how we can decide whether we know things. Bishop Berkeley was the most extreme of the empirical philosophers, and brought his enquiring, sceptical philosophical approach to Newport, Rhode Island and New York in the 1720s. Then, after nearly twenty years as the bishop of a remote Irish diocese, he died in Oxford, with his mystic-minded wife reading to him from St Paul's Epistles. He thought that you could not prove the existence of matter. (And Dr Johnson famously kicked a stone and said, 'I refute him thus!') But you can't kick away an interesting idea. Berkeley, and even more David Hume, left behind a trail of scepticism about how we can know *anything*. The difference between the two men was that, whereas Hume thought this was a reason for discarding religion, for Berkeley, it was religion's chief justification. For Berkeley, we are God's dream. We can only 'know' that a table is there by touching or seeing it, or, if you are the Great Cham, kicking it. Existence itself can only be explained if there is a consciousness holding it all together, a Creative consciousness. *Pace* Descartes, we cannot even know that we exist. Only God can know that.

But in that productive century with which Josiah Wedgwood had so much to do, Sukey was not alone in having a different way of laying hold upon the truth. While her Pa and his friends were digging canals and constructing turnpike roads and spinning jennies and steam engines; while the worthy Quaker Cookworthy was devising soft-paste porcelain to rival that of Meissen; while Messrs Jefferson and Paine were inventing American democracy, and M. Lafayette and His Majesty King Louis XVI and M. Mirabeau and M. Voltaire were watching the progress of the American Revolution with considerable interest; while Meinherr Haydn and Meinherr Mozart performed their own revolutions in such a peal of tragic-joy that some believed their effusions to be no more than tinky-tonk hurdy-gurdy, and could not see the change which they effected and reflected in the human spirit; and while Sir William Hamilton dug up antiquities and Robert Adam and William Chambers recreated classical architecture in the Strand; and while Wilkes called for Liberty; and while Mary Wollstonecraft had Thoughts on the Education of Her Daughters which were not without their influence on daughters and sisters not as yet conceived, Sukey might wish us to remember that other great production of her century, the English Novel. From the age of seven or eight, she was never without one or another of these productions hidden about her person. Since her mother was so often lost in her own illnesses and sorrows, and her father was the busiest man of business; and since neither her mother nor father were good at choosing servants, and therefore did not have governesses in the house who would regulate her reading, Sukey read freely. From her earliest years, she had travelled in Lilliput and Brobdingnag with Gulliver, and been marooned on the island with Robinson Crusoe. Far too young, she had been lost in the epistolary explorations of the human heart which Samuel Richardson had extended through many volumes. She had known the heady combination of classical learning and ribaldry, of riotous comedy and moral seriousness of *Tom Jones* and she had sampled the slapstick of Smollett.

The novelists of the older generation – Swift, Sterne, Fielding, Richardson – were part of her inner life. As for the novelists of her own generation, they had been, some of them, the companions of her youth. Papa's friend Mr Edgeworth, whose marital adventures so amused the Lunar men, was the father of little Maria, who used to come and play at Etruria with Sukey when she was a child of ten. Such was the Wedgwood genius, not unvexing to their humbler cousins and fellow potters in Staffordshire, for knowing 'everyone'. And then there was the niece of Mrs Bentley, Ann Ward, who in her twenties was destined to become the prodigiously popular novelist Mrs Radcliffe.

Sukey sometimes wondered, a trifle wistfully, why she herself, stuffed full as she was with the fictions of other people, had not ventured out and become one of these novelists. Perhaps her perpetual meditation upon her family, their characters, exploits and adventures, constituted some kind of unwritten novel inside her head? Were this the case, and were this a three-decker novel of the eighteenth-century pattern, this might be the moment where the author would bring her first volume to its close. We leave Tom Byerley in America (but he will soon be home); we leave his old mother in the shop at Burslem. But we must elbow our way into the public display, in the Wedgwood showrooms in Greek Street, Soho, of the completed Frog Service, before it is carefully packed and crated and sent to the Empress in St Petersburg. It will be a grand occasion, the most stupendous advertisement to the world of Wedgwood's genius, his aesthetic and commercial flare. And it will be a royal occasion, the Queen herself is certainly coming, and there is even the rumour that the King, to console himself for the bad news which is now coming across the Atlantic, will come to see these views of territory which has not yet slipped from his grasp.

But let us go back to the morning of that day, shortly before

Christmas 1776, and let us get things in perspective. The world has seen the convulsion which it will call the American Revolution. Britain has received a political buffeting which will change it for ever. The great firm of Wedgwood and Bentley has produced a stupendous work, and it is about to be shown to the monarch, or at least to the monarch's spouse. All London is invited, and as many of the great world as can be squeezed into the showrooms will shortly do so. But let us get things in perspective and recognize what is important. Mrs Wedgwood's hair needs to be dressed.

The dressing of hair is a painful, wearisome exercise, and the hairdresser is summoned to Little Cheyne Row immediately after breakfast, though why he should suppose that meant half past nine rather than half past ten is anybody's guess. Presumably, it had been his malicious intention all along to make Mrs Wedgwood suffer, though quite how much she suffered no one could plummet, least of all her husband who, as she took pains to remind him as he dragged his wooden leg sheepishly out of his dressing-room, did not care.

The hairdresser had brushed Sukey's hair and tied it in pale blue silken ribbons. He had formally dressed Mrs Bentley's raven locks and attended to the other women in the household before Sally Wedgwood called him up to her boudoir. It was all very well for the others to have had their heads dressed in the drawing-room, but they had not endured the night as she had done; they had not tossed, they had not turned, they had not been visited by dreams, or if they had been, their dreams were not so cruel; nor probably, when presented with their breakfasts, had they felt such revulsion; nor had they wondered, or if they had wondered, they had done so with less anxiety, whether a headache were on its way. If it were on its way, could anything be more appalling than the visit of a hairdresser?

In deference to Mrs Bentley's importance in the scheme of things, the hairdresser had piled upon that lady's head an extraordinary construction, two or three feet in height, with a wire frame, a small cushion and much silver and gold lace. It would clearly be an insult not to adorn Mrs Wedgwood with comparable elaboration; equally, it would be typical of the thoughtlessness of the human race that the dresser might suppose his client could endure such adornments without suffering. They would be, in short, martyrdom. The young man, a Corsican, tried to smile at her in the looking-glass as he did his work, but she looked daggers back at him. First, the hair had to be teased or 'frizzled' with tongs. Next came the wire crown, with its cushion; then a wig and ribbons and a bird's nest and a silver ship. Had ever human beings suffered so?

Sukey, who watched the dresser at his task with some admiration, thought, but naturally did not express it, of an answer to the rhetorical question, considering it indelicate to weigh the plight of slaves in the sugar plantations, or press-ganged sailors receiving the cat o' nine tails, with the veritable Golgotha which her mother's dressing table had become. Sukey noticed the black hairs on the young man's fingers as he crimped and pushed, and as his victim sometimes winced, sometimes, as the headdress developed, she could not stop herself smiling. She noticed too the smell, the combination of some sweet scent with that of garlic. Sukey noticed that her mother, while seeming to hate it when the young man touched her, also visibly enjoyed it.

But this was a perception of a split second, and the lackeys and carriages were at the door. Mr Bentley escorted Mrs Wedgwood, and Mr Wedgwood escorted Mrs Bentley, and the rest − children, and managers of the works − followed in lesser conveyances, as they rattled along the river, where a pale yellow winter light shimmered through the mist, up Whitehall, where King Charles I on his horse looked a little anxious about the way the world was going, and as if he would like to offer some advice to the Hanoverian monarch at present occupying his throne, and across Leicester Square, where men looked out of the windows of coffee-houses, and where there was a queue of men carrying sedan chairs, and through the narrowing, bricky streets of Soho until they reached Greek Street and the showrooms.

If they were practising their gestures of deference for the moment when the Queen arrived, the staff at the showroom could not have shown more respect than they now display to the great partnership of Wedgwood and Bentley. And old Mr Jos is both easy and smiling, and at the same time nervous. His eye is glancing round the room, where the stupendous service is arrayed on shelves, anxious that nothing should be out of place; and Bentley, who knows that nothing is out of place because he went round the exhibition yesterday afternoon, is gentlemanly and condescending to the staff, who incline their waists and twiddle their hands and bow their wigs like decorative figures on an Austrian clock.

—Well, Mr Wedgwood, he laughs, we did it!

—We did it!

And Jos holds his friend's upper arm and strokes it, and Sukey reflects that she has never seen either of her parents make such an affectionate gesture towards one another.

For on display is a wonder of ceramic invention, and a vision of Britain: a parson, fishing on the calm lake at Welbeck Abbey; a punt is moored; three swans swim, all towards the same slope of the tureen. The other great landscaped lakes extend their glassy surfaces over plates and chargers. Two little skiffs drift across the great lake at Holkham to the rim of a plate. At Wilton, stillness beneath the Palladian bridge. At Painshill, the little wooden bridge, as though painted on Chinese porcelain, crosses the water. In the Marylebone Basin, swimmers reach out bare arms to the all but cloudless sky. By the waters of England, we sat down. In Lulworth, two men stare across the cove where sailing ships bob in from the Channel. At the Block House in Plymouth, a soldier, by the look of him a toy soldier, is firing a cannon. Off the Scotch coast, fishermen drop anchor beside the prodigious basalt Pillars at the Island of Boo-sha; the ruins of Iona brood over the empty island; and at the tip of Skye, Duntulm Castle looks out to the north and the brightness of rocky islets. In Wales, two tiny figures await the Britton Ferry at Neath unaware of their fate, which is one day to be covered with Russian potatoes and gravy; by the bridge at Rhuddlan Castle, a man is fishing, and on the cover of a sauce terrine, Kilgarren Castle sheds its shadow on the tranquil waters, waiting for an Imperial helping of sturgeon in a *Sauce Nantua*. The most impressive of Cornish geological formations, Logan Rock, Lanyon Quoit, Zennor Quoit and the Tolmen at Constantine, await their anointing with turtle soup. Snowdon, as depicted by Richard Wilson, will meet its veal chops and the White Horse Hill in Berkshire its capons at some Russian banquet; St Michael's Mount, the Isles of Scilly, the Covenhope Valley in Herefordshire and the crags of Dovedale, the sheer cascade of the 'Dropping Well' at Knaresborough will all find themselves obscured by Imperial beefsteak and mushrooms in a creamy ocean. On the lid of a soup tureen, we stand on the top of Richmond Hill and watch the Thames meander towards London. Here are the Abbeys and Churches – St Thomas à Becket in Winchelsea, Faversham Abbey in Kent, Holy Island in Northumberland, and the ruins of St Joseph of Arimathea's chapel at Glastonbury. Here the palaces of noble lords – Stowe, West Wycombe, Shugborough, Stourhead, Chatsworth, Haddon Hall, Woburn, Blenheim. Here are manor houses and castles. Here, on fish platters and meat chargers, are the great scenes of London, the Royal Exchange, St James's Palace, Westminster Hall. Here is Eton, where two or three young gentlemen in tricorn hats amble leisurely on the lawn before the chapel. And here is a newer England, more industrious and industrial, which will one day make war upon all the rivers and mountains, forests and lakes so picturesquely immortalized: here is Darby's coke works at Coalbrookdale. Here is the glassworks at Prescott, Lancashire, still surrounded by fields and leaves. Here is the paper mill at Rickmansworth. Industry as yet is submerged and surrounded by a triumphant Nature as the barges drift up the Bridgewater Canal, as smoke puffs from a bottle over by the Thames at Chelsea. But one day, just as the Views will be covered in gravy, the Originals will languish under the industrial storm clouds which Josiah and friends had unwittingly summoned up.

But, untroubled by such knowledge, and his own household and history with storm clouds of his own, the King of England is entering the room, heavy of brow, double-chinned, full-lipped, in a startlingly white periwig, with a cravat at his neck no less snowy white, white breeches, white silk stockings, and a scarlet coat which alludes to the military.

Josiah had not expected his monarch, and it is a relief to see that King George is followed by his Queen. Though more than happy when discussing politics with Joseph Priestley to foresee a republican future, Josiah has bent low before his King, who moves from exhibit to exhibit making jaunty little comments to his consort.

—Mrs Queen, you remember Stowe? You remember, what? What, what? Now, that paper mill is interesting. Mr Watson, wasn't he, the man who ran the paper mill at Rickmansworth, what, what?

And Mr Bentley and Mr Wedgwood are being quizzed.

—A lot of work, Mr Wedgwood?

—Indeed, Your Majesty.

—My wife swears by you. The Queen wouldn't drink her tea out of anything but a Wedgwood cup.

—Highly condescending of Her Majesty.

—Oh, and Mr Wedgwood?

—Your Majesty?

—What sort of stock do they have at Shugborough?

—Stock, Your Majesty?

—Cattle, man. That cow on the what-d-ye-call-em of Shugborough.

—On the compotier, Your Majesty.

—Looks more like a damned buffalo, what? But if it's meant ter be a Chillingham cow, they only have 'em at Chillingham, and they're wild, man. Yer can't *farm* a Chillingham. On the other hand, if it's meant ter be a Kerry, they have long horns, but ye'd be hard put to find a Kerry in Staffordshire, what? What? Might have ter get yer fella to trim the horns a bit before you send the, what did you say it was called?

—The compotier, Your Majesty.

—Might have to get him to trim the horns before ye send it off to the Empress. Don't want to mislead her. I suppose it might be supposed to be a Dishley Longhorn. Who is the fella?

—Fella, Your Majesty?

—Who painted the darned thing?

—Mrs Willcox – the lady to whom I just had the honour of presenting Your Majesty.

—A woman? Ye got a woman to paint cattle? What, what?

—She is the best decorator in the kingdom, sir.

The monarch was deaf to this. He was still laughing about it when they took their leave; and his entourage sycophantically joined in the merriment.

—A woman to paint the cattle! No, no, Mrs Queen! The fella might know how to make a cup and saucer, but he couldn't tell the difference between a Dishley Longhorn and a Kerry!

# 19

THE SERVICE WAS PACKED IN STRAW THE NEXT DAY. FIFTEEN barrels, specially constructed in Etruria, had been brought to London by Caleb Bowers. And it was Caleb, when the expert packing was complete, who took the cargo to St Katharine Docks, where they were taken aboard a Russian frigate called the *Archangel Gabriel*. She was a three-masted vessel, built some twenty years ago in Sweden, where she had been launched as the *Venus*, but now belonged to the Russian merchant navy and plied her trade in the Baltic and the North Sea.

Caleb felt an awestruck sadness as he watched the stevedores swing the barrels aboard the frigate, where men in seal-skin caps called out incomprehensible foreign words. His old boyhood protectiveness of Josiah returned to him as the last rope was disentangled and the Frog Service was stowed in piles together with the Indian tea, and the spices, and the stuffs which were being transported from London to St Petersburg. Some hours after Caleb had left the Docklands, the *Archangel Gabriel* made her way down the river. She had a choppy, cold journey northwards, putting in at Antwerp, Copenhagen and Malmö before crossing the Baltic and coming to Helsinki in time for the Russian winter. The sailors were drunk for three days. Some of them managed to stagger from the harbour the short distance up the hill to their Orthodox Cathedral to celebrate the Christmas solemnity; but others of them marked the arrival in the world of their saviour by yet more copious applications of vodka.

The Gulf of Finland was thickly frozen, and the *Archangel Gabriel* was preceded, for the last day of its slow voyage, by a Russian ice-breaker. Pyotr Nikolaevich Garilov, the official of the Imperial Chamberlain's office who had been designated to accompany Mr Wedgwood's barrels from London Docks to St Petersburg, never felt more glad in his life than when, by the brilliant light of a January dawn, he saw the pencil gleam spire and gilded onion dome of the Peter and Paul Fortress shining across the expanses of ice, and his eye took in his magnificent native city, the sharpness of its icy air, the incomparable spaciousness of its prospects, its colours and lights.

It was known that the Empress was agog to see her purchase. A banquet, if possible before the Christmas season, had been planned, making use of the new service. The noise of the ice-breaker, crunching the great glazed expanses at the ship's prow, filled the anxious chamberlain's heart with foreboding: each crunch and crack seemed to him like the sound of broken crockery, and truly terrible would be the sovereign's wrath if so much as one egg cup were to emerge from its straw with a chip on its rim.

In the event, the tyrant Empress decided to delay the pleasure of eating off Mr Wedgwood's masterpieces. Ensconced until long after Easter in the Winter Palace, Catherine had each barrel unpacked before her excited gaze, reaching out a plump, moist hand to hold now a soup tureen, now a platter, now a coffee-can.

—*O! Z'est belle, za!* She would often exclaim in her Germanic French, which all the courtiers imitated in private.

—*Non, Hans, viens, viens, z'est tres mejant!* to her greyhound, who nuzzled into the barrels for mouthfuls of straw, while courtiers listened anxiously for the sound of dog's jaw biting teacup.

It was not in fact until the Feast of the Ascension, four months later, when she was installed in her Finnish 'Frog' Palace that the service was used for the first time. It was assumed by everyone that the Empress privately entertained her friend M. Voltaire's views of religion. (And much good they had done him, reflected the more pious of the courtiers, as they thought of the wicked old man's death in Paris.) But she had kept up appearances, upon her marriage to the late Tsar Peter III, and before performing the political necessity of having her husband assassinated, she had undergone conversion to Orthodoxy. The feasts and ceremonies of that Church were piously observed by the court. And when the lengthy, repetitive liturgy had been undergone, and the bearded, bejewelled Patriarch and his acolytes had made their mysterious exits and entrances through the great six-tiered iconostasis of the royal chapel, the guests had assembled in her newly built state dining-room in the Frog Palace to see the products of the Potter's Hand.

The works of the cooks that day could not be over-praised. Small slag-heaps of caviar, piled upon ice, were carried down the glittering tables. Sturgeons which had produced these luxurious egg-clusters had themselves been stuffed and roasted and were spread out on chargers. Beeves, swans, hams, wild boar, encrusted with the most ingenious pastries, and glistening with sauces and marinades, were carried to the greedy guests by impassive, powdered, bewigged waiters. Up and down the tables, generals, ambassadors, bishops and great landowners took in the extraordinary visions of England displayed on every dish and plate.

Happy near the Empress herself was the British Ambassador, who, having removed some smoked trout from his plate and swallowed it, had revealed Blenheim Palace and was able to tell Catherine of the glories of Vanbrugh, while his good lady sat next to Prince Grigory Potemkin, and by lifting a bread roll could reveal to the General the playing fields of Eton.

# INTERLUDE:
# AN EARLY ATTEMPT AT
# PHOTOGRAPHY – 1803

FLOATING. THEY WERE ALL FLOATING ON THE PUFFS OF smoke which emerged from bottle banks, out of Etruria, up the hill, towards the spire and rooftops of Hanley. The spire, no more than a darning needle from a distance, took the unmistakeable shape as you approached it of the well-crafted wooden leg which Pa had had made in Hanover Street a few weeks after his leg had been amputated. The wooden leg waved jauntily, kicking into the air with irrepressible energy. You had to swoop upwards on white-feathered pinions to avoid being kicked by it. And the swooping filled you with angelic joy, such joy, that you never wanted to descend. But there was the earth, and it had to be revisited, its brown ploughed, enclosed fields, its courtyards, its bordellos and universities, flickering in their impermanence, a collection of ever-varying, ever-changing impressions. Nothing was fixed. Black and white cows came into focus, on deep green fields, and then became blots of ink on white paper on the green baize tablecloth. Tree-tops flickered, as he flew to earth, and became the flickering of the curtain, as he slumped in the low-slung chair. And was it Pa's wooden leg, or his own right calf, which he saw, dancing, balanced on his left knee, both clad in worsted stockings the colour of grey doves, and dark blue breeches? And had he been sitting there an hour or a hundred years?

*Perhaps a century or so later, after which his mood had depressed itself to despondency as he landed once more on the planet of the present, he was blinking at Sukey, since she said, or at some stage she was saying,*

—*Show me, Tom. Show me the phenomenon. I am so very interested in it.*

—*I've been asleep.*

—*I know, my dear. But you've slept so long. Tom, you do not look well.*

*Tom Wedgwood rose from the chair, rubbed his face with his fists and then rubbed his fine hair so that it stood up on end. He was a thin, intense man in his early twenties. His sister was six years his senior. She too had a raw-boned, intense face, but whereas Tom was wispy, sallow and perpetually sickly in appearance, Sukey, who was as tall as he was, still retained the capacity for sporadic interludes of good health. None of them had ever been quite well in their lives. Health was not a Wedgwood 'thing'.*

—*Another time, Sukey.*

—*No, you said today.*

—*Did I?*

—*You said you would go to the laboratory and set up the equipment. There it is on the stand.*

—*Is it?*

—*It was an hour and a half ago. I worried that an accident had befallen you. I came to investigate.*

—*Well, well.*

*He knew she knew. She knew he knew she knew. But the opium was not mentioned between them, not on that occasion.*

—*The experiment which I have been pioneering with Davy, he said, is a simple one. Since I am demonstrating it for you, Sukey, I've chosen this glass plate.*

—*Where did you take it from?*

—The chimney piece in the saloon. It's the doodle on glass painted that day by Mr Stubbs, do you remember? When we were children?

—Of course I do. Do you remember how we were scared of his big horsey eyes, and we felt he was one of the men coming to disrupt our lives by falling in love with Mama?

—I don't know about that. What nonsense you talk, Sukey.

—I liked Mr Stubbs because he told Pa he must buy me a pony. How could I not adore him after that? I'm sure he was a little in love with Ma. Many men were, you know.

—He was trying to explain something to Pa about their difficulties when firing enamel paintings, and he took this pane of glass.

—Caleb had been going to mend the window. You and Jack had broken the pane with a cricket ball.

—He took this pane of glass and executed a likeness of Pa. Normally, Davy and I work simply with coloured plates of glass on which we have daubed shapes. But I thought you would prefer this, sister.

—And you can transfer Pa's image from that glass to a sheet of paper?

—In this dish, I have prepared a solution of one part nitrate of silver to ten parts of water. I dip the paper in – so! And I place it, thus, so that the brightest rays of the sun can penetrate the painted glass and fall on to the paper – so!

—But . . .

Sukey's voice was failing. Though a woman past thirty, her voice had become once more that of a young child in its rapture. For as the sun streamed through the painted image of her father's face, a sepia version of it appeared on the coated paper.

—It's Pa! You have performed a miracle! You have recreated Mr Stubbs's sketch! Oh, Tom, this is quite the most exciting thing which ever happened. Think what you will be able to do. Now, you are just copying through glass, but soon you will be able to capture images on the glass by coating it with some chemical solution. Oh, Tom. All the faces in

A. N. Wilson

*history, all the men and women who have ever lived, have vanished from sight. And you're . . .*

*—Thereby, as if he had not been listening, I should be able to fix images of the evanescent moment on to paper. But that is what I cannot do. Look!*

And as they spoke, old Josiah Wedgwood's oval face, now some years dead, its sideways blue eyes which took in everything, its full lips, its honesty and innocence, had died a second time and faded into a smudge on the page.

*—Imagine if you worked out how to make it permanent! Think what it would have been if such a thing had been invented long ago, and we could look into the face of Julius Caesar or Oliver Cromwell! Do you suppose ours will be the first faces in human history which do not fade with death?*

*—Davy can't think of a way of making the image permanent, said Tom. And nor, for the life of me, can I.*

*—It will replace the printed word, pursued Sukey. Hitherto, we have only biography to tell us about human life as it flits across the world's screen. And in a very few cases, of the privileged, such as we have been since Pa made his fortune, we have painted portraits. But most human lives have simply vanished, gone, flitted away like shadows. Oh, Tom, think of all the faces to whom you will give immortality. Think of preserving people's youth, Tom, before they lost it! Imagine Mama young – or Caleb, or Heffie!*

A dizziness had come over the young man, and his greyish pallor had become sweaty. He looked at Sukey, and the opium, whose effects he had imagined had worn off an hour before, made a spasm of an impression in his brain. Her face was very large, and the mousey hair, tinged with the red which characterized their mother, was an aureole of burning gold.

*—Is that why I read novels with such compulsion? she was asking herself aloud, more than she was asking him, because they create the*

*illusion that human life can be fixed on the page, and that all the things*
*we know to be ephemeral, our passing humours, conversations of which*
*we do not remember more than four words in real life, can be somehow*
*made immortal, in the letters of Miss Clarissa Harlowe or in the appar-*
*ently inconsequential ramblings of Mr Shandy?*

*—Wasn't there a man in one of the books you read to me when I was*
*a little boy, a man who tried to extract sunbeams from cucumbers?*

*They both laughed.*

*—We thought he was like poor Mr Chisholm, Pa's secretary, do you*
*remember? I do not think your experiments in Natural Philosophy belong*
*with the satires and fancies of Dean Swift. We are both looking for the*
*truth, Tom.*

*—And you find it in fiction? That is a paradox.*

*—Perhaps I find its flickering image in fiction. Perhaps it then van-*
*ishes again.*

*—You should write it down! I'm sure you'd be more than an equal for*
*your author friends Mrs Radcliffe and Miss Edgeworth.*

*There was a silence in the laboratory.*

*—Is it morning?*

*—You must know it isn't. Soon it will be dinner.*

*He stopped himself from asking whether she meant dinner last year*
*or dinner next year. But curiosity forced from him an enquiry.*

*—And Papa, Sukey, is Pa . . . is he alive?*

*—Oh, Tom! What are we going to do with you? Pa has been dead*
*these eight years!*

# PART TWO

# A Family Portrait

We see domestic animals and plants, though often weak and sickly, yet breeding quite freely under confinement.

Charles Darwin, *The Origin of Species*

# I

—A BEAUTY, EH, SERGEANT?

—Beauty doesn't describe it, sir.

Sergeant Powell, a short plump man in his late thirties with bright pink cheeks and curly black hair, stroked the field gun as he spoke.

—She's light, sir, she's elegant, she's got a hundred round of shot in her and thirty o' grape, and against that kind of fire-power, Captain Gower, sir, no Froggie stands a chance.

—It's not the Froggies who worry me. It's those damned Americans. And my name is Gore, man, Gore.

—Begging your pardon, Captain, I thought you were spelt as in the peninsula.

—I may be spelt like a fucking peninsula, but I'm pronounced Gore, Gore, Gore.

He was a tall, languid youth, the captain, with springy blond hair, very blue eyes, and the blotchy complexion of adolescence, although he was probably about twenty.

—Very good, sir.

—And that's what we'll be seeing before much longer. Let's hope it's American gore rather than ours.

—Very good, sir.

The sergeant laughed sycophantically.

—I expect that's where you come from, eh, Sergeant – the Gower Peninsula?

—Not far off, sir. Nearer Llandeilo way.

—Nearer Llandeilo way.

The young man seemed to be playing with the sergeant's words as if to tease him.

—Well, the sooner we bring this bloody war to an end, the sooner we can all get home. What'll you do when you're out of uniform?

—I've hopes of an alehouse, sir.

—Haven't we all?

Again the sergeant felt he had been tricked into absurdity by the drawl of his commanding officer.

—Running a small alehouse, sir. Running a tavern, maybe telling a few tall stories to the regular customers, telling them about the time I was at the Heights of Abraham with General Wolfe.

—And the time you were at the Battle of Camden with Captain Gower?

—Very good, sir! Very droll!

—I'm sure my cousin Lord Gower in Staffordshire could find you an alehouse on his estates.

—That's Staffordshire, way, sir? By the Potteries?

—My people would not mix with potters! We'd make an exception for Owd Wooden Leg Wedgwood – great character. My cousin has him over to Trentham. I'm going to go to m'cousin with the begging bowl when this show's over, I can tell you – just as soon as I get the family niggers settled. How d'you think they're shaping up?

—The niggers, sir?

—Some of them seem dreamy beggars to me.

—They're a good lot of men, sir.

—We took a gamble, offering them their freedom in exchange for a red coat and a Brown Bess, the captain continued to drawl. I'd feel safer giving a gun to a fucking monkey. I'll tell you one thing for certain, Sarge. As soon as this fucking war is over, I'm rounding up all ours and putting them back where they belong. In chains. You're not one of these abolitionist johnnies, Sergeant?

—Good heavens, no, sir.

—As soon as we've won the war, and you've marched back to the Gory Peninsula, I'm marching this little lot back to the family plantations in Virginia.

The sergeant burst into a silvery tenor laugh at the disclosure.

—Oh, very good, sir, the Gory Peninsula.

—See what we can do about that alehouse, eh, Sergeant? You'd not mind living in Staffordshire rather than the Gory Peninsula?

The captain heard the sergeant going down the line, listened to the perfect tenor peal as he told one man not to put his kit bag on the wet grass, asked another a question about the quartermaster's stores.

—And I don't want to hear any of you talking about Captain Gower, see.

He made the two syllables of Gower so pronounced as to be almost three. Gow-uh-er. His Welsh voice was like a song.

—Captain says it's Gore, see, not Gower. Now give me that Bess, see here, boy. Oh, dear, dear, dear.

(Dee-uh, dee-uh, dee-uh.)

—Some little nigger boy's not been cleaning his rifle. See here, what's your name?

—Tobias, sir. Tobias Gower, sir?

—Like the Captain, eh?

—We're all called Gower, sir, on the Gower plantations. We take the owner's, that is, we take . . .

—Take your owner's bloody name? Jesus fucking Christ! Well, see here, Tub-eye-us: you got to keep the barrel squeaky clean, see. You got your flue there. (He said 'fl-you'.) Your little bit of gunpowder down there, see. And that's where your ball goes. Then you have your wadding. But that Brown Bess isn't going to do her business of shooting a fucking American head off if you don't keep her clean, see?

Tobias Gower laughed, and there was a ripple of laughter down the ranks as the sergeant went on. The sergeant was popular with the men. They liked his jokes. When he was drunk, they received the sharp end of his tongue, but unlike the foremen in their plantation, he did not whip them or cuff them, or interfere with them sexually. Far from it. The rumour going round was that the sergeant had a fancy woman – had managed to befriend a native American woman, who had joined the great entourage of camp followers who stayed as close to the British forces as possible. The war now hung in the balance, and the general thinking was that, if the British won this war, it would be helpful to stay close to them, rather than be among the defeated Americans. If the British were defeated, however, their troops would almost certainly be evacuated quickly, and there was the hope, among the Loyalist Americans, among some of the native Americans who sided with King George, and with the runaway negro slaves, that they might escape too with the retreating British forces. It was assumed that the sergeant's 'fancy woman' belonged to this category.

There were about fifty freed slaves in the company, all of them from the Gower Virginian plantations. Back in England, the Parliament had debated the question of whether the American negroes should be promised their liberty in exchange for help in putting down the rebellion. It was a highly unpopular idea. Those who favoured the abolition of slavery altogether feared that the liberated slaves would rise up and massacre their masters before joining forces with the European redcoats, and that the whole scheme was, to use John Wilkes's words, 'too black and too horrid to be adopted'. Those who supported the American Revolution, such as Edmund Burke, thought that the arming of the negroes was nothing better than licensed murder. Those who represented the slavers' interests in the ports of Bristol and Liverpool were horrified by the prospect of unrest spreading to the sugar plantations of Jamaica.

But in war, needs must; and the offer of freedom to the slaves by the British commanders fighting the Rebels in America had been met by an overwhelming response, with tens of thousands fleeing their 'owners' and enlisting in the redcoat army. So great had been the swell, that the American Congress had been obliged to counter-attack, creating its own black regiments on the American side, though with no undertaking to liberate the black soldiers when the war was over.

The British-born soldiers in the company – nearly all from Staffordshire – enjoyed complete harmony with those they referred to as the darkies. They messed together, joked together, and showed no signs of racial tension, as would undoubtedly have been the case had the unthinkable occurred and a black man had found himself as a member of the officer's mess. In this company at least, there was a feeling that they were all in it together. And the 'it' implied by this phrase was a palpable atmosphere of fear which, that particular morning, as the dawn rose over the undulating landscape of North Carolina, had begun to grip all the men with the approach of engagement with the enemy.

If I get out of this alive . . . That was the thought in every head in the unit. Some of the men were still drinking stew from billycans, or polishing the ends of their rifles, or peering with an apparent air of purpose, but actually, with no purpose at all, into the middle distance. Some were making jokes. Others were praying. Nearly all of them thought of home, or of their mothers, and felt the simple paralysis of pure fear. They were no longer dreading pain – the thud of the shot as it hit some part of their bodies, or the wrench of stinging agony as the surgeon tried to dress them afterwards. It was a much more generalized and much deader pain than that, a fear of the cold emptiness which would engulf them if this day were to be their last. Death was what made them afraid. Death awaits everyone, but for the most part human beings disguise the fact from themselves with business, or drink. For the soldiers, especially soldiers on the eve of conflict, there was now no disguising. They looked upon death coldly, like the moon gazing upon the earth.

—What steet d'yer reckon we're in, Sambo?

It was one of the foot-soldiers who put the question to Tobias Gower.

—We're near Camden, Tobias replied, over there's the Wateree River, down that slope beyond the woods.

—D'you hear that firing durin' the nate? Don't know what's worse – wakin' up and hearin' the guns or wakin' and 'earin' this fuckin' silence. Listenin' to them waiting for yer, lahk. You know Geets 'as got a fuckin' greet army over them 'ills?

—Gates?

—Well, if Gates az a fuckin' great army, soze Lord Cornwallis got a fuckin' great army, man. We got Charleston. And with this fuckin' great army we're gonna knock them bastards to hell, man.

—Sure is! said the British boy, whose name was Billy Breeze. There was a croaking yelp as he said it, signalling that his voice was about to break. The escaped slave-boy, who was aged seventeen, realized this little redcoat boy from England was probably no more than fourteen.

At dawn, they went into the attack. Orderly squares of redcoats, all four companies drawn by Cornwallis from the Ninety-Sixth Infantry, made their steady advance, each man with his Brown Bess primed and cocked, and with bayonets fixed. The first attack killed hundreds of Gates's American army. Captain Gower's company saw little of it, just smoke and a haze of heat. They heard explosions, roars, groans, screams, the whinnying of dying horses, but it was impossible to see what was happening. Then, towards late morning, Major General de Kalb, an illustrious German cavalry officer serving in the French army, led a cavalry charge of mixed French and American troops (the Maryland and Delaware regulars) up the slope towards the English guns.

Sergeant Powell, under orders from his English captain, was standing beside Tobias when the charge began.

—Steady, he said, at first in a low voice, and eventually, as the noise of the approaching horses thundered, he yelled.

—Wait until you have them in easy range – WAIT! Steady, now, NOW FIRE.

The Welsh lilt of FF-Eye-YUH was repeated, as the sergeant moved down the line at running pace. The 'elegant' field gun gave a shuddering report and exploded its ammunition against the approaching French and Maryland cavalry. The sergeant saw first a flash of flame, then a cloud of asphyxiating smoke, and then, as the smoke momentarily cleared, he saw a horse rearing up only some ten to fifteen feet away from him. He saw terror in the animal's face, and then he watched it being dismembered in mid-air, in a spattering of blood and a shudder of artillery, and with the noise of shouting and screaming around him. The cannonball had hit the horse full square in the chest, tearing it open, and all but ripping off its head. Blood gushed in a fountain over the rider, who was thrown into the air and fell a few yards from young Tobias's feet.

—Shoot the bugger! Powell called. He has a sword! He'll cut you to pieces, boy.

In the seconds during which Tobias hesitated, the dragoon lifted his sabre. The sergeant ducked, but he was severely wounded in the shoulder. Tobias, his rifle by now ready, shot the dragoon dead, but not before he had shot the wounded sargeant.

Beside him, the boy-soldier in a redcoat with whom he had spoken that morning fired more shots at the advancing horsemen.

One of them held up his hand, as if five fingers and a palm could withstand a bullet. Was it a gesture intended to sue for ceasefire? Still the boy shot him, and the bullet caught the man's arm.

As this happened, a French officer called out, in heavily accented English,

—Please, I am Colonel du Buysson. Do not shoot the Commander. Zees ees le Baron de Kalb.

—Shoot him, it's a trick! called out one of the redcoats.

But their commanding officer, Captain Hambright, shouted,

—Hold your fire!

They had, indeed, shot and wounded Baron de Kalb, one of the most illustrious soldiers to fight in the entire American campaign. Tobias did not see much of the Baron, nor of the French *aide-de-camp*, Colonel du Buysson, who had saved the German's life, for Captain Hambright turned to him and said,

—Gower.

—Yessuh!

—It looks as if the Sarge has copped it. See to him, will you? Get him on a stretcher if you can.

Sergeant Powell had been wounded by a bullet in the shoulder. Tobias and Breeze, the Staffordshire boy whose voice had scarcely broken, lifted the injured man on to a stretcher. As they did so Powell let out an eldritch screech of pain, followed by an automatic mutter of,

—Sorry about that, chaps.

They almost ran with the stretcher into a shady spot, below the trees of Smallwood, where a rudimentary field hospital had been set up.

—Hey, hey, Sergeant Powell was able to say from the stretcher. None of that.

For Tobias had begun to sob.

—I'm the one who oughta be cryin', boy!

The surgeon was working fast. The smell and heat of the tent where his makeshift operating table had been set up was utterly nauseating.

—I'm going to look at the wound. If there's anything I can do, I shall do it now. Then I want you — he turned to Tobias — to be in charge of this man. There's a small town not far from here, Camden it's called. Take your man there for the night. If he lives, we'll get you both taken down to Charleston in the morning. If not . . .

Even as he spoke, he had cut open the shoulder of Sergeant Powell's coat and revealed the sodden crimson gore of the bullet wound.

—A reading man? The surgeon held up a tiny Bible which the sergeant had kept in his breast pocket. By the look of it, the book saved your life, Sergeant. It diverted the bullet from your heart. But this is not a good wound. I'm going to remove the bullet for fear of worse infection.

Even as he spoke, two orderlies placed a gag between Sergeant Powell's upper and lower jaw. The wounded man did not have to be told to bite on the cloth. The surgeon's knife, without warning, went into the jammy wet redness of the wound. He put down the scalpel and with some already bloody tweezers, he yanked. The sergeant's legs kicked Tobias so hard that he himself yelped with pain while Powell, the gag notwithstanding, let out deafening shrieks as the surgeon, with great expedition and skill, swabbed the wound as best he could and stitched with deft and deliberate movements.

—That's all we have time for with you, he said briskly. The best of luck to you.

He turned to Tobias.

—And you, when he's better — if he lives — here's the bullet which nearly killed him. And his poetry book, or whatever it was.

The boy soldier pocketed the Bible and the bullet. Already, before they had left the tent, a new patient had been heaved on to the table, and the surgeon was saying to the orderly,

—Now, that arm is going to come off at once, so hand me the hack-saw.

By the end of a hot summer's day, corpses littered the purplish mud of the fields as a violent red sunset lit the sky. Tobias and Billy Breeze had managed to get their sergeant lifted into a covered wagon and taken into Camden, a small town which had been largely deserted by its terrified inhabitants, and now was occupied by the military and their followers. Among these they somehow managed to find the person designated by Powell's Company as the sergeant's fancy woman.

—Is he going to die? Tobias asked her.

Powell had by then developed a high fever and was semi-conscious, but he was aware of their presence.

—Not if I can help it, he murmured.

—Do not weep, young man, said the woman. Fetch me water, and we will save his life.

The woman, whom the sergeant had by now known for a few weeks, stroked his head with her long, honey-coloured hands. Her blue-black hair was plaited neatly, and reached to the small of her back. She was kneeling beside the bed, her hair all but touching the floor and the soles of her white, beaded moccasins. She was murmuring to him a song, or perhaps an incantation. Her hands, which stroked the sergeant, so large, so strong, appeared to send him by hypnotic massage into a calm sleep.

---

Blue Squirrel both was, and was not, there among them. When the small township of Old Kowes had been lain waste by fire, rape and pillage, when dawns had risen and suns had set, when she had awoken, and slept again, awoken and slept, under hedgerows and beside the encampments of Cherokee refugees – Cherokee people from other townships which had been despoiled, and whose names she did not know – she had found herself within reach of the red-coats. How long this had been, how many days or weeks she had wandered, what she had eaten, what she had carried with her, she would have been quite unable to explain. The deep shock from which she was still suffering, and would suffer for years to come, left her in a trance; it was a detachment of mind in which movement was essen-tial. She was now incapable of stillness. She never slept for more than an hour, she was always pacing, striding, folding, tidying, brushing, grooming, performing actions as if sleepwalking. Sometimes, images of the raid would come into her head, and she would think now of this child murdered, now of this particularly desperate shriek of pain, now of the smell, the terrible smell, as the closed huts burned with people inside them. Sometimes, unbearably, Tom Byerley would be present to her in dreams. Sometimes, with great cruelty, the dream would trick her into believing that he was still beside her, that all was well, that he loved her and she loved him and would bear his chil-dren. And then, with cold cruelty, waking would remove his image, and replace it with a dark hatred of the man, a dread, a sense that everything to which she had given her soul had been false.

It was in this confused state that she had arrived, hungry and exhausted, at the redcoat encampment in New Jersey. The first soldier who greeted her, when she reached the camp, had been kind. In the normal course of things, that is to say, in the past, she would have been much more chary of approaching a strange European man in uniform. But she had blundered towards him like an automaton, scarcely conscious of the words which passed between them though she had been able to speak English. It seemed that the soldiers needed cooks, nurses – servants, in short. Bleary somnambulist, she felt no humiliation in being treated as the welcome skivvy. She accepted what was happening as if it were a dream. For the first few days with the British army – they had requisitioned a small street of colonists' houses – she slept, allowing herself to be visited by a soldier who also appeared to be a doctor. Later, she woke, ate, sponged her fringed deerskin dress, and became the useful, capable person which it was her nature to be. But throughout the weeks she had spent with the soldiers – now tending the sick and wounded, now cooking, now washing – she had moved about as in a dream, unable to distinguish between the passage of minutes and the passage of whole days.

Then had come Idris Powell, the talkative sergeant, whose merriment sustained the spirits of the men. The first impressions he made were not of himself, but of his effect upon others. It was years before she realized this. She was aware of the men laughing at some quip Idris had made. Right to notice their high spirits, and right to suppose it was the sergeant who had made them laugh, she made the false inference that the qualities he evoked – laughter, good humour, fellowship and good cheer – were his own qualities of soul. The merriment could not penetrate the deepest places of her sorrow, but it became possible to join in the laughter. It was like approaching a fire from a cold distance, and joining those who huddled around it. The warmth and the light were not in fact the sergeant's own, but this was not apparent, for where he was – with his jokes, his talk, his high-pitched mellifluous singing voice – the men were happy. And it was a convivial, comforting happiness. It was a comfort, and she took any comfort. Now the sergeant had been wounded, and the laughter was stilled. The atmosphere of fear among the men was palpable, as though the fire they had all approached for comfort was dying; and as its embers smouldered, the surrounding cold and dark resumed their habitual power.

# The Potter's Hand

Tobias gave her the bowl and the cloths, and she began to sponge the man's red, sweaty face. Her own face, with its high cheekbones, calm brow and sculpted mouth, was one of detached classical serenity.

—You are Tobias, she said, without turning. And you are Billy Breeze?

—How did you know?

—Idris often speaks of his men.

As she stroked the sergeant's head, she intoned something in her own language. It appeared to be the words *Let-tsi-yo-le! Let-tsi-yo-le!* Much later, she told him it was a charm used by the shamans to heal those who had been shot by gunfire.

—What is your name? Billie Breeze asked her.

She ignored the question for several hours. She chanted, she stroked Powell's head, she chanted some more.

—I have sung, she said at last. I sang to Idris, *Just lend me your bones and I will put you to sleep, dear man.*

—Are you gonna marry the sarge? persisted Breeze.

—Billy Breeze. You come from England, no?

—Staffordcher.

—You make pottery?

He turned to her sharply.

—Me Da's a potter . . . ee, owdya knaw thut?

—Many potters work in Staffordshire?

—Ay, but, owdya knaw?

She looked at him curiously.

—Your Da? He works for a man with a wooden leg?

# 2

—SO, WHO WERE THE MUSES?

There was general hilarity at the enquiry. Cousin Byerley chose to ignore young Jos's ridiculous intervention.

—No one we know! as if the mystic Nine had been the proprietors of some humbler pottery than their own, perhaps in Fenton or Hanley.

—Jack? Name one of the Muses.

But young Jos, unstoppable aged eleven before he became the shyest of grown-ups, spoke over his elder brother.

—Cleopatra.

Everina Wollstonecraft, one of Sally Wedgwood's aviary of lame ducks, a fourteen-year-old child she had lately imported into the household as a companion for Sukey, smirked,

—He means Clio.

—Cleo for short, no doubt, was Jos's confident reply. I'm not so familiar with the lady as Jack would appear to be.

Whoops of laughter came from all the older children, including Everina, who nonetheless, in her puzzled pallor, was visibly anxious for the mistakes to be corrected.

There was quite a houseful in that summer of 1780. Sukey, nearly fifteen, was back from her year with the Bentleys. The elder Wedgwood boys had been brought home from their boarding school in Lancashire because of the riots – the good weavers of Bolton apparently not sharing Pa's enthusiasm for his friend Mr Watt and the advantages of mechanized looms. While these northerners smashed wheels and windows with as much destructive force as was practicable before the arrival of the local militia, the twenty-nine-year-old Lord George Gordon, in London, was whipping up the Protestant frenzy of the mob against the new legislation. Desperate for more Irishmen to enlist in the army against America, the House of Commons had modified the oath which each serviceman was obliged to repeat before the collection of his shilling. A mere assertion before God of a loyal submission to His Majesty, without reference to His Majesty's Protestant religion, was, by the rigorous standards of His Lordship's riotously theological friends, a step towards acknowledging the sovereignty of the Pope himself. Time for more broken glass, more torchlight and arson in the small hours of morning, more ominous reminders that beneath the quiet surface of the English idyll, depicted by the skilled brush of Mrs Willcox upon the Empress's dinner service, there lurked a surface as fragile as an earthenware plate.

Mrs Byerley, as her son Tom had been amused to observe, did not consider smashing her neighbour's windows of necessity to be a patriotic thing to do; Mrs Byerley was even generous enough to assure her son that there were probably Eye-talians and Sardinians who meant no harm. In their Mediterranean place. Those ruffians over in Ireland were another matter altogether. But if the Pope ever had the temerity to come looking for a yard of silk taffeta in Newcastle-under-Lyme, as she had assured Everett, she would have preserved the politenesses, but felt it her duty to let him know where she stood. It was one thing for foreigners; but in England, it (by which monosyllable was denoted the unmentionable religion observed by three-quarters of Europeans) was not quite . . . She would not normally wish to ally herself with the late Mr Voltaire in his views, but in this instance, 'infamy' fitted the bill. Not quite wishing to say so out loud, she had left Everett puzzled, and half-wondering, as her mistress withdrew for the ritual of the morning 'tidying', how to conduct herself should any of these Mediterranean gentlemen, the Pope included, present themselves at the counter of M. Byerley in the absence of the proprietress.

So while the boys escaped the riotous loom-workers, and the Bentleys with their household escaped the Protestant fervours of London, Etruria Hall had become what, in its early months and years it had somehow refused to become, a family residence and a house of hospitalities. And a school. For Cousin Byerley, who had taught Latin and French in New York while 'resting' from his theatrical labours, was engaged to help M. Potet, their tutor, and Mrs Wedgwood in the instruction of the younger Etruscans.

Miss Everina Wollstonecraft, her elder sister and her father no enemies of mayhem, had reminded the company in the schoolroom that Clio was the Muse's name, not Cleopatra.

—Good, good, said Byerley. Clio is the Muse of?

—History, said Sukey quickly, for fear that the new girl should say all the answers. She added, quoting from Tooke, She is named from glory, and takes her name from the excellence of things she records.

Sukey was already her full height, and already beginning to be aware of the family as others might see it. The others – including Pa, she often thought – were so much *in it* that they could not see it. Their lack of self-consciousness half-appalled her. She could watch, as Mrs Bentley, with her greater worldliness, half-patronized Pa, or as the gawky peculiar Everina took everything in: Mama's languid moodiness, Mama's cleverness, the fact that the Wedgwood boys were spoilt, and that they lorded it over poor Cousin Byerley who, in addition to working for Pa at the works and taking sales orders up and down to London, had been enlisted to supplement the role of the French master in the schoolroom. Jack, and the fact made Sukey wince, had inducted Jos into the sense that Aunt Byerley's small shop, and their comparative poverty, made them ridiculous.

—Who can think of another Muse? urged Byerley, not to be deflected by the boys' obstinacy. How about you, Jack?

But John Wedgwood, the eldest boy, already at thirteen was a little superior to his surroundings. His manner suggested that everything was slightly absurd, slightly beneath his dignity.

—I don't know. Erotic? Error? Some silly name.

This reduced the others to fits. Little Tom, only eight, was too young in some ways to be taught with the others, but he had pleaded, and their mother had said she saw no objection. He it was who remembered.

—Erato.

—Well done, sir! exclaimed his namesake, Tom Byerley.

—She invented poetry, Sukey supplied, and she takes her name from love. And, she suddenly flared at the oafishness of the brothers, it suggests very great folly to find her so amusing.

—*Mais oui*, said Jack maliciously. Then he spoilt the joke by adding, in case she had missed his reason for speaking in French, That's 'cause you're in love with M. Potet.

His reference to the French prisoner of war who had been brought over from Lichfield by Dr Darwin was cruel because true. M. Potet was not yet twenty. Very pale, with raven black oily hair and wispy, long fingers, this elfin figure in a bottle-green cutaway coat had been offered his exchange at the end of the last war; but he had preferred to remain in Staffordshire, and now Mr Wedgwood offered him fifty pounds per annum to teach seven hours *per diem* in the Etruscan Academy. They were hours, for Sukey, of the most exquisite agony, not least because she suspected M. Potet, as he read to them from

Racine, of being in love with her in return; but their love was far too sublime ever to be declared.

—Anyway, said Byerley, perhaps we have had enough for one day of the Muses. Just remind me of the name of their mother.

—We've forgotten, said John, speaking for them all, as he liked to do.

—Scarcely an appropriate thing to do, said Sukey, since their mother was Memory or Mnemosyne.

But the boys, far from being put down by this, were simply provoked to further hootings.

—We are all to go down to the saloon, said Cousin Byerley. I have to speak to your father.

—You're paid to, said Jos. We don't have to.

But this was too much, and Sukey protested, and Tom gave Jos a punch and they descended the stairs in a tumble of half-playful acrimony. Only a few weeks since, Sukey would have said that Jos, aged ten, would have been incapable of such asperities and that when he came out with them, they were lines 'fed' him by John. Now, she was not so certain. Though neither Jos nor John learnt fast in the schoolroom (Tom was very different), they were swift adepts at the social skills of put-down, sneering and snooty jokes.

—Too right, added John with approval, still reverting to the subject of Byerley being there because he was poor. You talk to Pa because you are paid, but we're not. We can please ourselves.

—I never heard anything so preposterous, declared Sukey.

—You all get on so well, said Everina wonderingly, and artlessly, if a little domineeringly, taking Sukey's arm as they descended the swooping stone stairs. In our muddled house, it is all hate and shouting. All sixes and sevens.

—Of course we do not hate, said Sukey protectively. But we do fight a bit.

The Potter's Hand

Byerley followed them, now an avuncular figure. He had been home six months. It had taken no time, no time at all, to be absorbed back into family life. He lodged with his mother two miles away, though there was little enough room above the shop in Newcastle. He appeared at Etruria each day in the morning at seven, and he was still there when the children retired to bed in the evening. He had become his Uncle Josiah's right hand, his Aunt Sally's companion, his cousins' tutor, and, when need arose, the firm's salesman.

Coming back to it all, after five years away, he had been struck overwhelmingly by what money did. In the year he left England, there were still traces of the modest beginnings. His Uncle Jos still divided his time between the Brick House Works in Burslem, presided over by his cousin Useful Tom, and the new splendours of Etruria. But now, Useful and Decorative were both, in ever greater and more lucrative quantities, produced from the Etruria Works. Jesse Grocott, the skilled cooper who made the barrels in which the ware was stowed for transport, was filling several dozen a week and more, not only with dinner sets and tea sets, but with decorative vases, candlesticks, busts and medallions, for disposal in their Bath and London salerooms, and for export beyond the seas. The prodigy of the Frog Service, which had personally cost Josiah and Mr Bentley over three thousand pounds, was an investment which had paid prodigious dividends. For the English Views, painted so delicately by Mrs Willcox and her friends in London on plates, dishes and tureens, and exported to the icy Neva, had excited a Wedgwood frenzy throughout Europe. Jos continued to toil – at his scientific experiments, at his supervision of the works, at his pursuit of trade in Britain and abroad. The Etruria Works was itself a mighty well-oiled machine such as Mr Boulton or Mr Watt might have devised. Trucks with carefully cut lumps of damp clay, of precisely the right consistency, trundled to their apt destination at the modeller's benches and wheels; ware, once moulded and thrown, was wheeled towards the kilns, and wheeled out again, often beneath his uncle's watchful eye, who waited with his gnarled stick to smash anything unworthy of his name. The barrels were loaded by Caleb Bowers and his team into barges, and the horses and boys took them smoothly on their path to London, where the decorating studios were kept ever more busy in Chelsea, and where the showrooms in Greek Street never knew a week of slack trade, though trade was not so brisk as it was before the crisis in America.

The revenues from this ceaseless activity produced money, money, money – it was almost something you could feel beneath your feet or smell in the air, this sense of solid, tangible, ever-growing wealth; and it was the more remarkable since, skilled as Josiah was in the commercial arts, he gave no appearance of interest in money for its own sake, still less of avarice. What was that mot of the great Dr Johnson, which Mr Bentley had heard in London? *There are few ways in which a man can be more innocently employed than in getting money.* Uncle Josiah was an innocent. He believed in the future. He believed in improvement. He believed in these things because he had personally brought them to pass: better working conditions for the men and women whom he had brought from Burslem to become the first Etruscans, in the little model village he had built for them, better roads, a canal system which now enabled the products of manufacture to be transported and exported, and, more nebulously, a spread of reason and decency which would surely advance in conjunction with prosperity.

Uncle Josiah was apparently deaf and blind to the posturing snobberies of his two elder boys – where did they learn such tricks? He never seemed to notice himself being patronized by Mr and Mrs Bentley, nor by Dr Darwin – even quoting with some approval Darwin's reproach to him that his manners in the presence of grandees such as the Duke of Bridgewater were like those of a tailor.

He was innocent about such matters in part because they did not interest him, as the making of pots interested him, and as geology, and improvement – social and scientific – interested him, or as the family interested him. Such horrors as Byerley had seen in America, such evidences of human hatred and baseness and sheer bloodlust, had never been set before his eyes. For Uncle Josiah, the American question had been a simple matter of justice. The colonists had justice on their side, the Ministry in London had not; therefore, one supported the Americans. He had been proud to hear of his nephew's brief encounter with Washington and the heroic men who fought under him – and he was already, before the war ended, commissioning John Flaxman to make commemorative medallions of Washington and Lafayette – but he had no desire to have his mind twisted, as he would have put it, with complexities. Naturally, he felt sorry for the negro slaves who had come into the King's Service, and were now in danger, as the war dragged on, of being faced with the cruel choice: a return to slavery, or a life of abject poverty and exile. And slavery was one example of human turpitude to which Josiah's eyes were not blind. He never forgot what he and Bentley had seen with their own eyes in Liverpool – the lines of men and women in chains at the docks, the crack of the foreman's whip, the bloodied welts on enslaved, naked shoulders: it was an iniquity which must be expunged, of that he had no doubt. But he was sure, equally – and nothing that Tom Byerley said would shift his opinion – that it would only be a matter of months, were the colonists' victory in America only assured, before the Americans themselves abolished slavery.

—I have met Mr Franklin, my boy, with the Lunar men. He is as opposed to the vile trade as we are. Depend upon it, once this unnecessary war is over, we shall see the slaves and the Indians made fully fledged Americans, like the colonists themselves.

Perhaps, Byerley reflected, Josiah needed to entertain such inno-cent points of view because there was no time, in his busy life, to entertain thoughts of any complexity. Born with a sunny disposition, preternaturally energetic, intellectually inquisitive about the proper-ties of minerals under firing, when turned into ceramics and glazes, he could not afford to be inquisitive about the cause of women's tears, any more than he could afford the disagreeable complication of knowing that few political situations were either entirely good or entirely bad. It was easier for Josiah, the nephew saw that clearly, simply to embrace the American cause as the bright future, as the side on which men of goodwill found themselves.

For Byerley, the homecoming after five years' absence had brought life into perspective. Only upon his return did he recognize how much he had missed it all: Staffordshire, the works, the sense of belonging to a family. Only upon his return did the vanity of his ambitions – to be a poet or an actor! – appear clearly to him in all their childishness. Indeed, on the long sea-voyage back, cast among strangers, his heartfelt yearning for home had made him wonder whether the whole sojourn in America had been merely for the purpose of sowing wild oats away from the embarrassed or disap-proving eye of the family. Those oats now sown, he would offer his services to his uncle, and when his prospects were assured and his usefulness to the enterprise of Wedgwood and Bentley made certain, he would be in a position to marry and himself procreate.

It was Sukey, ahead of the other children, who opened the doors to the saloon and presented the tribe to their Mama and Mrs Bentley.

—What have you been teaching them this morning? Sally Wedgwood asked Byerley.

—We have been doing the Muses, Mama, Sukey supplied.

—Doing them? Doing? Doing what to them?

There was half-humour in the mother's snappy retort, as if she wanted to conceal a natural petulance with self-parody.

Jack added, in case his mother might not be acquainted with the fact,

—There are nine of the bleeders.

—John, you must moderate your language.

—Memory was their mother, supplied the young Tom. And then, not quite understanding his elder brother's joke, but stealing it shamelessly, But they are no one we know.

—Cousin Byerley seems to have taught you to perfection.

—We approach perfection, said Byerley laughing, but there is some distance between us and our object.

—Clio is the Muse of history, said Jos, rather stealing the lines which Sukey had hoped to make audible. Because everything in the past is so bally glorious.

—You see, said Sally, amused, why we had to take the boys away from that boarding school.

—Yet we Londoners miss you, Sukey, said Mrs Bentley, now you have come back to Staffordshire.

Things were to be so different now that Cousin Byerley had returned, with the purpose – Papa said – of making them all Etruscans.

—And, said Mrs Bentley, you are all to have your portrait taken by Mr Wright of Derby.

Painting being the subject of their story, John could burst out with,

—Have you seen that loon Pa has got to paint the hall ceiling of the works? A screw loose if you ask me. He called down from his ladder to us some balderdash about the Daughters of Albion wailing towards the forests of America. And what was it? Orcs?

—Mr Flaxman brought him from London, Sally said, in a tone

which suggested this could explain anything. He exhibited with them all in that extraordinary exhibition in which Mr Fuseli's monstrous Dream drew such a crowd. He told me that he had seen an angel sitting atop the stagecoach as they pulled into the yard of the Crown at Stone. But there is something about the powerfulness of his drawings . . .

—His eyes stare, said John.

—That is what eyes are for, opined Sukey. And he isn't mad. He made a song and sang it to me:

> My mother bore me in the southern wild
> And I am black, but O! My soul is white.

No one took any notice.

Far from mocking Josiah for what he did or did not see, and for the world he had created around himself, nephew Byerley saw it all – the craft and the skill, the trade and the money, the large house and the family – as worthy barricades against the mayhems he himself had left behind in America, the storms of the heart, the anarchies of war, the frontier-uncertainties of uncharted territory, political and emotional. Here, by contrast, was a house built, if not on granite, then on the reassuring foundation of clay.

Mrs Bentley was a silly, over-talkative woman in Byerley's estimation, but he had learnt, after many a dinner in her company, and extended periods as her London guest, to handle her sillinesses as one might learn, when in charge of a small skiff, to tack through choppy water. He had found that 'That may be so, ma'am' or 'Indeed, ma'am' was a good enough response to most of her more prettified utterances.

—I can see why music is so called after one of them no doubt, that lady was remarking in a high-pitched voice, in response to the children's morning occupation, but quite why a-Muse should be said to make us laugh I am not persuaded.

—There was one of Comedy, said John, though I forget the name of the lass.

Sukey had not quite time to finish supplying the name of Thalia before Mrs Bentley relentlessly went on,

—And Dancing, though pretty enough, never struck me as an art – not an art in the way of Mr Bentley's or Mr Wedgwood's revolution in taste.

Byerley raised an eyebrow at the notion of Mr Bentley having much to do with the designs of his uncle's wares. As he had observed matters, Bentley, though better born, and arguably more widely read than Josiah, had always attended more to the business, while it was Wedgwood who pursued, with his mixture of instinct and surprising turns of knowledge, his aesthetic and philosophical achievements.

—What is this? said old Josiah himself, hobbling rapidly in. It would be a revolution indeed if I were to master the art of dancing at fifty. I could not dance well with two legs, still less . . . and his sentence died laughing.

He began to tell the anecdote about Heffie, on the Day of the Execution, assuring him that he would soon be able to stand on his own two feet again.

—Well, said Mr Bentley, we have accomplished a good morning's work.

There they stood, Wedgwood and Bentley. Bentley bald, wigless, looking much older than his half-century, with a sweat on his pale greyish face suggestive of a half-cooked suet pudding; Wedgwood rubicund, smiling, never quite still, moving his walking cane up and down as if testing the drawing-room carpet for secret hollows of water, or valuable mineral supplies.

—Whatever emerges from the American conflict, said Josiah,

there'll be a call for jasper medallions of Washington and of Lafayette.

—You can't imagine, said Mr Bentley, the demand for portrait medallions in Paris when I was there last year. And jasper dip is all the rage. Everything à l'Anglaise. And of course, the names of Vedgvood and Bont-lee are on every fashionable lip.

—And we are having one modelled of the poor Earl of Chatham, said Jos. And your suggestion, Tom – he looked up at Byerley – one of Garrick.

—Flaxman can model them for us, said Wedgwood.

—Or Mr Blake, spluttered John: apparently the mere mention of the muralist was a perfect substitute for wit.

—They'll sell everywhere, said Bentley. No doubt about that.

—And the outlay is nothing, said Josiah. The merest quantity of white china clay set against the jasper dip. Each portrait can be made for a few pennies and sold for a guinea apiece. A guinea for five minutes' work!

—It can be suspended by the chimney, added Bentley, laid in a glass cabinet, inlaid into furniture in the French style – there are all manner of decorative uses to which the medallions can be put; and each purchaser can build up his own gallery of heroes.

—Or her gallery of heroines, said Sally.

Mrs Bentley laughed at this outrage.

From such propositions and brainwaves, Tom Byerley reflected, had the fortune accumulated, and from it, the slopes of the park, the substantial brick hall, a house worthy of a minor nobleman, with its high ceilings, cool interiors, its tall looking-glasses icily reflecting the characterless elegancies. More, the money had enabled them all to change. His cousins were gentlefolk, a transformation, manifestly, which caught Josiah two ways. On the one hand, it was one of the goals for which he had earnestly laboured – to spare the seven surviving offspring the hardships which he and his brother had passed through in the old Churchyard Works. On the other hand, were the new Wedgwoods still potters? Could you imagine these little gentlefolk with clay on their hands?

—We are all so excited, Mr Wedgwood, by the prospect of Mr Wright of Derby immortalizing your tribe! exclaimed Mrs Bentley.

—Yes, said Josiah sheepishly, and looking at his wife with the expectation of an explosion. The expectation was met at once with Sally's,

—What is it *now*?

—I've disengaged Mr Wright.

The mother's repeated *What* was drowned by a chorus of Oh, Pa, but you said, and Was he too costly, and Cousin Byerley, attempting to pour oil on troubled water with cleverness, saying how much he had looked forward to a shadowy depiction of all of them by candlelight, all peering, perhaps, at Cousin Sally's embroidery or Uncle Josiah's latest medallion of a radical hero.

—I think you should have told us. Mrs Wedgwood needed to ascertain before witnesses that her husband had been in the wrong.

—I have engaged Mr Stubbs, said Josiah.

—I suppose you think I'm a horse, was his wife's retort, which made them all laugh.

But the implications were not lost on Sukey. For weeks she had been imploring her father to buy her a pony. Never would there be a better moment to press home her advantage.

—Pa, she said, you can hardly expect Mr Stubbs to paint us unless we are on horseback.

—Nonsense. A man wants a change. Mr Stubbs won't thank us for casting him as a man whose only interests are equine.

He leaned back on his stick a little, pleased with the epithet.

—I have been perfectly plain with him. Two paintings, accomplished in three weeks. The first is of young male Wedgwoods – yes you, Sir Jack – you, Jos! It will be the three boys conducting a chemical experiment. We'll have John at the retort, and Jos maybe lighting the flame beneath it, and Tom . . .

—Yes, Papa, asked Sukey, what will Tom be doing?

—He'll be clapping his hands in wonder.

—It sounds more like a subject for Mr Wright, said Sally relentlessly.

—What will the other picture be of? Of the girls? What will they be doing? This was Miss Wollstonecraft. Embroidery? Playing the harpsichord?

Old Josiah looked nonplussed. He could tell that the answer he was now forced to give was somehow the wrong one.

—But, yes, he said puzzled. I thought that was precisely what the girls might be doing.

—If Mary Ann is in the picture, lisped Kitty petulantly, Mr Thtubbs won't hear himself paint.

—Poor Mary Ann, said Josiah with an anxious look. And asking his wife, he said,

—Has anyone been up to see her this morning?

—I've left her with Heffie.

# 3

ALL HAD CHANGED IN THE FIVE YEARS OF TOM BYERLEY'S absence in America. He had changed, the family had changed. The sapling Lombardy poplars, planted to shut out the offices to the side of the mansion house at Etruria, were now recognizable as trees. The acacia near the house itself had doubled in size. The shrubbery beyond the gravel walks, which had been a few small bushes when he went away, was now a shapely profusion of rhododendron leaves and blossoms.

There were seven children instead of four, and although this had not entirely removed the languor and pettishness of Aunt Sally, it had somehow changed her. She had ceased, very conspicuously, to be a victim of circumstance. When Cousin Byerley had gone away to America, she had been (as nearly always, it appeared) with child. She had wept when they parted. Of that, he had painful memories. They were tears . . . of what? Of anger, it seemed. His memory of his aunt was of her swollen gown, her perpetual burden of maternity, and of her sallow, infuriated facial expression. But now, with seven children scampering around her, she gave off every appearance of having come through the worst.

This was apparent, in spite of the sickness of Mary Ann. The very fact that all was not right with the child, for all the excruciating pain and disturbance this caused the household, was for Sally, or so it seemed to Byerley, something of a release. Even in the midst of the poor child's screams and puling, he sensed that Sally's warfare was accomplished.

The illness of Mary Ann had stopped Sally from persecuting Uncle Josiah. They were together now in their anguish. An apparently healthy baby at birth, Mary Ann had never been 'right' since. Her screams were not the ordinary weeping of an infant. They turned into convulsions. Much to Caleb's consternation, Heffie was persuaded to leave her family at Stone and come to sleep several nights a week at the Hall to help out the nursery maid. By the time teething began a year or so later, the convulsions had become stupendous. Dr Darwin experimented with an electrical shock, and taught Josiah how to apply the electrolyzed metal to the infant's gums. It was essential, in Dr Erasmus's view, to keep the wounds in the gums open, or the teeth would not come through. Only Josiah had the steadiness of hand to do this, using one of the sharp ivory modelling tools from the works normally used to pick out leaf designs on the black basaltes vases. The baby's shrieks, as Heffie held her and Jos prodded, were so awful that Sally could not bear to be in the room with them, but she would return, when the prescribed jabbing was over, and together the mother and father would bathe Mary Ann in warm water.

Josiah would say that he feared that the electrical treatment which Darwin was pioneering would affect her intellects. It is true that, though she was now over two years old, she showed absolutely no sign of having a linguistic sense. Sukey at that age could almost recite poetry. Poor little Mary Ann.

Yet, the sorrows of the child, so loud and so obvious, were often confined to another part of the house. And with her sick little presence in the family, and the return of the other children to form the Etruscan Academy, a new era had begun. Sally would not be required to go through the humiliations of childbirth again. Of that, Byerley was mysteriously certain. With this freedom, Sally was able to begin what had never been present in the past fifteen years, her forgotten friendship with her husband-cousin. One sensed, without anyone having made any remark, that a phase was over and that Sally Wedgwood's independence as a woman was about to commence.

Twenty years older than he she may have been; she was magnificent. Her strength of character, like her colouring, was all the more powerful for being understated. Sandy hair was drawn back from a large intelligent brow. It was the colour of a hayfield in high summer. Her skin had a bloom upon it. When her eyes met his, Byerley felt her gaze seeing the whole catalogue of his emotional adventures in America; she saw – or so his fancy painted – the German lady in the New York inn, she saw Polly Dwyer's huge creamy nakedness and Mrs Aylmer's urgent undressings, and that lust which had almost something desperate about it. She saw deeper. She saw the romance with Blue Squirrel. Or so it would appear, as his eyes met those of his aunt and cousin. Had she always conveyed this perfectly open preparedness for – what? This was not the simple bodily lust of Mrs Aylmer; it was something much slower, much quieter, much more prepared to wait and see. The lingering way in which she held his hand, quite brazenly, in front of the rest of the family; the calm looping of arms when they went into meals. Josiah could look on, lightly baffled, but pleased in her pleasure. She had gained something. It was disturbing to be so completely aware of this. Byerley did not know how to handle the new state of things. There had been enough in the previous few years of experience to tell him how quickly such impulses, if acted upon, led to chaos.

In any event, he knew that he was not returning to the old life. The return meant a very decided change, and this would mean not merely that he left behind the acting profession in the New York theatre, and embraced, once more, some kind of work, at present all somewhat vaguely determined, for his uncle; but that he must also consider the broader question of himself: marriage seemed inevitable, and desirable. But there was the question of whether he would follow the Wedgwood custom of looking for a cousin, or whether he would fish in some other pool.

Sukey Wedgwood was now all but a woman, and one he liked enormously. When, among his other duties, Tom had undertaken the education of his young cousins, he had immediately been engaged by the quickness of her mind, by the breadth of her reading, by her grasp of matters as diverse as Latin grammar and chemistry. The pert facetiousness of her brothers, on the other hand, was a shock. He did not know whether it was something which was obvious to his uncle. Jos's manner with the family – an ironical air of mild exasperation, a breeziness of humour, a bustling in and a bustling out of rooms – did not allow even so close a student of his character as Tom to guess what was passing through the great man's mind in relation to his children. With regard to Josiah, Tom had returned to the old question, and come no nearer to a satisfactory solution: whether a man so astute in chemistry, commerce and practical skills had a comparable cleverness of the heart. Was he aware of the children growing up to regard him, at least in part, as a half-joke?

They were all gathered at Etruria for a few weeks: the two business partners, Bentley and Wedgwood; Dr Darwin, who had become almost an extension of the family; Mrs Bentley, with her 'Lahs' and 'Lors', her London affectations and her name-dropping. And everywhere the children, scampering, chattering, squabbling, showing off.

Bentley, in his airy chatter with Dr Darwin, had spoken of the amorous history of the painter Mr Stubbs. Married young, in Liverpool, where Bentley had first met him. Father a currier, ran a prosperous little business. Stubbs always a boy who had played his cards close to his chest. Something of a mystery. A budding natural philosopher, interested to the point of fanaticism in anatomy, both human and animal. Married quite young, had children. Went to Rome to study painting, but came home again in quite a hurry. The English in Rome – Joshua Reynolds had been there at the time, and William Hamilton, and Chambers and Brettingham – had all been in pursuit of the Antique. Stubbs deplored it, though it was obvious from his paintings that one piece of antique sculpture – the Horse being attacked by the Lion in the Palazzo dei Conservatori – had made an impression. Its violence appealed to the man, who was, Bentley had insisted, a strange one. Dr Darwin had observed how a passion for violence can lurk behind the calmest of masks, that the glossy tranquillity of Mr Stubbs's depictions – now of racehorses, now of their owners, or their prize hunters posed beneath the shimmering summer of English trees – had the quality of mask. In his wild animals, and in the depiction of lions sinking their teeth into terrified horses, realism itself was abandoned. The expression of the horses' faces in these pictures, which he had executed over and over again, had something in them which was . . . Dr Darwin's chuckle had left no doubt that the unwholesomeness related to beneath the waist. He had mentioned a French nobleman.

—Not a name I know, Bentley had said. And a Marquis, you say?

—A fascinating case of a d-deranged mind substituting p-p-pain for p-pleasure, said Darwin. You see, in order for the species to repeat itself, Nature had to implant in m-mankind an urge which was irresistible: overwhelming. At the same time, it needed to force upon each young *tabula rasa*, each human infant, an object of d-d-desire.

—I had supposed that that propensity was not one which needed to be learnt, sir, had been Bentley's jovial rejoinder.

—But that, sir, is where we differ. I should m-m-maintain that the child at its mother's breast learns to love what we should all love – t-t-titty, sir, titties!

Dr Darwin rubbed his hands together as they walked through the shrubbery.

—I hope you're listening, young Tom.

—With rapture.

Both the older men had laughed.

—But take the child away from its mother's tits. Smack it when it soils itself, smack it when it cries, smack it when it requires l-l-love, and what will it do? It will respond to the scalding pain of the punishment as a normal infant would respond to its mother's n-n-nipple. The man who grows up from that childhood will only derive his erotic satisfaction from the b-b-birch or the harsh word.

But at that point, Uncle Jos had come stomping up with a question.

—Who are you talking about?

And rather than answering 'Stubbs', Darwin answered,

—Mr Barville.

Bentley yelped in recognition. Byerley took a moment longer to catch the reference, his acquaintanceship with *Fanny Hill* evidently being less profound than that of Wedgwood's business partner. The flagellation scene. Byerley noted, now he was treated as a man among men, that the other men treated Josiah as a child.

—It is a curious thing, said Uncle Jos.

But the curious thing had been of a chemical, rather than a psychological character. For some time now, Stubbs had been beholden to Wedgwood for the manufacture of ceramic tablets. They had even made him a glazed earthenware palette. But Stubbs had required something larger than this, as a substitute for the copper on which he had essayed some of his glossier enamelled paintings. The first dozen or so earthenware tablets had cracked under firing.

—What we needed – Jos broke into the conversation to tell Bentley and Darwin – and you listen, young Tom, because this will interest you, was a new body, flatter and thinner than our usual earthenware, which would not warp or crack when it was fired. Glory be!

He threw back his head and laughed at the memory of the experiments.

—The trouble it took me to come up with the blessed stuff! But then, last year, I was able to write to Mr Stubbs and tell him, We have done it, sir! We have done it! We made three tablets. On the first he painted a naked Phaeton riding his horse-drawn chariot too near the sun. Not entirely suitable to show to Mrs Wedgwood, and certainly not to Sukey. In the next, there was a horse frightened by a lion. A somewhat morbid composition – almost as if he derived pleasure from the sheer gruesomeness of it . . .

Mr Bentley shot a glance at Dr Darwin.

—And another, pursued Jos, was of Hope nursing Love, a gentle scene of a young nursing mother, but if you were talking of the Marquis . . .

—You know of him?

—Lafayette? All the world knows of him. His victories against His Majesty in America have done nothing to diminish his popularity with the English public, I can tell you! We sold twenty portrait medallions of Lafayette in the London showrooms last week.

The theme of Stubbs and his strange tastes, of more interest to Byerley at that moment than the soaring turnover in the Wedgwood salerooms in Soho, had been resumed a day or two later between the two old gossips as they walked in the shrubbery at Etruria before dinner, Tom Byerley strolling behind them.

—As a natural philosopher, I admire Mr Stubbs.

—It was in that capacity that I first became aware of him in

Liverpool, said Bentley, gentle in his refusal to emphasize that it was in fact he, with his Liverpool connections, who had been the first of the circle to meet this phenomenon.

—An anatomist, sir, said Darwin. Your great l-lords and your landowners pay for pictures of their g-grooms and their jockeys and their spaniels and their race-winners. Stubbs has flayed them all, catalogued their bones and m-m-muscles, seen the way they all fit together, in the same way that a surgeon would go to work.

—No soul, you mean, Darwin?

—You know what scares me about his pictures?

—No.

—It is like reading *Gulliver's Travels*, and finding the horses superior to the human Yahoos. I don't think 'soul' is a w-word with any meaning in the world of Mr Stubbs. There is just the English sky and a few carefully arranged t-trees, and this succession of perfectly executed exercises in animal anatomy. But, ye Gods! There is expression in the horses' f-faces!

—I wonder how he will anatomize the Wedgwood family, laughed Mr Bentley.

And Jos, once again hurrying and hobbling, between a breeze around the modelling rooms in the manufactory and a visit to the schoolroom to check on M. Potet's performance as a French master, could tell the answer to that question in some detail.

—Poor Sal is angry with me. Wanted me to engage Mr Wright of Derby. But Stubbs in effect owes me money. I have made him his tablets. When he had painted on 'em, we fired 'em, with total success, in the kilns behind the showrooms in Greek Street. I have made him his palettes. There could be a real market there for enamel-painted tablets by Stubbs. He owes us. I have commissioned him to do two works, of the children only. Sally can be painted anon by Wright – or by Sir Joshua if she wants, but I want my pound of flesh from

Stubbs first! I've told him, one picture of the boys conducting a chemical experiment, and another of the girls gathered round Sukey at the harpsichord, playing some girlish air.

—And what does Sally think of that design, Jos? asked Darwin with a chuckle.

—The tone with which you ask the question makes it clear that you know the answer, said Jos with a rueful smile.

—Mr Barville, repeated Bentley with a laugh.

—Who's that, Bentley? asked Josiah. I do not think I have the honour of Mr Barville's acquaintance.

At which they all laughed.

# 4

BLUE SQUIRREL LEANED ON THE RAIL OF THE QUARTER-
deck. The warm breeze refreshed her face, and played through her
thick hair. She had just been baptized. The ship's captain had insisted
upon this.

—I'll not marry a Christian man to a heathen.

—She'll be happy with that, had been the sergeant's view of the
matter.

There was no easier passage to England than to go as Sergeant
Powell's wife. The discovery, soon after her encounter with the redcoats, that Captain Gower, and most of the men in B Company –
the sergeant's Company – were from the region of England near
Wooden Leg left her in no doubt. She must go to England. If Tomtit,
as she feared and suspected, had betrayed her, and if he had been
responsible for allowing Boone and his men to return and perpetrate
the massacre, then revenge must be taken. And if it turned out that
she was mistaken, and that Tomtit was not responsible, then she
wanted to see Wooden Leg. Who knows? She might fashion
Cherokee clay in Wooden Leg's pottery, and learn the technique
which Tomtit had tried to describe to her, of 'throwing'. She could
not easily envisage how a potter's wheel could work. One thing
was certain: there was no returning to her old township in the
Appalachian foothills. It was in ruins. Most of her relations had been

killed or scattered. The Americans had taken control of the destiny of the Cherokee.

The scenes of panic at the dockyards had been terrifying. Hundreds, thousands of human beings had milled and swarmed, trying to get aboard one of the ships. From New York, she heard, they were sailing to Nova Scotia, and even to Africa, to enable some of the Loyalist negroes to start a new life. In Charleston, things had been otherwise. Captain Gower was not alone in wanting to reclaim ownership of his slaves, once the British defeat in the war had been recognized. There had been many hasty, makeshift little auctions all over Virginia and the Carolinas. Gower had expressed himself satisfied to have rounded up seventy. The promise was that, if they managed to get to the Bahamas Islands, any former owner who had repossessed himself of his slaves would be given estates by the Crown – ten acres per slave. The cargo they were now carrying from Charleston harbour would guarantee the Gowers the best part of a whole island to themselves. The Bahamas were not as fertile as the good arable land they left behind in Virginia, but they were able, at least – this was the captain's view – to salvage something from the wreckage. Now, as she stood alone by the railing, she could hear the cargo below decks roaring out a hymn:

> Nothing in my hands I bring,
> Simply to thy Cross I cling;
> Naked, come to thee for dress;
> Helpless, look to thee for grace.

Sometimes the crash of the waves, and the heaving of the boat, and the cries of the sailors drowned out the hymn, but still it came back, and still they sang. The ship was a chorus of voices: shouts from the maindeck, of sailors giving orders, haloos from sailors clambering up the rigging with the ease of monkeys, and calling down from one or another of the old Indiaman's three masts.

No longer a heathen, Sadloli repeated to herself her new name.

—What sort of a name is that? had been the captain's question.

She had been reading the bullet-charred Scriptures, the book which had saved the sergeant's life. She had enjoyed the stories: Abraham and Isaac, the Burning Bush (this was especially beautiful – the voice which came from the Bush, the fire which burned but did not consume the foliage); Jonah and the Whale. The later parts of the book, the parts called the New Testament, she liked less well. It was surely wrong to forgive enemies? The sergeant had told her that this part of the book was the most important, and that Our Saviour's words were the most sacred parts of Scripture. But none of the Christians she had met had seemed to be influenced by these very important words. They did not forgive their enemies; they did not turn the other cheek when they were smitten; they did not show indifference to money or to material possessions; they were not meek, but they thought they should inherit the earth. Sadloli thought it better to admit that the advice of the Saviour was all wrong: that we had a duty to avenge our enemies, and a duty to lay up treasure to protect our children and our old people.

The sergeant had found several names for her in the New Testament.

—You could be Priscilla – now there's a nice name.

And licking his forefinger, he had turned a page and added,

—Mary's nice and simple. Or Elizabeth – why not Elizabeth?

The names had not appealed to her. It was agreed between them that since she was being given a new name, she should be allowed some choice in the matter, whatever the captain of the ship might say. The displaced people of the Hebrews, who had followed Moses into the wilderness from Egypt as refugees, grumbled perpetually.

Some of them wished they could turn back to their old slave-owners, with whom they had known security. Others feared they would die in the desert. There came a time when they were thirsty. They asked Moses for water. God told Moses to stand before a rock on the mount of Horeb and strike it with his staff. Water gushed forth. For some reason which Sadloli could not understand, God decided to punish Moses for this. He would be allowed to see the Land of Promise from a mountain top, but he would never be allowed to enter into it.

Now, the place where he struck the rock was called Massah and Meribah, because of the chiding of the children of Israel. 'And because they tempted the Lord, saying, Is the Lord among us, or not?'

Sadloli thought this was a deep and important story. This is the water of Meribah, because the children of Israel strove with the Lord. The Cherokee people spoke of God as a Great Buzzard. His whims could not be gainsaid. He was Destiny. He swooped in the sky, and for the most part allowed the other creatures to go about their occasions. Sometimes he descended to rearrange the smaller creatures or to devour them. But there was no striving, no quarrelling with him, no wondering whether he was there or not, no taking charge of one's own destiny.

Sadloli thought of Wooden Leg, who had wanted good white clay so badly that he had sent messengers across a mighty ocean and into the land of a strange people in order to buy it. She took the name of the Waters of Strife, feeling a quiet, sad conviction that it would be an appropriate harbinger of her married condition.

—I can always call you Merry, bach!

And the silver tenor laughed.

An hour or so after the baptism, when the sergeant and the sea-captain seemed tipsy and smelt of rum, the marriage service was performed. *I Idris take thee Meribah . . . to have and to hold from this day forward.*

The great ship lurched, and the slaves continued to sing their hymn from below. Added to the human voices could be heard the noise of the overcrowded, overburdened ship itself, the creaking of its timbers, the smack of rope against mast, the crash of ocean water against the bows.

The afternoon sun was going down in the sky. From where they stood on the quarter-deck, the rigging of the ship was a vast stringed instrument, an Aeolian harp through which the wind played its spirit-music.

The sea was a rich bright blue, and it was very clear. The breezes were strong, but there was no danger of a storm, and their crossing to the Bahamas Islands was not going to be long. They had already sailed twenty of the hundred miles' journey.

*I Meribah,* she said, *take thee Idris, for my lawful wedded husband.*

So clever was she at languages that already she had begun to adopt his Welsh lilt.

As she spoke her wedding vows, Meribah Powell felt an intuitive consciousness of all the other wanderers whom the Great Buzzard or the God of Israel had thrown together on the ship. She was visited by an overwhelming awareness of all their varied expectations, hopes, memories, pains. Probably, one of the voices below was that of Tobias, the boy who had so believed in the sergeant, but who had been arrested as soon as they heard of the end of the war and impounded by the captain as his personal property.

This huge shipload of men and women was a fraction of the vanquished multitudes. All their lives had been affected by the defeat of King George. Some would settle on the islands whither they were bound. Already, on the Bahamas Islands, there were Chicksaw and Cree who had fled the Spanish in Florida. For all she knew, there were Cherokee there, though she had not heard that this was so.

She did not allow herself to hope for a reunion with any of her people. From now onwards, Sergeant Powell's people would be her people, and Sergeant Powell's God would be her God. The God who had fought for King George, and sent soldiers into battle for him, this God she could understand, and she would strive with Him, asking Him why He had allowed the King to be defeated, and the Cherokee towns and farms to be destroyed by vandals. But she could never worship a God who was a weakling, the second God in the Bible – the man-God who allowed himself to be captured by his enemies and tortured on a Cross. The slaves were singing to that God now, and that was why they were slaves. How can we forgive our enemies when they destroy our babies, our old men, our crops, our lives? This should not be forgiven. The law of vengeance was quite clear among the Cherokee people. If a Mohawk killed a Cherokee, even by accident, that death must be repaid by a death. If her Tomtit had been responsible for the massacre, then the price must be paid, and she alone was in the position to fulfil the Destiny.

—I wish I knew what was in your heart, wife of mine. Merry. Merry as a cricket, isnit? I feel gratitude that I met you, I do really. And longing for my brothers and sisters in Wales to meet you, and longing to see us set up in an alehouse. Captain Gower says he can write to his cousin, Lord Gower, about us. Get us fixed up. Says he is very grateful to me.

Grateful for helping to round up the slaves. Tobias had called out to the sergeant, when he was put back into chains and they shackled his ankles.

—Sarge! Sarge! It's me, Tobias!

Meribah remembered how the tearful boy had prayed for the sergeant's deliverance when he was wounded in battle, how he had sat beside him as she sponged the wounded man's brow.

—Come on now, you niggers, no talking in the ranks.

That was how Sergeant Idris Powell had answered his young friend's plea.

*Simply to thy Cross I cling.*

—There is a part of all of us which is secret, she said quietly to her husband, allowing him to hold her hand. You have such a part, Idris, and I have such a part. It is so secret we cannot share it with another person, not all at once.

—We don't have any secrets any more.

But he was having to shout because the wind got up as he said the words.

She thought, to Tomtit I did pour out my secret soul. In total simplicity and trust, I opened up my secret heart and shared it with him. I drained myself, I gave my whole being, freely and spontaneously and without reserve, to that man. I was drunk with love, I was drunk with sex. We soared together to the bright stars where we were king and queen. He said he felt the same.

Other Cherokee had warned her – he is not one of us. Even Swan's Wing, who was a good man, and a good judge of character, who liked Tomtit, had looked anxious as her love for Tom deepened.

It was now impossible to know what to believe. Clearly, Tomtit had been lying to her, else why should he have vanished during the raid and never returned to search for her? A spy had told Swan's Wing that Tom Byerley had gone back to live in Philadelphia. He had lodged with the Rebel Printer who helped to distribute that pamphlet, *Common Sense*, the one which made fun of King George. So much for loyalty! Tom had joined General Washington in his expedition across the great river when it had very nearly frozen, and no one had heard of him since.

She knew by instinct that Tom would have returned to Wooden Leg. She knew so much about him! As they lay naked in one another's arms, he had told her the story of his life over and over again. She knew about his mother, and the shop selling silks, and the need for her to tidy herself twice a morning. (This joke she never quite understood, but supposed it was some euphemism to do with defecation.) She knew about Wooden Leg standing beside the ovens as the men went past him with their saggars on their heads. She knew about him smashing defective china with his stick. 'Not good enough for Josiah Wedgwood.' She knew about the gloomy man on the canal, Caleb, who thought the worst of everyone, but who was secretly kind to children, and who protected his sister, Heffie.

Had Tom invented all these people? Surely not.

> Not the Labours of my hands
> Can fulfil the Law's demands . . .

That might be true for the man-God, the God of the slaves. But for the Older God with whom she was at strife beside the waters of Meribah, it was not true. She must fulfil the Law's demands, the demands of vengeance. She went to the world of Wooden Leg with no bloodlust, no exultant heart. The burning houses, the raped children, the butchered women, the reeking animals, the dead braves, the scorched corn demanded vengeance. Without vengeance there could be no justice, no morality.

It could not be done without deep pain. If Tomtit were to be killed, she would be killing the man she had loved, loved so deeply. A man could not have done those things to a woman, spoken those words to her, stroked her and cherished her and made love to her so passionately night and day without loving her. Could he? Or was he simply what he had been in New York, an actor?

She feared so much about the future. She feared meeting Tomtit again and being unable to fulfil the Law's demands. She feared loving him again. He would have found another woman by now. That thought was simply unbearable and it stabbed at her, as the ship swayed and as the sergeant, with his arm around her waist, said,

—Now, my darling. Now we must go below.

She feared the future and its implacable demands. She felt sorry for the sergeant in that moment, sorry for his stupid face which did not know he was merely the instrument given to her by the Great Buzzard to bring justice to pass.

# 5

CALEB BROUGHT HIM OVER IN THE WEDGWOODS' NEW
barouche, having met the London mail coach at the Crown Inn,
Stone. While Bowers unloaded the extensive luggage, an easel,
several large wooden boxes for paints, as well as his portmanteau of
clothes, Stubbs said to him,

—You have a fine face, sir. I would happily be painting you.

—Aye, and I can guess what Jos Wedgwood 'ud have to say about
that!

—But it's what I have to say about it which interests me. We'll see
how we progress, said Stubbs.

He was a bald, wigless man, just approaching the age of fifty, with
curling grey hair at his ears and nape, suggestive of the bottom part
of a periwig. His attentive eyes were very dark brown, almost black
like currants. He was extremely closely shaven, his cheeks were sleek
as a woman's, his oval face divided by a hawk-like nose and very full
sensual lips.

In answer to the usual enquiries about the comfort and conveni-
ence of his coming, Stubbs said to Jos and to Bentley who stood
beside him,

—Are you racing men? I came straight from Epsom yesterday.
You never saw such a race. A new race, just inaugurated, named after
Lord Derby. A mile on the flat. I put money on Lord Egremont's filly

Assassin to win, but in the end it was a splendid animal of Bunbury's who collected the prize. Over a thousand pounds. Diomed, she was called.

Both the men of business affected, out of politeness, an expression of admiration; but at the same time, Byerley could perceive in their features a shock which could not be entirely disguised, at the rashness of risking such a sum.

—The filly, she was called Diomed. I think the Derby will now be run each year. It was a great success. Over twenty runners in the contest, and some truly wonderful horses. Bunbury is a great man. You know Bunbury?

—I have not that honour, sir, said Jos, without irony. As always when Jos took on the manners of a shop-man, his partner looked uneasy.

—Steward of the Jockey Club, said Stubbs.

There was no grandeur about Stubbs's manner. His voice was that of his father, a Liverpool currier. He had not, as Byerley had at first suspected, come up with the account of the Derby in order to lord it over the two traders. Rather, he had plunged in out of a natural enthusiasm.

—I knew you weren't a racing man, said Stubbs.

Later, in the saloon, when the painter had been shown his rooms, chosen a studio in the newly built stables, expressed admiration for all he saw, the anatomist was introduced to his subjects: Sukey blushing uncontrollably, little Sal, four, shy, and, hiding her face in Sukey's skirts, Kitty, a pert six, smiling with the air of a confident princess. Annie Johnson, the nursery maid, trying to stop Mary Ann wriggling, had to take her upstairs until, as she put it, she'd recovered herself.

—In that case, said John Wedgwood knowingly, we shall all have a long wait before we see her again.

Sukey winced at the sense given off by Jack that Mr Stubbs was a subordinate who had been hired for a task. The boy addressed him, not as the man of genius she believed him to be, but in a tone which would have been more appropriate in condescending to a groom, or a man sent to tune the piano.

Jack, who had never in fact attended a race meeting, had picked up enough sense at boarding school in Lancashire of the importance of these things to begin,

—Cousin Byerley says you were at Epsom, Mr Stubbs. I suppose hired to sketch the nags in the paddock before the race.

Stubbs's cold amiability of expression did not desert him as he asked, with an irony instantly caught by Sukey, and missed by Jack,

—Did you have a horse running?

—Good, good, getting to know one another! said Josiah, who put one hand on Mr Stubbs's shoulder and addressed his children collectively.

—Now, brats, this is a busy man, and we are very fortunate, very fortunate indeed, that he can spare a few weeks of his time. He will be doing two paintings. In the first instance, I think that was what we agreed, sir? Two paintings, one of the boys. I've told you, Jack, you're to be looking into a retort. Jos should be looking on, and we thought, Mr Stubbs and I, that Tom would be clapping his hands in delight at your experiment being so successful. Then we thought, correct me if I am wrong, Mr Stubbs, that the girls—

—Far be it from me to correct you, said Stubbs. But I think we shall wait until I have made a few sketches, had a few thoughts, before we make final our choice of subjects.

—But, you understand what I have in mind, said Jos.

—Perfectly, sir. It is simply that our positions are not reciprocated. While I understand what is in your mind, you do not always appear to understand what is in mine.

Sally smiled quietly at this triumphantly successful broadside.

Later, while the painter was setting up the studio in the stable, the boys were playing outside and the younger girls were having their rest, Sukey, at work on a sampler, sat while her mother and father conversed.

—If you had wanted a picture of a little group conducting an experiment, you should have engaged Mr Wright of Derby, as originally agreed.

—I have tried to explain, my dearest, that Mr Stubbs is under an obligation to us. The ceramic tablets on which he paints in enamel were—

—You've told us about the tablets. We know how clever you were in producing samples which did not crack. That is your expertise and no one will deny it. Depicting scientific experiments is Mr Wright's expertise, and painting pictures of horses is that of Mr Stubbs. Depend upon it, Jos, by the time he has finished he'll persuade us all to sit for our portraits outside, and he will not care tuppence what any of us look like! We shall finish with some very pleasant portraits of our horses and ponies – and maybe of Hotspur – yes, darling, maybe of you, maybe of you, maybe of you! she said, pulling the ears of the Springer spaniel and smiling adoringly into its eyes.

# 6

AS FATE WOULD HAVE IT, SUKEY WOULD MARRY DR DARWIN'S son Robert the year her own father died, in 1796. But the younger Dr Darwin was not her parents' first choice. As a married woman, much later in life, Sukey could look back upon the past, and various conversations with her mother about the condition of wedlock and the plans her parents had made for her. These conversations began when she was younger than sixteen. Was it – she fancied it was – during the extended visit of Mr Stubbs that summer that she had that embarrassing conversation with Sally about Cousin Byerley?

—I do not know what you find to object to in the proposal, Sally Wedgwood had said. You know that neither your father nor I would ever force you into a marriage.

—But you and Pa have discussed it.

—A man and a woman may discuss the marriage of their child.

—Before you discussed it with me. Does Cousin Byerley know of this scheme?

—We mentioned it to him. How could we not? There is the possibility one day that your father will give him a position, a proper position in the firm. If he were married to you, well, we could consider him becoming a partner. If he married outside the family, naturally, the position would be altered.

—You make it seem like a business contract.

—Marriage is a contract.

Silence was all that Sukey could offer as a reply to this. Since Ma and Pa were cousins – albeit distant ones – she could scarcely object to the idea on the grounds of consanguinity. Sally broke the silence with,

—What is wrong with your cousin?

—I did not say there was anything wrong with him. I do not love him. I am not . . .

So, Sally put both hands to her ears in a little mime of blocking out all hearing. She said,

—You will say you are not in love with him! Good heavens, Sukey, I've allowed you to read too many novels.

—How many is too many?

—You expect that such emotions could lead to a stable and happy domestic partnership? It is better to take account of shared tastes, a joint outlook, a comradely, and indeed a familial, bond of friendship. Surely you can see that? Oh, Sukey, don't cry. Don't. It is so . . . uncalled-for, pet.

Sukey had not wanted the tears to come to her eyes, and she was able, for the remainder of that uncomfortable conversation, to retain her composure. But when the opportunity allowed, she took her leave and, cold and damp as it was, she walked out into the garden to be alone with her thoughts. All their lives, they had made a joke of poor Mrs Byerley, her false gentilities, her forthright views, and her shop. Part of the indignity of the current proposal consisted in this: that if the plan went forward, Mrs Byerley would be Sukey's own name also.

Perhaps Mama was right and they had allowed her to read too many novels. Since she first found herself marooned with Robinson Crusoe, and then went voyaging in strange lands with Gulliver, there had been no moment of her life when she did not have some work of fiction beside her. She had seen the world through the novelists' lens. But was this altogether a bad way of learning? Her father's friends had learnt more of the properties of matter, more about the constitution of the world, and of the universe, than any previous historical generation. But Mr Boulton's and Mr Watts's machinery were not the only developments of human ingenuity to have happened in her century. The discovery of dephlogosticated air, or the development of the spinning jenny, had happened while Mr Richardson, with his patient exchange of letters between female friends, had shown the workings of that contraption even more ingenious than industrial machines, viz. the human heart. Perhaps another way of viewing the matter would be to say that the reading of novels had refined her sensibilities, and allowed her to hope, and expect, from her only conjunction with a member of the opposite sex, rather more than – what was it Mama had spoken of – familial bonds? Shared tastes? Friendship? Wasn't Sophia Western right to run away from her father when he tried to force her into marriage with Blifil when she loved Tom Jones? Naturally, one hoped for a love, such as Sophia and Tom's, which was blessed by fondness and wealth; and any sane person would dread the ill consequences of a love match such as Clarissa's for the unscrupulous Lovelace.

The existence of the Wedgwoods – this was a given fact. Sukey had never asked herself whether things could have been otherwise, whether Mama could have married someone else, still less whether her mother and father were 'happy'. But the illusory joys of novel-reading had allowed this young person the false pleasure of believing that she could decide her own destiny. Papa had none of the bullying of Squire Western, but the conversation with Mama, in which it seemed as if Sukey was destined, will-she or nil-she, to become Mrs Byerley, made her the unhappy heroine of a modern romance, forced to obey her parents' will and to smother the instincts of the heart.

She had not gone so far as to hope that she would ever become

Madame Potet. The lank-haired, pale young Frenchman with whom she read the plays of Racine, and with whom she exchanged silent, profoundly meaningful exchanges at the dining table, had occupied the position of a semi-fictitious being. She yearned for him. She had conducted innumerable conversations with him inside her head, and penned thousands of letters in her mind to some imaginary friend about his sad eyes, his homesickness, his voice. She felt protective towards M. Potet when her oafish brothers mocked him, or when Pa asked him questions, which no one outside the world of commerce could answer, about French trade.

When she ran out of the drawing-room, through the stone-flagged corridors at the back of the house, and out into the stable yard, it was for air. Tears came fast. Her love, her pure, ardent love, for M. Potet was only one of many things which her mother was brutally destroying by this talk of marriage with Cousin Byerley. It was her whole inner life that they had been clumsily arranging for her, Ma and Pa. They seemed to suppose that the question of her future husband was a public, practical family matter: quite as much theirs to dispose as the question of who came to dinner or where they should next seek a water cure for their interminable ailments.

She felt wrenched, invaded, beaten about by their insensitivity. And yes, when a quarter of a century later she remembered the whole episode with fond smiles at her earlier self, she was confirmed in her memory that it had happened while Mr Stubbs was staying.

She opened the back door with its rattling bolts and ran out into the yard. She smelt the horse dung and the straw. She was not sobbing, but tears were flowing down her cheeks. And there he was, Mr Stubbs with his big glossy eyes, like those of a very intelligent horse.

—Your pony is too small, he said.

Of course, Mama had been right. Mr Stubbs had not even begun to paint the Wright-of-Derbyish painting of the boys conducting a chemical experiment. After some preliminary sketches of individual children, and after two very accomplished portraits of Mama and Papa, executed in enamel on ceramic plates, he had plotted a large family portrait, out of doors, and with dogs and horses.

—I . . . I know.

At the time, she supposed that Mr Stubbs's mind had been solely upon ponies, and that he had been unable to resist speaking of it. Almost instantly, she had stored up this 'hilarious' fact, and wanted to communicate it to some other student of the painter's mysterious character, to Heffie, who spent hours chatting to him in the stables, or to Mama herself. Later, as an adult, Sukey saluted Stubbs's delicacy. Of course, he had seen the tears, and knew the way to shake her out of whatever adolescent despondency was making her miserable.

—See here.

He led her into the stable which had been made into his temporary studio. The principal canvas, a huge picture some four feet by six, was balanced upon the main easel. But there were a number of sketches lying about on the tables and easels which he had arranged around the stable walls. One of these depicted Sukey alone, on Gumdrop. He had made it almost a caricature, so that her feet nearly reached the ground as she sat side-saddle on the little bay.

—You've made my legs twice as long as they are in reality, and poor Gumdrop's legs twice as short.

—That is true. But you should be on a proper mount at your age, young woman. You are, after all, a young woman now.

So, they all noticed it. She looked up at him with some horror, but he smiled, and then laughed and this made her laugh too.

—You will survive, he said through laughter. Most young women do, and when they have survived, they look back on the experience with some nostalgia.

# 7

—A FINE WOMAN, MRS WEDGWOOD.

Bentley's words had been addressed to that lady's nephew, but Mrs Bentley, who was ever-mindful of her husband's promise to endow her with all his worldly goods, included this remark in that abundant category, and replied as if it had been presented to herself.

—It will be interesting to see which of them wins the battle of the portraits!

—That, my dear, is a foregone conclusion, said Mr Bentley, affectionately. The affection extended both to his wife, whose legs he habitually patted or stroked as the coach sped over the new-surfaced Stafford road, and to the friends whom he had lately left.

—The more Josiah attempts to control Mr Stubbs, Mr Bentley continued, the less success he will have! I know that man. No mule is more stubborn. The whole family will end up depicted as dolls in a landscape, and the horses will take pride of place.

—And Mrs Wedgwood will get her way, Mr Bentley?

—If you mean, will Josiah engage Mr Wright of Derby to paint something for her, yes. But, depend upon it, my dear, Owd Wooden Leg is not as acquiescent as you suppose. There will be something about it which shows that, in spite of all, he is the master.

—I'm a Derby girl, so of course I support Wright of Derby versus Stubbs of Liverpool!

# The Potter's Hand

Mr Bentley rubbed his wife's knee and said she spoke of the painters as if they were racehorses competing at Epsom Downs.

They rattled along in the Bentleys' coach. Tom Byerley, wanted for the business in London, had hoped it would be possible to travel to the capital alone, by the mail coach. But the Bentleys were travelling home from Staffordshire to Turnham Green with their coach and four; Mr Bentley, as much as Uncle Jos, was Byerley's employer; the journey with the pair of them was free of cost. There was no getting around it, even though, left to himself, Tom Byerley would not have elected to spend two and a half days in a tightly enclosed space with Mrs Bentley, and to share her unstoppable conversation over breakfast and dinner for three days running at the coaching inns where they reposed upon the journey. By the time the coach had reached Stafford it appeared to Tom that she had run through her repository of reflections and anecdotes; and there was little for her to fall back upon except malice about his own kinsfolk. Whatever thoughts he allowed himself about Josiah, Sally, their children, or their household, it was quite another thing to hear the unvarnished spite of this mannered young woman.

—I distinctly heard him break wind before we went into dinner.

—Really, my dear.

—I do not mention it to be unkind. But this is the man upon whose partnership you rely for custom from the titled, and indeed crowned, heads of Europe!

—They buy Josiah's ware because of its beauty and perfection, not because of his manners. Besides, you exaggerate his coarseness and totally overlook his genius.

And so they rattled by.

—I wonder, Mr Byerley, that you are not yet married, said Mrs Bentley roguishly, even going so far as to lean forward in the barouche and touch his knee with her fan.

It was one of the questions uppermost in the young man's mind, but Mrs Bentley came low on any possible list of persons with whom he would have chosen to discuss its ramifications.

—No Americans took your fancy?

—I was very busy in New York, ma'am.

—But you must have had admirers. Surely all good-looking actors have their followers?

—Mary, stop persecuting Tom, I entreat you.

—Mr Byerley enjoys being persecuted. I am a good judge of these matters, she said with a coquettish smirk. Her husband looked gloomily at the spires of Lichfield scudding past the windows in the dying light.

That night was passed at an inn in Birmingham, Mrs Bentley countermanding her husband's suggestion that they should invite Mr Boulton to dine. She had had her fill of manufacturers.

The inn supplied a decent enough supper, of cold fowl and claret, in a private dining-room. The change of scene allowed Bentley to quiz Byerley further about the American situation.

—I will be candid with you, Tom, the war has been ruinous to English commerce: our own business is badly shaken by it, and were it not for the ingenuity of Jos selling the Frog Service to the Empress, we should be, I would not say we should be ruined, as some have been, but we should quite definitely feel the pinch. We shall have to see if the peace brings a revival of trade.

—It seems to be a stalemate, said Tom.

—And did you really take up arms on the side of the Rebels? asked Mrs Bentley. We were all – what were we, Mr Bentley?

—I think we were rather proud of you, laughed her husband. But we were glad your career as an insurrectionist was of short duration.

—I took part in one small exercise. He smiled at the recollection now. It was nothing. As I told you, my first impressions were in favour of the Americans, when I yet resided in New York. It seemed clear that the Ministry was quite unreasonable in expecting to tax the colonists, and the severity with which hired German and Irish soldiers were used to suppress the democrats of Massachusetts only confirmed my hunch. Later, however, when I had set out for the Carolinas, I felt horrified by the way in which the colonists treated the Cherokee people, who had been the excellent custodians of the land for hundreds of years, and who were now being driven out, and actually massacred by individuals who were little better than Yahoos.

—So you became loyal once more to King George.

—Back in Philadelphia, I stayed with a family of printers of a radical persuasion. They gave me Mr Paine's pamphlet to read, and I do not see how it can be gainsaid. It is true that I offered my services to the American army in that one small engagement. It had never been my intention to serve with them for the duration of the war! They offered, if I accompanied them across the great river to New Jersey, that I could have safe conduct back to New York and find my passage home, and this was indeed the case.

—But you did see action! said Mrs Bentley, her cheeks flushed.

—We were under the impression, I think, that by crossing the Delaware by night, General Washington would take a garrison at a small town called Trenton. In fact, when we got there, we found a few German mercenaries, who were easily overcome. There were few casualties. The Americans took some prisoners and went back to Philadelphia. I, as promised, was put on the road to New York, which I reached after a few days. I was never, as such, a member of the American army. Once back in New York, I received another package of letters from my mother and uncle, and Uncle Jos implored me to come home. So I did.

He smiled a broad, innocent smile.

—But you would have been prepared to fire a shot at the King's soldiers in defence of these Rebels?

—I did not get the opportunity. In the end I felt a little foolish. It was hardly a momentous event. When the annals of America come to be written, I do not think anyone will remember the incident of one Virginian squire crossing a river as the ice formed! There have been much bigger events since then. The last we heard was that Lord Cornwallis had taken Charleston.

—And you really think he will beat the Rebels? Bentley asked.

—No, I do not, said Tom. I think there will be a military victory for King George, but that nothing will quench the desire of the Americans to be independent, free, running their own affairs.

—I think you are right, said Bentley, eagerly. A very faint colour had come into his sickly grey complexion with his second glass of wine.

—Ever since I was a young man, I have known that we were on the verge of extraordinary changes. The superstitions of the past would be replaced by the rational pursuit of virtue. Privilege would be replaced by Merit. In England and in America, we should learn systems of political improvement which would allow cultivated men and women of merit to choose their laws and their law makers. What Jos says about America is true – they complain about not being represented in Parliament, but *he* is not represented in England. He has no vote! A man who has done as much to foster the inventiveness and improve the wealth of England as any man in the kingdom! We must have a system of Government which allows for annual Parliaments, and a widening of the franchise.

Such talk was of no interest to Mary Bentley, who lost no time, when the waiter had come in to clear away the things, to abandon politics and to return without relent to the theme of themes.

—I know nothing of politics, and her tone suggested this was a matter for congratulation. Much more important to me, while he is in London with us, is the procurement of a wife for Mr Byerley!

It should not be difficult, for a bachelor so well favoured, to find a positive queue of heiresses.

—If you carry on at this rate, my dear, you will drive him into a monastery.

Bentley clearly found his wife's ceaseless badinage a source of amusement, even though, as Byerley conceded in his defence, Bentley patently did not share her desire to embarrass him.

—You Wedgwoods have all married cousins.

—Sally is only a very distant cousin of Mr Wedgwood, my dear.

—Even so, I am sure that they have you lined up to marry the gangling daughter.

—Oh, come, said Bentley, we'll hear no unkindness about Sukey.

—Nor did I intend any. I have come to love the child since she lived with us, and she loves us. It is scarcely unkind to observe that the girl has shot up like a bean-pole; and neither parent will do any-thing to educate her for society. Why is her complexion so muddy? Her brow is a gleaming sunset of spots and moisture.

—That is unkind, Mary, unkind.

—Oh come, Mr Bentley, there is such a thing as pearl powder and if Sukey is not old enough to purchase it for herself then her mother could for once take her nose from her book and her feet from her sofa to dab the forehead of her own offspring.

—Sukey will be her own woman, said Tom Byerley, firmly.

—Until she marries, said Mrs Bentley, for whom conversation was a battledore match. No shuttlecock would be allowed to remain in her court if she had the chance to lob it back over the net.

So Tom Byerley was to stay with the Bentleys while he was up in town. By the time the long journey was over, and at varied intervals in the carriage, as at breakfast and dinner in inns, Mrs Bentley had openly discoursed about the marital possibilities which remained open to Tom. Her candour as she embraced the theme had been as painful as it had been pertinent. And the fact that he had responded only with smiles and blushes to much of her talk was not to deny that it had hit its mark.

The prime purpose of Byerley's extended visit to the capital was that he should be more deeply initiated into the 'London end' of the business by Mr Bentley. Since his return to England, he had been a useful Jack of All Trades, by turns teaching the children in the ever-expanding Etruscan Academy, working as his uncle's clerk and doing small pieces of trade. He had ridden to Derby, to Liverpool and to Shrewsbury, offering ware for sale in the small china shops he found there, and he had discovered some aptitude for the task. In short, he had put behind him the lure of the footlights and the smell of grease-paint, just as he had abandoned the lure of literature. The future, whatever its detailed architecture, was to be one of business and practicalities. Poems and plays were to be for his leisure hours.

Far from finding this a disappointment, Byerley found it both a relief and a stimulant. Both reactions surprised him. Only when he had decidedly abandoned any hope for a creative or an imaginative life did he discover what a drain on his nerves it had been. He had never been more than a jobbing actor, and he knew that his success as Macheath owed more to his youthful good looks and the shape of his legs in white tights than it did to any hope of his being another Garrick. Each performance on stage, and each attempt, by the light of a guttering candle in a cheap American bedroom inn, to write tolerable verse or plausible scenes of his next play, brought with it the fear that he might not pass muster. There was a futility in being either a second-rate actor or a third-rate writer, which he had been too proud to acknowledge to himself until the aspiration was set aside. Hence, his relief.

# The Potter's Hand

The stimulant of ordinary work had come as an equal surprise. He already knew that he was quite a good teacher, and, in spite of the puppyish ways of his young male cousins, he had enjoyed taking the children through their conjugations and declensions. The discovery that he could sell his uncle's ceramic wares, and that he could derive positive pleasure from Bentley's instructions in the ways of business, was more unexpected. Aged sixteen, writhing in shame and discomfort on his clerk's stool, Byerley had felt that Art was the only escape from the humiliation of having been born a poor relation, having been born, as are most human beings, into a humdrum family. The calamitous effect of the American war on commerce on both sides of the Atlantic bore home to Byerley the central importance of trade to the smooth running of the world and the maintenance of peace. Every cup and saucer which Uncle Jos manufactured and Mr Bentley managed to sell contributed to that smoothness and that peace.

Besides, having accomplished a business transaction, however modest, even if it were to sell twenty teapots to a china shop in Liverpool, allowed him to eat his dinner, take his leisure, and repose upon his bed with a peaceful sense, as each day closed, that no more was demanded of him until the morrow. The leisure hours did not merely become sweeter in consequence. He found in a strange manner that they were the first leisure hours he had ever enjoyed since his original childish dreams of being an actor and a poet had fashioned themselves in his brain.

Leisure, for Byerley, meant walks in the Staffordshire countryside, sometimes with a rod with which to fish the Trent, or a gun with which to pick off the rabbits and the pigeons in the fields between Newcastle and Burslem. It meant an enjoyment of his reading, which he had never really had while he anxiously supposed that it was his vocation to join the ranks of writers whose excellence he could never match. It meant music, playing upon the harpsichord with Aunt Sally or with Sukey. It meant conversation.

But above all, as was plainly evident in different ways both to Aunt Sally and to Mrs Bentley, it meant the desire for feminine companionship. He knew that he had reached the age where it was not merely expected of him, it was on all rational levels desirable, that he should find a life partner. At the same time, there remained the much more general, unappeasable appetite for experience, for simple gratification, which the proposed six weeks in London had quickened to the point of frenzy. Indeed, so strong was that appetite that the very word 'London' acted upon his imagination as an aphrodisiac, and by the time they had refreshed the horses at an inn in Brentford and clattered the last ten miles of the journey into town, his body was tingling with appetites and demand which could not be overcome. Each avenue and street, each gated square, with its watchman awaiting with a lanthorn on a pole, each yellow-boughed plane tree in autumn moonlight, each barge on the river, each ripple on the Thames as the coach approached Turnham Green (where the Bentleys now resided, having moved from Chelsea) served as promises to him of a crowded programme of erotic pursuit.

The proximity of Soho Square to the Greek Street showrooms gave the young man repeated opportunities to wander about, tormenting himself with the wide range of visual stimulants on offer. On the eastern corner of the square was the enormous brick face of Carlisle House, Mrs Cornelys's Fairy Palace. Inside, there was a Chinese assembly room where music played from the early evening, and where tea, coffee, orgeat and negus were being served. It was possible to sit at a table while consuming these refreshments, but it was preferable to stand, the better to see the swarms of people crowding into the mirrored interior, winding up the stairs and admiring the various rooms and apartments, all fantastically decorated with a wallpaper of climbing plants and flying birds, with grottoes and lamps and chandeliers. Many of the visitors wore masks, and a great number of the women were so provocatively dressed that the very shape of their nipples could be seen through silk and taffeta. He had found himself in a kind of trance, as one woman, dressed in a male Pierrot costume on her nether body, and with her face heavily masked, had stood before him and stroked her breasts, and then moved her fingers slowly, slowly towards her groin.

—Do you like what you see, pretty man? she had asked.

Husky with lust, he had tried to reply, before she laughed, and was lost in the crowd.

The Fairy Palace was only the most glittering of the many places within a short walk of the salerooms which offered sinful ways of filling the idle hour. All the streets which led from Soho down to Covent Garden were lined with women. In one tavern, where he in all innocence asked if there was a bill of fare – intending to eat a veal chop or a plate of bacon and eggs – the waiter brought him a list of more than a hundred names of young women resident in the vicinity, with the most exact descriptions of their physical qualities and the range of activities on offer. 'Miss Jannice Burton has such elasticity in her loins that she can receive even the most distended of gentlemen and cast him into an extasie' . . . 'Miss Riley of Cranbourn Alley gives music lessons, and prefers to help gentlemen with their duets. They can play upon her instrument with their tongue or if they have a larger tool that can be used to tune her strings' . . . 'Miss Dingley has two large dumplings which she would like to display to a discerning connoisseur of her culinary favours. A perfect cherry sits . . .'

Having read this list, and been told that the starting rate was two guineas, Byerley had hastily swallowed his porter and walked out into the street in a daze of confusion. After this, every woman he passed on the crowded pavements looked like a commodity, a notion which was both infinitely exciting and infinitely depressing to his soul. At some turns of his evening walk, he allowed his mind to reason along these lines: he, and Mr Bentley, and Uncle Jos were in London because they had wares to sell. They had paid the best craftsmen and women in England to produce vases, obelisks, busts, dishes, tea sets and dinner sets of the highest quality and they arranged them in Soho in order to make the greatest amount of money.

The blowsy old harridans with their puckered expanses of bare arm and neck and breast, offering younger women to sale to any gentleman willing to part with two guineas, were not so very different from any of the other traders in this wicked old city? So he had allowed himself to ask. And the question had led on to frantic exercises in mental arithmetic: that if he were to save a week's wages and drink no porter in taverns, he could enter into just such a contract, with none of the complications which love had brought him in New York. Here could be a simple transaction, devoid of Mrs Aylmer's demanding tears or Mr Aylmer's wounded anger.

But one turn of the street, and one encounter with a cheaper version of the same 'commodity', was enough to make him feel sick with self-hatred even to have entertained the idea. Coming down an alley behind St Paul's Church, as the evening shadows fell, she called out to him, 'Two shillings for a glass of gin!' He turned, for a moment the businessman superseding the amorist in his brain, as he considered the outrageous overcharging proposed.

—Give me two shillings and I can buy a glass of gin, she said again.

The face which looked at him from its bonnet was scrawny, the teeth were black, the arm which waved its tattered sleeve was little more than bones. But he could see with horror that this apparition was no older than he was himself, even though she appeared to have lived through an infernal eternity longer than he.

Much to his alarm, she had advanced upon him, and such was

the narrowness of the alley, he could not avoid physical proximity.

—Please, give me money! she said through the stench of her rotten gums and fangs, and as her hands clawed desperately at his groin. You can fuck me, ducky, fucky duck. Two shillings!

He tried to get away without making a reply, but when she began to repeat her offers, and when her offers became demands, he said,

—Clear off!

She was so emaciated that as he pushed her away, he felt there was a danger of cracking bones, and as he ran away down the alley, she let forth a stream of furious obscenities.

All the way back to Turnham Green, his head throbbed with the ugliness of the scene. Although he had not actively compromised his virtue with any of these women whom he had seen on that or any previous London afternoon, he felt, nonetheless, that he had done wrong. He wanted bodily gratification so much; he felt so painfully frustrated. The painted women who had excited in him so wide a range of feelings from dizzy excitement to abject fear, from scorn to pity, were all enslaved; but so too were the men, who most definitely included himself, who could think of nothing, as they paced the streets of London, but the allurements of Eros.

—We wondered what had happened to you, young Mr Byerley. Your walks home from the showroom take you longer and longer, said Mrs Bentley at dinner.

And there was no surprise when, towards the end of that repast, she repeated her badinage about his being in need of a wife.

He agreed. But London was disturbing, erotic in a way that Newcastle-under-Lyme was not: fascinating in the activity of its streets, windows, squares and – even if all the women of the taverns and the streets were discounted – full of the energy of life itself. These facts could not be laid to rest simply by Mrs Bentley's zest for matchmaking. During his first month in London, when his admiration for Mr Bentley grew with each passing day, Mrs Bentley arranged for a succession of visitors, all more or less unsuitable, to be brought to dinner, bringing their daughters with them. He would retire from such scenes of embarrassment, his sexual fantasy still immovably fixed upon some dream-woman encountered in the streets. It was several weeks, for example, before he forgot the Pierrot met at the Fairy Palace.

And then, one day, during an interval at the salerooms, his life changed. Mr Bentley and Mr Bell, the rather lugubrious saleroom manager, had received a new consignment of vases, brought down by Caleb's barge in their barrels. It was an especially elegant selection, and Bell had decided that the vases would be shown to best effect if they could be arranged on a series of shelves, of different heights, draped with a deep blue cotton velvet. This being agreed upon, Byerley was asked if he would go down to Meard Street, where he would find a little draper's shop supplying just such velvet as Mr Bell's visual fancy required.

To be asked to visit a draper's shop was, to the son of M. Byerley of Newcastle-under-Lyme, an assignation which brought a combination of feelings: a tender awareness of how little effort he made to write letters to his mother; amusement at contemplating her apparently irrepressible (but who should want to repress it?) self-confidence; and awkward shame at being the son of such a small-scale and unprestigious establishment. Happy as he was, when introduced to strangers, to own himself the nephew of the great Josiah, Byerley was always slower to acknowledge that he was in fact the son of a small shopkeeper.

The shop in Meard Street, easily found, was smaller than M. Byerley. Behind the counter was a young woman whose hair was the colour of sun-scorched timber, so blonde as to be almost silver, drawn back from a pale face. Her eyes were bright blue, the colour of Love in a Mist. She seemed like a girl in a song, every facial quality so perfect as to call forth the most commonplace of epithets, her lips cherry red, her teeth white pearls.

—Yes?

—I . . .

—Is there anything I can do to help you?

—I was looking for . . .

—Are you lost, sir? Maybe you are a stranger in town? Where was you trying to get to?

—Velvet, he at length was enabled to say. I was looking for velvet. The rose-red lips broadened into a laugh.

—I thought you was lost for a minute there.

—So did I.

Mr Bell found it unaccountable that Tom should have come away from the shop with green velvet, when a deep blue had been specified.

—I distinctly remember mentioning the sky at night, said Mr Bell.

—So did I, now you say it, Mr Bell.

—And yet you are able to come here with green. It is almost as if you wanted to be sent back to the shop – for I fear that is what I shall have to ask you to do, to return to Meard Street directly.

But his return to the draper's shop was not to happen that afternoon. He was on the point of setting out there, and he had in his head a whole paragraph of excuses and gallant requests for an extension of his acquaintance with the young woman – even the hope that they would meet again out of shop hours – when the door of the salerooms burst open and Mr Bentley, his face furrowed with anxiety came in.

—Tom, I'm afraid there's news from home.

—Oh?

—Bad news about your mother.

# 8

TWO WEEKS LATER, BYERLEY CAME BACK TO TURNHAM
Green an orphan. His mother's distaste for 'fuss', her neatness, her
desire for meals or games to be tidied away almost before they were
done, and her scorn for displays of emotion had all, in her lifetime,
been emphatic. Byerley, however, could have hoped that her family
should not have been quite so much her imitators when confronted
by her own demise. Everett had showed more emotion than any
relative: an unmistakeable redness in the eyes, as she locked the shut-
ters, and draped the upper windows above the shop with the best
black crepe (the silk warp and worsted from Norwich). The family
had been plunged into mourning clothes, but none of their faces
had betrayed any mark of grief as they presented themselves at the
Unitarian chapel in Newcastle for the obsequies. Uncle Jos had
impatiently looked at his watch, both in the chapel and at the
cemetery.

The sermon by the minister had imparted to the small congrega-
tion various pieces of information of which they were already in
possession: such as, that death came as an end of life, and that it
made no distinction between persons. As to what lay beyond it, the
minister regretted being unable to provide any information, but he
believed it incumbent upon all of them to hope: to hope for a
reunion beyond the grave in a place of light and reason.

—It were a cartload of cant, was Caleb's judgement. He had put on a smarter coat than usual, and wore a black crepe armband.

It was Caleb Bowers who conveyed the coffin, in a black hearse hired for the purpose, to the cemetery. He and two other men from the works drove the coaches which conveyed the dozen or so mourners back to the shop for the baked meats. As was customary in those parts and those days, women did not attend funeral services or interments, but when the men and boys returned from the burial, Heffie Bowers was on hand to help Everett dispense the Madeira and biscuits which were laid out on the counter of the darkened premises where customers were wont to feel lengths of stuff. No one touched Tom. Even Uncle Jos nodded at him, and stiffly held back from so much as stroking his arm or patting him on the back.

—She were right as neenpence when she went upsteer, Everett told the subdued company.

The narration of the proprietress's last moments had been recounted several times, but Everett, who had been kept silent so long by Meg Byerley in life, was not to be silenced now that lady was dead. Besides, the silence which had fallen on the company demanded to be filled.

—Ah luked at t'clock and ah thought, it's not lahk er tubbe two minutes leet, and so ah called oop steer, Are yo aw raight, Mrs Byerley? Silence.

—Oh! Fancy!

Heffie was responding to the narration with the rapt attention appropriate to high drama.

—Mrs Byerley! Ah called and ah called. Eventually, ah thought it canna be raight.

—Na, said Heffie, of course not.

—Ah went oop steer – though she never lahked anywun in er room.

—Bless 'er.

—And she were sitting at 'er dressing table wi' one mob cap in 'er 'and and t- tother . . .

But this point of the story being too poignant for utterance, Everett was unable to finish the sentence, leaving her listeners in a condition of suspended ignorance as to the other cap's whereabouts.

—Bless 'er, added Heffie, awestruck.

Byerley, too, felt no little reverence and fear at the thought of his mother, so solitary and contained to the end, sitting there before her looking-glass, in the very process of her mid-morning change of caps. At one moment the eye which looked at the glass could see its own trim figure, its strong features and pointed chin. At the next, the nothingness was indeed awe-full. In death, he had been even more conscious than in life of her smallness. The stiff, white person in a shroud into whose presence they had ushered him when he came post-haste from London had seemed little bigger than a doll. The shroud, with its white tucks and pleats, its trimming of good Nottingham lace, framed a serious waxy little face which would never again break into that self-protective laughter. The lips were stiff and dry which had formed their ironical *moue* when contemplating human folly, and which had so often been pursed with indignation when confronted with bad taste.

Byerley felt the smallness of life in the presence of that corpse. Uncle Jos and his friends were leaving their mark – in canals, roads, vases, great enterprises. Jos Wedgwood's sister, like almost all human existences, would leave nothing behind it beyond the memories of her son, and of a few others.

For all the others, with the possible exceptions of Everett and Heffie, these memories would be comic, or semi-comic. It was not so much that anyone mocked Mrs Byerley, as that they accepted her own ironies and protective laughter. Absurd too, in the eyes of the others, was the tyranny with which she ruled the passing hours and minutes, and the vicarious pride she had in her brother's wide circle of clients and acquaintance. Affectionate, too, would be the smiles which remembered the High Toryism of the little woman whose brother was so noted a radical. But what was this? A breath! Byerley had some sympathy with the minister for having nothing new to say about this strangest, most unavoidable and calamitous phenomenon.

Between Byerley and his mother there had existed a bond whose profundity was hidden from the rest of the world. Humour, which was both a manifestation of the bond and a part of it, hid from their cousins both its depth and its seriousness. Until a fortnight since, until his departure for the Bentleys in London, she had been relishing every detail of the Portrait drama, of the comings and goings of Mr Stubbs, of the war of wills between Stubbs and Aunt Sally on the one hand and Josiah on the other. When Byerley had told his mother that the children would be depicted with horses, there had been a splutter of laughter.

And now the laughter was stilled, and there was no one left in the world with whom he could enjoy such jokes: for with anyone else, with Mrs Bentley, for example, they would be merely malicious. Meg Byerley had felt no malice towards her brother, her pride in him was unalloyed; but the day by day and week by week comedy of the Wedgwoods' domestic life, and the easy manner in which all Josiah's family patronized her and her son, could all be enjoyed as a gentle joke which had now been silenced for ever.

Jos, as he stood among the small handful of neighbours, cousins and his two eldest sons, all black-coated and pale, allowed himself a small chuckle even as the Madeira and biscuits circulated for a second time. He remembered her forcing a customer to buy mourning crepe which he could not afford, and another, one of the first patrons of the establishment when it had opened in the early days of

Mrs Byerley's widowhood, who had been unimpressed that a particular damask had been favoured for a bedroom at Trentham.

—I don't know where Trentham is and, this intrepidly ignorant passenger (a southerner from her speech) had added, I do not care.

It was one of the many trivial interludes in Meg Byerley's life which had been immortalized as anecdote. For anyone not to have heard of Trentham was, in her scale of values, equivalent to not having heard of the moon. Not to have heard of Lord Gower! Not to have heard of a great house, where Lord Gower and the Duke of Bridgewater had condescended to entertain Mr Wedgwood, not merely for dinner but for the night! Where had such a creature been living?

After the dismal ceremony in the cemetery, and the semi-silences which punctuated Everett's account of his mother's death, Byerley had shared a coach back to Etruria with his uncle. It was then that Josiah first allowed himself a display, if not of emotion, then of fraternal piety.

—Dear Meg. I was very fond of your mother. You know that, lad.

—I do know it, Uncle.

—It is a terrible thing to lose your mother. I wasn't yet nine years old when I followed my Dad's coffin to its burial in Burslem. I were eleven when my mother died. But whatever age you are . . .

—I know, Uncle.

—And now you are alone in the world, young Tom.

The two bays ran gleefully side by side, sometimes nuzzling their cheeks together, and visibly enjoying the speed which their joint effort affected. The carriage swayed calmly as the wheels sprung along the new tarmacadam up the slopes to Burslem and then down, towards Hanley and into the parkland surrounding Etruria.

—You will have to decide what to do about the shop. We must give Everett a pension if you decide to close it down.

—I had not thought about it.

—You must think about it. There are so many things you must think about. Your shop – because it is your shop now. Your future with us, Tom. All our futures.

Byerley knew this was true. In some senses of the word 'think', he thought about it all the time. That is to say, an uncertainty of what was coming next, and a feeling that he should be doing something to direct or shape his own destiny, came over his mind whenever, somewhat ineffectually, he tried to form ambitions or plans.

—You are eight and twenty.

—I know, Uncle.

—Easily old enough to marry.

There was now a very long silence. This was a line of talk which he had not imagined – not for this day.

—I was a good deal older when I married your Aunt Sally, thirty-four years of age and she herself was past thirty. We do not always marry early.

—We?

—In the family, sir!

Josiah's eyes rose heavenwards for help, and he chuckled, as if 'we' could be anyone else.

—We'll have to decide whether you should wait a little, to see how things develop. But there is no one . . . *outside* the family you had in mind, is there, lad?

—Not exactly.

—No secret betrothals? The light laughter which accompanied the enquiry was devoid of any mirth.

—No, none.

—Good lad.

Josiah patted his knee.

—Sukey is a spirited young girl.

Tom Byerley now spoke quickly. He felt dizziness in his ears, and he could feel blood coming into his head, as if he might faint. The strangeness of losing his mother, the painfulness of it, had made him light-headed, and deprived him of the ability, for some days, either to eat much or to sleep. The notion shocked him, that Sukey Wedgwood, still on some mornings of the week his pupil, his little child-friend, now not yet fifteen, should be proposed as a bride to him, with all his range of experience.

—Your Aunt Sal and I have discussed it, Tom. We feel we should like you – especially now your mother has been called away from us – we should like you to be closer, more a part of the family. It would make it easier for you to get a foothold in the firm, boy. Naturally, I hope that my own boys will take over the firm when it is my time to go.

—But there will be many years.

—You never know, boy. Your poor mother's departure makes us realize how suddenly it can come to any of us. In any case, I do not always feel very robust. I get tired, with my old peg leg!

He laughed.

—The boys are good boys, aren't they, Tom?

—Tom in particular is a clever boy, said his namesake.

—You're worried by Jack and Jos's airs and graces? Tom asked. Uncle Jos laughed.

—I prefer to be honest, he added. You have shown yourself a safe pair of hands, Tom. I know you had your adventures in America. But you are back with us now. You are back. You are part of the family. And your Aunt Sal and I just wonder, as you become more and more part of the firm, whether it would not make sense. Sukey's only a lass, but she's growing up fast. Your Aunt Sally's dad put money in the way of our marrying young. But I'd not do that to you, Tom. You'd be araight.

# The Potter's Hand

Was it nervousness, or a sign of how deeply, at that moment, Jos felt their kinship, which led his tongue into the dialect?

—You'd be araight.

The carriage was conveying them now up the sloping drive towards the circle of gravel outside the house. Sukey came running towards them.

—Answering his nephew's silence, the uncle elaborated, changing back into Received English. I mean, you would be all right for money. I'd see you right, my boy.

She was still a half-child, her hair loose behind her, and tied with black ribbons in deference to the solemnity from which Byerley and her father had returned. But Sukey's face was contorted with mirth as she spluttered out,

—Mr Stubbs gave Jack a real wigging for his cheek, and then he said he'd rather paint Gumdrop than a little pup with no manners. And he is going to paint me up on Gumdrop. Mr Stubbs says Gumdrop is a dull little pony and much too small for me. So, you see, I *do* need a new pony! Oh, but, Pa, Cousin Tom, you never met such a rude man! It's killing, how rude he is.

Certainly, the death of Mrs Byerley, at less than sixty, concentrated her son's thoughts. Principally, it renewed his consciousness of how much depended upon his uncle's existence. Owd Wooden Leg had not merely thrown pots, pioneered glazes, sold tea sets, dinner sets, vases, busts and medallions by the score; not merely perfected creamware, black basaltes and jasper; not merely nurtured the skills and artistry of an ever-expanding workforce; not merely given his seemingly irrepressible energy to such schemes of social improvement as the canal system of England, the turnpike roads, and the schools and hospitals for the working people of Burslem; as if this were not enough, he was himself the lynch-pin of the whole vast machine. It was difficult to imagine Mr Bentley carrying on without

Josiah. Mr Bentley was a clever man. And the more time Byerley spent in their company, the more he liked both the Bentleys. Indeed, he had sensed, in the latter stages of the Bentleys' stay at Etruria that he might be the only person in the family (except Sukey, perhaps) to like Mrs Bentley. He recognized that the partnership with Bentley had helped to create Uncle Jos's fortune. Bentley had brought to the partnership a social polish which Jos never felt the need to acquire; and he had already established, before linking his commercial enterprises with Wedgwood, a prosperous export business. But Bentley, clever as he was, knew nothing of the manufacture of ceramics. Bentley could not oversee the works, still less pioneer new ware, new shapes, new glazes. He could only promote the genius of his friend, and, were Josiah to be snuffed out with the suddenness which had removed his sister from the scene, and while the boys were all so young, it was difficult to imagine the enterprise continuing. And yet, it must continue! That was Byerley's growing conviction. Only months after his return to the old country from America, Byerley discovered that it had become his core belief, the centre of his being. The quest for fame by his acting or authorial skills was a dream which had faded like the steamy rise of dew on a summer day.

There was an element of rivalry, that is, rivalry with his puppy-ish young cousins, when he thought the matter through. But such emotions were only flickering at the edge of consciousness. Much stronger was his sense of a wider whole; his vision of a calling. Josiah had built up so much. It was their duty, collectively, to carry it forward. And Mr Bentley could not do it alone. He was not family, for one thing.

Therefore, when Byerley returned to London with the Bentleys after his mother's funeral, it was with a quickened imperative to learn Mr Bentley's skills. He visited the Chelsea works with great regularity. He attended the Greek Street showrooms daily, and began to learn, from Mr Bentley's instructions, how to read balance sheets, how to keep stock, how to notice or predict a run on any particular item, duly alerting Josiah by letter of any need to re-order. In spite of the slump in American sales, there had been brisk sales at home of medallion portraits, and the numbers sold suggested an evenly divided political outlook among the customers: about half rushing to buy souvenir portraits of Franklin and Lafayette, and others expressing loyalty by the purchase of jasper reliefs of the King and Queen.

—It is bad for trade, Tom, bad for trade, was Mr Bentley's almost daily saying. Not only have sales to the Americans died down to almost nothing, it is months, and in some cases years, since we received payment from the shops in Williamsburg, Philadelphia, Boston, New York.

By the end of another month, Byerley felt he had advanced, not only in Mr Bentley's affections, but also in the mysteries of trade.

—Since your Uncle John died, we needed one of you, by which Bentley meant he needed a Wedgwood, to look after the London end.

The more that Byerley felt himself settling into the business, the more rational it appeared to him that he should follow his uncle's advice in his matrimonial ambitions. The quagmire of emotion which he had left behind in America would not be repeated in London. That he promised himself. What could be more practical than to keep things in the family, and marry young Sukey when this became practicable? She did not love him, and he had no thoughts, until his uncle raised the proposition, that he could love her, in the manner normally expected of husbands, rather than cousins.

Returning to London, he felt that an extraordinary hollowness, a coldness, an emptiness had come into life. He wondered, without being able to answer the question at all satisfactorily, whether his mother had been lonely. She had hated what she called 'drawing attention', and hence, emotional display had been foreign to her. When he left for America, he had not allowed himself to contemplate what she felt as he kissed a powdery cheek. When he returned, and kissed the same cheek in the same spot, she had merely said, as the eight-day clock chimed twelve,

—Everett said it would be two o'clock before you arrived, but I think I know Tom Byerley better than that.

The withdrawal of his mother was a further reminder that life must be pursued before the generalized phrase 'it is too late' became applicable to all its choices, professional and emotional. There was no future with the young draper's assistant of Meard Street. Her beauty was simply a distraction now.

Her skin, of the very white, slightly moist fingers (he found the moisture disturbing in their allure) and of the white brow framed by the pale straw hair, was what captivated him, almost more than the eyes, the lips, the general positive demeanour. She was a young person saying an unambiguous YES to life, and for a woman of eighteen to be saying this from a darkened shop in Soho, there was something heroic: at any rate, if that adjective were too much to apply to someone so jolly and smiling, at least it had the quality of heroism, it was a defiance of all the melancholy things which Byerley had already encountered in the last year: a defiance of death, a defiance of cruelty and conflict.

—I thought you'd forgotten me, was her greeting, with a display of pearl teeth, when he returned to the shop with a spurious request for ribbon.

—I had to go away.

—Lucky for some to be able to! she had quipped. And no good purpose would be served at that juncture of things to explain the reason for his absence in the north. And when he came out of the shop, with a coil of silk ribbon which her moist fingers had wrapped for him in a twist of paper, he felt the familiar shudder of conflicting emotions. On the one hand, he wanted her, and it did not especially trouble him on what terms this possession might be accomplished. She seemed pertly willing enough, so he did not have any sense of guilt; here, surely, was no case of the exploitation of innocence. On the other hand, things had changed. And after the purchase of the ribbon, he turned to one of the new bookshops in Golden Square, and tried to remember which novels Sukey had told him she wanted to read when she had finished *Joseph Andrews*. He lighted on a prettily bound set of *Evelina, or the History of a Young Lady's Entrance into the World.*

# 9

AS THE BARGE HAD PULLED AWAY FROM THE QUAY AT Etruria, Mr Stubbs's great glossy Houyhnhnm-eyes had focused, first on the eyes of Hotspur, who ran backwards and forwards barking and laughing at the movement of the boat and at Caleb's shout – *Give over, Hot, get off with yer bother* – and then Stubbs's eye had seen the munching cows over hawthorn hedges. Their faces, as vivid as the dog's, their moist noses, their large contemplative eyes, as they looked up at the passing barge, and waited a moment as ordure splattered the sward at their hooves, were in the sharpest, brightest focus. The boyish figures of Jack and Jos Wedgwood, who yelled from the bank to Mr Stubbs to be sure not to be late for dinner – for their Pa had invited the Quality to dine with them to meet the famous painter – these human dolls were as dull as hay-stooks. He saw their pink faces and heard their voices, but nothing in their personalities was conveyed to him as he savoured a few hours' relief from their company. They passed Trentham, Lord Gower's place, a backcloth of dolls' house and trees against which could be seen the lustrous sheen of four splendid chestnut hunters with cropped tails in emerald fields.

Caleb, as sensitive to another's mood as the Wedgwood boys were indifferent, allowed the painter to absorb what he saw in silence, only occasionally calling out routine instructions to his nephew. June in all its profusion burst on either bank its sprays of Queen Anne's Lace, cow parsley, red campion, hawthorn white and pink. It had lately rained, and the billowing white and charcoal clouds promised rain again as they brooded in the pale blue sky, and the hedges and bushes of privet and thorn were slick with moisture. Beneath, around the towpath, the red sludge of clay and the bright emerald tufts of grass grew thick against the muddy wetness beneath the hedges, dank with leaf mould and the animal life of rats and voles. With the speed of an eye-blink a kingfisher swooped from a low-lying beech branch over the greenish, flat water. From the canal itself there came the richest smell of summer dampness. Roach and chub jumped to the surface. By the time Trentham had been left behind, and following the magnificent tail and haunches of the shire horse who dragged them, they slowly approached Stone, the sky had quite clouded over; and by the time they moored behind Caleb's cottage, and Dandelion was being given her nosebag of oats, great drops of water had begun to fall once more, causing more fish to leap and kiss the canal surface with open lips, more rats to scurry out from bank holes to swim across the surface of the water, and more of the delicious odour of dampness and weed to come from the canal, more of the half-rank, almost uriney smell to come from the thorn bushes around the garden door and the currant bushes which grew in such abundance at the edge of the kitchen garden. The small door was set in a high, new-built red brick wall. Leaving the boy with rudimentary instructions about the horse,

—Tie 'im oop 'ere, Ted, an' we'll go down t' Henshaw's when I've been in ter see yer mother,

Caleb led the way through the door. It gave Stubbs satisfaction that the sudden cloudburst, which was in fact pleasant, not least because of the exciting smells of moisture which it all but instantaneously enhanced, provoked in Caleb none of the foolish expressions of shock, or disappointment or self-pity which town-bred or the would-be genteel let out whenever it rained, and they squawked for their fool umbrellas.

—Tryin', was what Caleb said when Stubbs noted that they were growing some apples.

—Those trees there are russets, as you probably recognize. That there's a Bramley, for pies. And we're growing some Conference pears, see how they'll go along.

The orchard was set a little apart from a handsome kitchen garden in which potatoes were already well grown, and peas and beans were halfway there in their ascent of neatly made triangles of ash. Netting covered the odiferous currant bushes and the raspberry canes which grew against the wall opposite, beside a clump of hazel trees. A tidy brick path crossed the greensward and led to Stonefield Cottage, a pretty twenty-year-old house of three storeys, symmetrically constructed of red brick, with brightly painted white windowframes and a shiny back door.

—I'm leading you in through the back offices. We don't stand on ceremony.

—Nor do I.

Caleb did not say that, apart from rather stilted calls from members of their immediate family in which aunts or cousins would sit bolt upright at the tea table, or the necessary calls of tradespeople, or the physician, and in earlier days, the midwife, this was in fact the first time that he or his sister had ever entertained a visitor to the cottage. They entered by a small tile-covered corridor, on either side of which were back-kitchens or sculleries; in one of these laundry was suspended from various ingenious racks and devices, and in the other, crockery, pots and pans, all gleamingly clean, were hung from hooks or arranged on orderly shelves. The tiled floor led on into the front hall, where, to the left, there was a small panelled dining-parlour and to the right a living room in which a kitchen range filled the chimney. From this room emanated the delicious mingled odours of baking – a rabbit pie, and some fruit stewing – from the oven, and of Heffie herself, sweaty in face and armpit, as she looked up, a little anxiously, but with a warm smile as the two men entered.

Caleb saw Heff, as usual, at work at the range. He also sensed immediately what he had previously only half-suspected, that she welcomed the painter's attention. A range of unconnected thoughts ran through his brain: the unavoidable sense of exclusion born of his sister desiring a man (this was a familiar emotion to Caleb since youth, but it never failed to sting him, and today it stung particularly because it came as a surprise); this thought, this immediate readjustment to a new situation, this recognition of what, emotionally, was going on in his small house, brought with it an amused sense of the Wedgwood tragi-comedy. It required no gift of clairvoyance to see for whom the baking had been undertaken; nor to guess the end of the rabbit pie and the stewed bottled plums. Nor was it difficult to imagine the fluster and botheration at Etruria, as the Swynnertons and the Gowers, with their lady-folk, drew up in their carriages at the dinner hour to be met by their hosts and no celebrated artist.

—Thee's bin bakin, Heff!

—Making pies – thought I'd make one for thee – thee's off tomorra?

—Ay, dine ter London agin.

Heffie had known, more or less from his arrival at Etruria, that Mr Stubbs was available to her. Her attitude to the comings and goings of erotic pleasure and possibility had, since the death of her last lover and the father of Ted, been entirely matter of fact. She had her three boys, two of them employed down at the works by Josiah and one of whom helped Caleb on the barge. The five of them, Uncle Caleb, Ted, William and Joshua, had formed a family. She was aware, without the matter ever having been discussed, that she was now 'with' Caleb for life or until he chose to take a wife. This, as he approached the age of fifty in a state of complete celibacy, Heffie regarded as something he was unlikely to do.

When they were adolescents, Heffie had ribbed Caleb about his fastidiousness towards sexual activity. Later she had come to see that 'it', the whole strangeness of her brother's character and his 'attack' on existence, had mysteriously to do with the death of their mother, the repeated calamities of their early life together, the smallpox, the poverty. 'It' also mysteriously had to do with the prodigious success of Josiah – but, as far as sex was concerned, there, thought Heffie, was another on 'em. For all Josiah's eight children, she knew, from the sobbed confessions of Sally, what had and had not gone on there.

But for Heffie, things had always been different. She had initiated Hardy, Ted's dad, into a life of regular and satisfying performance. It would be wrong to say that it was central to her life, since, so obviously, it was her sons and her brother, and her duties of kindness to Sally Wedgwood (in some ways her best friend) which were the central things to Heffie's existence. On another level, however, sex had provided, more or less since the onset of puberty, the well of hidden joy which consoled, excited and rejoiced Heffie's life.

She had set up with Wilbraham when she was seventeen, but she was not a virgin even then. Love, of the kind sung about in tavern songs and recited in ballad sheets, had never so much as flickered across her heart. Love – as she understood the term – was for Caleb and the boys; it was for her mum and dad, and for the poor old Wedgwoods. She shared Caleb's view that, were it not for herself and her brother, the Wedgwoods would 'fall to bits', and on a practical level there was much truth in this. The dullness of most of Heffie's daily routines, the washing, scrubbing, slicing, peeling, rubbing, flouring, baking, ironing, pressing of material objects, which took up so much of her waking life, made it almost inevitable that she should seek an outlet of physical satisfaction whenever this was offered. It first came to her when she was working as a twelve-year-old girl at Neale's works in Fenton (she forgot why she had gone to work at Neale's, rather than at one of the Wedgwood works nearer home). There was an established code at most of the Potteries in those days – though such a code would never have been tolerated for a second by the puritanical and orderly Wedgwoods, either at Brother Tom's Brickyard Works, or at the ever-expanding empire of Josiah. In many of the pot works, the men and women divided into two distinct camps. Some, when the work was done, went home to their families, to reappear the next day when the horn blew for work. (Owd Wooden Leg had pioneered the use of the bell to summon his work-force in Burslem but nearly all the other potteries used horns for the purpose.) The rest remained behind at the works, wherever the works happened to be. It was then that the bottles and barrels were pro-duced, and, when drink had been taken, that the frolics began.

In after time, especially when Methodism had swept through the Potteries, there were those who spoke of dissipation, corruption, and all the sins about which the Bible is so salaciously eloquent. For Heffie, from an early age, it was one of those things, a lark lahk, why not.

The sight of old Mr Farley, the best modeller Neale ever employed, calmly lowering his breeches after a pint or so of porter, and calling out, Raight, lassies, who'd lahk ter sample a luvly bit o' Farley's cock?, was to Heffie purely comic and charming. The animals in the farmyard chased one another around, nuzzled against one another's bottoms, rutted, as season and Nature decreed, without any obvious feelings, except those of bodily pleasure. Why should we, also the creatures of Nature, presume that we were so superior?

That was Heffie's view. When Caleb had found out about the

'orgies' – such was the word used by the scandalized who took no part in them – at Neale's works, he had insisted upon her leaving. She had lied to Caleb of course and said that she had seen nothing and done nothing. The truth, however, was that after one of these afternoon revels, she had, before she was thirteen, lost her virginity to a sturdy thrower called Cyril Sawyer. He was about sixteen, and she would never forget the pleasure of seeing him undress – she had not removed any clothes, simply lifted her skirts, for she had never worn breeks or knickers – and allowed him to initiate her. The first time had hurt a little, but nothing you'd mention; thereafter, for a year or so until Caleb sensed that all was not right, she had enjoyed not only Cyril Sawyer, but also Abe Wright, James Wilson, Sol Adams and George Watson. She had begun to develop a sense of what pleased her, and never for one particle of a second did she feel guilt or awkwardness or self-hatred.

Neither she nor Caleb was religious, but when she came across the conventional viewpoint, expressed either from pulpit or in the secular conversation of the Wedgwoods, that there was something shameful about this area of life, she simply thought they were 'avin' a laff. It seemed to her supremely ridiculous to attach moral significance to what happened in your drawers. Some liked one thing, some another. Some did not need it so much as others. Some wanted it all the time. That was all. There were no need to go on 'baht eet.

Such was Heffie's view. Clearly, since the demise of Hardy, the last attachment, the opportunities to indulge herself were few and far between. When they arose, she did not turn aside from the possibilities of pleasure.

———

At Etruria Hall, the anticipation of Lord Gower's arrival for dinner had an effect upon the atmosphere comparable to one of Dr

Darwin's or Mr Franklin's harnessings of natural electricity. The air fizzed, as Josiah clonked from hall to drawing-room, from drawing-room to dining-parlour, from dining-parlour to kitchens, to make sure that matters were in order.

—Mrs Hassall, thee hast ow a' raight?

—Ay, Mr Jos, everything's a' raight, ta very mooch, dinna thee fret theesel, Mr Jos.

—Thee hast sowp onta booble?

—Ah'm joos pootin the mooton patties inter ceek nie, Mr Jos. Ellen, lass, pass me that plate . . .

—Ah' hope ah'm not in thee road, Mrs Hassall.

—Well . . . Politeness wrestled with the bustling need to get from one side of the kitchen to the other without having to squeeze past her employer, and the professional's longing for him to go away.

—So, we 'ave mooton patties . . .

—Lahk Mrs Wedgwood sed, yo 'ave three sort sowp – turtle, asparagus and Palesteen; then theers they patties – mooton, if they ever gets ter t'oven, and beef, and mushroom; then there's they joints rowstin as thee can sey, Mr Jos – we've the turkeys, the mooton, the chickens as thee can sey, Mr Jos. Boot, eef thee disna mahnd na, a woman needs ter be left alorn in her ine kitchen!

It was the same in all parts of the Hall. Footmen, who only hours before had been labourers in the works, carrying saggars on their heads, now reeking with nervous sweat under unaccustomed wigs, stood on liveried guard in the Hall a full hour before His Lordship's arrival. The place settings in the dining-parlour were checked a dozen times by Josiah: new silver gleamed on the white damask cloths. Sweet peas clustered beside the Corinthian columns of basaltes candlesticks. There was an undoubted grandeur, a solemnity, about the black basaltes candelabra on the dinner table, and the black vases, topped with a pine-cone shape and adorned with drapery swags, which stood upon the brand-new mahogany pedestals either side of the serving tables. These tables, groaning with foods, and the pedestals, and the austere Adam chimney piece were all encrusted with jasperware medallions: nymphs and deities, frozen and dead.

Seeing it all reflected in the crystal of the torchieres and the huge oval looking-glass, gleaming in its glossy new gilt, Sukey anatomized with an attention to detail which would have done credit to the painter – had he returned from Stone to witness the august occasion.

The room itself, designed for show, had not quite shaken off the feel and appearance of a showroom. There was nothing domestic about it. Nor was there much domestic about the studied formality of the diners who sat, as the afternoon sun began to blaze in the windowpanes, like bored dolls, while Mrs Hassall's attempts at a *grande cuisine* came and went, largely untasted. (The fricassee of soles was rank and rubbery; the little pasties, whether of mutton or beef, all tasted of nothing; and everything, from soup to entrees, was lukewarm and greasy.)

—I do indeed, sir, I do indeed mean what I say, Lord Gower was saying. There is no reason why we should not reconquer the colonies! Why, sir, we have a standing army in the Bahamas Islands. We could capture Florida from the Spaniards tomorrow and fight back to win the Carolinas and Virginia for the Loyalists, and indeed all thirteen colonies for the Crown. But we must see what our young Prime Minister has to say on the subject!

—Young Mr Pitt has troubles enough at home, surely, said Dr Darwin, and he made his views on America clear on many occasions in the House of Commons.

Lord Gower, a prune-faced man of sixty, had been spoken of as the next Prime Minister when, only a few weeks earlier, Lord Shelburne's Ministry had fallen. The King had in fact offered him the post, though no one round that table knew of this fact at the time. Instead, he served as Lord President of the Council under the younger Pitt. He was accompanied on his visit to Etruria by his wife, Susannah, whose fantastical hair, dressed and piled as high as Mama's had been when she was presented to the King and Queen in London, towered towards the crystal chandeliers; and by his young son George. The party, who had arrived in a splendid equipage from Trentham Hall, with two powdered footmen on the outside, were perfectly friendly, but it was not an easy occasion. Sukey watched her father attempting a gentlemanly demeanour and achieving only what Dr Darwin mercilessly called shop manners. Mama, talking to Lord Gower as best she could, felt evident nervousness, and her voice was quiet and quavery.

—There is no accounting for the artistic temperament, I am afraid, my lord. Mr Stubbs has gone to Stone and forgotten the time.

—That, said Mr Stubbs, as she was saying these words, is the best rabbit pie I ever ate.

Caleb had tactfully finished his dinner in a rush and gone out with Ted to attend to the barge and the horse. Stubbs held out his hand across the kitchen table, and Heffie enclosed his big soft-tipped fingers in her red palms. She smiled, enjoying the feast for his eyes which was provided by her loosely laced, large and quivering bosom.

—Not since last year, Sukey said, when George Leveson-Gower asked her when she was last in town, and whether she had seen *The Spaniards in Peru*. He gave her a somewhat laborious account of its plot, and then, with many a happy laugh, tried to repeat the plot of *A School for Scandal*, the last play he'd seen before *The Spaniards*.

Sukey was too polite to tell him that he had mistaken the name of two of the characters. It was Sir Peter Teazle, not Sir Peter Thistle, and Sir Benjamin Backbite, not Sir Benjamin Slander. But they both laughed when they recollected, more or less accurately, 'Your ladyship must excuse me, but I leave my character behind me.'

George was about to go up to Oxford, but he did not appear to have read many books, and having inadvertently discovered his ignorance of *Sir Charles Grandison, Evelina* and *Tom Jones,* Sukey abandoned literature as a topic and spoke of local families known to them both.

Dr Darwin was having scarcely better luck with Lady Gower.

—When my husband represented you in Lichfield.

—Before my time there, ma'am, and now we have left dear old Lichfield behind us. We've moved to Derby. My daughters run a school there.

—Indeed, my good Doctor, I cannot for the life of me imagine why any young girl whose parents have pretensions to gentility should wish to fill her head with books.

—Perhaps because she has to fill it with something, ma'am, he said, and, upon noticing her ladyship's shocked expression, he added, Or again, perhaps not.

—And what of you, young Sukey? Lord Gower suddenly asked. You are the person at this table most affected by the question of the education of young ladies.

—I think it desirable, my lord, that a woman should be the companion, if not the equal, of her husband. My Mama . . . here she faltered, but Lord Gower, with a kindly courtesy which surprised her, said,

—Go on, my dear.

—I think my Mama would not have been so good a companion for my Pa had she not been well read and rational.

—Bravo! called Josiah, and they all laughed as Sukey blushed.

When the laughter died, Sukey ventured,

—At first, Pa, you commissioned Mr Stubbs to paint the boys doing a scientific experiment, while we girls sat at the harpsichord as decorative as those.

She pointed at the centre of the table; whether at the sweet peas or the frozen black basaltes nymphs who upheld the candelabra, it would have been hard to distinguish.

—I'm afraid I lost that battle, said Josiah. He's painting Sukey on her pony, as Mrs Wedgwood predicted.

And they all laughed.

Lord Gower was far from being a fool, and when the atmosphere melted sufficiently, talk around the table became general, with Lady Gower's haughty imbecilities and young George's giggling asides drowned by a discussion of Dr Darwin's latest design for an artesian well which he had dug and designed near his new house in Derby. Gower immediately grasped the principle and said,

—But this could provide clean water for half the houses in England!

And they had fallen to talking of decorative fountains, and how these might be set in motion by natural pressure if the water came down from a sufficient height.

—Now at Chatsworth, sir, or Haddon, I can see such a scheme in operation, for there you have heights. But at Trentham, with our calm undulations and gentle-flowing Trent, I see no chance of another Versailles!

The men, prompted by the mention of the French King's palace, fell to discussing European politics. Dr Darwin and Josiah were optimistic about the American spirit of equality and democracy spreading through the continent, while Lord Gower viewed events with alarm.

—Consider, sir – sirs! You see a continent of Benjamin Franklins, sanely debating their future and spreading abroad literacy, decency and rationality. What if the mob were less reasonable? What if they saw the chance, in reform, for revenge on a thousand years of what they considered to be oppression?

—If it were oppression, my lord? asked Josiah.

—Is oppression always a bad thing? asked young George with an idiotic laugh.

—If the cruel oppression of the people provokes violent outrage. Sukey could scarcely believe her ears, and her own response, which burst spontaneously from her, was incoherent, less because she did not know what she thought, than that she could not absorb the possibility of George's imaginative limitations.

—You applauded the Americans shedding the blood of His Majesty's soldiers? asked George.

—I never applaud the shedding of blood, she replied indignantly. But injustice; one of the first principles of physics is that action and reaction are equal and opposite. The American war came out of English intransigence. We will only have a peaceful world when we have a just one. Until then,

> Air, earth, and ocean, to astonish'd day
> One scene of blood, one mighty tomb display!
> From Hunger's arm the shafts of Death are hurl'd,
> And one great Slaughter-house the warring world!

George looked at her as if she were a madwoman.

Sukey, who knew she had said too much, sank back into silence. She reflected, with a mixture of horror and amusement, that one day, perhaps not long after he had spent three years at Oxford drinking too much and keeping a hunter in the college livery stables, this young man would ask a young woman to marry him, and they would stay together for the rest of their lives according to God's holy ordinance.

—Well said, were the words at her left, from Cousin Byerley.

—Well said, he pursued, in quoting the great doctor's lines. Well said earlier, about the happiest marriages being those where men and women are equal companions, and where their shared experiences, their shared reading, their shared . . .

—Where they can be little more than friends? she asked glancingly. And then she felt she had said too much, and she was grateful for Mr Stubbs, bursting into the dining-parlour unannounced.

—Mr Wedgwood, your grand dinner table! And here I am in my working clothes. Lord Gower, sir, Lady Gower! I have just been conveyed past Trentham Park in a rowing boat by young Ted Bowers.

—We thought you had forgotten us, sir, said Josiah, not without asperity.

—I dare say you did, said Stubbs, not to be put down.

Apparently oblivious to the potential dismay brought on by his absence of ceremony, he had reached himself for a chair and, lifting it, placed it between Sukey and Lady Gower.

—As you may know, my lady, he said, I have my hands full here. Mr Wedgwood wants me to paint his children, and we are still at the discussing stage.

—Indeed, sir? asked Josiah.

—Sketches, studies. I have too many obligations to Mr Wedgwood to think of hurrying the work. But while we contemplate the final design, I have been looking about me, so to say. Today I did a pencil study of Bowers's head – you know Caleb Bowers, the bargee? A fine man. He took me down to Stone, and I shall return there.

—Poor Papa, murmured Sukey to Cousin Byerley, and they both

smiled conspiratorially at the exaggerated comic exasperation on Josiah's face.

—But if, while I mull over the best way to paint the Wedgwood family in all their glory, said Stubbs, there would surely be the opportunity to come over to Trentham and see the inside . . .

He leaned towards the magisterial, statuesque figure of Lady Gower, whose bulbous grey eyes and rolls of chin seemed comically to forbid such ribaldry.

—You'd let me, ma'am, would you not, if I asked you very politely, you'd allow a man to have a surreptitious glance inside your . . .

—Inside my what, sir?

—Inside your stables! said the painter with an air of triumph.

# IO

THE SERGEANT HAD GONE BELOW, LEAVING HIS WIFE stretched on the bed, with one hand nursing a bruised cheek. It was the first time he had struck her. Sadloli, or Merry as she perhaps now had to be called, had only a limited experience of men. There had been young braves in the village, and there had been Tom. The difference of feeling between her early experiments as a young girl and her mature love for Tom was immense. But in no case had there been difficulties.

Each time the attempt had been made with the sergeant there had been failure. She knew that her own body was not responding to him as it should, but her sense of justice told her that she must try to make it a success. When she knew, or suspected, that he would make another attempt, she had therefore made herself ready as best she could. So there was no actual difficulty of entry, as there had been the first time, on board the ship, on the day of their being married by the ship's captain.

The first failure she had attributed to drunkenness, and to his inexperience, and to the strangeness of their being alone and naked together on a ship – though with another man, the strangeness of the cabin and the heaving of the vessel and the noise outside the porthole of the crashing ocean would all have been a stimulus to the act of love. But now there had been enough failures for her to be unable to blame external factors, such as drink. There was something within this man which made him unable to be fully a man.

Part of her felt immense relief. He was her means of coming to England, and she had married him solely for this reason. To deny him marital rights, however, would have been a base act. To offer herself to him was, in the circumstances, the least she could do. She tried different approaches. She tried gentle stroking, she tried the stimulus of hand and of mouth, she tried pinching, squeezing, hugging, but all to no avail. The cloud of his self-reproach descended between them and turned swiftly to anger. On some occasions when she was trying to please him, he would shrink – call her crude names, accuse her of being a whore. On this occasion, he had pounced upon her and tried to perform the act quickly, but there was an unwonted semi-tumescence, it wasn't enough to be effective, and when she used her hand to try to guide him inside her, the small serpent had shrunk to a timid slug.

—Why, you . . .

He had been furious and struck her face. And then she was alone in the room, and he had gone downstairs and next door to one of the many alehouses with which they were surrounded in Wapping High Street.

Soon, he had told her, they would find an alehouse of their own to run. Since his discharge from the army, they had both subsisted upon casual labour. She served in one of the alehouses, he in another. He had been asked by Captain Gower to work as a slave-catcher, but since the Somerset case, there was less mileage in that.

Slave-catching was now quite definitely illegal, but it still went on, and men like Captain Gower, whose chance of expanding their holdings of land in the Caribbean were directly consequent upon the numbers of slaves they owned, were intent upon catching as many runaways as possible.

Sergeant Powell reckoned there were about twenty of Gower's slaves at large in the capital.

—Poor men, his wife had said.

—I'm not saying, the sergeant said, as I'd approve of enslaving my fellow man, poor devils. Not if we started with a clean slate. But the Captain, he paid good money for those darkies, see. There's no use wearing that sad face, Merry, my girl. Slavery's a nasty business, but there's no changing the world.

So, that was how her husband spent his days when he was not drawing ale at the local taphouse, the Dockers' Tavern. Looking for runaways, an illegal trade, but he was paid half a crown a time by those who enlisted him. He had found three so far. Two were working as stevedores, downriver in St Katharine Docks, and one he had apprehended in an apothecary shop, where the former slave was working behind the counter. And now she lay, in a tiny, cold room beneath the eaves of a creaking old house in Wapping, with damp plaster and the wattle of the ceiling visible, and held her hand to her cheek.

She was numb with misery.

In America, her grief and rage about what had happened had pro- vided a strange kind of energy. It had felt as if she had a purpose in life: to get to England, somehow, to find out the truth of what had happened in her village, and if necessary to exact the proper revenge on her former lover. The presence, so near the ruins of the Cherokee town, not merely of redcoats, but of Staffordshire redcoats who knew of Wooden Leg, had been an opportunity which she could not turn down. She had worked as a servant in the barracks, doing their chores, washing their shirts, serving their meals. The jolly Welsh ser- geant who had so ostentatiously 'taken a shine' to her provided her with her transatlantic passage.

Since her arrival in London, however, her perspective on

everything had changed. She longed to escape. While her husband was out, she would walk down the stairs which led to the water's edge and look across the river at the numerous ships with their masts and rigging. Surely one of them would take her back to America? The whole journey, the whole revenge-exercise, the whole pursuit of Tomtit and Wooden Leg, seemed like an act of madness.

Rising from the bed, she splashed her scalding cheek with some of the cold water in the basin on the dressing table. She put on her slip, and over that, the small hoop which she wore round her waist, and the dark blue dress and white apron which she wore for working in the tavern. How strange was the European costume! She felt she would never get used to wearing stays as she tied herself into them. She wound her plaited hair into a bun, which she pinned against her scalp, and she squeezed it into the grey cap, frilled with white lace, which was now her daily wear. One of the only presents Powell had ever given her was a plaid rug, woven by Scottish islanders, and this she wrapped round her shivering shoulders.

Outside the tavern, she walked along the High Street to a spot of lawn, where there were some well-built houses of gentlefolk dating from early in the century. A low-lying silvery mist hung on the water. She walked on, past tavern after tavern. In this part of London there was a great preponderance of black men and women. Some were escaped, or liberated, slaves. But there were many who were working as shopkeepers, innkeepers, free household servants, dockers. Others were employed as entertainers, pugilists, tumblers, conjurors, Punch and Judy men.

She had no particular aim in mind as she walked. The Tower of London loomed up on her left as she entered the City, and from the hill above it, she could look down on the gloomy, all-but-frozen winter scene, of silver mist and grey rooftops and gelid, dripping masts and dank water. It was a strange walk, which took her into the centres of commerce near the Bank. She passed many churches. Frequently, she became lost, but then she would get a sense of direction once more. She reached the great domed Cathedral and gasped at its beauty. Then she walked down to the river again, and shiveringly made her way eastwards along its banks. Strangely, this walk gave her strength. Her spirits were still unutterable in their sadness, but she still had her spirits. She arrived half an hour early for her shift in the tavern where she worked, because Solomon, the African tapster whom she had befriended, was teaching her to write, and she was making good progress in her lessons.

—What's this? she asked, before they began.

—What do you think of it?

She held in her hand what Solomon had offered her. It was a small ceramic button. Yellow biscuit ware, with a black relief. It depicted a negro in chains, and round its perimeter were the words, AM I NOT A MAN AND A BROTHER?

—They are giving them away, he said.

—Who are?

—The man who made them. He is a potter, an English potter. He is very well known. He has come to the help of our people. He is against the slave trade. He has made these buttons – also medallions, with the same device. A black man in chains asking the question, Am I not a man and a brother? That must be a remarkable man, must it not, an Englishman, a white man, who gives away these buttons and medallions in Soho?

—Does he, she asked, does he have a wooden leg?

It was this encounter which led Blue Squirrel to learn the craft of throwing on a potter's wheel.

While her husband was out in his gruesome pursuit of runaways, she herself went upon the quest for Wooden Leg's showrooms in Soho. In the normal course of events, this would have led her to meet with Tom Byerley, but as it happened, he was away on one of his business trips, a tour which involved a visit to Bath and a replenishment of the company's showrooms there. She had asked of Mr Bell, the manager, whether there was a chance to see the workshops at the back of the salerooms. Bell was under strict instructions from Mr Wedgwood and Mr Byerley not to allow strangers to snoop. There were poor imitations on the market of Wedgwood jasper, Wedgwood creamware and Wedgwood black basaltes, and Josiah was right to suspect his rivals of industrial espionage. Something about Meribah Powell's face, and the gravity of her enquiries, however, made even the serious-minded Mr Bell relent, and he took her to the back of the showrooms in Soho, to the yard where there were throwing and modelling rooms.

—I am a potter, she said, but I never saw this.

It was a miracle to her eyes! A man sat at a wheel kicking a treadle which operated a fly-wheel. As the wet lathe spun in obedience to his feet, he threw a lump of clay into the centre, and, with the quickest of manual squeezes, it became a bowl. With a wire, he detached it from its base.

All shyness left Meribah Powell.

—But this is wonderful! We only made our pots, built them up by hand. We had no wheel.

The potter looked up and smiled at her.

—What sort of pot works is that?

Mr Bell looked at the potter, and the potter looked back at Mr Bell. Their looks seemed to say, 'This woman is not a spy. She comes in a spirit of innocence.'

—May I try it? she asked.

All three, Blue Squirrel, the London potter whose name was

Morrel, and Mr Bell, knew what was going to happen next. The atmosphere of the moment made it impossible for anything other to happen. She was helped into an apron, and she rolled up the sleeves of her frock. She sat at the stool before the wheel, and kicked the treadle into action. Mr Morrel stood behind her, guiding her hands. The first bowl was a little wobbly, but the second was near perfect. Then, with a strange swoop of her right hand, as if her hands knew things which had not yet been taught them by her brain, she made a little vase, very much in the shape of the vases which she had hand-built in Old Kowes.

The three human beings were silent when she had finished. They knew something very strange had happened. They knew that a woman from nowhere had walked into the shop and, never having thrown a pot in her life, had been able to do so.

It was from this experience that Blue Squirrel, before her husband was offered the proprietorship of a public house in Staffordshire, had acquired the skills of an English potter. There was no work for her at the Soho works, and Mr Bell said that he had no authority to employ her in the absence of Mr Tom. She had noted the name, she did not need to be told his identity. But they gave her the address of a small pottery in Clerkenwell, nearer her Wapping lodgings. Sergeant Powell forcefully objected to the idea of her taking work, but he recognized that they were not earning enough from his activities as a slave-catcher to save for the longed-for hour of release when they got a 'pub of their own'. So, he allowed her to go out to the Clerkenwell works, and it was there that she learnt to throw pots. It was a small firm, which made cups, saucers, coffee-cans, teapots and other domestic items. When she came to the master, Mr Wigg, after only a few months in his employ, to say that she was moving to Staffordshire, he told her he was sorry to see her go.

—I never saw a better modeller, he said, and I mean that,

Mrs Powell. Is there nothing we can do to persuade you to stay?

She knew that she could at this moment run away from the sergeant. London was full of runaways – why should she not join them, and settle for the life of an obscure potter in Clerkenwell? But she did not do this. When Sergeant Powell, with a brief return of the old cordiality which had marked his nature in America, told her, she took his strange words as her destiny:

—Lord Gower's as good as his word – it's not Wapping we're staying in, Merry, girl, it's in Lord Gower's estates, Staffordshire. The Rising Sun, my girl – you and I are the proprietors of the Rising Sun!

# II

AT TURNHAM GREEN, WHERE THE BENTLEYS NOW RESIDED, there was ample discussion of literature, not all of which would be suitable reading for Byerley's young cousin, and intended bride, in Staffordshire. The Bentleys' great friends in this genteel suburb were the Griffithses. Mr Ralph Griffiths, brother of Thomas, Wedgwood's agent in New York – the man who first bought china clay from the Cherokees – was editor of the *Monthly Review*. The Griffithses were a Burslem family, but Ralph had made his fortune in London as the publisher of John Cleland's novel *Fanny Hill*. If this lubricious tale scarcely stood, in the annals of literature, on a pedestal of comparable dignity to Wedgwood's place of honour in the story of English craft and manufacture, it nevertheless offered a bond of some intimacy between the two families. Jos Wedgwood had used his increase in wealth and fame to build the substantial mansion house of Etruria with its park, its ornamental lake, its walks and shrubberies. The elevation had left the whole family somewhat isolated from their poorer cousins and childhood companions. Nor could the swift acquisition of wealth alone supply the inward confidence that they mixed as equals with the real grandees of the vicinity, with Lord Gower or the Duke of Bridgewater or the Fitzherberts of Swynnerton. With the Griffithses, another family of Burslem boys made good, it was otherwise. Josiah's brother John had lived happily, and all but *en famille*, in the substantial house in Turnham Green until his untimely and mysterious death. There was a fellowship, both in the memory of the smaller houses and lowlier avocations of their Burslem childhoods, and in the newly acquired taste for powdered footmen, huge mirrored saloons, butler, housekeeper, maids and pages; marble-topped hall tables, gilded looking-glasses; likenesses by Sir Joshua of wives in the bloom of their youthful good looks. Sharing the experience of a sudden acquisition of riches mitigated the apprehension that *richesse* so *nouvelle* could only cause envy in the lowlier, and mockery in the more sophisticated, quarters in which they still had to walk. Birds of a feather flocked together.

Bentley, whose gentry family in Derbyshire had been a cut above all this, was very much not inclined to sniff at the prodigies of riches. Byerley, who tiptoed at first, awestruck, through both households – the Bentley and the Griffiths – noted the relish with which Bentley loved every luxury which the new money brought. Whereas Mrs Bentley affected to take it all for granted, and to behave as if acquaintance with the celebrated and the nobly born were as much to be expected as the glimmering of silver and gold upon her dining table, Bentley was devoid of affectation in his enjoyment. The pleasures of the table were especially indulged and celebrated: turbots in rich cream and brandy sauces, cutlets, glistening hams, golden pies and fatty beeves and capons appeared in course after course, and long after Byerley's appetites had been satisfied, and others at the table had sent the serving-men away, Bentley would be still eager to heap his plate. Moreover, when the cloths were removed and they sat over their Burgundy, Madeira and port, his glass was replenished with a speed which left nearly all the other drinkers at table with their glasses scarcely broached, unless Dr Darwin happened to be in town.

It was on one evening, towards the close of November, at the Bentleys' table, that Byerley noticed his friend was suffering from a heavy head cold. The condition seemed to have come upon him in the course of the meal. They had all – Ralph Griffiths and his wife, Mrs Bentley and two other couples – taken their seats at dinner in a mood of some conviviality. Conversation had ranged from 'shop' to gossip, from art to the political situation both at home and abroad. Mrs Bentley had finished telling the guests about the Stubbs portrait of the Wedgwoods, which had more or less come to its conclusion. When laughter had subsided, Bentley, beginning to cough and sneeze as he spoke, had told them the less amusing, but perhaps more impressive, fact that after many a long year of struggle, Josiah had persuaded Mr Champion of Bristol to sell the patent and dispose of the secret of how to make porcelain. It was an extraordinary development, and they had spoken, all of them – even the strangers, who had nothing to do with the Potteries – of how they should all like to visit Cornwall and see the china clay quarries.

—Old Jos, said Bentley affectionately, always wants to go one better. He writes that if we visit Cornwall, he'd like to see Land's End.

—I do not know why you say old Jos, said Ralph Griffiths. Both he and you are no more than fifty; you both seem like boys to me.

A tremendous sneeze was Bentley's answer to this compliment, but he continued to fork in a succulent, dripping mouthful of crispy mutton fat.

Next they had laughed about the elopement of their friend Edgeworth.

—I declare, said Mrs Bentley, he will be like Henry VIII before he is done.

In after time, Byerley could never remember at what stage of Edgeworth's marital Odyssey that dinner had occurred, nor how many of his four wives had died, nor how many of his twenty-two children had been born.

There was satirical talk of the late election. In Newcastle-under-

Lyme, a pocket borough in the gift of Lord Gower, the two seats went, respectively, to his son, Lord Trentham, and his son-in-law Archie MacDonald. In Stafford, rather more money had to pass hands to secure the election, by the tiny number of voters, of Richard Brinsley Sheridan.

—Not many Rivals there, then! quipped Mrs Bentley.

And Griffiths had got in with,

—But a School for Scandal that could teach the Americans they are not the only beings in the planet who do not enjoy the blessings of democracy!

And so, inevitably, the conversation had led on to the disastrous war, and the plight of the refugees, especially the slaves who had been promised their liberty if they fought for the Crown.

—Since Jos had the idea of giving away the Am I Not A Man medallions and buttons, we have not been able to manufacture enough of them! And, cunning old devil that he is, when the customers come in for free medallions, one in ten o' 'em stay on and make a purchase – here a medallion of poor Garrick, there a teapot.

After dinner, a small concert had been arranged and Miss Tillson, a popular young soprano, engaged to sing airs from *The Beggar's Opera* – strange memories for Byerley there – from Handel, and from Dr Arne's *Masque of King Alfred*. Everyone joined in the choruses of that masque's most popular air, which had become, almost instantaneously, the great anti-slaving anthem 'Rule Britannia', and it was difficult, even given their sympathies with the colonists, not to feel some consideration for the redcoats posted in Massachusetts, New York and the Carolinas, nor to have a sense of patriotism about the humiliations which would almost certainly be visited upon them.

Wine had been taken, and retaken, faces were rosy, Arne's music and the rousing words bore repetition, and the volume increased, so that Bentley's coughs and splutterings were drowned, and he eventually left the room. Only when the little party broke up, and his absence was remarked by Griffiths, did Mrs Bentley send a servant to see after his master. Innes, the footman, came hurrying back with an expression of dismay upon his face. The physician was sent for, but by the time he had arrived, it had become obvious that they were attendant not upon mere sickness, but upon a death-bed.

The breathing was irregular, and in its irregularity and its stertorous volume it announced to those gathered round the bed how difficult it had become. As the small hours turned to dawn, the watchers found themselves awaiting each breath, hoping for the next, as a sign of life, yet in some ways dreading it as a sign of pain and struggle. By the time full daylight had come, at around eight, the balance of hope and dread had altered. Relatively young as Bentley was, forty-nine, they all wanted nothing for him but peace. The death rattle, raucous, struggling, terrible, came at mid-morning, and then all was still. Byerley was with him when he died. Mrs Bentley came back into the room shortly afterwards, and knelt beside the bed, with her head silently buried in a sheet. When she stood, it was to embrace Byerley, fully and completely. So complete was her giving of her lips, breasts and kneecaps to him in this embrace, that, with some absurdity, he wanted to turn with embarrassment to Bentley as he lay on the bed; or to draw the wife's attention to the silent witness who lay there, white, pasty, moist, immobile. He afterwards wondered whether it was in fact the presence of death itself which had brought on this life-affirming instinct upon both their parts, for the embrace was a consensual expression of rather more than two people consoling one another for the loss of a husband and a friend.

Byerley's first words were, We must tell old Jos.

She kissed him again on the lips.

—I know, she said.

It was agreed that the intelligence was too shocking, too crammed with import, to be entrusted to paper. Byerley must go to Stafford-shire in person. This was something which he did at once, travelling post, and changing at Oxford and Birmingham. Wakefulness, and something very like excitement, coursed through his being as the coaches shook and sped through the dank England of November, with cold rain falling on leafless trees, and the sun setting early behind the rooftops of Birmingham. A whole mixture of thoughts churned in the young man's head: awe, which was a variety of thrill, at death itself. Coming as it did so soon after the death of his mother, the departure of Bentley forced yet again the recognition of the sheer strangeness of it: those corpses, of Mrs Byerley and of Mr Bentley, both were, and were not, the departed. The very word 'departed', which seemed in ordinary parlance to be a feeble euphemism, an undertaker's gentility, seemed to mean something when one was in the actual presence of death. For simply, where were they? These waxwork hulks left behind were not they.

At times, in the future, the actuality of death would produce long passages of melancholy, and occasional horror. In the aftermath of Bentley's death, this was not so. Byerley found it exciting. Perhaps this was for the obvious reason that the removal of Bentley from the firm changed the whole ethos and shape of Josiah Wedgwood's enterprise.

For seventeen years – ever since Byerley's childhood – Bentley and Wedgwood had worked together. The prodigies of their inven-tion, the magnificence of their prosperity, had come about through the alchemy of partnership. Bentley had not been able to throw pots, or to design new ones, or to manage manufactories, or to instruct hands. But even in Wedgwood's prodigious skill in all these areas, Bentley had been of assistance. He had helped Josiah, by conversa-tion, and by willingness to experiment and to try out new schemes, with, for example, the decision to move so much of the decorative work to the Chelsea works and to the Greek Street showrooms. He had made Wedgwood and Bentley a London phenomenon, and it was he who had driven forward such ambitious schemes as the sale of Queen's ware, the manufacture of the great Frog Service for the Empress, the huge expansion, in spite of the general depression of British trade owing to the war, of their domestic trade, the development of the European outlets.

The range and size and potential of the business were the result of the partnership. Wedgwood, its great name, its works, its output, would continue without Bentley, but it would continue on a different footing.

Byerley knew that Josiah's first instinct would be to draw the family closer to him. It was the old boy's hope that he would be able to keep the works thriving until the three boys – Jack, Jos Junior and Tom – were old enough to take over the business. Jos himself had been apprenticed to his elder brother Tom. His own father had worked for *his* father. So it had been in the past. So, too, surely, it must be in the future.

Byerley knew that this was the way his uncle's mind worked. And yet, when Jos and his brothers grew up in the Churchyard Works and the Brick House Works, no famous painters came to paint them. Caleb Bowers was the playmate, not the attendant, of Josiah. The celebrated Josiah Wedgwood of Wedgwood and Bentley could not ask his three sons to work as apprentices in a trade. He had made them into gentlemen, or semi-gentlemen, and he had thereby endangered the future of the firm. What did the flowered lawns and mirrored drawing-rooms of their new friends have to do with a manufactory?

Jos would hand them the works, and the business, and all the money which derived therefrom, but he had educated them in a way which made them only half-competent, or -desirous, to indulge in trade. None of them could replace Bentley. But nor would Josiah wish to replace his friend and partner with any of the managers, in London or Staffordshire, who had worked under him. As Byerley changed coaches for the last time at the Crown in Stone and awaited the mail coach to Hanley, he realized that the death of Bentley had made his own destiny. The three boys were Josiah's heirs, but they could not, alone, carry on the Wedgwood tradition. Byerley must do that. Byerley in large measure must step into Bentley's shoes. Byerley, perhaps, should take very seriously the wisdom of Josiah and Sally, so recently expressed: he must find himself a wife, and begin wooing Sukey in earnest. He thought regretfully of how little she attracted him; how happy he would be, entwined in the arms of the blonde draper of Meard Street, whose name, he had discovered, was Miss Peck.

The coach reached Hanley at midday and he took a fly over to Etruria. He knew that at that hour, Jos would be at the works, and it was there that he found him, in the Counting House.

—This is a surprise! he said, looking up from his table and rising awkwardly.

—My dear Uncle Jos.

The table, neat as always, was laid out with experiment books, and a number of mineral samples, about which Jos had been making notes.

—Bentley told you the wonderful news? We've bought the patent from Mr Champion! We can start making porcelain in earnest, and with our very own china clay. I shan't be sending you off to the Indian country again, my boy.

—Uncle, I . . . Oh, Uncle Jos!

It was almost shocking to Byerley that the news took no time at all to sink in. Jos, steady now upon his wooden leg, immediately began to delegate, to plan, and to consult the calendar.

—We were to have gone down to Bristol on the fourth of

December to finalize the sale of the patent. There was also business in Liverpool to conduct. Bentley was to go on to Liverpool from Bristol. We need to renew the lease on a warehouse there, and Campbell needs to be informed about those American sales. You know the rogues in Jamestown and Williamsburg are refusing to pay our bills even though the war is over? It is a sorry state of things. We'll need to go up to the house, and tell your aunt.

They crunched slowly over the moist gravel path. It was as if the pull up the hill was causing his uncle some difficulty.

—How did Mrs Bentley take it?

—She is much shocked.

—Poor woman! I'm afraid it will upset your Aunt Sal. It will upset all of us. Oh, Tom, Tom! Why should this have to happen!

They found Heffie hovering in the hall with the two younger girls.

—So, it's complete! said Byerley.

For there hung the Stubbs portrait at last: Jos and Sal sitting to the right of the canvas, a table before them, on which stood a First Day's Firing black basaltes vase. Behind, a smoking factory chimney hinted at the source of the wealth which paid for the finely tuned leg, the finely woven clothes and the seven finely bred surviving children.

—Yes!

He let out a bitter sort of laugh.

—I commissioned him to paint two pictures of my children. I assumed it would take him three weeks. Four months he stayed in my house, and we end up with neither of the pictures I wanted – and instead we have that monstrosity! Mind you – his voice took on the hushed tone often used when his wife was under discussion – the portrait he did of your aunt, the enamel thing, that's a master-piece. And he painted her Dada – caught him exactly!

Tom noted Heffie staring at them with a fixed vacancy while they discussed the painter. Her mouth hung open to reveal terrible teeth.

—I liked the one of you, Uncle.

—That thing!

—You've brought Tom Byerley back from London, stated Sally Wedgwood as she greeted the two men. She was swooping down the stone staircase and found them in front of the Stubbs portrait.

—Sally, my dear,

—Oh, Jos, what is it?

For the first time in his life, he saw Aunt Sally regard her husband with a look of tenderness.

—Oh, Jos, love.

The husband all but fell towards his wife. He put out his arms, and she enfolded him, as if he were a hurt child.

—What is it, love, what is it?

—Oh, Sal, oh, our Sal.

In the presence of the dead Bentley, Byerley had felt awkward to be embraced by the new widow. Now he felt equally awkward to be the third party in a scene of such tenderness. Jos had given over to emotion and was weeping freely.

—There, she said, while rubbing his back and shoulders.

And after a while,

—Oh, Jos, love, give over!

When he stood upright and drew apart from her, he told her the news. There was a strange impassivity in her features when she received them. Sometimes, that highly sensitive face took on the knowing and almost cynical expression of her father the cheesemonger which Mr Stubbs had caught so precisely.

# 12

AFTER THE DEATH OF BENTLEY, JOSIAH RETREATED INTO the world he had created at Etruria. He felt no inclination to travel to London. He spent hours alone in his laboratory in the cellar up at the Hall. New building schemes were undertaken. He decided to expand the 'village', which consisted then of seventy-six houses which he had built for the workers at the same time as the erection of the Hall. The new terraces he built were on the same pattern as the old. Each house had two downstairs rooms, a living room and a kitchen. There were earth floors, plain board doors and casement windows with small panes of leaded glass. The only room in the house with a fire was the living room, and it was here that all the cooking was done. Above, there were two small bedrooms.

There were now eighty-seven houses in the 'village', as well as the bakehouses and ovens, where tenants could cook larger items and heat pies. There was an inn, the Etruria Inn, on the edge of Fowlea farmyard. Sheep and cows grazed behind the inn, and there was still a sense of Etruria being out in the country, even though the manu-factory was humming with the activity of the three hundred employees – men, women and children. All that winter and spring, mists lay on the wooded hillsides. For two months it was so cold that the pools in the estate froze over. So did the canal, and children skated as far down as Trentham. There then followed a moist, foggy

February and March. Wind blew across the cobbled yards of the manufactory, white fog blending with the billows of chalky smoke from the frit kiln, which coated the clothing and the lungs of those who worked there.

Almost as if they were cogs in a machine of Josiah's invention, the workers produced pottery with automatic skill. The modellers modelled, the throwers threw, the painters painted. When ware had been prepared for firing, it was placed in heavy round saggars, which the men placed upon their heads, carrying them across the yard to the bottle kilns. Inside these ovens, the saggars were piled up almost as high as the chimney flue at the top. The upper levels were reached by ladder. When the brick bottle was filled, the entrance was sealed and the oven was stoked. There were now about a dozen of these bottle kilns at the western edge of the factory site, and there was scarcely a day of the week when at least half of them were not sending out darkened smoke to the pure sky. The ware was fired for upwards of thirty-six hours. When it was ready, the cavity at the bottom was opened, and, with an iron bar, a man would come to remove a few samples to check whether the firing was successful.

Then the glazing process could begin, with half a bushel of salt being thrown through the holes left at the bottom of the brick ovens. This salt-casting was repeated every half-hour every six hours.

Josiah wanted to make kilns hotter and hotter. Sometimes the men dreaded the appearance of Owd Wooden Leg, waiting impatiently for the saggars to be removed from the kilns at the end of the glazing. He was never satisfied, and they all became aware that 'summut wuz oop' as he shook his head sadly at what appeared to be flawlessly glazed vases and bowls.

The difficulty was his inability to measure the temperature beyond three hundred and sixty degrees. Of course, in the days of his apprenticeship at the Brick House Works, the experienced potter simply guessed the temperature of the kiln by removing one of the small plugs in the brick wall and peering through. His cousin Useful Tom still did this as they came to the end of each firing process at Etruria. A good man 'knew', partly from the colour of the flames, partly by instinct, whether the oven was unduly hot, or not hot enough. But there were many mistakes, and even Useful Tom wasted a lot of ware. And Useful Tom would never be able, as Josiah aspired to be able, to bake ever more delicate, ever-whiter jasper, or to make experiments with jasper slipware which would enable him to imitate cameo-glass, with delicately applied fine reliefs.

So, it would seem, as Josiah disappeared into the cellar, and as Mary Ann screamed, and as the women tried to calm the child, as if he had only one thing on his mind, the invention of a new type of pyrometer to measure the fire's heat.

—We miss you when you are inventing, Papa.

It was Sukey, one night at dinner.

—And I miss you, my dear, but at least we are all together. At least we got each other, eh?

—Something tells me, said Dr Darwin, that you have not been working on the pyrometer today, Mr Wedgwood.

—Dr Darwin's a magician.

—Well, I think if you were just playing down there, you should have come up and helped while Dr Darwin was giving Mary Ann her shocks, said Sally sharply.

Sukey knew how to deflect an unpleasantness, and on this occasion, she was genuinely interested to know.

—What have you invented now, Pa?

—Well, it's not very delicate, and perhaps we do not need to discuss it at the dinner table, said her father, his normally pink complexion deepening to scarlet.

—My giddy aunt! What can it be? Jack asked, clapping his hands.

—Well, since we're all family this afternoon, except you, Doctor, and I count you as family.

—I take that in the complimentary spirit in which it is meant.

—It is the Jakes! said Josiah proudly. No one yet could visit the Jakes without, shall we be candid enough to admit it, producing, well . . .

Tom's giggles were so uncontrolled that even Sukey felt that they were entering the territory of what Sally called the 'unsuitable'. She nonetheless could not avoid being interested by what her father had to say.

Later, at Stonefield Cottage, Caleb laughed too, when Heffie told him.

—Whatever next! Only a Wedgwood would think you could visit that particular room and not make a smell.

—It do sound ingenious, said Heffie.

—Aye, I'll give the bugger that.

—It's called an air-closet, said Heffie. Tha sits dine and duz tha doings and they fall dine, lahk, and summow – I know not ow – the doings is drawn away and consume they-sels. Combination, 'e say it were.

—That would be combustion, lass.

—Ay, combustion, lahk ah say. And the air, it draw out the stink.

—Give over.

—E's putting them in oop at 'all.

—Give over, 'e isna. Shittin' indoer? It doesn't seem hygienic.

—'E is. Four air-closets, one near the dining-parlour, one out at back, and two near bedrooms.

—By 'eck, our Heff. What will that bugger think on next?

—Oh, but our Caleb, if you could see Mary Ann, it would break your heart.

# 13

IN THE EVENT, IT WAS DR DARWIN WHO SETTLED TOM
Byerley's marriage question, as he settled so much else of a practical
character in the Wedgwood family. It was Dr Darwin who found
Josiah his new secretary, a chemist named Chisholm. It was Dr
Darwin who arranged for Sally Wedgwood to have her Wright of
Derby painting after all. And it was the resourceful doctor who found
a wife for Cousin Byerley.

The last two achievements were connected. Erasmus the medical
man-mountain had, having been widowed, abandoned Lichfield for
love. Almost certainly (though none of them could be sure), he had
begun his attachment to a patient, Elizabeth Pole, before the death
of her husband. Upon the colonel's demise, Erasmus had moved in
to Radburn Hall, in the county of Derby.

> If false to thee my perjured bosom prove,
> To thee, my sweet Eliza, and to love;
> That hour – oh Heaven, that guilty hour avert! –
> Shall plunge a dagger in my worthless Heart.

Both Sukey and her mother had read the verses with some smiles,
but since his wedding to Mrs Pole, there were fewer fumblings
beneath their petticoats than there had been in the past. When he

had pressed his ear against Mrs Wedgwood's chest, she had, it was true, been laid up with an unpleasant suspicion of bronchitis. In his old self, Erasmus would have thought nothing of examining her chest even though her complaint had been a sprained ankle.

Radburn Hall had been admirably suited to the late Colonel Pole, who had enjoyed pacing its acres, and in due season tempting its trout from streams and blasting its partridge and pheasant from the branches of his soothing elms. It was less obviously the ideal residence for a busy physician, and in time, as Elizabeth began to bear the doctor infants to add to the children he had sired by his first wife, they moved into a handsome townhouse in Derby.

The marriage changed the doctor. He all but abandoned his scientific friends. His world was now concentrated upon his wife and children, upon his poetry and his philosophy, upon his patients, and upon a few close friends, of whom Josiah was the closest.

—We'll be the next to be dropped, predicted Sally. Because she's an Earl's by-blow, he's got no time for your Birmingham manufacturers, your natural philosophers and republicans!

—You're very hard, sometimes, Sal! I couldna think of circumstances in which Erasmus would, as you so inelegantly term it, drop us.

Jos was proved right by events. When the interruptions of childbirth permitted, Elizabeth Darwin accompanied her husband on the journeys to Etruria. When not, the doctor came alone, both as physician and friend. And Josiah, sometimes alone, and sometimes accompanied by Sally, visited the Darwins at Derby, which was a handsome town, full of smart new houses, of which their substantial residence in Full Street was one.

—Poor Wright, I never knew a worse c-case of hypochondria.

—Not Dr Johnson? asked Jos.

—Poor old J-J-Johnson. Erasmus shook his head. It w-w-was

p-p-painful, that night he c-came to dinner at my house in Lichfield. Were you there?

—Of course, said Jos. It was too much of a London performance. He came out with his famous sayings and sat back, expecting us to admire him. I was surprised. I'd never have expected that so great a man, used to conversing with Mr Burke, or Sir Joshua, should have behaved with all the vanity of an actor. And the ill-mannered way in which he slapped you down.

—He said that my theory of the origin of plants undermined the teaching of the Scriptures. Why sir – Erasmus adopted the Lichfield accent of the great lexicographer – this is Lu-Lu . . .

—Ludicrous? Jos annoyingly supplied.

—Lucretius r-redivivus! If life can appear on earth without a Creator setting it here, you have destroyed r-r-religion, and left m-mankind w-without h-h-hope! That is what he said.

—Arrant nonsense, said Wedgwood.

Darwin paused, as if he supposed that the Great Cham's rebuke had perhaps contained some justification.

—It is true that Johnson suffers from melancholy-m-m-madness. They even say, you know, that he is ch-ch-chained up by his f-f-friend Mrs Th-Th-Th-rale, though whether – a chuckle – that were for r-recreational or medicinal purpose, we are not informed. But poor Wright's is the worst case of hypochondria I ever m-m-met among m-m-my patients. My dear Elizabeth was s-so kind to him at Radburn, had him to s-s-stay for w-w-eeks on end, got him to paint her p-p-portrait, had him d-decorate the hall. You should c-come over to Derby and c-c-commission him to do more work, Jos.

—I know I should.

So, the journey to Derby was fixed, and for some reason, Jos was accompanied by his nephew Tom Byerley. On the way, Byerley watched his uncle's ruddy, clever face become animated by a new idea. It was no surprise, therefore, when the barouche pulled up outside the house in Full Street, to watch him thrust his wooden leg out of the carriage with manic eagerness to meet the painter, to heave himself upright, as he clutched the side of the coach, and start speaking almost before the front door had been opened.

—Mr Wright, I have a commission for you!

Wright was a staring, timid man, whose eyes were the saddest Tom Byerley ever saw. He had curly hair, no wig, and plump cheeks. Erasmus said that when the melancholy was worst, Wright did not console himself with drink, as other men would, but with cream, and bread and butter, and cakes, which he consumed in remarkable quantities while the black mood held him in its thrall.

The painting was to be a surprise for Sally, and it was, for Josiah, a rather delicate joke. Byerley, whose matrimonial life was (though he did not know it) just about to begin, took it as a kindly object lesson in marital tolerance. Wright was asked to depict Mrs Wedgwood as Penelope unwinding her tapestry by night. Wright made a few preliminary sketches of the composition, and Mr Wedgwood approved them. This was not going to be a repetition of the Stubbs impertinence! They would agree a subject, and the painter would stick to his commission. Penelope/Sally was to be seated in a shadowy bedroom. To her right, Hotspur would be sitting as the patient dog Argos. A mysterious light would be falling upon the son and heir – Telemachus, asleep in bed. Wright could get Tom Wedgwood to model this if he liked – or one of the younger brats if he so chose. And the whole scene would be shrouded in the shadows of night, with a great brooding statue silhouetted in the foreground, and nearblackness at the edges of the canvas. The scene would say – though of course, Jos did not need to spell this out – Etruria is besieged by 'suitors' – not necessarily trying to persuade Sally to be unfaithful to her absent wooden-legged husband, but tempting her to think them more amusing company than Josiah: Dr Darwin himself and Tom Byerley were both charmers to her, Jos knew that. She had basked in the somewhat lecherous flatteries of Mr Stubbs. As for that puppy Flaxman – his flirtations were outrageous. And there was the faithful Caleb who gazed at her with more abject adoration even than Hotspur. But Jos knew she had always been a good wife to him, and what she was looking at on the bed was not just an heir: it was the business, the family firm which would go on in spite of all the rivals, all the 'suitors', all the business rivals, all the politicians in England who failed to see the importance of trade and the New World.

That was what the painting would say, and so began Mr Wright's visits to Etruria to capture 'Penelope's' likeness. How well he did it, though, as Sukey said when the painting was done, you could not have a greater contrast with the work of Mr Stubbs. In the Stubbs portrait all the Wedgwoods looked like a display of waxworks among living dogs and ponies. In the Wright painting of Penelope, the mother and child are almost painfully alive, and poor Hotspur, the true old hound sitting in the nocturnal shades, resembles apprentice-work by an amateur taxidermist.

—Those two painters should go into partnership, said Caleb, when he saw Wright's 'Penelope'. Friend Stubbs could paint all cats and dogs, and horses: leave Wright to do the folk.

He and Heffie had been too tactful to tell the Wedgwoods that Stubbs had painted his own likeness to perfection.

Byerley sensed the progress of his aunt and uncle's arranged marriage. While she was still having the children, there had been so much rage and melancholy. Josiah's unstoppable preoccupation with work, with inventions, with the firm, with the great affairs of the world, had driven Sally more and more into herself, her books, her private thoughts, her sometimes bitter jokes. But as the children grew up, and as her friendship with them deepened, so too had her friendship with Jos. It was love of a kind – perhaps it was the best sort of love, this deep feeling of family loyalty and kinship. Byerley would never forget her taking her husband in her arms on the afternoon he heard of Mr Bentley's death.

And now it was Byerley's turn to begin the great adventure. He was on the edge of thirty. Time to do what his uncle wanted, even though the more he contemplated his cousin Sukey, the less able he was imaginatively to think of a sexual life with her. Such a life with Miss Peck, the pert, blonde draper of Meard Street, was all too readily conceivable. He sometimes thought that he should begin an intrigue with the draper, and hope that his uncle would eventually accept the girl as Mrs Byerley.

He feared that if he married Sukey, he would simply be unable to be faithful to her; and, oh, the rumpus this would cause when the reasons for her unhappiness came to be known in the family! On the other hand, if he did not marry Sukey, and he married Miss Peck, there was the danger of estrangement from the family. And it was while his mind, and whole consciousness, was torn on a daily basis between the alternatives, that he was rescued by Dr Darwin.

It was on that first day in Derby, when he and Uncle Jos went over to discuss the painting of Penelope with Mr Wright. They were staying to dinner – eaten in the Darwin household at two. At half past one, Erasmus Darwin suddenly seized Tom Byerley by the elbow and walked him into the large walled garden at the back of the house.

The lawn sloped down to the River Derwent, which, after an especially wet September, was in spate. Fish were jumping and bubbling in the swift-moving greyish silver water.

—Byerley, I hope you like m-m-my guests at d-d-dinner.

—I'm sure I shall, sir.

—B-b-but I hope you'll like Miss Bruckfield especially. J-J-Josiah has h-h-hinted to me the th-thoughts he has about Sukey.

Many a time in later years, Byerley would remember this conversation between himself and the man who was going to become Sukey's father-in-law. Had he already ear-marked Sukey as a wife for his son Robert? It was hard to believe that the doctor left anything to chance. On the other hand, Byerley had no evidence that Erasmus forced the pace between his son and Sukey. The two came together – marrying after Josiah's death – quite naturally, as childhood friends whose love for one another blossomed into something more. Yet, in Byerley's mind Erasmus had a mythic status, not unlike that of the deities in Homer or Hesiod, controlling the destinies of the mortals.

—The c-c-cousinage . . . the c-c-consanguinity. It is m-most inadvisable. Jos and Sal are cousins. I know they are d-d-distant cousins, but Sal's parents are also cousins. You and Sukey are f-f-first cousins . . . As your m-m-medical adviser I would advise you against it. I sh-share Josiah's wish to see you happy, my lad, happily settled. N-nothing like m-m-matrimony, nothing like married love. So, look kindly on Miss Bruckfield, Tom, look kindly on her.

The river rushed by, the leaves of the sycamore which overhung the bank where they stood shook raindrops down upon their heads. They did not feel it through their wigs, but Fanny would tell him, when they repeated to one another, as they so often did, the story of the day they met, that she had wanted to laugh at the sight of his surprised face and his wig drenched with rain.

The Bruckfields had already arrived, and been shown into the drawing-room when Tom and Dr Darwin came back to the house. To say that he was surprised would be an understatement. At first, he thought he was in a dream, for the resemblance of Miss Bruckfield to Miss Peck was uncanny.

Later – when he had married Miss Bruckfield and settled down to life with her – he edited Miss Peck out of his memory altogether, and had anyone told him that his secret devotion to the draper's assistant of Meard Street had formed a major part of his inner life for so many months, and that it had prepared his heart and imagination for his future life with Miss Frances Bruckfield, he would have dismissed the very idea as an absurdity. For the truth was that, even before the end of that first dinner at the house of Dr Darwin, he realized that destiny had played a card. He had not made up his mind to marry Frances, still less did he make it his aspiration. He saw, by contrast, that it was something which was inevitable: his future life with her, his long marriage, his many children, seemed – at any rate in retrospect – to be something over which he had all but no control: as if he had been hired for a part, handed his script, told to learn his lines, and to appear for the first performance at Drury Lane in a few weeks.

# 14

FAN BRUCKFIELD HAD THE BLESSINGS OF SOUND HEALTH,
a happy temperament, and decent, hard-working parents who had
prepared her well for life. It would have been difficult to find a
woman less like Sally Wedgwood if you had scoured the three kingdoms. For whereas Sally was someone to whom almost every day
presented some ill to be endured, or some minor domestic crisis
which swelled in her head to the proportions of a calamity, Frances
was one of those extremely fortunate human beings who accepted
what came, and found much of it – most of it – amusing. Nor, when
she came to read the writings of Sally's friend Mary Wollstonecraft
– sister of the 'lame duck' Everina – did Fan Byerley feel for a
moment that her existence as a daughter, as a wife or as a mother
had in any sense infringed her rights.

She had never known want. Both her parents, being musical, lit-
erate, and neat in everything, had brought her up to imitate these
virtues. She played the forte piano, she had a wide selection of songs
in her repertoire, she sketched adequately, and by the time she was
sixteen she had mastered all the necessary domestic skills – necessary, that is to say, to be able to get by in life without everything
falling into chaos. Had she suffered Sally Wedgwood's misfortunes,
in her early married life, of being entirely without servants, she would
have managed perfectly well, being a good cook and an efficient

manager. As it happened, she and Tom Byerley, when they married, were able to afford a cook and a maid.

Frances had a happy acceptance of her family, while recognizing that her sisters, Lydia (the eldest, now married to a doctor in Leek) and Elizabeth, and her brother Henry, destined, like his father, for the law, could sometimes irritate her. With Lydia, who bossed and scolded her from infancy, she felt frequent provocations to rage, though, once childhood years were behind them, these provocations had not been yielded to and it was years since they had come to childish blows.

From the age of eleven, Frances had known that she preferred the company of men and boys to that of her sisters and their female friends. She enjoyed playing whist with her brother and his friends, she enjoyed the attentions and flirtations of male visitors to their two houses (in Derby and in Soho). Since she grew, after her sixteenth birthday, into a person of great personal beauty and charm, there was no shortage of admirers. Only with Dr Darwin had there ever been anything like a feeling of discomfort. His purportedly medical examinations had been increasingly unnecessary in a young woman of near-perfect health. This did not stop the doctor, if she had a winter cough, from pressing his old ears against her exposed chest. Nor, when the stomach cramps and associated pains of womanhood began, could he be restrained from demonstrating, with fingers rather than words, how the nether garments might be loosened.

After this episode, she had (laughingly) implored her mother to be present during any future consultations with the doctor.

—Fan, you almost invite it, had been her mother's response.

—Mama, I do not!

—Not by coquetry, of that no one could accuse you, but by seeming so childish, so young for your age. You could at least pretend to be sophisticated.

But of course, as Sally Wedgwood was very quick to notice when Fan joined the family, it was precisely in Fan's naivety that there resided her abundant charm. Beautiful, indeed stunningly beautiful, as she was, she was quite incapable of vanity. And although Tom Byerley was bowled over by the beauty, enchanted, unable to believe his luck, almost his first thought, when he met her that day at Darwin's house for dinner, was that she would be a mother.

As soon as Nature allowed for this to happen, the phenomenon took place. The courtship was very short. Frances appeared delighted with Byerley, and, whether by good luck or by an act of will, was in love with him by the time they were married – an event which took place in St Anne's Church in Soho.

—We won't be round your necks, her mother promised their son-in-law at the wedding breakfast at the house in Dean Street. My husband conducts more and more of his business in Derby, and I believe he only retains his London clients out of kindness to myself, to give me the chance to attend the theatre and to buy clothes.

The silvery laugh, so lovely in the daughter, was just a little frightening in the mother, who, like Fan, was blonde and well proportioned.

Tom and Fan used to laugh that no one could ever have instructed her Mama to be more sophisticated. She seemed the essence of sophistication – poised, powdered, a little too grand and a little too well attired to be the wife of a provincial solicitor. Tom, whose own mother had brought him up to speak a southern form of English, and whose career on the stage had honed his voice to that of a gentleman, retained a slight nervousness in the presence of real gentlefolk, all of whose family – even when residing in Derby – spoke southern. Uncle Jos had never gone in for such nonsense, alternating a northern-accented standard speech with dialect Staffordshire without any affectation. The rest of the family, even the three sophisticated sons of Josiah, spoke with a distinctly Staffordshire timbre, and many words, such as castle and rascal, in their pronunciation had short 'a's.

Frances, from the way she spoke, could have been the sister of a Duchess. Yet she was without hauteur, and by the time the first two babies had arrived, Byerley felt that she had always been awaiting their arrival, that her physical fondness for them, her ease with them, even when they were sickly or fractious or when she was sleep-deprived, had this completely unaffected quality of feeling truly meant. Indeed, as their erotic attraction for one another grew, Byerley occasionally asked himself the sly question, whether part of the attraction was that he felt he was indulging a love affair with his children's beautiful young nurse, rather than making yet more Byerleys with his wife.

We have emphasized her good luck – Fan's beauty, health and comparative wealth (though this should not be exaggerated, as she did not come with a great dowry, nor would she ever feel wealthy by the standards of her husband's Wedgwood cousins). But her mother had missed elements in Frances Bruckfield's nature which must not pass by the more attentive reader, who will know her better than her mother.

Frances was not 'sophisticated' in the sense that her mother would have liked, but nor was she so childish as the elder woman, or her husband, imagined. It is true that she liked playing with babies, just as she liked every aspect of the activities which led to these babies coming into the world. She performed the duties of the wife and housekeeper with absolute good humour. But this is not to say that she did not notice what others thought of her: she noticed, without resentment, that Sally Wedgwood considered her a fool. On the first occasion they met, Mrs Wedgwood had asked her, quite idiotically Fan thought, whether she had read . . . oh, Fan forgot even the name of the author. But it was a trick question to show off cleverness, and

Fan decided that she never wished to play such games, nor to resent those who did. She became aware very early that Sally had loved her nephew-by-marriage in a very unauntly way, and that in consequence, Mrs Wedgwood would have resented anyone he eventually married. The younger Wedgwood cousins – John, Josiah and Tom – simply seemed to her like dozens of the boys she had met while growing up in Derby, the sons of rich merchants, or manufacturers who had risen a little socially above their fathers, and were a little too conscious of it. She also quickly established a feeling of friendship for all three – for scientific John, a boy with whom she instantly sympathized, since it was obvious he did not want to be a Master Potter and would do anything to be able to escape into the great world; for shy, kind, smiling Jos the Younger, who was emerging from John's shadow and becoming an all-but-silent young man, perhaps prepared to take on the firm, but nonetheless yearning to study at Edinburgh University; and the bright, sickly, brilliant young Tom, who was so full of questions, and jokes and whose face, when he coughed, looked as if he was about to die.

But chief among the Etruria set, Fan liked Sukey. As soon as she had become engaged to Cousin Byerley, Fan found herself being taken up by Sukey, who was exactly her age. They rode together in the park at Etruria – Sukey now had a magnificent grey called Priam – and they established themselves immediately as Best Friends. In every large extended family there is a pivot, one with whom all members remain on terms even when they are at odds with the others, one who bridges generations, ignores coolnesses and rivalries, who calms anxieties and, on the simplest level, remembers anniversaries. This figure, even when she was just a young woman, was Sukey. It showed Fan's instinctual good sense with people that she made friends with Sukey and thereby conquered the Wedgwoods. And even though she had read none of Sukey's favourite novels, she shared her passion for music, for Telemann and Handel and Albinoni. Neither woman ever spelt out, either in these early raptures of friendship – which were akin to the pleasures of first love – or later, when they matured into an older generation, a primary reason for Sukey's immediate fondness. The arrival of Fanny had put an end to the preposterous idea that she should herself marry Cousin Byerley.

# 15

—WIV SCARCE HAD SATE O' THEE, OUR CALEB, THESE FO'
or five week – these allus oop poob in Burston.

—Who told thee that?

—Well, it's true, intit?

—Conner a mon goo dine inn without folk minding 'is business
fo' 'im?

—Our Caleb, it's so unlike thee, love. They disna tak our Ted wi'
thee so often as thee din.

—Well, dinna bey sa nowsy and I needna bey sa close.

They were quarrelling as they had never done as adults, which
presumably explained why Caleb, who normally spoke Standard
English, had slipped into dialect. Caleb did not walk out of the house
without saying goodbye. He did not slam a door. But as he left the
little orchard at the back of the house, and closed the door in the
garden wall, he thought of all the times when he had turned a blind
eye to his sister's pursuit of love. During the whole of the Mr Stubbs
summer, Caleb had tactfully kept his distance, taken Ted to London,
generally made himself absent. Now that, to his astonishment, he
found himself to be possessed by amorous yearning, he felt that Heff
should have played fair, and not expressed her natural feelings of
curiosity.

Since his youth, for nigh on forty years, Caleb Bowers had

doggedly and persistently loved Sally Wedgwood. Loving her and hating Providence had been his inward religion.

—It's a receipt for trouble – yo're askin' fo' it if yo' tell God yer plans!

This had always been his bitter jest. First, Caleb had lost his mother, and Jos had survived. But Jos had in turn been visited by a whole series of misfortunes – the loss of eight siblings, a child, his business partner. His brother John had died in peculiar circumstances in London. And there was scarcely anyone close to Caleb to whom comparable calamities had not occurred. Life was, as Caleb had once read in *The Rambler*, a state where little was to be enjoyed and much to be endured.

The deity who presided over this painful condition was plainly not the Jesus in whom Mr Wesley taught his sentimental followers to believe. On the contrary. When Caleb thought of Heff's grief at her own lost babies; when he thought of old Jos's face as he carried his baby Richard to his grave, or their worries about Mary Ann; when he thought of the burying-grounds of Stone and Burslem and Hanley full to bursting, almost literally, with the rotting corpses of children, he thought that the President of this Vale of Sorrow was no God of Love, but a child-devouring demon like Moloch in *Paradise Lost* –

> horrid King besmear'd with blood
> Of human sacrifice, and parents tears

In Caleb's mind, if there had been a God, that is what he would have been like: no other deity would match the reality of things. What softened the gruesome universe for him was, or had been, Sally Wedgwood, her sandy-gold hair, her rounded bosom, her smiles – when they came! – her moods and humours, her cleverness. She was his goddess. It would almost have spoilt things had she known quite the extent of his worship, though of course she had always known, since they were children, that he had 'a soft spot' for her. This knowledge was all part of the strange dynamic of the friendship between Jos, Sally, Heffie and himself.

But now everything was changed, everything was up in the air. For the second time in his life Caleb Bowers had fallen in love: this time, with the wife of the new publican at Burston.

She was called Merry, and never had nomenclature seemed so inappropriate. Her long face, which still bore the bruise where her husband had struck her, was suffused with melancholy. Only lately had he discovered that Merry had undergone baptism before her marriage. The name she had taken was Meribah, which meant 'The Waters of Strife'.

Her marriage was evidently a strife. Whenever he visited the inn, he heard the publican's abusive words. Sergeant Powell made no effort to disguise the strife in the presence of strangers. Nor did Caleb's presence do anything to sweeten the sergeant's temper.

One day things came to a head.

—If you think you can come in by 'ere, sniffing around, you can clear off now, I'm telling you.

This was how Caleb was greeted as he tied up the barge and the horse, before he had so much as stepped into the inn.

—I'm not in 'abit o' sniffin'.

—Sniffin's what I said.

It was clear that even by his own inebriated standards, the publican was very drunk.

—Sniffin' round my woman.

Merry now came out on to the towpath and, when she saw Caleb, she paused. No one who had seen Caleb in recent weeks could doubt that he loved her. It was obvious. Merry was both pleased, even a little awestruck by the fact, and at the same time frightened of the effect that it would have upon her husband.

It had all begun one very wet winter day, when the rain was coming down in sheets on the barge, and the horse itself seemed lashed, punished by the downpour, its great wet, gleaming shoulders bowed by the splashes of water which fell from its back and its haunches, and when the tarpaulins and covers on the barge had collected great pools of water, and when the surface of the cut was bouncing with the wet, almost as if a mad regiment of soldiers were shooting the surface with bullets, but no fish jumped, it was so cold, so dank, so wintry, on such a day, Caleb was coming back to Stone past Burston Bridge. There used to be a small inn there, the Rising Sun, though from the look of it that day, the sun had not risen on it for weeks. Caleb was murmuring in the ear of the horse that if they could only endure another hour's walk, they'd be back at Stone. He promised her oats and warmth. But even as he said the words, with water dribbling down his neck and through his sleeves, and down into his chest, he yearned to be out of the weather.

He was travelling alone that day, for the task of fetching a small quantity of crates and cargo from just south of Stafford and bringing them back to Henshaw's yard in Stone had not made it worth the while of two of them – as he had put it to Ted – getting bloody soaked. Besides, he sometimes liked to be alone, as did the lad, and what was the virtue of being a Number One if you could not sometimes work alone?

The Rising Sun was used by quite a number of bargees, and there was much traffic on the canal in those days, in spite of the war and the slump in trade. Several barges were drawn up at the bank before Burston Bridge, and there was smoke coming from the little tiled roof of the inn. Caleb wondered why he had not stopped at this inn for so long, and the answer was it was just too far to be a 'local', but too near to Stone for it to have been worth stopping for. The old innkeepers had the name of Bowers, funnily enough, though they had been, so far as he knew, no relation. He did not know who the new people were, though he'd heard they weren't from round here.

In spite of the wet, he gave Dandelion her nosebag. The dried oats in it had turned to a kind of muddy porridge, but she mouthed some of them gratefully.

—I don't like doing it to you, lass, but I must stop a while. I canna stand this bloody rain.

He loosed the old girl from her tether, and led her towards the stableyard at the back of the inn, for the great thing about the Rising Sun, used by so many of the boaties, was that it provided accommodation for the barge-horses. The stable was full of steaming animals, grateful to be in out of the downpour.

—Wi' straw and a roof for thyself an' a noggin o' grog for meself, we'll see out the storm, eh, lass?

And with water coming through his hat and making cold splashes on his skull, water mingling with his body sweat, water in his boots, he pushed open the door of the bar parlour.

A smoky little interior greeted him. There was a good coal fire in the small grate, and two or three men, evidently bargees, sat at low tables, smoking pipes and drinking what looked like a rum punch.

—Only, careful where you come with that wet, dripping coat, if you don't mind.

It was a peremptory greeting by the man Caleb took to be the landlord, and he nearly turned on his heels and retreated to the horse, and the downpour. Something made him obey, even though he sensed that the landlord was drunk. He removed his outer mantle and his hat, and, trying not to shake them too vigorously in that small space, he hung them on the hooks near the door, where a number of other hats and coats were steaming malodorously.

—No, well; the landlord was clearly in the middle of a monologue and the others, five or six men, some grizzled, some youthful, drank in obedient silence.

—No, well, said Mine Host, if they made the mistake of invasion in winter, see, then they'd be ready for them. Heard they've been building the fortifications.

What was the accent? Welsh?

—At Dover. If the bloody Frogs tried coming over, they wouldn't stand an earthly . . .

At some juncture of the tapster's talk there was a pause, during which Caleb asked if there would be the chance of partaking of the hot toddy or punch which had been dispensed to the others.

—I'm coming to that, said the host. And at a moment agreeable to himself, when he had expressed a few further thoughts about the disposition of the French army along the northern coast of their country, he went behind the bar and into the private part of the house.

A quiet murmur could be heard – presumably the voice of his wife – and then they heard their host's voice raised in anger.

—What's the fucking kettle for!

Another quiet murmur, and then more shouting from the landlord.

He came back into the saloon, rubbing his fist.

Shortly thereafter, a woman entered, bearing a steaming tray with a punch bowl, a ladle and several small glasses. The smoky little room was filled with an odour of sweetness. The woman who carried the tray was of middle height. She wore a very clean mob cap and a starched white apron over a muslin pinafore. Caleb noticed her hands, which were long and of great elegance. Her high-cheekboned face was . . . The first adjective which came into Caleb's mind was 'noble'. Although she was a serving-woman carrying a tray, she had about her a quality of majesty. Her back was remarkably straight.

In low tones, she asked him how he should like his punch to be prepared. The husband, who was, as Caleb realized, in an advanced state of inebriation, hurled further insults at her.

—He doesn't want to produce a fucking receipt. Make the bloody drink, and add some rum by here.

He advanced, waving his own glass at the woman, and, as she lifted the rum bottle to replenish her husband's glass, he fetched her a blow on the side of the head.

—Ee, have a care, said Caleb strongly.

—I beg your pardon?

—I think you heard, sir. There's no call for that. Are you all right? he asked her.

Her silent expression seemed to implore him not to enter into any altercation with the landlord.

—How my wife is . . . her husband's business, I think . . . no business of a stranger, were the slurred observations which, not without belligerence, were delivered.

Caleb Bowers could not fight him there and then. Nor could he walk out without paying, since she had entered with the tray, and to leave now would be to subject her to further punishments. So he drank down two measures of rum, sugar, hot water and lemons, and felt them scald his throat. The warmth which returned to his blood-stream, as the rain lashed the widows of the inn, was very welcome, but he felt great disquiet as he sat there, not least because the other bargees in the saloon were clearly oafish fellows who did not merely tolerate the landlord's abusive tone, but even appeared to relish it. One of them had laughed when the blow was delivered to the beautiful woman's cheeks.

And a beautiful woman she was. Glowing with rum, but disturbed in his heart as he walked the horse back along the towpath to Stone, Caleb found himself thinking about her. Who were they? Why were they there? How did this noble woman, this great woman (as he already thought of her) come to be serving rum punch in a small inn in North Staffordshire, matched with a drunken buffoon?

Some answer to this was supplied, when Caleb had drunk down two small tankards of punch and the rain had begun to abate. He mentioned his horse tethered in the stables, and the woman followed him out into the yard. Caleb did not adopt, or 'put on', as he would say, a voice, in the way that Jos Wedgwood did when speaking to the Quality customers. But he often did moderate his accent and vocabulary, for example when travelling in regions where the Staffordshire was a strange dialect. He spoke now in an accented version of the King's English.

—You are not from these parts, then?

—I'm from very far away.

—Wales, I reckon?

—The Sergeant – Mr Powell – he is from Wales. I am from America.

—You never!

He grinned, and to his immense satisfaction, she smiled back. It was hardly a grin, but it was a warm, glowing smile.

—It was chance that we came here, really, she said. If anything is chance. When my husband came out of the army, he had the idea he would become the proprietor of a little inn, perhaps in Wales, perhaps in London. And then we met Captain Gower again – he was his officer in America, see. He put in a word, as you might say.

—Ay, well we know the Gowers.

—You *know* them?

—I know on 'em, I mean.

—Lord Gower owns this inn, and the villages round about. He offered it to the Sergeant – to Mr Powell – if he would like it. He told us it was in the Potteries. I asked him, when he condescended to make us this generous offer, whether the inn was near the Etruria Works.

—Thou'st heard o' Etruria, then?

—Wooden Leg, she said quietly.

Caleb threw back his head and guffawed.

—Why is that funny? We were told that was his name. Mr Wedgwood. But those who love him call him Wooden Leg.

—Well, it's true in a way, but I wouldna try saying it to his face, he laughed.

—Mr Wedgwood, then. He bought clay from us, from . . . She looked at her feet as if she'd said too much.

—He bought clay from your husband?

—From my people. In America. In America, I was a potter. It would be wonderful to visit Etruria, it would be wonderful . . .

—You made pots, you say?

All at once, Caleb Bowers had a vision of a future with this woman. He imagined her working at the Etruria Works, and him drawing up in his barge when the bell was rung and escorting her home. The drunken, angry sergeant had been wiped out.

—I make vases – I made vases.

She wanted to tell him of her new-found skill, throwing at the wheel, but she was held back by an intuitive sense that this knowledge must be kept secret a little while longer.

—I'll take thee in to meet Mr Wilbraham, the foreman at the works.

—And you know Mr Wedgwood?

—Ay – with a smile – you could say. Now, Dandelion, lass, how are you?

The horse turned, as if she sensed that something had happened to the master while he had been in the inn.

—You docked her tail? asked the woman.

—No, it were docked when I bought her – owners thought she'd be put into shows.

—She's a fine one, said the woman. Good solid quarters, a good sloping pastern. I bet she never goes lame.

—Nor she does, our Dandelion!

—She's a fine, fine horse, Dandelion, said the woman.

—And you're a fine judge of a horse. And a potter. Didst thou mean it? Would you like me to ask Mr Wilbraham about work? What kind of work would you be able to do?

—As I say, I can make vases.

—I don't know if they have a woman modeller. Normal, like, the women paint pins.

—Paint pins?

—Or help with the dippers, like, or paint plates an' that, but not so many as modellers, not at Wedgwood's works.

—You could ask Mr Wilbraham, she said quietly and seriously. I am a very good potter.

He had never heard quite such a statement on any human lips, male or female. The words were not exactly boasting, since it was clear that she was merely saying what was the case.

—Right, he said with a smile. Next time I see old Wilbraham, I'll put in a word. And, he looked back across the yard, if the Sergeant . . .

—Please, she said quietly.

She did not need to say much more than to repeat the three words, Ask Mr Wilbraham. But he had not done so, not at first, because he wanted an excuse to return to see her at the Rising Sun.

It was soon clear that Caleb was in love with Mrs Powell, and that the publican was, in a sense, right to accuse him of 'sniffing around' her. It was clear, too, that this was not something which would be resolved without a crisis. The way he saw it, there was nothing which could now stop him loving her; though how this would develop, and whether she would accept his love, he could not tell.

Blue Squirrel, for her part, could not mistake his feelings. She had no wish to cause scandal. And in a small part of herself, she felt that she had used her husband as the means for coming to Staffordshire and meeting Wooden Leg. She was now within a short space of her goal. To love this new man, Mr Bowers, would only cause trouble. She did not love him in return, but the knowledge of his love caused a strange mixture of emotions in her heart: excitement, joy, fear, and – something of which she had experienced not a glimmering since the destruction of Old Kowes by the Americans – she felt hopeful about her future.

# 16

ALEXANDER CHISHOLM, A SNOWY-HAIRED SIXTY YEAR OLD, was engaged as Pa's secretary, and the younger Wedgwoods' chemistry tutor during that summer. The success of the appointment was apparent in the fact that all the older children were soon perfecting their Chisholm imitations, revealing, as they did so, how quickly he had sharpened their scientific curiosity.

—And so, my friends, my great friend, your father's great friend, Dr Priestley – what is it? What is it he has discovered? Nothing less, my friends, than dephlogisticated air! What did he do, what did he do? He REDUCED a mercury calx without charcoal, and he produced this infinitely more breathable so to say, my friends, an eminently respirable AIR! And what is this dephlogisticated air, my friends? It is what M. Lavoisier, greatly indebted to our friend Dr Priestley, calls OXYGEN! Mr Priestley calls this the French heresy! But what Monsieur calls Oxygen Gas is to all intents and purposes the same as Mr Priestley's dephlogisticated air. Now by studying this Oxygen Gas, you see, my friends, we begin at last, after thousands and thousands of years of human inquiry, to see how things are – how the universe hangs together . . .

And Tom, no less anxious than Josiah Junior to 'be' Mr Chisholm, could take up the tale with,

—So you see, my friends, although there are some among us who have been looking for a FRENCH Revolution, something along the lines of the AMERICAN Revolution, you could say that the FRENCH REVOLUTION already occurred here; because, inspired by the discovery of Oxygen Gas, or Dephlogisticated air, what have they done? What have they done? They have discovered the properties of matter, the properties of matter, my friends. We can begin to single out different types of gas, types of AIR, so to say. Why, already in France the brothers Montgolfier have learnt how to fly in a balloon! And our own Mr Watt – Mr Watt, my friends, with Dr Priestley and M. Lavoisier, what have we here? Spark together your Oxygen Gas and your inflammable air. What do you have, my friends – water? And now what has Mr Cavendish discovered for us, my friends?

—Qu-qu-queer fish, Cavendish, said Dr Darwin. Lives near me in Derby. So shy of women, he's had an extra staircase built in his house so he never has to see his housekeeper. Communicates with her by l-l-letter!

—And he has discovered, said Tom in his Mr Chisholm persona, that water is one third part Oxygen Gas and two parts inflammable air. Now these gases can support combustion. We know the properties of water, we can harness it, harness it, my friends, and make an engine. The energy of the water so combusted can become steam and drive an engine. Think of Mr Arkwright, using the power of water – water, you see my friends – Mr Arkwright in his mills in Lancashire. His water-frame can make the spinning jennies work ten, twenty, thirty at a time! Out come the cotton spinners from their cottages in small villages – and into the manufactories they go! In their dozens, their hundreds. Ten years ago, Mr Arkwright had three hundred souls in his mills – now it is three thousand! Energy, my friends, energy! Dr Darwin even has it in mind to make a steam-propelled carriage.

—It'll c-come! insisted the doctor against their childish laughter.

So, from the cellar laboratories there now proceeded the pops, bangs, explosive bursts, puffs of smoke which might be expected to emanate from a wizard's cave. When Josiah returned from his next business visit to London, Tom and Josiah asked, and received his permission, to discontinue their music practice since chemistry was 'a good deal pleasanter and more useful'.

—What is chemistry? Sukey asked Mr Chisholm one day at dinner.

—Why, my dear young woman, it is how one thing CHANGES into another thing.

—Metamorphosis, in short?

—Precisely, my young friend.

—And how can we tell that what you are doing is any more true or less true than the stories told in Ovid?

—Because Ovid, my dear young lady, did not produce a steam engine, he did not produce a hot air balloon!

—B-b-but he could expand our m-m-m—

—Minds, sir? With mythology?

—Certainly! replied Darwin with some heat. That is w-w-w-why I am writing my poem about the plants – 'The L-Loves of the P-P-Plants'. N-n-natural philosophy and m-myth are not separate. Botany, chemistry, all branches of Natural Philosophy are the new m-mythology of our age.

—But they're myths which happen to be true, said Sukey.

—All myths are t-t-true for those who live by them, said the doctor. Our age is advancing so much faster than any other in history because we have s-s-seen the m-m-mythological use to which chemistry, botany and so forth can be p-put. The ancient Egyptians h-h-had no idea about oxygen or the F-F-French heresy but they invented the s-steam engine.

—Truly, my dear sir? You astound me! said Josiah.

—Oh, yes, Philo of Alexandria knew about steam engines. The difference b-b-between him and me is that he could not th-th-think of a use for them and I can imagine a st-st-steam carriage which would take me from here to D-D-Derby in half an hour!

—Pa, is that true? asked Sukey. Are we really different from our ancestors?

Josiah was silent for a space. Then he said, with a little laugh,

—Ask Dr Ovid here.

Darwin and Chisholm laughed.

Josiah added,

—Ay, lass. We're different from our Dad's generation, different from what went before. We're metamorphosed, you maht say.

And his face resumed the sadness which had possessed it for months, ever since the death of Bentley. After they had eaten and the cloths were removed, Darwin said,

—I can see you are t-troubled by neuralgia, sir. Your jaw is so fixed. There is p-pain in your jaw.

—There is pain everywhere, said Josiah Wedgwood.

—Then you should increase the dosage of opiates.

But it was by an almost visible act of will that Josiah lifted himself out of his melancholy. He announced one morning at breakfast,

—For twenty years, afore even I met Mr Bentley, the life of this family and the life of this firm have been held back by Cookworthy and Champion and these other troublemakers. And now, when it is too late to tell Mr Bentley of our good fortune, we are rid of them, and we all – all the potters in England – have access to the Cornish china clay.

Tom looked up. The other boys continued to saw at their mutton chops, or eat their cold chicken legs with their fingers.

Sukey turned to her father and said,

—So, Pa, you have made a decision?

—I have, lass, I have! And we're *all* going.

—Lord save us, exclaimed Mrs Wedgwood, where in the world is he taking us now?

—Guess!

He had that look of almost idiotic, boyish glee which they had not seen for months. It was an expression which Sukey so loved and which could make Sally slam cutlery in exasperation.

—Where, do you guess, Tom? Timbuktoo? The Great Wall of China?

—Somewhere where there's clay?

—Well done, lad! Somewhere where there's clay and then beyond. We are going to Land's End.

And so they went, the whole family, except poor Mary Ann, who was left behind with her nurse. Sally and Heffie, Sukey, John, Jos Junior and Tom, Kitty, Sarah, the whole tribe with Owd Wooden Leg. It was the last great enterprise which they all undertook together, before the metamorphosis of John and Josiah into gentlemen.

They went in two parties by mail coach to Bath. Sukey had never seen that city, though her mother went often for the cure, and Pa had showrooms there. It was a revelation to Sukey, even more spectacular than London itself. The town was so new, and so perfect. In London, beside the new splendours, there were old squalors: but here, all seemed to be as the architects had intended. The sun was bright when they arrived at their inn near the Pump Room and the Abbey. She saw the carved angels who ascended to the throne of God above the west door of that church, and clambered down the stone ladder to the right. She saw, with Tom on her arm, the severe Grecian terraces, the fudge-coloured crescents, the squares and the King's Circus. Walking about in the middle of the Circus on the austere paving, she felt she was in ancient Rome, only a Rome devoid of its cruelties. Here, in this Coliseum-like structure, were no bleeding gladiators or fighting beasts, but gentlemen in wigs, walking their valetudinarian, bonneted wives in the golden sunshine of the afternoon.

The town was a dream, and one which satisfied them all. For while Sukey and Tom paced about, and noticed a poster for a tempting concert in the Assembly Rooms, Josiah was enabled to visit the showrooms and conduct some business. There was a concert – a delightful performance of a concerto grosso by Handel. Next day, while Sally, Heffie and Sukey took the waters and admired the clothes of those visiting the Assembly Rooms, and while Tom nursed a bad cough in his bedroom at the inn, old Josiah developed a brief but intense preoccupation with buttons.

—Why, you could sell Wedgwood buttons by the pocketful! he told the assistants in the salerooms. Buttons with emperors' heads, buttons commemorating great events . . . why, we could reach the happy position of finding all the gentlemen and ladies of Bath adorned with Wedgwood buttons and medallions.

Sukey, when she heard of the scheme, had laughed, but such was the good humour which the journey had uncharacteristically inspired, there was no scorn in the laughter, or not much.

They were near a week in Bath, and from thence they progressed to Exeter. Beyond Exeter, the roads deteriorated into rutted, dirty tracks, and the advance into Cornwall was slow. The difficulty of the journey, which caused Sally's spirits to swoop down, and which seemed to be half-killing Tom, only inspired Josiah to go further and further. Outside St Austell, he insisted upon clambering up the chalky white clay-pits and waving his stick in triumph.

—We did it! We did it!, he cried.

—Now can we go home? moaned Sally.

But he needed to go on, on, on. They were in two coaches as they attempted to cross the bridge at Penzance. The wheel of the first carriage descended into a pothole so deep that there was a danger of the whole vehicle overturning.

—Oh, please let's stop!

—Not now we've come so far! And look! Look! Look at the Mount! St Michael's Mount! And the glittering sea.

To Sukey, it was indeed the most beautiful view, and Penzance the noblest and most beautiful town she had ever seen, surpassing even Bath – for Bath had no sea, and nothing could match this Cornish light. She squeezed her mother's hand in a consolatory gesture.

—Them in tother carridge nearly went ower, lahk!

Though Heffie affected amusement, there was as much fear in her voice as there was tiredness in all their faces.

But Jos, puce-faced with ardour, drove them on. Beyond the bridge, the hill became sheer, and they all had to get out and follow the carriages to the brow. And now the hedges, bright with gorse, stood out against the blowy wind and the bright sky, and the horses themselves seemed to sense Wedgwood's excitement. And for the last seven miles, cantering and galloping down narrow, high-hedged lanes, the Wedgwood family made their way to Land's End.

Heffie was wondering if they'd see a 'mermeed'. But though they were not so fortunate, when they reached their rocky destination they had some compensation.

—We're here, Wedgwoods! We're here.

—Watch yosen, Jos Wedgwood! called Heffie.

—I can't watch him, said Sally, untruthfully, pressing both cheeks with gloved fingers.

The one-legged man, with his walking stick, was hopping from rock to rock, out into the ocean. Sukey stood with her mother on the shore and watched the strange sight of her red-faced father in his grey coat, and his wig askew, treating the ragged rocks as stepping stones. Little by little, the family joined him, Sarah and Kitty dancing like fairies.

—Dunna fo in! Heffie was laughing now as the sea foamed.

Tom, in spite of his cough, jumped energetically after his father, and Jos and John had removed their shoes and stockings and were wading in the waves. There was a line of brown-white foam where the sea crashed on to the sand, and beyond that a line of purest turquoise, and beyond that still a blue-black rolling wave of ocean ever-heaving, ever in movement, ever-dappled with little flecks of white foam. Out to sea, beyond the glimmering grey-blue and the streaks of white, were more islets of jutting rock where the ocean foamed and broke, sometimes sending up white fountains into the clear air. And to greet this remarkable family, who stood there at the furthermost westerly tip of England, and stared towards America across the Atlantic, there bobbed up a family of seals, their great doggy eyes staring quizzically at their human visitors.

# INTERLUDE:
# A BURIAL IN TRAFALGAR YEAR

ABOVE A GREEN BANK IN A DORSET CHURCHYARD, GREEN BANK
notes fluttered from the twigs of an old elm. A bird sang in the pure azure.
*The Bank Balance Ascending* by Charles Darwin. *The Origin of Larks*
by Ralph Vaughan Williams. *The Trial of King Charles Darwin* by C. V.
Wedgwood. England expects every man to claim his duty, with interest.
Money, like genes, rolled down the great river of life towards the future.

In 1805, the dynasty gathered in Tarrant Gunville to bury Tom
Wedgwood, photographer Tom, in white clay. Owd Wooden Leg was ten
years dead. Cousin Byerley and his enormous brood of eleven children
lived at Etruria now and ran the works. Owd Wooden Leg had died in
'ninety-five. The variants and mutations of his genes and Sally's stood
around upon the greensward watching the coffin of his son Tom, photographer Tom, being carried to the open grave of white clay. Money and
Genes drove on the March of mind and music. From this group of individuals, who gathered to bury their ingenious thirty-four-year old Tom,
sprang the great pedigree of Victorian intellectuals – scientists, musi-
cians, politicians. The tribe who had scampered about in the Brickyard
Works in Burslem in 1730, and contracted smallpox in 1741, and carried
saggars on their heads into the brick chimneys of the pot banks in that
still rural village bore as little relation to their Victorian intellectual
descendants as did the orang-utangs and gorillas to the human race.

## A. N. Wilson

*Was it money, Josiah's money, the catalyst which metamorphosed them? When photographer Tom died, in Trafalgar year, his sister Sukey was forty, and by now married to Robert Darwin. Sukey and Robert still lived in the north Midlands, though in genteel Shrewsbury rather than honest Burslem. Robert, the doctor son of Dr Erasmus, was, in addition to being a physician, also a financier who multiplied their fortune many times over. Owd Wooden Leg had left Sukey her share of the huge inheritance: twenty-five thousand pounds. Robert's income as a physician was three thousand pounds a year. His flair as a banker and broker outstripped even his medical accomplishments. They, who in four years' time would become the parents of Charles Darwin, had accumulated a fortune of close on a quarter of a million pounds. Reader of the twenty-first century! Multiply it by a hundred for an idea of what it would be worth to you.*

*The old doctor, Erasmus Darwin, had died at a little over seventy in 1802. By then, this beloved physician and ever-enquiring natural philosopher was the most famous poet in England. A year after he died, there was published posthumously his masterpiece* The Temple of Nature *in which he explored his scientific enquiry into the origin of things. The poem saw life beginning asexually and purposelessly, beneath the surfaces of the Ocean –*

> *Hence without parent by spontaneous birth*
> *Rise first the specks of animated earth;*
> *From Nature's womb the plant or insect swims,*
> *And buds or breathes, with microscopic limbs.*

*From these mysterious life-forms, came the capacity to reproduce –*

> *The Reproductions of the living Ens*
> *From sires to sons, unknown to sex, commence.*

*The stronger genes drive out the weaker.*

# The Potter's Hand

*The feeble births acquired diseases chase,*
*Till Death extinguish the degenerate race.*

The key ingredient in the survival of species was, according to the poem, sexual rivalry, in which the stronger expels the weaker male. Nature is seen as a battleground –

*The wolf, escorted by his milk-drawn dam,*
*Unknown to mercy, tears the guiltless lamb;*
*The towering eagle, darting from above,*
*Unfeeling rends the inoffensive dove.*

Sukey, among her kinsfolk in that Dorset churchyard, recollected these lines by her father-in-law and thought of her poor, drug-crazed genius of a brother Tom, whose coffin – how painfully light it looked as it was hoisted upon the shoulders of his brothers and cousins – was now carried to burial. If her thoughts were a little woozy, it was because, in common with the rest of the family, she had taken a few drops of laudanum an hour before the ceremony to give her strength. It was the first funeral she had ever attended. Pa having died in the Potteries and been buried in Stoke, she had observed the customs of his class and place. Now, swathed in black bonnet with a thick crepe veil, as were her mother and sisters, she stood a little distant from the men.

Into the unfeeling world of Nature, where the triumph of 'the living Ens', or being itself, was itself a battle, stepped humanity. As they increased and multiplied, humanity would have gobbled itself into starvation had not war and famine culled its surplus.

*So human progenies, if unrestrain'd*
*By climate friended, and by food sustain'd,*
*O'er sea and soils, prolific hordes! Would spread*

*Erelong, and deluge their terraqueous bed;*
*But war, and pestilence, disease and dearth,*
*Sweep the superfluous myriads from the earth.*

Her genial father-in-law, who had been her doctor and friend since early childhood, had concluded that in such a universe, humanity alone could bring benevolence, morality, kindliness. It was his hope

*That man should ever be the friend of man,*
*Should eye with tenderness all living forms*
*His brother emmets and his sister worms.*

It was an estimable ambition, which she shared. But if this were the true state of Nature, where was the great Creator? Voltaire had erected a Church for Him, but Voltaire was dead. What would Sukey's children make of the Author of the Universe?

Sukey had never discussed religion with her father. Every few weeks, he would escort the whole tribe of them to the Unitarian chapel at Newcastle where Mama's grandfather had once been the minister. Unitarianism allowed the mind its freedoms. It asserted the existence of the First Cause, and a due reverence for the moral code, but it had separated itself from those who would attempt to divide three into one, or worship the inspired carpenter-prophet of Galilee as a member of the Trinity. And yet, Pa's funeral had been in church – at Stoke – and now again, the Unitarian tradesfolk of the north Midlands had mutated into Church of England southern gentry.

—I know.

Sukey now spoke this word, 'know', with her lips formed into an O. Pa had said 'I knaw', and among her surviving siblings, there was a just-discernible variation in the way this vowel was pronounced. The effeminate-sounding, Eton- and Oxford-educated southern parson whinnied,

*—I knyow that my Redeemer liveth . . .*

*A very delicate breeze shook the elms and beeches above their heads and lifted the lily-white linen bands at the parson's throat.*

*—I syed, I will take heed unto my wheeze; that I offend not with my tongue . . .*

*But the man did offend Sukey with his tongue.* She felt completely alienated by this voice, his white surplice, his white bands, his white hands. She gasped at the felt implications of this burial: Pa, Mary Ann, little baby Richard, had all been buried in Staffordshire. This was the first of them to be buried in alien clay. They were the first Wedgwoods since the time of William and Mary not to be Potteries folk.

*—Eshes to eshes, dust to dust.*

*Potter's clay to Dorset clay; Burslem dust to Tarrant Gunville earth.*

It was the clay which had drawn them there in the first instance, Pa's need for clay. If Cookworthy and the Bristol works prevented him from going to Cornwall, and if the American war made it impossible to get the purest Cherokee kaolin, it must be found somewhere else. Josiah, who had been conducting mineral experiments since boyhood, had an almost instinctive sense of where clay could be found. Explorations in the country of Dorset led to the fields near Eastbury, beneath which lay the deposits of sticky white clay suitable for his trademark jasperware.

*—Tom in his coffin,* thought Sukey. *My baby brother in his coffin, with all his chances exhausted. Tom, the man of genius. What had Coleridge written, damned Coleridge,*

*—He is gone, my friend, my munificent co-patron, and not less the benefactor of my intellect!*

*A pretty way of saying that young Josiah and Tom Wedgwood had bank-rolled the lazy, pretentious, unscrupulous Coleridge for the last five years!*

*—He who beyond all other men known to me, added a fine and ever-wakeful sense of beauty to the most patient accuracy in experimental philosophy . . .*

*Of all the siblings, it was Tom who had been the keenest inheritor of Pa's scientific curiosity, his sheer genius. The fading of the heliotypical images on the silver nitrate page now appeared to Sukey like the cruellest of metaphors for her brother's weak, pallid face, which had now faded utterly from their vision.*

*—We give thee hearty thenks, thet it hath pleased thee to deliver this our brother out of the miseries of this sinful world.*

*No, no, no, Mr Parson, I do not give thanks, or thenks either, for the melancholy, or hypochondria, or dejection of Tom's life, which interrupted all his study, all his capacity for enjoyment, and crippled his talents and capabilities; I do not give thanks for the congenital physical weaknesses which he shared with his all his family; I do not give thanks for a life pointlessly cut short, in part by mental and physical illness, in part by addiction to drink and narcotics, and I would thank you, Mr Parson, not to put words in my mouth.*

*The birds above sang with heartless joy, indifferent to her rage. The sun shone. There was complete peacefulness upon the scene. It was hard to believe that a mere thirty miles away in the Channel, the French Navy was poised to invade England.*

*White cumulus lolled in a jasper-blue firmament. Against the churchyard wall thick cow parsley burgeoned shoulder high. Behind it, cabbage moths dipped and fluttered in the abundant red valerian. The hedges frothed with dog roses. Red campion and sneezewort edged up in the thicker grass around the older tombs. Upon the turfy graves near Tom's, daisies, clover, buttercups, all bright from the previous night's shower, were heartlessly beautiful. And in the cornfields beyond the stone walls of the cemetery, dotted like drops of blood, the poppies, the fateful poppies, which were the cause of Tom's undoing, nodded mockingly at their victim as they laid him to earth.*

*I heard a voice from hivven, saying unto me, WRITE.*

# PART THREE

# The Portland Vase

Are those her ribs through which the Sun
Did peer as through a grate?
And is that Woman all her crew?
Is that a DEATH? And are there two?
Is DEATH that woman's mate?

Samuel Taylor Coleridge,
*The Rime of the Ancient Mariner*

# I

—WE HAD THOUGHT OF YOU, MR WEDGWOOD, AS THE friend of free trade.

—And so I am, Prime Minister.

—Except where the Irish are concerned?

—What we, what the General Chamber of Manufacturers of Great Britain, feel most strongly, *most* strongly – Josiah could feel his voice shaking, partly from conviction, partly from nerves at being in so august an assembly – is that these measures will damage British trade at precisely the moment when we most need a recovery. The effects of the American war have been calamitous upon all British mercantile life. Wholesalers in the former colonies are still not settling accounts for goods exchanged three, five, even eight years ago. It will take a decade for us to recover our strength.

—But there are no significant pottery manufactories in Ireland, Mr Wedgwood.

The observation came from the drawly voice of the Duke of Rutland. Josiah looked for help to the one member of the Parliamentary Committee who might have been his friend, Lord Gower. But since the disastrous Stubbs dinner there had been a perceptible cooling of relations between Trentham Park and Etruria Hall; and, in any case, Gower was a politician and, as the Lord Privy Seal, he was not going to quarrel publicly with the stiff, impassive youth whom the King in his wisdom had just asked to form an administration.

William Pitt the Younger's challenge, after the termination of the American war, was very largely an economic one. Trade had indeed been very badly affected by the eight years of American conflict. The war had cost Britain over one hundred million pounds. Not only had it deprived Britain of American trade, but – because France had been at war with Britain over the American issue – it had produced a catastrophic effect upon continental trade. Pitt, the twenty-seven-year-old Prime Minister, now proposed to fuse the Irish economy with the rest of Britain, to allow free trade, without tariffs, between Britain and Ireland as a way of relieving Irish poverty and stimulating the economy of that island.

—Cheap Irish labour, Wedgwood was saying, will undermine our capacity on this side of the water. We cannot compete with the Irish if they pay their hands a pittance! The General Chamber of Manufacturers, which I had the honour to form, and which I represent here today before Parliament, could tell you the same story, gentlemen, whether we were discussing the sale of buttons, or gloves, or china, or machinery.

Josiah had expected the Prime Minister to respond to this paragraph. He had practised saying it several times before his shaving mirror that very morning, and he believed it had a force against which it would be difficult to argue. But Mr Pitt merely said,

—Thank you, Mr Wedgwood.

Lord Gower looked sly as Josiah scraped his chair, and bowed and took his leave of the Parliamentary Committee. On his way out of the ancient panelled room, one of the many which made up the warren of the old Palace of Westminster, he met Charles James Fox, William Eden and Lord Sheffield, the trio of politicians who had put him up to giving this evidence to the Parliamentary Committee. Fox was Wedgwood's political hero – a radical who believed passionately in human freedom.

—That'll scotch the young shaver!, said Eden.

The three politicians all laughed.

—We must offer you refreshment, Mr Wedgwood, said Fox. Come into my rooms for a glass of wine.

—I am heartily obliged, said Josiah with an obsequious bow, but I must decline the generous offer. I have—

—A rival attraction? asked Lord Sheffield.

—I think I know what it is, said the fleshy-faced Fox, more kindly than his two colleagues.

And again, the three men laughed, as though Wedgwood had walked into a trap.

After the bowing and the farewell, Wedgwood felt a sense of inner misgiving, wondering whether he had been right in the matter of the Irish trade agreement. Important as it was to the future of his business, however, there was something else upon his mind. He could hardly contain his excitement as he walked down the corridor outside the Committee room and made his way down the strange medieval and Tudor maze of the Parliament building. Before Pitt had been the King's choice for Prime Minister, for a few months in 1783 it had been the Duke of Portland who had held together, as Prime Minister, a precarious Whig coalition, with Mr Fox as Foreign Secretary. It was to this musically minded and artistic Duke that Wedgwood was now making his way. At first, he got lost and found himself on a stone staircase being accosted by a Yeoman of the Guard, clad in the flat hat, ruff and doublet of the Henrician soldier. You would have believed it if told that this white-bearded man, rather than being a veteran of Göttingen, had seen action at Flodden Field.

—Oh no, sir, you've quite come out of your way. You're nearly in the White Chamber, sir, and His Grace is up near the Court of Requests.

—I have been up there once, and nearly found myself in a kitchen.

—Then you were very near it, sir. Their Lordships' House is next to the House of Commons kitchen.

Josiah could feel himself sweating under the strain. Part of this was the sheer physical difficulty of hobbling about these uneven floors and stairs upon his peg leg. Part was a nervous reaction to having just been under public scrutiny in the Committee room. (Josiah was one of those who suffered from attacks of nerves after, rather than before, trying events.)

But the chief cause of the sweat and the palpitating heart was the letter which he carried in his pocket.

*I wish you may soon come to town to see Wm Hamilton's Vase, it is the finest production of Art that has been brought to England and seems to be the very apex of perfection to which you are endeavouring to bring your bisque & jasper; it is of a kind called 'Murrina' by Pliny, made of dark glass with white enamel figures. The Vase is about a foot high & the figures between five & six inches, engraved in the same manner as a Cameo & of the grandest & most perfect Greek Sculpture.*

Flaxman's letter had come to Etruria on a dank, cold day in February. A raw day, a freezing mist so thick that the works were hardly visible from the house. Holding the letter in his large red fingers, Josiah felt the stirrings which always accompanied the beginning of any great matter. He had felt these prickings of excitement years before in Liverpool, when there was a chance of going into business with Bentley. He had felt like this when the chance came to buy the Ridge House estate and move to Etruria. Flaxman was a man who, personally, revolted Josiah Wedgwood: an arrogant, near-anarchic sensualist. But in Flaxman, there had come again to earth some of the Greek genius, the divinity of Phidias. Excepting perhaps the Stubbs bas-relief of Phaeton driving his chariots too near the sun, the finest reliefs and sculptures in Wedgwood's catalogues were all Flaxman's productions. These large hands which held Flaxman's letter, and the brain which read the words . . . Josiah felt all but detached from them, as if some *daimon* flowed through them, as if he were an instrument. Yet, for him the whole glory of the Antique was not that they were irreligious in the modern way of Voltaire, so much as that they were able to have a religion, or a series of religions, which avoided 'the Infamy'.

For them, in sun-scorched Athens and primitive Etruria and sturdy Rome, their mythologies and theologies were organically linked to the realities of life, not hysterically at variance with it. War, lust, the cycle of seasons and the abundance or the dearth of crops, as well as the greater metaphysical mysteries of life and death, were contained in their stories of Gods, nymphs, heroes. Beside the mythology was their unfolding sense of historical destiny, and their serious application, in the Letters of Cicero, for example, to the ethical requirements. The need to lead a good life. But it was all in their hands: their hands fashioned the artefacts, erected the temples and the agora, tilled the vineyards and devised the laws.

When John Wesley came to the Potteries, Josiah had been to see the famous orator. It was like something in the Bible, as when the prophet Elijah gathered together Israel to witness his contests with the prophets of Baal, or when Moses drew the Israelites to the foot of the mount. The prophet Wesley had drawn a crowd of nearly a thousand men and women, and as he spoke, of their sinfulness and their neediness and their redemption through the Saviour's blood, extraordinary waves of enthusiasm had passed through the crowd.

Josiah had been repelled. Some of the men were weeping, groaning, even shrieking for forgiveness. Their maenad wives were shouting alleluia! And when the hymns began, it had been time for Owd Wooden Leg to take his leave. But as he had done so, and hobbled back to the coach, the whole hillside had reverberated to the words and music – poetry of a kind, but poetry of a kind which seemed uncivilized.

> Visit us with thy salvation,
> Enter every trembling heart.

The collective hysteria had been nothing to do with reason. It had nothing civic about it. It was all concerned with the mishmash of emotion inside these confused individuals. It was the same phenomenon which made them lurch in and out of taverns and fuddle their wits with gin. No wonder Wesley made his disciples forswear gin – he was peddling a rival mind-rot. Now some of the hands at the works were asking if they could build a Wesleyan chapel at Etruria. It seemed like a contradiction of everything he stood for.

To Josiah, all he had done from the beginnings of his professional and family existence had been with the aim of making life better – better organized, more rational. His fascination with the Antique had been very largely technical. He'd heard Erasmus Darwin and Bentley talking about him, and saying he knew nothing of the real classical literature, such as an educated man would know. Caleb mocked him likewise, pointing out that Jos got all his classical learning from Tooke. Maybe he did.

He had lived to see the world turning away from superstitious hierarchies, and towards a juster, more rational basis for society. He had lived to see, and rejoiced to see, the American Revolution. He had seen the ingenuity of his friends Boulton and Watt transform the manufacturing industry of the country. With friends Brindley and Bridgewater he had helped construct a canal system which made it possible to transport manufactured goods from one end of the kingdom to the other smoothly and efficiently. Above all, in his own sphere, he had not only outstripped all rivals, he had become better and better at his craft.

The sale of Bentley's goods in London when he died had been a revelation to the world: twelve days in the auction rooms selling his personal collection of Wedgwood stock – vases, urns, busts, bas-reliefs. Many of the Wedgwood pieces had been inspired by the illustrated engravings of antiquities excavated by Sir William Hamilton around the Bay of Naples. Some were of Wedgwood's own design. The assembly of the whole achievement in the auction rooms, however, was in its fashion a demonstration of what he and the more enlightened men and women of his generation had chosen to do with existence. These ceramic objects had made a statement about life, as did the architecture of William Chambers or Robert Adam.

Theirs was an age when Reason could once more rule the human race, when Cicero – a 'new man', wasn't he? – could be heard in the Senate. The ancients did not grovel, as Wesley's Methodists grovelled. Their hearts were not mean altars: their hearts did not tremble, they were open to reason, their hearts were open to the light of Mount Olympus. It was through humanity that the divine *afflatus* flowed, creating order and decency. Josiah's unstoppable energy was something which he himself scarcely understood. Sometimes, when his exhausted frame was racked with the familiar series of medical problems – neuralgia in his face, diarrhoea, and in general a weak digestion, phantom pains in his 'lost' leg, sleeplessness – Jos could have wanted the divine breeze to stop blowing through the strings of his particular Aeolian harp. But ideas kept coming, ambitions did not cease; and as the End of All approached, he wanted perfection – the physical perfection of the Great, the Ineffable, the Sublimely Beautiful Artefact.

Flaxman's phrase – 'It is the finest production of Art that has been brought to England' – that was what triggered this new frenzy of desire in Wedgwood. He would see it, he would copy it, he would outstrip it in its beauty. And, even as he had the thought of how he would do so – modelling the Vase himself, and rebuilding a kiln to fire at hitherto undreamed-of temperatures – even as he thought of the technicalities of glaze, and the fascinations of resolving all the technical problems, he had also seen, in his mind's eye, the inevitable consequence. He would reach a summit of perfection, aesthetic and technological: and the pecuniary emoluments would come down like lava from Vesuvius. The strange glow of satisfaction caused by the knowledge of his own success both tingled and exhausted his very limbs.

Josiah had business in London in any event. He needed to visit young Byerley and his wife – oh, she was a delight, that lass! – in Greek Street. He was summoned to appear before the Committee of the House to defend the interests of the General Chamber of Manufacturers. And he needed to see that Vase. Within hours of receiving Flaxman's letter, Wedgwood had applied to the Duke of Portland, the Vase's owner, and now he was going to view this object, which had taken shape in his head as a grail, an aesthetic and technical perfection to which he would devote the rest of his life.

—Ah, Mr Wedgwood.

—Your Grace.

The third Duke of Portland was seated at a writing table as the manufacturer was shown into his room. He was somewhat younger than Josiah: sharp, bright eyes, a quizzical mouth, a small aquiline nose, very smooth, arched eyebrows, almost like a woman's, Jos thought, and a neat bob wig. Lace cuffs frothed from the sleeves of a dark crimson coat. He wore matching crimson breeches and hose of a silvery grey, encased in very soft shining black shoes with silver buckles.

—I've finished my business here for the day. We can travel home together, he said.

Josiah did not bow exactly, but he fumbled with his hands. He had been told to meet the Duke in Westminster, but he had not expected the Vase would be here. Quite where he was to view it, he had not exactly envisaged. As the carriage trotted across St James's Park from Westminster towards the Duke's residence in Berkeley Square, Josiah, feeling and smelling himself sweat disturbingly, envisaged the Vase. He knew it was of Alexandrian glass. His mind made the venerable object tall, perhaps with some of the elegance of his own agate creations, with a sibyl finial and swagged with gilded drapery; or perhaps austere and cool with a gadrooned body, such as the pair he had made for the Duke of Chandos. The more vases he had made, the taller, the more elongated they had become. This was a shape he increasingly favoured, so that by the time the coach had reached Berkeley Square, and the two powdered postilions had leapt from the outside of the chaise to open the doors, and the footmen at the front door had flung wide the entrance to the house, Josiah's mind had made of the Barberini Vase – or the Portland Vase as he supposed it must now be called – something almost in the shape of a flagon.

—I can tell you are eager, Mr Wedgwood.

Did the Duke mean, Josiah wondered anxiously, that he could smell Wedgwood's eagerness?

—We'll go straight into the library. The Duke spoke with complete indifference to the servants, who bowed to right and left, and to the doors which opened with apparent automation.

They entered the beautiful library, which was to the right of the front door across a marbled floor. There were a number of vases atop the grilled bookshelves. Jos recognized two very fine urns of his own on the side tables. On the central table, which was of French design,

gilded walnut, inlaid at the top with marble, there stood an incon-
siderable pot, or so it seemed to Wedgwood's eye, a black thing
engraved with beautiful white figures, but squat and flat-topped; not
at all a shape which would have passed muster at Etruria! No word
escaped his lips, but he realized shyly that his eyes were still darting
around the room to find the Vase, and there was a twenty-second
awkwardness as the Duke recognized this.

—Well, there you are, sir! My mother's Vase.

Accurate as this description was, or had been, until the Duke
himself had recently bought it in an auction of his late mother's
effects, there was something in the phrase which was comically paro-
chial, given the Vase's long, prodigious, European story. Like many
insatiable collectors, Sir William Hamilton had bought it in Rome,
had paid more than he could afford, and he was happy to unload the
Vase on to the Duchess of Portland – 'a simple woman', Horace
Walpole said – 'intoxicated only by empty vases'. She only owned it
a year, before she died, and in the sale which followed, her son the
third Duke bought the Vase for nine hundred and eighty guineas. But
this was the termination, not the beginning, of its long journey.

When Jos's eyes accustomed themselves, the Vase, whose shape
had at first surprised him, worked an enchantment on his heart. Less
vulnerable than windowpanes which were blasted by Vesuvius, and
durable as the Roman bottles which so mysteriously, sea-green
and luminous, survive all over Europe as tokens of the legionary
presence, the glass Vase, which had perhaps been fashioned by
Greek-speaking Egyptians in Roman Alexandria and brought to the
capital in the reign of Augustus, had performed the miracle of survival; Achilles-like, stronger than its maker. The Imperial purple was
adopted by the overseers, or bishops, of the new superstition; and
the old Gods and heroes, revered in Corinthian and Doric temples,
faded to fragments of half-remembered verse and old tales which

were piecemeal refashioned, here from Ovid, there from an old frieze. The faith of the purple-clad bishops itself transmogrified from anarchic pacifism of the primitive times lampooned by Gibbon to the new rule of European law; from frenzied expectation of the end of time to rivalry with all Imperial powers, from ascetic monks to violent crusaders. From the chaos of medieval Rome, the Renaissance Popes built new domes, new columns and new friezes. The Gothic and mathematical mysticism of the medieval cracked and fell, replaced by unabashed classical form. Princes of the Church like old senators chose once more to derive pleasure from the pagan aesthetes. They had not died, they were sleeping, the old Gods and heroes. The Trojan Priest Laocoön, wrestling with water-snakes, whose statue was admired by Pliny, was rediscovered, walled up in a vineyard on the Esquiline hill. Callipygian Venus and great-muscled Hercules, Apollo and Daphne, and Meleager were rediscovered, to adorn the palaces of Roman aristocrats and cardinals.

At about the time the English Queen Elizabeth was dying, a Barberini cardinal, who knows how or where, acquired the Vase, the great Vase, and once again its mysterious shape, its shimmering figures, were admired by appreciative eyes. Its power had slept. Now it awoke. But great and rich as the Barberini might have been – did not Maffeo of that name, who entertained the young John Milton when he was in Rome, become Pope Urban VIII? – few Italian grandees could resist the lure of English gold, once the grand tourists came. Old Donna Cornelia Barberini-Colonna, weighed down by dusty wigs and by her papal and aristocratic surnames, and last of her line, spent the 1770s playing whist and ombre and losing the remains of the family fortune in crumbled marbly corners of her old palace, encrusted with the family emblems, the bees. The grand tourists, English milords, were brought to her piano nobile. Much bowing and inspecting. Some of the young milords behaved with decorum, and others might have been wandering around a saleroom, as they eyed and fingered the stupendous, the antique Barberini collection. And enterprising architect-salesman James Byres bought the 'Barberini' Vase, for a sum he did not disclose, and persuaded Sir William Hamilton to part with a thousand pounds.

So the third Duke paid at auction some forty pounds less than Sir William had paid for it in Rome.

—You alone in Europe have the expertise to copy it faithfully, said the Duke to his visitor.

—Highly condescending of Your Grace.

—It's true, man. What will you use? Black basaltes, like those urns over there?

—It will be a problem for me, said Josiah, trying to keep the disappointment from his voice.

—You can scarcely spare the time to copy it in London. You must take it to Staffordshire.

—Are you sure, my lord?

He remembered too late that 'my lord' was not the correct way to address a Duke. He was thinking of the temperature he would need to fire the basalt. White porcelain slip for the figures? But how to reproduce the luminescent quality of those exquisite figures?

—I can barely express . . . gratitude . . . in Your Grace's trust.

—Nonsense, man. We can't have Sèvres and Meissen overtaking Mr Wedgwood. This will be a crowning achievement. Think of the wonder of it! Sir William bears the Vase back in triumph from ancient Rome. But it is the British, sir, who will be the new Rome. What is it the poet says?

> Other Romans shall arise,
> Heedless of a soldier's name;
> Sounds, not arms, shall win the prize,

Harmony their path to fame.
Then the progeny that springs
From the forests of our land,
Arm'd with thunder, clad with wings,
Shall a wider world command.

—Eh, Mr Wedgwood?

—Quite so, Your Grace. Well, if you'll hazard it, I'll take it back to Etruria.

—I like the sound of it! said the Duke with a strange smile.

Even as he left, Josiah could hear the Duke practising his cello.

# 2

WHILE JOSIAH WAS HAVING THIS CONVERSATION WITH THE
Duke of Portland, about the possible hazards of transporting the Vase
to Staffordshire, the normal tranquillity of Etruria was being dis-
rupted. The poverty and hunger which Mr Pitt hoped to diminish in
Ireland were suffered in England too. Josiah was a believer in free
trade when it suited him – except when the low wages of the Irish
might threaten to drive down English prices and the English manufacturers' profits. The English landowners and agriculturalists were
confused by no such double standards. They insisted upon Parliament imposing tariffs on cheap imported corn. Their own profits
from poor harvests over three years were not to allow the price of
British cereals to decrease. The result was that the price of bread was
scarcely affordable for the poorer classes.

There were mass meetings in most of the Staffordshire towns. At
the Billington Works in Hanley, the hands were particularly active
politically, radicalized, it was thought, by one Barlow, keenly supported by his friend Boulton. They had demanded higher wages,
and for several days Billington's had been closed. There were similar
disruptions at many of the other potteries, and Josiah had placed
his works manager, Wilbraham, on the alert for any signs of radical-
ism among the Etruria workforce. Sukey and her three brothers got
Richard Hall the coachman to drive them into Newcastle to a

meeting addressed by a Major Sneyd on the dangers facing them. The meeting was held in the Guildhall, and the major was accompanied by the militia of local reserves, overseen by Sergeant Powell, a veteran of the American and Canadian wars who now ran an inn some ten miles south down the canal out Burston way. The major was a short man, with double chins and a brown bob wig. He wore a blue coat and grey breeches. About two hundred people had come to hear what he had to say.

—Every property owner in the district, said the major, must be aware of the dangers we face. The mob attacked a warehouse last week in Stafford, and the other day there were disturbances around Lord St Vincent's barns at Meaford. There have been troubles at Billington's, only a hop away from Mr Wedgwood's own manufactory at Etruria. Any shop, any canal barge, any manufactory is vulnerable. Now it is quite clear what we need.

—To give food to the poor? responded Sukey quietly. But her brothers looked at her furiously, as the major continued his harangue.

—to raise a subscription. We have raised a hundred pounds so far, and this should keep – what, Sergeant? A decent troop of men for a week?

—I should say so, Major.

—We've got a good platoon in Newcastle, and how many men from Stafford and Stone, Sarge?

—Oh, a good twenty, thirty men.

—But the militia can't do it all on their own. We need vigilance. We need, if necessary, to board up the manufactories, the houses of gentlefolk, the bigger shops.

Then they trotted home in the barouche. They noticed that M. Byerley, the shop which Everett was now managing, had boarded up its windows, as had most of the shops in the High Streets of Newcastle and Hanley.

—If people are hungry, persisted Sukey.

—It is still no excuse for mob rule, said John.

She supposed he must be right, but it was with feelings of some guilt that she felt herself salivating as they entered the hall at Etruria, and savoured the fumes of roasting mutton drifting up from the kitchens. Dinner was potato and leek soup, veal pie, roast mutton and a syllabub made from last summer's bottled damsons, served with an egg custard.

—Major Sneyd seems to have everything under control, John told their mother.

—Well, that's more than we have, said Sally. With your father in London, and Caleb on one of his canal jaunts. I went down to the works when you were out.

—Mother, you shouldn't. Pa's told us it's not safe when the hands are restive.

Sally ignored this ridiculous remark.

—Wilbraham says it is perfectly true. There is actual hunger, even among those with work. Lord Gower, and the Duke, and the rest of them are adamant that the price of grain cannot be lowered, and I am afraid there is, she murmured the word, well, resentment.

—I don't know what Wilbraham thinks he knows about it, said John.

—Very little, I imagine, said his mother sarcastically. He merely lives among these people and pays them their wages and notes that a dipper or a saggarmaker's weekly wage scarce covers the price of three loaves, some scrag end, milk for the bairns, by the time they've made clothes for them, and bought a few coals for the fire. It has been very cold lately, and it is six months before the next harvest. Your father is as generous as he can be, and, as you know, nearly all the workers at Etruria are paid more than the hands in other potteries.

# The Potter's Hand

—And what is Wilbraham suggesting? asked John with the elderly testiness of the late adolescent being affectedly grown-up. He dolloped more syllabub on to his plate as he put the question. That we ruin ourselves by paying these people more than we can afford? Hasn't Wilbraham heard of the war with America and France? Has he not heard of the slump in trade?

Even John's voice slightly faded as they all looked about the dining-room, with its gilded looking-glasses, swagged pilasters, gleaming floorboards and marble chimney piece. He put down an exquisite silver fork.

—Does he think we're made of money?

The mob did not come for them that day, however. On the following day, the bread sold out in the four bakers in Hanley, and someone chucked a stone through one of the bakers' windows. A small crowd collected in the marketplace in Hanley and a rumour began to fly through the town that a bargeful of grain was being transported up from Trentham even as they spoke. The words themselves seemed to make the crowd who heard them double in number, and they swarmed down to the bank of the cut.

It was a raw day. Solid-quartered Dandelion, with her good sloping pasterns, walked the towing path. Her breath was steamy. Dawn had begun with a deep frost, and Caleb Bowers, standing upon his long boat, wore a leather jerkin and a woollen cap knitted for him by his sister. It gave him something of the look of a Turkish corsair. Since falling in love, he had – Heffie noted with something approaching despair – begun to look much younger, almost preternaturally so. You could have mistaken this wiry pessimist in his late fifties for a man of forty. She had been unable at first to believe it. She had ribbed him about his devotion to the Welsh lady in the Rising Sun, and then to her horror, she had seen that this was something serious, transforming.

Like everyone else in the district, Caleb knew of the food shortages and the rumours of mob action. He knew he was at risk because he was carrying a cargo of flour and cheese which he had picked up at Fradley Junction, where the Trent and Mersey meets the Coventry Canal. The cargo had been loaded by the militia there, and the officer in charge had spoken to Caleb of disturbances all over the country.

—I'll do me best to protect it, since it's paid for, Caleb had said grudgingly. But I'll not fight any hungry man for food.

The captain had looked at him as if he were one of these dangerous republicans.

It was Dandelion, of the three of them, who first sensed trouble ahead. Caleb could see her ears come back in the way that happened if Henshaw in the boatsheds at Stone was in an especially foul mood. She'd been like that the first time they'd encountered Powell at Burston, and he'd come out into the yard and shouted at them in the rain. And now Caleb watched as the animal's instinct told her that there was trouble ahead, a full five minutes before Ted, who was leading her as usual, called back to his uncle,

—Ey, oop!

—Ere it coom!

—Eet's Caleb Bowers!

—E's nobbut slave t' Wedgwoods.

Our proud friend smiled haughtily to himself when he heard this judgement of the crowd, which consisted of about thirty or forty people waiting on the quayside in front of the Etruria Works. Most of them were women in flannel petticoats, with shawls around their faces, shouting, as far as he could make out, any nonsense which came into their heads, and waving at him indignantly.

Old Wilbraham was there, with a phalanx of Etruscans to defend the works against invasion, but they would have had difficulty resisting had the mob grown larger and decided they wanted to break into the manufactory. And now Caleb saw that, over the brow of the hill, to the right of the works and away from the Hall, a much larger crowd of people, several hundred, perhaps a thousand, had broken into a run. The smaller group, by the water's edge, the shouting women in shawls, was still recognizable as a number of individuals who happened to have come together. The larger crowd, however, no longer seemed like individuals. They were indeed the Mob, a many-headed organism of impressive power. Some held forks, staves and what, in the misty distance, could easily have been guns. From where he stood it was difficult to see. They moved, letting out shouts and cries, with great speed down the side of the factory, becoming for a while invisible, and then swarming down the towpath towards him – evidently they'd streamed in through the alley at the end of the Lamb Inn in Ford Street.

Ted had stopped some hundred yards from the factory and stood protectively stroking Dandelion's nose and ears, while she nervously trod the frosty turf with one hoof, and whinnied slightly.

A man – it was that prize Charlie, Parson Sneyd, the major's brother – was leaning out of one of the windows of the works attempting to address the crowds. Caleb could just hear 'Disperse . . . go to your homes . . . one hour . . .' Young John Wedgwood was out on the canalside shouting at the men. Caleb nearly ran to him, conscious of how agonizing it would be for Sally if her beloved son was hurt. And another man, this time speaking from another window at the front of the works, was bellowing through an ear trumpet.

—The militia is on its way from Stoke . . .

The words were drowned by angry roars.

—We'll pay a fair price for the flour . . .

—We'll not let it go to Manchester.

Some of the women were shouting Nay, nay, that wunna do, that wunna do!

Amazingly, two men who appeared to be ringleaders of the mob had commanded their silence.

—We offer no violence! one of them was shouting. We jus' want bread for our littluns! That's all. If they offer us no violence in return we'll pay money for flour. But we're not permitting that flour or grain to go oop t' Manchester, where we have it on good authority—

But at the mention of Manchester, the crowd had begun once more to bay and shout.

The man through the window was reading what Caleb realized was the Riot Act. Across the frosty air could be caught the occasional word which made it clear that the rioters were given one hour to disperse. Thereafter, the militia would be justified in opening fire. You could just about hear the speaker say 'Fire!' before the crowd burst out in another roar of chaotic shouting.

Barlow, one of the ringleaders, was yelling, and pointing at Dandelion and Ted.

—They will NOT be permitted ter take our babbies' food ter Manchester!

The huge crowd – Caleb revised his judgement of one thousand and wondered whether it might not be two – were shouting, NOT, NOT, NOT. THAT WUNNA DO!

—We canna turn, said Ted to his uncle.

—No, we've got to wait and see what t' militia 'll do.

—'appen they'll sell t' corn.

—'appen they will, lad. If you want to come on board, I'll stand by Dandelion.

But Ted was a good lad who loved the horse, and he stood there for the full hour, stroking the animal and calming her while the mob raged and swelled, like troubled seawater which was now still, now boiling and heaving.

Long before the hour was up, the Welsh Fusiliers, with Major

Sneyd and Sergeant Powell, arrived in uniform, with rifles cocked and bayonets fixed.

The man with the ear trumpet, who was called Dr Falkner – he was the Rector of Stoke – was assuring them that the flour and cheese—

—Oh what in the name of God did he want ter go and tell them there's cheese as well? asked Caleb.

And in spite of the seriousness of the situation both men laughed, for the crowd now started to shout the words CHEESE, E GOT CHEESE NALL, with all the fervour of Methodists calling out the name of Christ.

Dr Falkner was trying to say that if they dispersed, there would be a peaceful unloading of the barge and they would sell the flour and the cheese at reasonable rates. This was indeed what happened the next day. There never had been any intention of taking either the flour or the cheese to Manchester. Both were destined for grocers' shops in Etruria, Hanley and Longton.

Now was not the moment for calm reasoning. The existence of the cheese, or the fact that the witching hour was about to come round, and the soldiers were being given orders by the sergeant, led to further movement of the crowd. Barlow and Boulton, the leaders of the protesters, were, as Caleb could see, trying to restrain the frenzy of the mob, but it was no use. As the soldiers fixed bayonets, the vast sea of men and women simply charged against them. There were some shots fired, but by an extraordinary chance none of the crowd was killed. But then, once again, the many-headed beast was stilled. Some shouted out,

—Get off out uv 'ere afore they nile eet on one of us.

—It wunna nubuddie's fault!

—Nubuddie's fault – 'e were jus' in t' wee.

Almost as fast as they had arrived an hour before on the

canalside, the crowd had now begun to scurry away and to disperse. Now some of the soldiers did fire their rifles, but this time it was into the air.

—Cease fire, cease fire! bellowed Major Sneyd. And then —Good God, they've killed him!

—They've killed a man.

—Mebbe e's aw raight, mebbe e's jus . . .

—Good God, he's not breathing.

As the crowds were now running away from the scene up the hill, towards Hanley, and as some of the soldiers gathered around the man who had either been hurt or killed, Ted and Dandelion deemed it safe to move forward. Caleb felt himself drifting towards the scene on the barge as if in a dream. Ever afterwards, he would tell himself that he knew before being told the identity of the dead man, who had been accidentally crushed by the crowds.

—It were Sergeant.

—Welsh bugger.

—I eerd 'im say fix bayonets – e'd 've killed uz, an no mistake.

—Aybut two rungs dunna mak a raight.

Many of these views, either at the time or later, were aired.

Caleb saw only the hunched backs of three soldiers kneeling on the ground. He saw Parson Sneyd, in his black gown, standing over the huddled forms, and then falling to his knees himself. He knew that Powell was dead. He knew that his own life had been changed.

Because he had been standing at a distance from the incident, Caleb considered himself a useful witness. There were two facts of which he was certain. One was that Boulton and Barlow had been nowhere near the sergeant when he fell. Another fact of which he was certain was that Boulton and Barlow, although the leaders of the protest, had done their best to control the crowds and to obviate the development of mass violence.

## The Potter's Hand

When he heard that the two men were to be taken for trial in Stafford, Caleb offered himself to the magistrates as a witness. The hearing was six days later.

**3**

—I DON'T KNOW WHY CALEB BOWERS WANTS TER BE getting involved in the due process of t' law.

—He writes that he was a witness.

—Nobbut, it's the man all ower, said Josiah testily. More and more, when his guard was down, he drifted into Staffordcher, especially with the family.

The boys' letters, and Caleb's, had reached London only three days after the riot. Little Tom wrote of it all as if it were a lark, a game, and the women shouting for bread as comic turns. John wrote in his usual measured tone. They said that Boulton and Barlow were to be hanged – outside the Billington Works where they had started all the trouble.

Caleb, though, wrote a slightly different story. He said that the men had been sent for trial before magistrates at Stafford and that, since he was one of the few people to witness the riot from a distance, he was obliged to go and see if he could not save the men's lives. He wrote that the reading of the Riot Act had been a provocation, rather than calming down the crowd, and that it was only the death of the sergeant which had made the people disperse. As soon as they saw the danger of being arrested for homicide, they'd scampered like frightened hares. Caleb did not know at the time of writing whether Barlow and Boulton were arraigned merely for causing an affray and sedition – for both of which they could be hanged – or whether they were also being prosecuted for murder. But they had been standing yards away from where the sergeant had been overwhelmed by the press.

—It's all a blasted nuisance, said Jos to his nephew.

They stood together in the salerooms in Greek Street. Josiah had spent three nights there now in the apartments above the rooms. With Tom Byerley, pregnant Fanny and two children, there was scarcely room for the maid. But stubborn old Jos would not admit that the living space was inadequate. He was determined that Byerley should prove himself, and part of this mysterious process was squeezing into the flat above the showroom with his ever-expansive family.

The old man – for this, in his mid-fifties, was what he felt; did not the Romans describe a man as senex when he passed his fortieth birthday?– was given a guest bedroom, very small, which looked over the street. He had not slept much, the four nights he had been there. It would have been kinder to put up somewhere else. Mrs Bentley, now established in Gower Street, would always have been willing to give him a bed. But there was some strange principle at stake, as if he were at war with young Byerley and trying to make a point. He actually heard Fan saying, *When he sees how cramped and confined we all are, he's bound to let us have somewhere bigger*. And he had not quite caught the reply, but he knew it was along the lines of *You don't know Uncle Jos*. For he heard her reply, *I'm beginning to do so!* And because she was such a good-natured, high-spirited girl, Fan had laughed. But, by Harry, it was uncomfortable squeezed into that little truckle bed, with his leg neatly placed within reach against the wainscoting! Oh, but you could hear too much through those little panelled walls! The rooms were no more than boxes. And he had grown nesh since living at the Hall, especially since his invention of the air-closet. The noises and odours of life were at times over-whelming.

He knew that he was somehow punishing Tom Byerley for the years away, the prodigal years in America. Josiah had no prodigal years. His entire existence had been a struggle and a consecration. The copying of the Vase would be the crown of that. The large sale-rooms in Soho, the painted name of Wedgwood above the elegant windows, the very fact that he was a household name, were his reward. His success and the abundance of his laurels increased his impatience with those who seemed to possess no such motivation to get on. Tom Byerley was an honest youth, and the acting and poetry nonsense was by now, surely, as well out of the system as the con-tents of chamber pots which their slatternly Jamaican maid, Sophy, sometimes remembered to empty into the privy in the back yard. But you got no sense of Tom Byerley being driven to succeed, any more, if the father was honest, than you got with those boys in Staffordshire. Why, when he was their age he'd been apprenticed, he'd worked through every process of the manufacture of pottery, he had begun his experiment books. True, he had been marked out by Nature or Good Luck for this extraordinary talent, this preternatural control over the clay. But it was more than that. His whole being throbbed with peculiar energies. He had no sooner completed one task than he felt heady compulsions to be on to the next. Most of humankind, he acknowledged this, were not so constituted. He knew, he absolutely knew, that when the salerooms closed for the night, and Tom Byerley went upstairs to play with the children in the smoky little parlour, and to hear Fan prattle about how she had passed the day, neither of them spent one minute thinking about the business. Likewise, his sons! They might be interested in a few of the chemi-cal problems which Mr Chisholm or their father had disclosed to them, about the glazes of a particular piece. They might have

sporadic bursts of interest in the progress of the war, or the movement of political events at home. But none of them seemed to have
any instinctual sense, as he, Josiah possessed, of the *business*. By this
word, Wedgwood meant not simply the making of pots, the transport of pots, and the sale of pots. He meant everything! He meant
the part which his own activities, both as a potter and as a merchant
and as a citizen and as a man of science, played in the changing face
of the great world.

Mr Pitt, now there was a man who had a sense of business! But
if he got his way in Ireland, the English manufacturers would be out
of pocket. Where was the wealth going to come from to pay for the
war, and not just the fighting of it but the calamities which resulted
from it? That's what Josiah Wedgwood would like to know. A figure
such as the Duke of Portland, with his effete delicate mouth, and the
fingers twitching to get back to the cello, had no conception at all of
the nature of the difficulty. Mr Pitt knew. Josiah regretted being in
opposition to him over this Irish matter. England must be made to
operate! Its mills, its factories, its canals, its hundred or so men of
genius who invented and devised new means of production, new
means of creating wealth – these were the hope of England! Not
Dukes in velvet coats. And yet, when Josiah thought of his friend
Mr Boulton, and the smoke belching from the iron foundries in
Birmingham and the coal emerging from the mines at Cannock
Chase, he knew that the business was more than simply the dirty, literally dirty, filthy business of making money. There was the sense of
achieving ever more beautiful forms. That was what they had accomplished, his generation – the new buildings of William Chambers
and the brothers Adam; the paintings of Mr Wright and Mr Stubbs;
the vases and medallions of Mr Wedgwood.

As these thoughts passed through the uncle's head, Tom Byerley
read over the letters from Staffordshire once more, and Mrs Tom,

attentive with the coffee pot, called to Sophy to control the children tumbling about at the other end of the breakfast table.

Suddenly, Sophy realized that the Old Gentleman was addressing her.

—Did you come from America?

—Jamaica, sir.

—You were never in America, then?

—No sir. My grandparents came from Africa. They came to Liverpool, where they were indentured.

Byerley and his wife looked downwards, embarrassed by the directness of Josiah's questioning.

—And then they were taken to the plantations.

—Yes, sir.

—How did they escape?

—They didn't, sir. But my father was killed by whipping. I was very young, I did not remember it. My mother had the good fortune to be a house-slave to Mrs Goodhart, that was the lady who was our mistress. Mrs Goodhart came to London, where my mother worked as a house-servant.

—And does so yet?

—No, sir. My mother was allowed . . . let free by Mrs Goodhart. She works in a shop, sir, in Covent Garden.

—My God! exclaimed Wedgwood. To think the evil trade still continues! I have hopes, Sophy.

He tapped the front of his coat, which was emblazoned with one of his Am I Not A Man And A Brother? buttons.

—Yes, sir.

—We should all wear these, Sophy.

—Yes, sir.

—We should all be optimists. We should believe in a better world.

—If you say so, sir.

—And you do not? There's Granville Sharp, an excellent man. And there's this Member for Hull, Mr Wilberforce. Mr Fox is on their side, and I have no doubt Mr Pitt also. It can only be a matter of time before they abolish the trade altogether.

—Yes, sir.

—And meanwhile, said Fan, they still go round the taverns arresting the negroes. Could you countenance such wickedness?

Later, in the showroom, Tom said to his uncle,

—Thank you for asking Sophy about her past. We'd never quite liked to.

—If thee disna ask thee disna knaw.

# 4

THE CASE OF REX V. BARLOW AND BOULTON WAS NOT considered sufficiently important to be worth putting before a judge and jury. The two men were therefore taken before the magistrates at Stafford.

—Our Caleb, be careful, love, said Heffie Bowers over their breakfast in Stonefield Cottage some five miles away in Stone.

—I just want justice, our Heff. That's all. Barlow was trying to quieten the rabble, not incite them. They were just asking for food.

—I knaw, love, I knaw.

A great sadness had descended between Heffie and Caleb since he fell in love with Mrs Powell. Naturally, Heffie had heard that the sergeant was now dead. Everyone in the district was speaking of it, many of them saying openly that Barlow or Boulton would be hanged for his murder. Heffie's immediate reaction, when she heard the news was, And now she's free.

Caleb, Ted and the horse had come to Stone from Etruria as soon as they'd unloaded the flour and the cheese. These comestibles had been impounded, with promises that they would be sold, at much reduced prices, via the shops which had ordered them from the wholesalers. Somehow the Master Potters, even in the absence of Mr Jos, had agreed on this singular occasion to subsidize the losses of the grocers who were selling the food.

Ted, over their evening meal, had poured out to his mother an excited account of the day, from the moment fear appeared in the mane and ears of Dandelion, to his Uncle Caleb's bravery (— no, Uncle Caleb, yo' wer), to the surge of people coming along the towpath towards them, their shouts, their despair, their anger – and then to the death of the soldier. Ted was either unaware that Sergeant Powell was the publican of the Rising Sun, where Caleb had been on several occasions during the last year, or he chose to speak as if he were unaware. Caleb himself commented upon every other aspect of the day, including the idiocy of Parson Sneyd (which made Heffie laugh) and the rashness of John Wedgwood shouting at the mob (which made her frightened). Of every incident he spoke, except the man's death. He was simply silent when it was mentioned, and throughout the evening, and all the next morning, he had said nothing. Heffie could not have asked for clearer confirmation from her brother that this was, for him, the centrally important event of the previous day: not that any man had been killed, but because this man had been killed: making *her* a widow and a free woman.

And why not? Heffie asked herself. Caleb had never known the love of a woman – did he not deserve a chance of happiness before . . . But the sentence could not form itself in her brain because it was not true. He had known the love of a woman, all his life through – hers, hers, his sister's. If her helping to bring him up when their mother had died of smallpox had not been love, then what had been? If her sharing her home with him for most of their grown-up life was not love, what was? If her endurance of his strange sullenness, silences, melancholy-madnesses had not been love . . . And oh, she loved this man, she loved her brother. In all her own escapades, including the recent summer of Mr Stubbs, she had taken it for granted that she could take lovers, safe in the certainty that Caleb would always be there for her when she returned, either in person or in spirit, to the hearth. Caleb had given her life its emotional flexibility. The rock certainty that her brother was always there, that he would not want, or take, a woman, had underpinned all her own emotional adventures, and actually made them a possibility. She saw that now. And the prospect of him and that woman . . . She felt an aching emptiness, a terror. Our Ted was a big baby, slow to develop, unlike his two brothers, who'd married and moved on. Of the lost babies, she could not speak. But one day Ted would go. Some woman would offer to mother him, and lure him away with cookery and laundry even if he was not especially interested in what she had to offer him in the bedroom.

In none of these insights or meditations did Heffie Bowers for one second feel entitled to hold on to either man. She knew it was her youngest son Ted's right to marry eventually – indeed, she hoped he would do so. She could see that from a point of view of justice there was absolutely no reason why her brother, though fifty-six years old, should not make himself happy with a woman, even if she were a Welsh woman and a witch, as some in the village at Burston had guessed. That's what they were all saying round about the district – that she were a witch.

But although Heffie's brain spelled out so clearly that she had no right to hold on to Caleb, her heart could not stop its panic. As he set out for Stafford in the governess cart (taking Juno – 'I reckon Our Dandelion needs a rest after yesterday'), Heffie envisaged, falsely, That Woman waiting for him at the Shire Hall, and their sitting beside one another in court as the case proceeded. It was this, really, as much as the possibility of Caleb getting himself into trouble with the authorities, which had prompted her 'Our Caleb, be careful, love'.

In fact, since the first disturbing signs, more than a year ago and more now, that her brother had lost his heart to the Woman, Heffie had no idea how often they had met. Sometimes she imagined them making love on the barge. Sometimes she thought of them walking out together, maybe on the Downs Banks. But she had no reason for thinking these things, and the truth of the matter – unknown to her, since brother and sister never discussed it – was that he had not so much as set eyes on Mrs Powell for about six months.

There was a hint, as the governess cart whizzed along the new road to Stafford, with Juno trotting cheerfully, of spring in the air: many primroses grew in the banks beneath the hedgerows, as well as clumps of celandine and snowdrops. A weak sun shone.

Telepathically conscious of Heff's anxiety, and, of course, conscious of its cause, Caleb had needed to get out of the house immediately, even though the hearing was not for hours. As he sat in the cart with the reins in his hands, he was abstracted with consciousness of Heff's pain. He was almost dazed by it. There was so much pain in the world, and Meribah Powell had endured more than the average share. He had no hope that she would ever be for him more than an idol in his heart, as Sally Wedgwood had been all these years. He had been unprepared for Heffie minding this – even this! – so intensely. The love he felt for Meribah was something so nebulous, so almost childish in its raw, pointless concentration. Her hair, her hands, her eyes, her voice, her whole being and personality, haunted him as a sort of holiness: he was in awe. But although he could not control these feelings, it was beyond possibility that she could ever reciprocate them, and, without having speculated in any detail, over the last day, what she would do now she was a widow, he was all but certain that she would wish to return to her own people in America.

This, he told himself, was what she would do: an absurd thing to think, as he recognized immediately, since he was incapable of imagining the real Meribah, or to guess what was passing through her soul, beyond a very broad sense of her having been unhappy.

In this miasma of thoughts, he sat upright in the cart, looking vacantly at Juno's bottom as she lifted her thick black tail and shat neatly. Caleb never lost his admiration for the manner in which horses evacuated themselves so cleanly, compared with the smeared stench which came from the human anus.

The repetition of the familiar thought, with its abrasive misanthropic tug towards sanity, recollected him to the day which lay ahead. He was riding to Stafford to do what he could to save the two men who had supposedly incited the riot.

There was already a crowd outside the Shire Hall and a gallows had been erected in the square. The rope dangled and swung gently in the morning air. It did not suggest ardour, on the part of the magistrates, for the principle of presumed innocence in the accused before proven guilty.

—Yo canna goo in, was the simple message of the constable on the door.

—I must. I insist. I have the permission of Major Sneyd.

—Yo wha'?

—I must speak to the advocate who is defending these men.

—Who are yo?

—That is unimportant.

—Yo's Caleb Bowers. All fowk knaw tha's difficult customer!

Caleb knew that if he lost his temper there would be no chance of getting through.

—Please. I ask you. As a Christian man. If there is the smallest chance that these men are innocent, it is surely the duty of any decent person to speak fo' 'em?

—Lahk ah say, difficult! said the constable, and, to Caleb's amazement, he was let through.

—Sam! called the constable to another official. Mr Bowers coom ter spake fur twa boogers what we're gine t' 'ang!

Before the trial, Major Sneyd came out into the lobby and barked at Caleb,

—Sedition, sir, is a capital offence.

—I know that.

—Riot and affray, damage to property, these are all capital offences – even before you come to the undeniable fact that an officer of the Crown, albeit a non-commissioned officer, was killed. That, too, is a capital offence.

—I know that, said Caleb, now varying his speech and making it so that it was all but southern. I know that there are two hundred and eighty-eight offences at present on the statute books of England for which a man may be hanged. All I'm asking is that Boulton and Barlow be not hanged for offences which they did not commit.

Major Sneyd stared at him as if he were mad.

—You are asking to be called as a witness.

—I am.

The major sighed. Caleb imagined that the man was going to refuse him permission to speak in court. Caleb had no idea of the legal rights and wrongs of the matter. He assumed that, in the cir-cumstances – the Riot Act, the gallows – the local magistrates had absolute power over the poor wretches who appeared before them. It was a surprise, then, that the major's stern features relaxed and he said,

—Very well.

Caleb was glad, when it was all over, that he had made the effort. It stimulated the magistrates into at least going through the motions of asking some reasonable questions.

There were three magistrates on the bench. Major Sneyd himself, a Mr Thompson – a parson who turned out to be the Rector of

Stafford – and a thin, bony-cheeked man whose name Bowers did not hear in the course of the proceedings. This thin man, who was either deaf or inattentive through sleep, occasionally leaned towards the parson and asked him to repeat what had just been said.

—So you are telling the court, Mr Bowers, said Major Sneyd, that Mr Boulton had turned away from the crowd even before the disturbance began.

—I am, sir. He were going up the hill, away from the works. I could see him from my barge. None of the others who were down near cut, down near t' works, could have seen him as I saw him. They were too near. From where I stood, I could see the grass which slopes away behind the works. As you know, your honour – he turned to Major Sneyd – it's white with clay dust for yards around the works, and I noticed that Boulton had got beyond the line where the white clay dust turns to green and he were on t' grass.

—And when was that? asked the major, who was plainly a fair-minded person, however strongly he felt displeased that this man of the people possessed the temerity to come into his court and recall what had actually happened.

—After the Riot Act were read. He – *and* Mr Barlow – were both urging the crowds ter see reason, they were both urging them to disperse, once the Riot Act had been read. I couldna hear their words . . .

—Ah. So you couldn't hear their words, but you are asking us to believe they were trying to calm the crowds! said the parson with some triumph.

The thin magistrate asked the parson to repeat what had just been said and the two whispered together, not really listening, as the major asked,

—Am I right in saying that in relation to Mr Boulton, which is the case we are considering at present – he shot a glance of irritation towards the thin magistrate – you saw him going away from the crowd *before* the real disturbance began?

—Yes, sir.

—So you saw Mr Boulton and Mr Barlow speaking to the crowds.

—At different times, yes.

—And it would be a reasonable inference to suppose that they advocated dispersal, since the first of the accused, Mr Boulton, actually began to leave the scene.

—Yes, it would be reasonable. More than that, Mr Boulton quite plainly did not have anything to do with the riot or with the accidental death of the soldier, sir.

—We'll be the judges of that, snapped Major Sneyd from the bench, causing the thin magistrate to lean over and whisper yet again in his ear.

The hearing of both men took little more than half an hour. They had called other witnesses. Mr Wilbraham from the Etruria Works was there, Dr Falkner was summoned, and old Billington, who owned the pot works halfway up the hill as you go into Hanley, told the story of the riot. But all three, upon cross-questioning by the major, were obliged to admit that they had not actually heard Boulton inciting anyone to sedition, nor had they seen him at any of the scenes of the crime. So Boulton was acquitted.

The sense of a deed well done should have given Caleb Bowers satisfaction. Naturally enough, it did so, in a way. But his partial success in defending these men was outweighed by the partial failure. Barlow was condemned to be hanged at once. When the sentence was pronounced, Barlow began to cry out.

—Yo canna – naw, naw, yo canna!

Caleb knew almost everyone in the region by sight, and to this extent, he 'knew' Barlow, though he had probably never exchanged more than ten words with the man in his life. But he knew of Barlow.

Josiah spoke of him as a troublemaker at Billington's, always complaining about the working conditions and the wages.

—We'd stand no nonsense of that sort at the works, was how Josiah had dismissed the stories of Barlow answering back to old Billington.

—'E wer telling Billington yo wer a better employer than he wer.

—Well, I am, Josiah had said proudly. But I'd dismiss any rogue who had the cheek to speak like that to my face.

—He wer saying how Wedgwood's works is the only place in the Potteries where yo' pay Mr Bent ter administer physic to the little ones in Etruria, how yo' pay their medical expenses. Jos Wedgwood, you's a cussed difficult man – Barlow wer jus' asking Billington if he couldn't have the simple decency, the humanity, to behave as yo' behave. And yo' say you'd dismiss a man lahk that?

—Certainly I would if he spoke impertinently.

That was how Barlow's name had come up in conversation, some time the previous year. Barlow – thirty-three, a rather plain young man, with the typical pallor of the potter; married, several children, Caleb forgot how many. No doubt some had survived, and most had been given to Moloch. And now his widow – Caleb recollected that she was called Rachel – would have to find her way in the world. She would probably become homeless, and the children would be taken to a workhouse.

As he came out into the public square outside the Shire Hall, he saw to his unsurprised disgust that the crowd had swollen to several hundred. There was a palpable excitement in the air, akin to the feeling he had known at fairs when a celebrated pugilist was fighting. There is nothing a crowd enjoys more than violence and death, and a public hanging was always popular.

Old Billington had apparently asked for the hanging to take place on the bridge in Hanley, near his works – to teach them a lesson, as

Caleb bitterly thought. At least Major Sneyd was a halfway decent man, for all his military pomposity, and Parson Thompson, and the thin pasty man who whispered in Sneyd's ear, had done the comparatively decent thing and prevented such a spectacle by decreeing that Barlow should hang in Stafford.

—Not stee-ing fur t' shoo? asked the all-but-toothless liveryman, when Caleb picked up Juno from the stables at the back of the Swan.

—No, Mr Lush, I am not.

—Tha isna, eh? Teach 'em a lesson, mebbe.

The man seemed to be deriving visible pleasure from the fact that another human being was about to suffer a violent and publicly humiliating end.

—Ay? And what lesson ud that be then, Mr Lush? That if yer ask fer bread ter feed yer children yer deserve ter die? That if yer have the courage ter spake oop fer yer brother workers yer deserve ter be 'anged? Useful lesson that be nall!

And he led Juno to the cart which was parked in the inn yard, and strapped her into her harness. When he came through the arch of the inn, he could hear the swelling noise of the throng over in the square. And though he urged the horse into a trot, so that the hateful noise could be inaudible to him, he did not get away quite in time. Behind him, he heard the great roar of the crowd, signalling the appearance of the victim on the scaffold. There was then a silence during which, no doubt, the ordinary of Stafford Gaol would have read prayers. Some silences are almost unbearable. A child falls over, and grazes its knee, and for a few seconds there is a silence which has no peace: it is a silence which is a mere preparation for the howls of agony which the child is about to give out. And this crowd-silence behind Caleb was similar, only much more awful. For after the prayerful pause, Caleb knew well that poor Barlow had been forced on to the block, with the noose around his neck. And then the block would be removed. That was what signalled the great roar of applause which echoed over the small market town. That hateful noise of bloodlust, that collective human sound, which has risen up from our planet from gladiatorial arenas in Roman times, from bullfights, and would be heard, long after Caleb and Juno were no more, at the Nazi rallies, that football-crowd roar came up into the air. And Caleb, anxious to put the sound out of his ears and such mindless mob-cruelty out of his consciousness, shook the reins and said,

—Git on, git on w' yer.

And Juno's ears went back and she broke from trot to canter, so that the governess cart was almost upturned as it went up the hill, over the country, and back towards Stone. A great circle of rooks, disturbed by the excitement of the collective human bellow, rose into the sky, singing the hanged man's Requiem with a hopeless cawing.

# 5

—YO'D LOOK A FOOL, JOS WEDGWOOD, IF THAT FELL FROM thee hands!

—I would and all, the Potter laughed, holding it.

So anxious had they been about the jolting of even the smoothest of carriages on the roads, that Caleb had brought the Vase from London by water. Strange journey from the Alexandrian glass-makers of old, to glide through Oxfordshire and Warwickshire, as unheeded by Mr Boulton's hands in the iron foundry, or the undergraduates of the University, as by the cows who chomped beside the meadow-lands of Meaford Hall, this masterwork had travelled from London to the hand of the Master Potter. And the carefully packed barrel had been carried with all the delicacy with which you would transport a pain-racked old father, up the steps of the jetty, into the Ornamental works. And then, with the near-clumsiness of an eager child opening a birthday present, Josiah had rummaged in straw and produced the often-wrapped, cushioned object, and held it, with the body of the Vase resting on his left palm, while he held one dark yet luminous handle with his large red fingers.

—But, Caleb, Caleb, and he carefully set the Vase down on the table in his small accounting room, we've made better shapes than this in the old days at the Brick House Works! Mr Flaxman said it was the finest production of Art that had been brought to England.

—And you say it's not so fine as a vase thrown by theysen!

—I say its shape isn't so fine as some of my amphoras, yes, I am saying that. It's so squat! But the colour! The moonbeam colour, Caleb! How in the name of Charity am I going to be able to imitate the effects of that cameo-cutter? How did they do it? They must have scraped away at the external crust of white opaque glass – it must have taken months, nay, years to make those figures! It's so thin, so fine, so full of light! That's never been done with jasper slipware. And if I put so little slip on to the vase and increase the heat of the kiln, it's gine ter pucker.

—What was it furr, d'yer reckon? Funerary?

—It would've taken so long ter make – it can't have been made for one individual. They'd 've waited years tubby put in vase, else. But I tell you one thing, Caleb, I wouldna 've trusted eet to any carrier, man.

—And I'm not a carrier?

—Na, Caleb Bowers, na.

For some reason, Josiah was visibly moved, as though the arrival of the Vase punctuated the last stage of the journey these two men had made together through life. Both became aware of the half-century they had spent together. Both thought of their mothers, and all the dead in the Bowers and Wedgwood families they had buried. Caleb, embarrassed at the possibility of any emotion being shown between them, looked away. He nursed the half-fear – but dismissed it as too absurd – that Josiah was about to stroke him or even to kiss him. Caleb looked at the Vase and read in it some of what Josiah saw: a last project. They might only be in their fifties, but Josiah looked so much older. How different the two friends were! Caleb never felt it so strongly as in this moment of silence. He was staring at an object which (whatever Josiah might say) was of stupendous beauty, in shape as well as decoration. For him, it was an object which did not need commentary. He was haunted by it at first glance, or would go on being haunted by it: partly by its beauty, partly by its antiquity, and its link with so many generations.

Owd Jos, however – the booger! – Caleb could feel, as he had done so often, the energy, the competitiveness, the hyperactivity in his friend as he hopped from real to false foot. Wedgwood was looking at this exquisite production of a vanished age as if it were the work of an industrial competitor. Wedgwood was going to beat it – he visibly felt it as a challenge. More than that, prematurely aged, slightly shaking, red-faced Jos saw the Vase as the Last Heave, the Final Task. When Jos was dead, Caleb would remember this moment in the Counting House, when it was just the three of them: him, his old friend, the Vase.

Caleb had another thought at that time, too. It was some months since he had himself been into the Hall, but Heffie went in several times a week to visit Sally Wedgwood and to help as best she could. Caleb knew his Jos, the infinite capacity of the man to blot out painful experience with work. This Portland Vase project – he'd embarked upon it to numb, or if possible to expunge, the consciousness of his poor little daughter's pain; to forget Mary Ann and her screams; more generally, to blind himself to the tears of things.

We begin to work without heed. Everyone needs to work. The thought flitted through Caleb's head. In youth it is a toil simply imposed upon us. Later, with families to feed, it becomes a necessity. But by the time a man reached their age, work had become something else: the best narcotic to keep at bay the spectre of death.

Escaping Mary Ann's convulsions, which confronted the women day and night, Josiah had bustled up to London – yes, to speak out for the manufacturers against Mr Pitt's attempts to help the Irish. (Caleb smiled at the mayhem this was so bound to produce!) Jos had gone to see to the salerooms, to meet the Duke, to borrow the Vase. And now he set himself the all-but impossible task: how to make a ceramic object as luminous and delicate as that Alexandrian master-piece; how to set radical Hanley and Burslem against Imperial Rome; how to make the white relief as translucent as the mysterious white on the Portland Vase; how to fire a black basaltes or dark blue jasper vase at a heat which would not crack. To put it all another way, the old bugger was trying to march on, to hobble on, blotting out the crushing misery of emotional consciousness.

These thoughts of Caleb's, which came in the silence, were echoed, like the repetition of a musical motif in a concerto grosso, when Dr Darwin heaved himself up the steps into the little Counting House to view the wondrous Vase. It was clear that the doctor, who now visited several times a week, had been at the Hall to see Wedgwood's youngest child. Josiah all but admitted as much, though they were supposedly discussing the Vase.

—I feel as if, in making this funerary object, I am saluting the ashes of all the friends and dear ones we have lost. The awfulness of death, Doctor!

—I've been meditating upon the figures on the V-V-Vase, said Dr Darwin, who held his friend's arm in a comforting gesture. Death is its subject. I do not know, Jos, if you have read Dr Warburton's theories about the sixth book of the *Aeneid*.

—I, er, I am afraid I . . .

—You are a busy m-m-man, Jos, c-can't read everything. Warburton th-thinks that the story of Aeneas being taken down into the Underworld is a poetical account of the future state in the Eleusinian m-mysteries.

—The mysteries were Egyptian, no?

—They b-began in Egypt, but they were adopted by Greece, and by Virgil's time, they would have reached Italy too.

—Of course, the Vase might antedate Virgil by centuries.

—T-t-try this f-f-for an idea. The central figure on the Vase, the d-dying female is, so to say, m-m—

—Maternity?

—M-m-m—

—Mortality?

—Mortal life, had been my idea. Don't f-f-finish my words for me, there's a good fellow. Mortal life. She holds the torch which is being extinguished. She l-lies beneath elms – you remember the elm trees at the entrance to the Underworld in the *Aeneid*. On either side of M-Mortality or mortal life sit the human race, m-male and f-f-f- – don't say it for me, I b-beg – female. They have their backs to death. They can not face it.

—And on the other side.

—On the other side of the Vase, Jos, you see, there is Im-im-immortality, immortal life. The serpent acquired immortal life from the ass of Prometheus. To the right, you have the bearded figure of P-p-pluto, with literally one foot in the grave. Immortality is stretching out to the t-timid ghost of humanity, who is coming to confront Pluto the God of the Underworld. He is being led along, you see, by the God of L-love, the winged figure. And above the Immortality figure, you have the evergreens, symbols of everlasting life.

—So, in an urn you have the ash. And outside the urn, you have the human soul: on the one hand, turning away from the fact of its own mortality; on the other, stretching out . . .

—Being led by love, Josiah.

They stared for a moment awestruck at the Vase.

—I'd like, if I m-may, to get an engraver to copy the Vase, as an illustration to my new p-poem.

—Who did you have in mind?

—Do you remember Mr Blake?

—Oh, ay, the young man Flaxman brought to the works. He painted very well, did the ceiling in the hall.

—That's the man. Interesting f-f-fella. He went to see the Vase when Sir William first brought it to London and placed it on public display. Blake's interested in my idea of the Eleusinian mysteries. He thinks the n-naked figures on either side of Mortality are Adam and Eve. Which in a w-way they are – they are primitive humanity, humanity in its original.

—My boys thought he was mad, Jos said with a chuckle.

—They were wr-wrong, my friend.

—Something about meeting Julius Caesar in the stagecoach? Seeing an angel? Josiah shook his head at the recollection. That's just so daft. How could a sane man say he'd seen such things?

—He thinks our friends are bringing an evil world to pass. He hates the machines, he's totally on the side of those who want to smash the new looms and the spinning jennies, he thinks Mr Boulton is an abomination.

—I dunna know what he thought of the works when he was here! laughed Josiah good-humouredly.

—The Albion Mills . . .

—The mill at Battersea? The great mill which Mr Boulton and Mr Watt constructed?

—You and I think it is a m-monument to the ingenuity of our friends Boulton and W-Watt. I even wrote a poem about it.

—Indeed so, Doctor.

—Blake does not think so. He says the mill is . . . 'satanic' was the word he used, I think. But he isn't mad. He's a great man, a good artist, a strange but beautiful poet. He's not really our enemy. He sees. We see, d-don't we, Jos?

Josiah looked at Darwin with a settled smile.

—I . . . he hesitated modestly. It clearly troubled him. He did not want to make claims for himself.

—I've tried to improve everything I've touched. I've tried to make pottery better, I've tried to introduce new techniques. I don't want to say I've . . . I'm not a poet, I'm not an artist.

—My dear friend.

Erasmus looked moved. His large smiling blue eyes danced in his fleshy face.

—My dear friend, he said.

# 6

THEY WERE ALL LOVED, ALL THE CHILDREN, OF COURSE they were, and the more that they all settled to becoming Etruscans, the deeper became Josiah's sense of *them all*, as a tribe, *contra mundum*. He had not known it was possible to feel even more tribal, even more family-minded, but so he did, with each passing month. And perhaps it was this feeling which strengthened the sense that to lose one of them would be unendurable. Perhaps, contrarywise, it was the sense of their being everlastingly on the verge of losing Mary Ann that quickened the sense they both shared, he and Sally, of the Etruscan family.

The teething horror, which had coincided with the Stubbs portrait, was followed by a period of comparative calm. The other children petted her and loved the little mite, but there was no life in her. It was so unlike a Wedgwood, the unresponsiveness, the incuriosity about life! Moods – the family could enter a competition in ill humour, in melancholy, in hypochondria! Sally would have outsulked any lady in the country, and no number of visits to Bath to take the waters, no number of consultations with Dr Darwin, no number of leeches or bleeding could shake her out of it when the fit was upon her. But she'd been better since the birth of the last child – somehow everyone now knew that Mary Ann would be the last child. When she was so sick as a tiny bairn, and the screams had filled the house,

Josiah had prayed to be delivered from the wish that she would die, just the wish that the noise would stop, and the pain would stop. They'd lost baby Richard and it had been a sadness, but life had moved its great stagecoach forwards. The machinery had started itself again. And then the little lass had lived, and entwined herself round his heart.

It wasn't weakness, such as Tom's physical weakness, accompanied by aliveness of mind which was dazzling, even when his melancholy cast over that brilliant mind a cloud of melancholy as deep as the mother's. It was not like the mother's sorrow at all, for Sally, sad and cross as she so often was, was ever-sharp in her wits. And little Mary Ann . . .

—She's not all there, bless 'er.

How they had both, Sally and Josiah Wedgwood, been bruised by Heffie's artless judgement! Josiah had held Sal in his arms when they were alone together. She had not wept on that occasion, but he had known her need to be held.

—Oh, why did she have to say it? Why couldn't she—

—Keep her gob shut?

She'd half-laughed, conspiratorially quiet against his shoulder.

—If only she'd *say* something, Sal had then added. Mary Ann had reached the age of six without uttering a syllable.

The air-closets had been installed and been a partial success. Tom and Kitty had made their mother exclaim at the sheer audacity, the coarseness, of their demonstrations, coming out on to corridors, and into the hall, with fingers clasped to their noses.

—More experiments required, I think, Papa! You won't get your patent yet!

—Not when you've been stinking us all out, Kitty Wedgwood!

—Tom, please!

—Oh, Sukey, don't be such a prude.

—Well, there is some improvement.

—When you sit down, it feels as if someone is blowing on your—

—Tom Wedgwood! – his mother overheard this – That is quite enough.

—Or, as I was trying to explain, *not* quite enough!

The conversation about the air-closets had caused such general merriment that even little Mary Ann, looking from face to face like a puzzled dog in search of a ball with which children had been attempting a game, had tried a smile.

—It's funny, isn't it, Mary Ann? Tom had said, picking his little sister up and whirling her around.

—Oh, Tom, be careful with her!

And Sarah, ten already, had said,

—Truly, mother, she likes it.

—But, darling Mary Ann, said Sally, bending towards her last-born, we can't tell what you like, can we? Come here, darling.

And she had done the only thing that could be done, and which she seemed to do a dozen times a day, clasp the impassive little face to her bosom.

But, more and more the child was in pain, as well as impassive. No one accused Dr Darwin, with his electrical contraption, of destroying the intellects. There had been no intellects to destroy.

—It's not because . . . Sally had not dared to finish the sentence, when she was alone with the doctor.

—W-wh-what, my dear?

—It is not a problem resultant from consanguinity?

—You are but third cousins. And many of you Wedgwoods have married cousins.

—And many of us are odd-bods.

—No odder than some. Jos is the child of cousins, and there's nothing wrong with his intellects.

—That's true. But I look at Mary Ann, and to tell you the truth, Dr Darwin, I look at Tom.

—His weakness is . . . it is not a weakness of cons-, cons-, cons—

—Consanguinity?

—It is p-possibly congenital, but it is not . . . But, my dear dear girl! There's no merit in holding this discussion *now*. You have a fine family. And poor Mary Ann, well, when the child is in pain, just continue to give her laudanum in a glass with water. Or even a few grains of p-pure opium.

—That's what you prescribe for Tom, and he is already, at fifteen, dreamy with it on occasions.

—There's no danger. Believe me, dear Sally. C-come here for one of our . . .

—I am not in the right humour.

—But I am . . . oooh!

And perhaps there was comfort, as well as an element of disgust, in being able to allow him to fondle her. Nothing which counted as unfaithfulness to her dear Josiah was ever allowed to take place. The doctor had assured her, as the intimacies progressed from one thing to another, he would never wish to compromise her, or to betray a gentleman in whom he reposed such a very high regard. She must regard these caresses as something in the region of the medicinal, and if he sometimes asked her to return the favour, and place her long delicate hand into his breeches, there was nothing serious in the game.

So, medical advice was followed, and Mr Bent the surgeon was, as always, of Dr Darwin's opinion. Tom's delicacy, Tom's breathing difficulties and Tom's rheumatics responded with wide-eyed smiles, and extraordinary swoops and elations of spirit to the imbibing of opium. And poor little Mary Ann, with her excruciating and unbearable pain, was simply numbed by having more and more of the drops of the laudanum mixture, Batley's Sedative lotion, added to the sweetened barley-water which Heffie spooned into her quivering lips.

There reached the time when Heffie said she didn't any longer like to be the one who gave the child her Batley's lotion, and Sally knew what Heffie meant. One spoonful too few spelt a sleepless night for whichever of them had taken turn to sit up with the writhing, screaming Mary Ann; but one spoonful too many would put her to everlasting sleep.

Sukey was nearly twenty-one years old when her little sister died. She sat with Sally and Josiah in the nursery all through the last two nights. Two dozed in chairs while the other, on the small, spindly upright cane chair beside the truckle bed, smoothed the sticky brow with damp cloths, held the tiny, taut fist, and, when she woke, or half-woke, with whimpers now, not screams, spooned more of the Batley's lotion on to her cherry lips. They had not wanted Heffie there; they had not wanted to put her through it. Caleb forced his tearful sister to come with him back to Stone, while the child whimpered, and then breathed, her last. Sally, who had one hand on Mary Ann's brow when she died, was holding, with the other, a small silver teaspoon with which she had delivered the last opiate. The child's eyes, a grey blue, stared dully at nothing. Sally put down the teaspoon, leaving a stickiness on the bedside table, and closed the eyelids.

Sukey had not been present at a death before. Pa had seen eight of his siblings die in childhood, and lived through the smallpox out-break in Burslem. He'd known the sight of a tiny child waxy and white in death. Had it been he who put baby Richard in his coffin? Sukey had not been present, and she could not ask her Ma. But she witnessed this. The coffin was brought over from Newcastle the morning Mary Ann died, and by then, the little waxwork had been washed and put in a clean shift and tied with a white cap round her head. They didn't use a shroud. Josiah's face was creased with grief as he lifted her, stiff now as an item of laundry left out by accident in the frost, and placed her in the quilted satin lining of the coffin. Sukey was especially horrified by the coffin lining. She thought of the lid leaking when they buried it, and the reddish clay mud seeping over it like shit. And she thought it would have been purer and better to wrap the little mite in a blanket and bury her in the earth without a coffin. But none of these things were said. They passed through her mind as her white, terrified face confronted the reality of death, and its power: its power, not only to remove Mary Ann. That was not much power. Any one of them could have destroyed the poor frail creature who had snuffled like a young puppy on that bed. Death's power was greater than that. It could reduce breezy, energetic Pa to this broken snivelling creature. It could melt Ma, and make her lean on Pa, with all her need-love, and coo like a very sad pigeon as he held her, uttering words of grief too low, too moaned, too inarticulate to hear, before he picked up the box from the bed and carried it down the main staircase. His lips were very tight. It was such an unnatural expression for him, who normally allowed his lower lip to hang almost open. Those lips of Pa's were almost the saddest thing that morning. And he put Mary Ann in her box in the back of the hearse. Jack, young Jos, Tom, Cousin Byerley, Caleb and Useful Tom went in two carriages to bury her in the old churchyard at Burslem.

All the women were deep in the hall, looking inwards and downwards; all the women, that is, but Sukey, who stood in the child's bedroom looking down, and watching the miserable procession – undertaker's hearse and two carriages, scrunching over the damp gravel, over the brow of the hill, over Fowlea Brook until, crossing Brick Kiln Field, they became invisible. Sukey did not know what to do. She went to her room and took out her oboe case. She played Albinoni, the oboe part from the opening movement of the Concerto in G Minor. At first she felt almost ashamed to be playing a tune which was so little, so in a way trivial, as a farewell to a departing human soul. And then, as she played the air again and again, it seemed to be saying, Death you cannot cow me. You have stolen our little sister. You have given her no chance of a future. But we will go on. Sukey played again and again, the repetitive little melody. The reedy oboe's voice, a sad deep-throated bird, filled the silent house.

—She's been playing that thing all the time you were gone, said Sally when she greeted Josiah. She took his large potter's hands in hers and squeezed them.

—Well, yes, was all he said. And then again, as a kind of generalized affirmation, Yes.

Words could not have lifted them. The oboe skipped, sang, led onwards all who heard it with sounds which did not give hope, but which defied despair.

# 7

ONE NIGHT, AS HE LAY IN HIS BED IN SOHO, WITH HIS arms around the belly of Fan, who was pregnant for the third time, Byerley remembered Blue Squirrel. Several years had passed since he and Fan had begun to make love, and the intensity of sensual enjoyment had grown, not diminished. Except when childbirth and its aftermath made such a conjunction impossible, they still made love each day. When tiredness, or the presence of wakeful babies near their bedchamber, made the night-time unsuitable, she would make sure that she could visit him in his office at the back of the salerooms. Anywhere would do. Tom had been born – yes, they had the sheer lack of imagination to name yet another of this large tribe Tom – and all but weaned, when, one summer night, they conceived their first daughter, Frances, leaning against the warm brick walls of the kiln in the back yard, with – Fan insisted for ever afterwards – a nightingale trilling from the branches of a London plane, as she lifted her skirts and guided Byerley into another small ecstasy. But it was in bed, some three months after this, that he woke, with her legs around him, and his hands on her belly. They normally slept in a spoon position, and much of each night, during the hours of sleep, their bodies, so accustomed to one another, so happy in the conjunction, would form half-acts of joyous union, her fleshy bottom pressing with exquisite softness against him, and keeping him in almost perpetual arousal. It was during one such semi-somnolent holding and caressing, when he would have been unable to tell whether he was slowly waking to a new arousal or falling asleep in the middle of an old one, that the memory came, sharp, poignant and clear. He thought suddenly of Blue Squirrel.

During the previous married years with Fan – six years it was now – he had developed a grateful sense that all his previous life had been a preparation for this life with her; that every expression and enjoyment of sexual feeling had been an anticipation of his marriage. On other occasions, he had been possessed by a joyful sense that in making love, two human bodies entered into an ecstatic creative state, making the world new with each copulation, and bringing new life thereby to earth. Byerley was not a man for church or chapel, but this filled him with reverence, and every sexual experience of his life seemed gathered now in the glorious, life-affirming joy of regular congress with his loving wife.

The recollections of these earlier unions were entirely vague. Very occasionally, he would put a name, or a face, to such a memory, but for the most part he was feeling 'the past' to be at one with the glorious present. And then, as if a visitant from the Cherokee territory had actually stolen into the Soho bedroom and touched his shoulder, he became aware of Blue Squirrel. It was almost as if the act of making love to Fan had conjured up Blue Squirrel's presence, and he remembered now – everything. He remembered his arrival at the township; he remembered her large hands at work building a vase. He remembered their conversations about Wooden Leg, about the art of pottery, about the American future, and about their future, together. He remembered his deep love for Blue Squirrel, and his horror, on the day of the raid, at losing her. There had been such chaos that night. He had ridden round and round among the Indians, aware to his intense dismay that some of them, seeing a white man on a horse, had assumed that he, who loved and revered them so much, and who so respected their traditions, was one of the Rebel colonists come to rape and pillage. But this realization, and this horror, had been subsumed in the much greater horror of losing Blue Squirrel. It had been agreed with them, as they made love and fell in love, that their lives would be together now for ever and always. He was desperate to find her, but she was nowhere to be found. When he came across the group of women scalping Mr Bird, he had been transfixed with horror by the scene, and yet had half-hoped to find her among the maenads with their uplifted knives: partly because Bird richly deserved his fate, and chiefly because he missed her. In the panic and the hurly-burly, he had missed her with an intense agony, but it could not yet occur to him that he would lose her for ever. And then, as he had deliberated and searched, he had found himself being led away, in effect the prisoner of the white raiders, but also – as they had surmised, partly falsely, partly too truly – their racial and cultural brother. And now, all these years later, suddenly very awake in his marriage-chamber, he was aware of Blue Squirrel. He thought of her body, which he had worshipped, as he now – so treacherously, it seemed in that nocturnal clarity – worshipped Fan. He thought of Blue Squirrel's breath upon his body. The breath of this woman, on his throat, on his belly, as she returned his worship, was the most beautiful thing he could remember, it was the breath of God.

Now, in bed with his wife, he could feel Fan weeping in the darkness.

—Why? he asked her. Why are you crying?

She did not reply with words, but with more tears.

—You weren't, he replied, because he thought she said, through stifled sobs, that she was being silly.

—It was different, she said, much later, when he was pretending to be asleep.

—What was different?

—Tom, you know. Our lovemaking.

The silence was eternal. She then said,

—I felt as if I was not there. You did not speak to me, as you usually do. You were silent. It was silly of me. I am sorry. But . . .

Once more, a silence which seemed longer than the night itself.

—You with someone else. I felt that your body was making love to mine, but that you were with someone else.

After more silence, during which the darkness seemed very dark indeed, she said, in a grown-up voice which rather terrifyingly reminded him of her mother,

—No, don't.

For he had climbed over her and was attempting, clumsily, to make everything all right by a repetition of what had made her weep.

—Let's go to sleep, she said.

Thereafter, they had many more children, and they remained together as man and wife. But something had changed between them.

It was during the morning after that sad night that the news came to Soho that the Bastille had fallen in Paris. Everyone in the sale-rooms cheered, and Fan and Tom Byerley raised a glass of wine that evening to celebrate. But something had gone from them. The old ecstasies never returned.

# 8

ONE WEDNESDAY MORNING, JOSIAH WAS MAKING ONE OF his regular tours of inspection in the Etruria Works. His head throbbed as he walked through the modelling room. He was not drinking more brandy than usual, but the pain on the top of his head was like the after-effects of cheap cognac. The pain was worse each day now. The only suggestion Erasmus could make was more opium. The removal of pain, however, brought with it the removal of other faculties. Jos was less attentive than he once was. The endless making of lists inside his head, the habit of a lifetime, was now done with a different purpose. In the old days, he listed his day's tasks, his week's tasks, his current ambitions, as a way of cramming more and more activity into limited time. Now he made the mental lists for fear of forgetting. Dispatch letters to lawyers, and pay bills in St Austell. Be at quayside eleven a.m. when Caleb draws up with new Cornish consignment. Try firing the new Portland Vase at twenty degrees hotter? Vary the consistency of the slip in two vases, and compare them. Write to nephew Byerley about the dishonesty of Philpotts, an assistant in the Greek Street showrooms. Certainly have Philpotts dismissed, but whether to prosecute him for theft? With all the time-wasting this would involve, and the possibility of Philpotts being hanged? Make quarter of an hour to listen to Sukey, who has been teaching Kitty and Sarah that Handel piece she used to play when she was their age (ye Gods – Sarah was fourteen, Jos was twenty-one, Sukey was twenty-five and still not married: the passage of Time, the most obvious fact of existence, remained the most incredible).

Discuss wages with Useful Tom – the lazy, greedy dogs at the works had asked him for threepence extra *per diem*! It might be time to harangue them once more. Consider the possibility of a Paris showroom, after the confounded Irish stopped buying Wedgwood ware? Now this wonderful Revolution had occurred, there was surely a chance of patching up our differences with France. Write to nephew Byerley about the dishonesty of Philpotts – oh no, he'd already said that.

Such mental lapses never happened in the past.

And there was something worse, something which caused almost the acutest pain of all. He could not quite bring himself to admit it, as he clutched and clutched harder at his stick. His hands had begun to shake. Reason, his God, told him that more brandy, and more laudanum, would only make the shaking worse. But the painful consciousness that his hand now shook made him reach for both bottles with ever-greater frequency. Besides, he was not deceiving himself. For an hour or so after taking two or three drops of laudanum in a glass of brandy and water, he could still make the best pots in Europe. Thereafter, the shaking began. He cringed to think of the botched Portland Vases which he had hurled in anger to the throwing-room floor.

—Ee, lad!

He put out his walking stick and prodded at a piece of wet clay which Isaiah Palethorpe was fashioning into a plate. Even as the stick went out, Jos was aware that he was being unfair. He was a good modeller, was Isaiah, and that plate could easily have been rescued. It was the pain which made Jos scoop the clay on the end of his stick and hurl it to the floor. Not just the physical pain in his head, but the mental pain of remembering his own botches – he who since the days of his apprenticeship had never made a botch!

—That's not a Wedgwood plate, not the way thee's messing wi' eet.

—Yes, Mr Jos.

The patient fury with which the modeller endured his humiliation in front of the other workers stuck into Josiah's conscience. But you couldn't apologize to them. It would give them ideas.

The works was pursuing its own life. He thought of what it would be without him, and he could imagine it all being perfectly satisfactory, like a well-made machine outliving its owner. But, even as he was having this thought, he spun round on his wooden leg and bellowed,

—Who said that?

There was silence from the modelling room.

—Somebody said a word!

He could feel the blood heating in his throbbing skull. His lower lip was trembling with the agony of the whole situation. He did not really want this situation to develop. If he found the culprit, he would have to dismiss him on the spot. He did not want to do that. On the other hand, he could not be seen to climb down in front of the rogues. And that sort of language, the language of sailors, was not to be tolerated at Wedgwood's.

There was no danger of a confession. No one was going to lose their work and their day-wage just for uttering a monosyllable. But it was conceivable that some of the more slavish young apprentices, resentful of their seniors, might betray them. Worse, there was the danger of ribaldry, enquiries by the younger hands as to the word's meaning. He must hobble on before the situation got out of control.

—There'll be no foul language in Etruria! he bellowed.

When he left the modelling room he could hear the rumble of laughter, and badinage being exchanged. Was that really what they thought of him now?

He was in the decorative modelling room now. He tried, this time simply as a mental exercise, to repeat the list of necessary tasks for the day. All seemed to be going well here. The funny thing was that, in spite of the slump caused by the wretched French war, there was not much diminution in trade for the decorative side of the business. It was in the useful ware that the slump had occurred, as if people were making do with chipped tea sets and dinner plates until the hostilities were over. The Quality, or the aspirant Quality, still seemed to have their appetite for luxurious items. Perhaps the toppling of thrones and titles on the other side of the English Channel had actually increased the desire of the nouveaux riches in England to mark out their territory with stupendous vases imitative of the antique examples in Sir William Hamilton's collection.

—Eee-eye-yi!

Josiah Wedgwood stopped short. In the ordinary modelling room, his exclamations and his pauses had been governed by the purpose of finding fault. But they now fell upon the most superb vase of volute-krater form. It could actually have been an Etruscan antiquity. Or better than that, it could have been thrown by the hand of Josiah himself in the days of his perfection and glory. Indeed, he paused beside it and looked, asking himself if, in this phase of opium-induced forgetfulness, he had in fact thrown this vase, and forgotten doing so. But it was still wet. It had been thrown that morning.

—Wilbraham.

He spoke to the foreman.

—Ay, Mr Jos.

—Who threw that vase?

Wilbraham's face took on a strange expression. If Josiah had been

asked to translate the expression into English, it would have said, I
have a surprise for you, Mr Jos, a very pleasant surprise; we have discovered a new modeller of genius. But there was something else in
Wilbraham's expression – amusement, or suppressed something or
other? In answer to Josiah's question, the foreman tilted his head
sideways and jerked it two or three times in the direction of the
wheels. A dark woman in a bonnet sat at one of the wheels.

However often he watched the process of throwing a pot, Josiah
was always interested by it. It must have been nigh on fifty years since
he watched anyone else at work on the wheel and thought they were
his superior. He could nearly always detect some kind of fault in what
was being done, even though it were easily of good enough quality.

This was something other. Here, once again, he experienced that
curious tingling of excitement which possessed him when he himself
threw a pot and saw emerging from the damp clay the very shape
which its creator had intended. Here was certainty of eye and hand.
The woman had propped up in front of her one of the engravings of
Sir William Hamilton's collection which they used in this room. She
had a particular trick, which Jos himself had never seen anyone else
use before. It was a fast little movement of the thumb-knuckle which
made the clay form the exact shape which she intended. She was
making another of the volute-krater vases, and it was identical to the
one he had just seen. Exactly identical, as if it had come out of a
mould. Here was a potter's hand which was the equal of his own!

When she had finished, the woman scraped the vase clean of its
base with a cheese wire and put it ready to dry. There was a loosen-
ing of coarse shoulder muscles which Jos could see through her blue
overalls. This relaxation told him how she, like all who have totally
mastered a craft, had been wound up to an extraordinary pitch of
emotional concentration while she worked. Muscles of neck and
shoulder had been as hard as leather, and now once more became

soft. He noticed the beauty of the nape of her neck, from which dark hair was gathered up beneath her cap. She could have been Spanish or gypsy. She kept her eyes down as he approached.

—I am your employer, Mr Wedgwood, he said as he stood over her. Mr Wilbraham hired you without consulting me. It musta bin while I was in London. What's your neam?

—I'm sorry, I . . .

Welsh. Well, he smiled a little and allowed himself the silent exclamation, which was on the edge of coarse language, well, I'll be jiggered.

—Your neam, ma'am?

—My name is Mrs Powell.

—Well, you are a very fine craftswoman and I hope you are happy here in your work.

—Thank you, sir.

Definitely Welsh.

— Weer d'you learn to throw a pot like that?

Her next words were incoherent, inaudible. She seemed discomposed. He could hear himself adopting – something which was all but unknown when addressing his workers – an apologetic tone.

—I merely asked weer you learnt to throw a pot, Mrs Powell. Because wherever it were, you are no ordinary potter. It canna 've bin Chelsea – we'd 've met befower. Bristow? Were it Bristow?

In reply to her quiet response, he asked,

—Yer what, lass?

Deaf as well as forgetful. Had the fateful poppy numbed his ears as well as his wits? It was as if she'd said America. But he did not want to press her in front of the others. He could sense her discomfiture.

—Well, thank you for such excellent work.

He looked at his own large red hand clutching the stick. If, before he had perfected the last Portland Vase . . . If opium, or disease, were to destroy his hand before his work was done . . . Had she been sent to him? By some kind Providence?

He looked once again at the two vases she had produced.

I should lahk t' introduce her, he thought with a smile, ter Sir William Hamilton hissel.

# 9

WHEN THE BELL RANG, THEY ALL DOWNED TOOLS AND LEFT the works. All the rooms in the factory felt, in that July heat, as hot as ovens, and there'd been many jokes shouted round, to the effect that the firemen did not need to heat the kilns, the pots would cook themselves if just left on the shelves. The heat, the clay dust, and the smell – both of the clay and of humanity – were oppressively strong. Everyone, therefore, mould-runners, throwers, plate-makers, paint-resses, handlers, in whichever part of the works they laboured, streamed out into the afternoon almost gasping for air. Even those lucky ones who were not in the various stages of potter's rot felt their lungs clogged, baked.

Meribah Powell came out of the works with the others. No one called her Sadloli now. She was Mrs Powell to everyone. There was no one who called her by her baptismal name. She had lodged with the Caul family, two streets away from the works, ever since she got her first job – as a handler – and that was some years ago now. Jo Caul, a kind man whom she had liked very much, had worked as a mould-runner. His wife, Hannah, was a paintress of great skill, a cleverer person than her husband, who managed, while doing a full day's work in the Ornamental works, painting teapots with flowers, to keep the family fed, clothed and up to scratch with their reading. The children – at the time of this momentous July day – were aged eight, nine and twelve. Hannah had lost two. The twelve year old, Shem, had started his apprenticeship at the works; she had hopes for him that he would become a thrower. As for the little girls, well, it was early days. Jo had died, aged thirty-eight. It was not an unusual age for a potter to die, not once the potter's rot had reached the lungs.

Mr Bent called it silicosis. When he'd pronounced Jo incurable, little Becky Caul, six, hearing her dad had silly causes, had wailed that she wanted 'em nall, supposing silly causes to be a treat. But most people just called it potter's rot. You could get it at thirty, you could get it at fifty. It got you in the end. Maybe – this was what both women thought, both Hannah Caul and Mrs Powell – maybe Jo had urged Hannah to take a lodger because he sensed he had not got long. The extra few shillings each week did not come amiss either.

The cottage, which was near the blacksmith's shop and the baker's – so handy for the heating of pies and other dishes – had a living room and a scullery downstairs, with earth floors. Upstairs, there were two rooms. Mrs Powell did not feel it was right that Mrs Caul should squeeze in to her small room with three children, but Mrs Caul said fair was fair and Mrs Powell had paid good rent. Sometimes one or other of the little girls came in to share the lodger's bed, which was a small truckle, all but filling the seven foot by seven foot chamber. They peed in ceramic pots, but there was a house rule that for anything more serious you used the privy in the back yard – something which was little more than a hole in the ground. The smell in summer was appalling, and when Mrs Powell walked through the clay dust of the yard to the stench of undrained Lord Street, she remembered the hay-smelling open spaces and the breezy open casements of her Cherokee girlhood.

Mrs Powell recognized, nevertheless, that she was lucky to be the lodger of the Cauls. They were a decent, utterly discreet family. None of them had ever asked about her husband, although they must have known she was the widow of the sergeant killed in the riots. By the time she arrived in England, she had grown adept at putting things in her mind behind her. At the forefront of things, there were the Cauls and their cottage; the children, of whom Mrs Powell had become extremely fond; and the works.

Mr Wilbraham had taken her on as a cup-handler at the works. He had believed her account of her working life. Many men would not have believed it, because it sounded so strange – that in America she had been all but in charge of a small pottery; that she had learnt how to throw pots in London, and even had some knowledge of glazes and firing, though less than she would have liked. She respected Mr Wilbraham. He had believed her, but he had not risked making a fool, either of himself or of her, by giving her work which was too ambitious; but nor, on the other hand, had he humiliated her by offering her work as a cleaner or skivvy.

As a modeller, she was required to make cup handles. The task involved filling two moulds, each representing a half-handle, with wet clay. When this was dry, the two half-handles would be stuck together with more liquid clay and affixed to the side of a cup. It was dull work, but – given the exacting standards of their employer – it was a craft. She learnt it quickly and, having worked patiently and quietly for over a year at the task, she had won commendation from all who observed her.

The throwing came about quite by accident. Harvey Wittaker, one of the best throwers of a pot in Etruria, succumbed to a stomach ailment one morning, and had run into the yard of the Ornamental works to throw up. Wilbraham had promised Owd Wooden Leg four stoneware vases by the end of the week – it was an order for a German client. Three of the magnificent objects had been completed when Harvey fell sick.

—If yo' d lahk ter try thah hand, yo'd help owd Wilbraham owta horl!

He had not meant it. She knew he had not meant it. She had known that the words had been drawn out of him by the World Spirit, drawn by the talons of the Great Buzzard. That was why she had said nothing in reply, but merely slipped quickly and quietly to the modelling room.

—Ee, lass, weer's thee gooin?

And she had seated herself on Harvey's stool and looked up at Wilbraham.

—Yo isna sairious?

—I could try.

For the first time in eighteen months, Wilbraham saw her white teeth. Her eyes also smiled.

—Well, that's the pattern-buke, he said, pointing to the document from which Harvey Wittaker had been working.

After this, there was no possibility of keeping her in the modelling room, and although she was the only woman throwing ornamental vases, no one seemed to mind. She was extremely careful, upon Harvey Wittaker's return, not to do or say anything which suggested she had displaced him. She behaved with perfect tact. She kept meticulous hours. She was not surly – she spoke when spoken to, exchanged pleasantries about the weather, was a perfectly kindly fellow worker; but no one at the works felt they knew her any better when she had been there eighteen months than on the day of her arrival, even though Etruria folk said she was wonderful with Mrs Caul's daughters when they were ill.

So life had gone on, and some of its painfulness had been concealed beneath the routines of work and the carapace of conventions.

She lost count of the evenings in the Rising Sun, when drink had been taken, when the sergeant would tell the patient boaties that Lord Shelburne should be ashamed of calling himself a bloody Englishman; he'd let himself down, his country down, twenty thousand good fighting men down and over a million loyal colonists. He never mentioned, during these diatribes, the fate of the indigenous population of America – the 'savages' – her people.

That part of her life was carried around perpetually in her heart. It emerged in dreams, it emerged when she had thoughts in her own language. It was there when she worked, and her hands felt the wet clay. The sense of exile was an everlasting sorrow in her heart which it was impossible and undesirable to expunge. She had never supposed that there was anything wrong in being sad if sadness was the appropriate response to circumstance. It would only be wrong to spoil another's happiness by letting her own wretchedness show. So, with the Caul children, for example, she was all smiles On the voyage to England and for many weeks after she had found herself, so grotesquely, working as a publican's wife in a small village miles from anywhere, she had quietly assumed that, since her heart was broken and she could never be happy, she must be on a quest, a mission. The only thing which could redeem the whole intolerable experience was revenge. She would find her lost love, Tomtit, and she would kill him, in revenge for all he had done, or not done, to her and her people.

She had managed to locate him, and actually to see him, remarkably early after their arrival in London. She had many long walks while her husband was carousing or blathering to his drinking pals, and it was not difficult, after judicious enquiries, to find the Wedgwood salerooms in Greek Street. Her body imprisoned in stays and hemmed in by European clothes, and with a slightly larger bonnet than was necessary, she was confident that she was almost unrecognizable. So emboldened did she become that she actually

entered the salerooms and saw the wares on display: work of astonishing quality, though there was none of what Europeans called
china. This was fascinating to her, since, if you spoke to an English
person about Wooden Leg they would always reply using the word
'china'. In fact, she could not see a single china object on display. It
was all varieties of earthenware brightly and beautifully glazed:
teapots in the colour and shape of cabbages, cups painted with
flowers, the famous creamware. Then there were the elegant black
objects – what she later learnt were called the basaltes ware. And
there were superb vases, urns and ewers of the most elegant shapes
and ingenious glazes.

Why had he needed the Cherokee clay, then, since he could get
what he wanted using English clay? Or had he ingeniously blended
their American kaolin with his whiteish English clay to make his
creamware? Or was the secret that he needed it for this . . . jasper.

Jasper was a revelation, this densely white stoneware: *that* was
where the Cherokee clay was used! She loved the white modelling on
the reliefs – a medallion of Medusa, modelled by Flaxman, against a
pale blue background, plaques of Gods and heroes and maidens; so
their mythology was not all from the Bible (a book she had now read
through several times, each time with greater degrees of puzzlement).
At this stage of her life, she did not know the stories which these
remarkable objects depicted. That would come later when she read
Tooke. There was an extraordinary jasper tablet of a youth riding wild
horses into the rays of the sun.

The beauty of the salerooms had shocked her; in a way, changed
her, taken the revenge out of her heart. Before she had seen any of
it, and when she was simply lying in misery in small malodorous
tavern rooms, or ship's cabins, she could rehearse her bloody
revenge. Face to face with the reality of the showroom, it seemed
impossible to use her potter's hand for anything but good: how

could she lift up her hand against Tomtit even if he were the deepest-dyed villain?

Later, much later, when she had been emboldened to visit Mr Wilbraham and to gain employment, she had the chance to meet Tom. By then, everything was different. The American experience would never go away – how could it? But the tragic past was over-laid by the misery of the present; the dignity of the Cherokee calamity was temporarily obscured by the ignominious farce of life with Sergeant Powell in the tavern, the tedium of his talk, the surli-ness of his drunken bad tempers, and the rough edge of his fists.

—If you think I'd permit . . . a wife of mine . . . to work!

But the culture of the Potteries was that women did work, and she had simply defied him. She had walked to Etruria from Burston. After Mr Wilbraham had taken her on as a modeller, she had decided at once to leave her husband, and she had found lodgings with the Cauls. Powell had yelled, but he was powerless to make her return.

Becoming an Etruscan was a much more momentous event for her than any of the recent transformations, such as becoming a member of the Church of England, or becoming a married woman. Since the destruction of her village, life had been experienced through a murk of pain. It did not lift now, but finally it became pos-sible to move forward. Sometimes, after two hours of doing nothing but affix handles to teacups, she knew she had been in a haze which was not a haze of misery. Work had become a narcotic. She would find herself with a full board of cups, each with its handle attached, and she would have no real recollection of having fixed them, as she carried the board across the brick-paved yard to the sheds where finished work was stored and dried before firing.

Later, when she had been allowed to throw vases, life had actu-ally blossomed. Work did not compensate for what could not be restored. But it was a worthy end in itself, and deep pleasure coursed through her at a vase well thrown, a bowl well crafted. There were days when her hands seemed able to make the clay do whatever she wished, not by conscious thought but by a profound instinct and a sure, steady skill. These days were very precious.

She always knew, of course, that the day would come when she was confronted by Tomtit, and she could not foresee the consequences of this. Her initial desire to fulfil the law of vengeance, simply to kill him, had evaporated, but she was not sure, quite simply, whether she could bear to see him. And once the connection had been made, once it was clear that he, the nephew of Wooden Leg, had found her, his former lover, throwing pots at the works . . . She would have to leave, wouldn't she? So she dreaded seeing him as many, perhaps most, ex-lovers dread seeing one another, and she dreaded losing the one occupation which was keeping her sane. Perhaps the solution would be for her to leave, to go to work for another pot works, in Derby or Worcester, to get right away, before the dreaded meeting with Tomtit so much as occurred?

She had almost reached the point where this did indeed seem to be the right solution, and she had almost decided to warn Mrs Caul that she would be leaving Etruria, when, quite suddenly, there he was: Tom Byerley. He had been waiting for her one winter afternoon when she came out of work. Normally, the movements of the Wedgwoods and the foremen and the other boss figures were noted by the workers. (*'Young Master John – almost Mister John now – 'as gone ter Scotland' 'E asna?' 'E bloody az' 'What's e want ter bloody go there fur?' 'Nehemiah Marow, less uv t' bloody!' 'Sorry, Mr Wilbraham – studying e says – chemistry nall.'*) It would be noted when Wooden Leg was in London, and also there was talk of Tomtit.

*—They sez Mr Tom'll be made partner, jes as soon as Mr John's of age. Owd Wooden Leg wouldna make iz nevvy a partner afore iz own sons.*

There was talk of Tom's marriage, his children, even hints at his racy life.

—*E were on steege, werny? Actors are all t' seem – they lahk a leedy! But that was afore e were wed.*

—*Ee, lad, yer knaw what thee see: wunce a leedy's mun, owees a leedy's mun.*

But there he was, lady's man or not, casually standing beside the canal one sharp January afternoon. Though it was only four o'clock the light was fading. Her bonnet was large, and she kept her eyes down demurely. Tomtit had aged. You could not mistake the tall carriage, the pronounced cheekbones and the hooked nose, but these could have been the marked characteristics reproduced by Nature in an elder brother, even in an uncle. His face was chiselled now, and all the youthful softness was gone from his cheeks. She saw this at once. He wore gloves, a hat, a wig, and a long winter great-coat with a cape at the shoulders. He was a dark apparition. She scuttered round the corner of the works when she came out at the canalside and was going to walk on, avoiding him, when she found that he had not merely drawn level with her but overtaken her, and was standing in her path, as the others, seemingly unnoticing, trudged home for their tea.

—Blue Squirrel.

—Mr Tom – it isn't . . . it isn't my name.

—Blue Squirrel.

—Please, no.

—I knew it must be you. My Uncle Jos. Wooden Leg told me, close on a year ago, that there was this wonderful woman. He thought she must be Spanish or possibly Maltese, but speaking with a Welsh lilt. Then, one day, I saw you in the modelling room, at work on the wheel.

He laughed, but she did not.

—Who else could it have been? He says that you beat him at his own game.

—Mr Jos is very kind.

They walked silently to the water's edge. She shivered, and not just from the wintry cold which crept up from the water. As light fell, grey mist hovered over the overhanging branches and the bulrushes were stiff as stalacmites. She said nothing.

—I wanted to come as soon as I heard. And then I was afraid to come . . . Blue Squirrel.

—Please. My name now is Mrs Powell. Mr Byerley.

—Mrs Powell – there was hurt, not satire, in his tone as he adopted her chosen form of address – I feared. I am married now. I feared loving you still. I feared what it would do to my wife, to my children. Obviously they must come first.

—Obviously.

He seemed unaware of her tone of voice, for he went on,

—That I knew you would see at once. But I did not want to . . . awaken old fires in you. I thought that you, who had also married – and I am sorry for your loss – I was afraid that—

—You were afraid I might find you irresistible? She asked it in a tone which even male vanity could not but hear. Mr Byerley. I do not know where this conversation will end, and it was perhaps a mistake for it to begin. Can you imagine what happened, that night in Old Kowes? The children raped? The numbers killed? My pot works in ruins? The crops burned? The houses, the Hall of Meeting, everything in flames?

—It was the worst night of my life.

—It was the worst night of *your* life?

Silence had to follow her horrified outburst.

—I looked and looked for you, he said. I searched about in the darkness. I thought you had run away from me . . . I was on a horse.

One of the men, one of the evil posse of men who wrought all that destruction, seized my horse . . .

As he spoke, she could hear his recognition of what, all these years, she had suspected. She could hear his narrative unravel, and test itself against another memory.

—My God, you don't think . . . you have been thinking . . . what kind of man did you think I was? That after all we had . . . that when we loved one another so much that I could betray you, your people, your . . . Damn it, I will call you Blue Squirrel. Blue Squirrel, you could not have believed that—

—Don't, she said quietly.

They walked for a while, silently. The canal turned leftwards towards Shelton. After an eternity of not speaking, she found her voice.

—I searched for you too. You were not there. Some of the braves, the few lucky braves who survived, saw you ride off with Boone's men. What were we supposed to think? Don't answer that, she spoke sharply and with authority. I loved you. I do not think it would be possible for a human being to pour out more love for another person than I poured out for you. In doing that, I poured out my life-spirit and gave it to you. I cannot just scoop that up and save it. I spent it. I followed the soldiers to England because I needed an explanation – yes, I believed . . . I see that was false. I am sorry. But can you imagine what I had passed through?

—Yes! No . . . I am sorry.

—If you want me to leave here, leave my position at Wedgwood's—

—Blue . . . Mrs Powell, why ever should I want that?

—Because of embarrassment.

Again, an eternity of silence as they walked, and, when shadows fell and it became dark, they paused and looked again at the gloomy, misty canal.

—My uncle has come to depend upon you. He often speaks of Mrs Powell now. He would be so puzzled if you left him. Of course he has no idea . . . of us.

—Of course.

They turned to walk back. There was no agreement between them. Neither said to the other, We have now moved onwards, we have left our old selves behind us. I will never mention to my work colleagues that you were my lover, my Tomtit, and you will never tell Mr Jos or your wife that I am Blue Squirrel. It will always be our strange secret, sometimes unbearably painful, sometimes numbly locked away like a hidden jewel, concealed in cotton-wool in a closed drawer.

Nothing was said, but all was understood and agreed. They had sometimes seen one another since that half-conversation, when Tom Byerley and Mr Jos did tours of inspection together. But for the most part Byerley was in London and that, she suspected, was how both of them preferred it. So life had gone on, and now on this swelteringly hot July day, eighteen months after the difficult conversation, she emerged with her work colleagues, as usual on to the canalside. She knew, as soon as she looked up and saw Caleb Bowers, giving Dandelion a handful of oats, that he was studying how not to look at her. And she knew with that instinct which is given to some human beings, that something important was about to occur between her and this man.

# IO

EVER SINCE CALEB BOWERS HAD COME TO THE RISING SUN
on that very wet day several years before, Mrs Powell had been aware
that he had fallen in love with her. She had believed at first that it
was a sexual attraction which, in part, she reciprocated. She imagined
that many of the rough men who worked on the barges took a fancy
to the women who worked in the taverns up and down the water-
ways, and that this was how many got their pleasure. There was not
even a particle of Puritanism in her nature, so this did not shock her.
It was simply not an indulgence which she was going to allow 'her'
bargee. Her marriage was too unhappy, her past was too complicated,
for her to imagine it possible to embark upon any new love. She
knew that, whatever satisfactions such an adventure would provide
the bargee, it could bring nothing but unhappiness to herself.

Nevertheless, 'her' bargee had taken to returning over and over
again to the Rising Sun to the point where his devotion was obvious
and embarrassing. She had exploited the situation to the extent of
asking him to put in a word for her with Mr Wilbraham. Otherwise,
she had no desire to get involved with him.

Little by little, however, she recognized that Caleb Bowers, who
was old enough to be her father, was not, in her husband's intolerable phrase, 'sniffing around'. She did not then know that he was in
fact a completely virginal man, but she responded to his devotion in

a way which recognized it for what it was: not a passing fancy, but something which was perhaps breaking his heart. Since she had been lodging with Mrs Caul, and even more strongly since she had been widowed, Mrs Powell had had very little contact with the curious, grumpy, brooding bargeman, although whenever they happened to encounter one another, it was obvious, from the look in his eyes, that the tragic devotion had not gone away.

Now, Meribah Powell's secret was that this had become part of her own inner life. It sustained her, and gave her tremendous joy. Next to her success as a thrower, she derived comfort in life from the knowledge that He – she frequently gave him no name inside her private thoughts – was worshipping her. She actually basked in his hangdog love, because she knew now that it was completely unthreatening.

Sometimes women at the works prattled. They spoke of the Wedgwoods as if they knew them much better than was really the case. Indeed, they spoke of them as if they were characters in a play or a novel, whose passing inner thoughts and whose emotional life could be known. They discoursed intrusively about how Mr Jos felt at the death of his little girl, what he thought at the prospect of Miss Sukey becoming an old maid (*Shame intit – though she's plain lahk, yewda thought somewun wud avver – I'd avver fer that munny* . . . and so on). Part of this running commentary or *roman fleuve* about the Wedgwoods which formed part of the conversation of the Etruscans was the thought that Mrs Wedgwood had, in her youth, been no better than she ought. No one had the slightest evidence for supposing that their employer's wife had been an adulteress, but the particles of non-evidence were gleefully assembled. Somehow, Caleb's love for Sally Wedgwood, and even his one teenaged kiss with her, now so many years ago, had passed into the legend. How this could be, neither Caleb nor Sally would have been able to say and when, much later, he found it to be the case, he was ruefully amused but also profoundly uncomfortable. Yet, as he knew, folk will talk. Nothing to be done to stop them.

Meribah Powell, who had heard these stories of Mrs Wedgwood, and who knew that Caleb had been her youthful swain, had concluded that Caleb and Sally Wedgwood had been lovers; she even wondered whether they were still lovers, which was what the wilder gossips at the works wanted to believe – even though, as with so much of the best gossip, there was not the smallest evidence to support it. Her whole approach to the man, therefore, was coloured by all this talk, which had been swimming about in the atmosphere ever since she took her position as a cup-handler. The reality – of Caleb's detachment from the physical experiences of love until he had encountered her – was only going to be revealed to her that day. Had she known of his virginity, and had she known the depth of his tragic outlook upon existence, she would almost certainly have been frightened away.

It was, as we have said, a very hot July day. The sun did not beat down on the sites of ancient Etruria with more scorching intensity than it did on that day in Staffordshire. The mud at the canal's edge was caked into biscuit. The air shimmered with heat. It had been even hotter inside the works, so that there was a measure of refreshment for all the workers as they came out at the end of their day's labour. But it was from heat to heat that they passed, such a heat as can make one light-headed.

Meribah did not know then, as she was unable to say afterwards, what it was which made her pause and walk to the water's edge, rather than joining in the general trudge round the side of the works and into Lord Street for the journey home. But she did pause, allowing her eye to follow the progress of a moorhen which was lazily scudding across the surface of the water, which was always powdered with grey-white clay dust.

—She's in t' best place, swimming!

Meribah looked up and saw that Caleb had joined her, that he was standing beside her watching the bird swim on the canal.

—That's true, she said.

The two had not spoken to one another for about two years, though she had caught sight of him from time to time ever since working at Wedgwood's, heard him calling to the men loading his barge, seen his strong arms holding barrels of ware which would have caused two normal men to collapse beneath their weight; and been conscious, all the time, of his gaze, flickered surreptitiously towards her.

—There's no working in this heat, he said. I'm knocking off.

—It must be lovely to be on the water.

—Have you never been on a barge?

—Never.

This was the closest this taciturn man was going to come to inviting her. Soon, she was greeting Dandelion, who stood patiently beside the barge, and he was holding her elbow as she climbed on board. The overpowering scent of his sweat as he did so, and the moisture of his brow beneath the curly, brindled black and grey hair were by no means disagreeable to her. She knew that she was sweating too, and that her simple grey dress was stained around the armpits.

After all her years of service, the aged Dandelion knew her job so well that, for the earlier part of the familiar voyage, she trod alone, while Caleb stood beside his guest, watching hedgerows and fields drift along behind them. Very soon, the industrial grime of the clay dust cleared from the water's surface and the boat drifted between passages of dark water, and stiller stretches where the entire surface of the canal was covered with duckweed, so that they were surrounded on all sides by brilliant green – the green of the duckweed, the green of nettles and grass at the bankside, the green of hedges and trees and fields. There were a number of vessels out on the water. They passed seven or eight barges, laden with various wares, from coal to vegetables, coming northwards. They passed Barlaston and Meaford, sleepy in the haze of heat. Conversation between them had been desultory, but this did not seem to matter. She felt that it did not matter whether or not they found things to say to one another. Indeed, sometimes when she thought that he had at last thought of some new remark to address to her, he was in fact calling out to Dandelion.

—Don't mind them, love!, if some boys were fishing on the bank and looking quizzically at the horse.

Or – and Meribah thought this was usually addressed to the horse, rather than to her –

—There'll be a lock coming up in a minute, remember!

Just before they reached the little town where Caleb lived they came to Siddal's Bridge and Turnover Bridge and the cluster of locks known as Stone Flight. Two boatmen were coming towards them on the canal, which necessitated their holding back, for the locks were extremely narrow – only just wide enough to take a seven-foot boat – and there was no possibility of passing there.

—He's letting in water far too fast!

It was hard to know whether this was addressed to Dandelion or to Meribah; maybe to both.

—Where's the sense in that? With all that turbulence, he'll have t' barge crashing against the lock and do damage to both. Better to do it gradual. Keep your barge intact. Slow and steady wins the day.

She looked at him and said,

—I want to swim.

—We canna swim here. Not with folk coming up and down, not with barges.

He was getting off the barge as he spoke, and mooring it to a bollard on the bank where there was sufficient space to allow the other long boats to pass when they had come crashing clumsily through the lock.

—Thee'll be raight as reen, he said quietly to the horse, who looked at him somewhat reproachfully as he tied her to the towpath fence.

—Come on, he said, and this, Meribah realized, was addressed to her.

They walked a little while in silence down a bridle path which wound into bushy, rolling, fertile fields, where the farmed land was hedged with crab apples, which nodded ripe among the foliage, and pink dog roses full in flower. Within a very short space they had come to a pool of water, whose edges, overhung with oak and ash and thorn, were covered with lilies. Ducks swam on the surface.

The man and the woman looked at one another. Afterwards, some years afterwards, she told him that at this moment she knew what it was like to be Adam and Eve in the Garden of Eden before the apple had been eaten.

—Crab apple, more likely!

Without any further words, she climbed the fence, and began to unbutton her grey dress. Her working costume was simple. If Caleb had chosen to go swimming that afternoon with a lady of quality, it is quite possible she would have been unable, without assistance, to disentangle herself from the paraphernalia of hoops and stays with which a genteel female person was imprisoned. She still was laced into stays and a petticoat beneath her dress and they were sodden when she removed them. She was soon naked, placing her bonnet on the top of her other clothes, and looking up at him with a smile which turned to a laugh at his expression, which combined rapture and terror.

—Come on, undress. Let's swim! she said.

He was a sinewy man, and although it was a body which had been put to much work and exertion over the years, there was no flab, no softness of skin. When naked, as if the best he could do to cover his shyness was to be in the water, he dived from the edge, head first through water lilies. Two ducks rose startled into the air. Stepping cautiously into the water, and feeling the delicious ooze of clay mud between her toes, she trod until the refreshing water touched her thighs and then she too plunged in.

At first they swam about separately, simply luxuriating in the experience of being cool. Once the weedy edges of the pond had been left behind, the water was limpid and clear. They could see that they were sharing their swim with little shoals of minnows, with perch and roach. Having swum on her front for a delicious ten minutes, she turned over and floated, looking at the sky. She knew then that he had drawn alongside her. She did not look at him at first. She could feel him taking her hand in the water, and she grasped his too. Then she turned, and saw the intensity of his love. She opened her mouth. Afterwards, he told her he thought she was about to laugh, and she said,

—Laugh? *No* – I was simply astonished, taken aback. I'd never seen emotion so clear on a human face . . . need.

But they said nothing at the moment itself in the pond. Merely, her hand clasped his even more tightly, as she moved towards him in the water.

Later, much later, as they lay on their bed of moss beneath the overhanging ash tree at the far end of the pond, seen only by the indifferent ducks, she murmured sweet amorous things in his ear, and stroked his cheek and licked him, and felt such boundless, rapturous joy that it could not at that moment be put into words. Afterwards, she said that she had supposed this would never happen to her again in her life. But this was not quite true, since she had not consciously supposed herself a finished being, sexually. It was merely that life had placed her in circumstances in which it was not quite imaginable how or where she would meet 'someone new'. It was during that beautiful hour, lying naked on the moss-bed, however, that she discovered the truth about her lover, that she was his first woman, his Eve, his Lilith. She whispered to him her real name, and she loved the way he said it with a Staffordshire accent. He made it sound like Sad Lawley. She felt a little ashamed – but again, this was 'afterwards', for at the time, the intensity, and the surprise, of the whole experience did not make it possible, precisely, to chronicle or record what either of them were feeling that afternoon – but at some stage, she felt ashamed at the intense pleasure it gave her to know that she was his only woman. It was this which gave the relationship its peculiar Adam and Eve quality. (She would soon come to love the books he loved, and few pleasures would match lying naked in his strong arms as he held aloft his little morocco-bound copy of the poem. They both learnt to recite passages to one another, and a favourite was the pregnant moment when the serpent glimpses the naked Eve performing her gardening tasks, and is so moved by her innocence and beauty that he for a moment forgets to be the devil –

> her heavenly Form
> Angelic, but more soft and feminine,
> Her graceful innocence, her every air
> Of gesture, or least action, overawed
> . His malice

Caleb would say that they had been Adam and Eve, that afternoon beside the pool, and she did not mind him, not at all, praising and caressing her 'heavenly form'.)

So there began their happiness. So Caleb changed. The unhappiness of his early life, and the horrors through which she had passed, would never go away, but they were both able, when he died in her arms as a beautiful old man with silvery hair a quarter of a century later, to look back upon the kind of happiness which very few people enjoy unalloyed and which he, for his first half-century of existence, had supposed the stuff of romance.

# II

—YOU S-SAY HE IS GONE INTO D-D-DEVONSHIRE?

Dr Darwin, Mrs Wedgwood and Miss Wedgwood were in the drawing-room at Etruria.

—We worry about him, don't we, Sooks? drawled the boy's mother.

Tom had never really been healthy. Dr Darwin diagnosed paralysis of the colon for the constant diarrhoea, and failure of the digestive system. Other physicians, such as Dr Beddoes of Bristol, had taken refuge in vague terms such as 'hypochondria'. But then, Dr Beddoes, an habitual sufferer in his lower gut, was, with Tom, an adept of the opiates. The languor and mental imbalance of her favourite sibling was especially distressing to Sukey, now in her late twenties, since she could not comprehend it. Of all the siblings it was she alone who possessed old Josiah's forcefulness, his effectiveness, his vigour of attack. Her formidable intellectual energies, however, were to be devoted to largely private accomplishments. Old Josiah, for all his embrace of progress and the rights of man, could not contemplate the prospect of a daughter having authority over the works or the business. Nor could Sukey herself. The Rights of Women could be left to their friends the Wollstonecrafts. Sukey, since reaching the years of maturity, had become the director of operations in the family, the focal point to whom all turned — mother, younger

children and the three boys. Had she been allowed to apply her energies and intelligence to the business, it might have fared better. John,
after a spell at Edinburgh University, had been drilled by Pa into a
partnership; but he had pleaded, after a year or so, to be released,
and Josiah had given him the money to set himself up in London,
with a partnership in a small bank and a house in Marylebone. Josiah
the Younger, quiet, introspective, as passionate as his father about
experiments and Natural Philosophy, had agreed to take over the
running of the works at Etruria, but his heart was not in the business. And they had been too well bred to make some aspects of the
work tolerable. In short, they had become gentlefolk. Young Josiah
could walk down from Etruria Hall to the works, oversee the
workmen, inspect the equipment. But he could not, as old Josiah
could do, throw pots. Still less could he appear in any aspect of trade.
Josiah had sent him, in Cousin Byerley's absence, to oversee the
London salerooms. After a day of it, Josiah had written to his father
to explain that the haughtiness of the customers, and the ignominy
of having to appear to them as a shop-man, made it impossible to
continue. There were men and women coming into the salerooms to
make purchases whom he knew, or knew of, socially. Tom, having just
finished at Edinburgh, where he made fast progress in his experiments, was impeded from doing anything with life, not merely by the
gentility which undermined his brothers' capacities, but by physical
weakness.

—You see, Doctor, said Sukey, it is not just the listlessness, or the
asthma, or the low spirits, it's the combination of all of them. When
Pa has been ill, he has always worked *through* it. The slightest setback
leaves Tom prostrate. He's so unlike Pa!

—So are most of the world, remarked the Master Potter's wife.

—Most of the world is n-n-not the better for it.

Dr Darwin had completed his examination of Mrs Wedgwood.

She, like her son, had been suffering from a lassitude which a visit to Bath and a prolonged dependency upon laudanum appeared to have done little to shake. Old Josiah, prematurely aged at sixty-two, worried by exhaustion and palpitations in his heart, had been sent by the doctor to Buxton, enjoined to imbibe a 'decoction of bark' of Erasmus's own decocting, with powdered rhubarb, alum and nutmeg. If the heart continued to palpitate, even after regular application to this restorative, and if Jos's face and jaw continued to ache with neuralgia, even after taking the Buxton waters, the Potter was to resort to the tried and trusted laudanum. Nothing better!

—Virgil t-t-tells us that J-Jupiter sent Care into this world to spare humankind the fate of something worse. P-p-perhaps if T-Tom had an occupation of some kind.

—Like all of you, he is never out of a laboratory, said Sukey. He is a philosopher and an inventor, but without either your or Pa's application, but he is more dedicated to the pursuit of knowledge than either John or Jos.

—He is dedicated, said Sally, when he is dedicated. Otherwise, he loafs about, feeling ill and feeling sorry for himself in consequence.

—He has this scheme of reproducing images. Do you think that there could be anything in it, Doctor?

—Yes, Sukey, I do. He and his friend Humphry Davy have worked out that if you coat paper in silver nitrate and project images from a glass plate, using a camera obscura, the image will appear on the paper. They have demonstrated that. What they cannot work out is how to make the images stick.

—It is an image of poor Tom's life, isn't it? A flash of something – something quite brilliant – and then it vanishes. He writes from Devonshire that he has made a wonderful new friend, and he longs to go into Wales with him to visit John and Jos.

—Well, he should do so, said the doctor. But n-n-not without treating the disorders which have laid him low. I had hitherto recommended one g-grain of opium *per diem* and a few drops of laudanum in addition, as required. I shall write to him today to recommend that he increases the opium to two g-grains. I think it should stimulate his appetites and bring him into a livelier f-frame of mind.

—He writes that his new friend, Coleridge, is also feeling languid, restless, dejected. They met one another because they were both being treated by Dr Beddoes in Bristol. A brilliant young man lately down from Cambridge.

—What is it about our young men, drawled Mrs Wedgwood from the sofa, that makes them so languid?

—I shall write telling him to give his friend C-C-Colingbridge some opium too. N-n-nothing better!

The doctor rubbed his hands together gleefully at the prospect.

—I believe that Mr Coleridge needs little encouragement to take narcotics.

—A few grains more each day – it will drive away bodily pain, it will have the pair of them skipping about like mountain r-r-r—

—Rams? suggested Mrs Wedgwood.

—Roe-deer, said Dr Darwin. All the way to Wales.

When years had passed, and Sukey was a married woman, she reflected upon many ironies of that momentary conversation with the doctor. He had already decided, though she did not know it at the time, that he should become her father-in-law, that she should marry his son, huge, clumsy, shy Robert Waring Darwin. Her brothers, it would seem, were free to choose themselves spouses. But although she and her mother had half-adopted Mary Wollstonecraft's sister, and half-adopted her ideas about the Rights of Women, it would seem that these rights did not extend to any such freedom as the liberty to select her life companion. It would not be possible, quite, to marry her off to a cousin in the time-honoured Wedgwood tradition. But they would do the next best thing. Erasmus Darwin had become so close to them all that he was, after all, very nearly family. Sukey would marry Robert.

But she had not known it, when Tom set off to Wales that summer, with his friend Coleridge, to stay with Josiah and John and the Allens. And there was another strange thing to reflect upon, years later, from her perspective as a married woman. This alliance, between the Wedgwoods and the Allens, which was to produce so high a proportion of the great dynasty – it was not the boys' doing! Unable to choose her own husband, Sukey had, in effect, selected her brothers' brides. For the Allens had been Sukey's discovery.

Had the Wedgwood boys married cousins, or had they sought wives among the children of Staffordshire industrialists, the gene pool would have remained in the region of petty bourgeoisie. Like pigeons being bred less for their speed than their plumage, they now took a turn which determined the social direction of the family for the next two hundred years. Old Josiah had bred them to be men of intellect, and this they were, and would be. He had hoped, unrealistically, that they could continue men of business. This, their alliance with the Allens made even less plausible.

During her year in London, staying with the Bentleys at Turnham Green, Sukey had befriended Bessie Allen, an animated, pretty girl, just Sukey's age, with thick curling auburn hair and an infectious laugh. Mrs Bentley, with her zest for amusing young people of good family, had met her at some evening or another, and seen that she would make a good friend for Sukey. Later they had met Bessie's younger sister Jenny. Both Allen girls were of high intelligence, as well as good-looking. And though their father was a squire who lived in the palatial Cresselly Place, Pembrokeshire, John Allen was not every gentry family's idea of the ideal father-in-law. Neither Bessie nor Jenny Allen had found a husband when Sukey introduced them to her brothers; and both the elder Wedgwood boys fell in love, not merely with the girls, but with their entire family.

John Allen was at present the master of a fine house and a large estate near Haverfordwest. His father, a Pembrokeshire yeoman of relatively modest beginnings, had had the good fortune to capture the heart of Joan Bartlett, the heiress to Cresselly, a fine new-built mansion house set amid many acres not only of good agricultural land but also of coal seams. Welsh sea coal, and especially Pembrokeshire coal, burns purely and all but smokelessly, so the mines beneath Cresselly were of prodigious value.

John Bartlett Allen, Bessie and Jenny's papa, inherited Cresselly when he was a schoolboy at Westminster. He was an exceptionally handsome young man in the swarthy Celtic manner, with surprised brows which might have been drawn by a pencil, a sneering mouth and a pretty nose. Apart from an undistinguished career as a captain in the Foot Guards during the Seven Years War, John Allen had spent most of his mature years as a squire and a mine-owner, fathering eleven children, and making himself much hated by neighbours and coal miners alike by his quarrelsome temper, his greed and his irregular life. His wife died, exhausted by quarrels and childbirth, and Mr Allen took up with Mary Rees, the daughter of one of his colliers, and a strapping young person the age of Jenny. One third of his neighbours had stopped speaking to him because of his irascibility; another third because he had made a pleasant estate into a colliery; the remaining third could now follow the majority of 'the county' in eschewing Mr Allen's society on the grounds of the sheer impossibility of meeting the daughter of a man who had burrowed under the earth and smudged his face with coal dust. Sukey, who had met Mr Allen only once or twice, and disliked his strong language and his bluntness of manner – *You're the crockery merchant's girl?* – could not

but admire him for defying the snobbery of his neighbours. Probably
the supposed lowness of Mary Rees's background actually enhanced
her attraction in the eyes of the old squire. The pair were married,
and Mr Allen sportingly agreed – for his sons and daughters somewhat shamingly shared the snobberies of the county – to install his
new wife in a little house nearby at Creswell Quay, promising faithfully that she never be brought to Cresselly.

As the family had now begun to enter adulthood, there was at
Cresselly an air of a party, with the young grown-ups having the run
of the place for their own amusement. A conventional gentry family
might have raised an eyebrow at marrying a daughter to the son of
a manufacturer. But no Allen, knowing their father to be immured
in a cottage with a miner's daughter, could plausibly find the connection unrespectable, especially since any alliance with one of
Josiah's children would guarantee a considerable income. Great as
the revenues were from Cresselly coal, most of this went to John, the
firstborn Allen, and to the estate, and the young heiresses had to
divide what Allen wealth there was by nine. The marriage of young
Jos Wedgwood to Bessie was a very happy arrangement, especially
to his sister Sukey, and no one seemed to mind the fact that she was
five years his senior. John, now working as a banker in London, followed shortly afterwards by marrying Jenny. Since Jos the Younger
was now nominally in charge of running the works, Bessie and Jos
resided at Little Etruria, the Petit Trianon of the Staffordshire enterprise, the house old Josiah had built for Bentley and which had never
been occupied. John and Jenny lived in London, but the young
couples and their friends and siblings spent as much time as was
practicable at Cresselly itself in a round of balls, parties and meals
with neighbours, pursuing seasonal sports and living lives which were
as little as possible like either of their fathers'.

It was to join such a house party at Cresselly that Tom was now bound with his new young friend Coleridge. They travelled by post from Bristol to Gloucester, where they picked up a diligence which took them into Wales – through the brooding dark purple of the Brecon Beacons into the dumpling-shaped green hills of Carmarthenshire, past Llandovery and the medieval ruins of Llandeilo and down towards Carmarthen Bay. There were many changes of horses and sojourns at inns, and all the way, Coleridge talked. He had a light Devonshire accent and a voice which was both low – you leaned forward to catch it – and animated. For everything interested him, and he appeared to have given his mind to, quite literally, everything: to the likely triumph of the Girondins in France, to the impossibility of the Trinity, to the necessity of accepting the Godhead, to Lavoisier's experiments with oxygen, to Plato's Theory of the Forms, to Dr Darwin's poetry (much admired) and his materialism (not so admired).

The pair of young friends, in their early twenties, made a puzzling appearance to the Welsh innkeepers and townsfolk whom they encountered. Neither of them had powdered or brushed their long hair. Coleridge was a fleshy-faced man with flashing grey eyes and a large mouth. Tom looked fascinatingly ill – so pale and greasy-faced that you would have supposed him to have just arisen, unwashed, from a bed of sickness. They wore rough workmen's clothes – trousers, rather than the breeches and stockings which would have distinguished them as gentlemen – and they carried canvas knapsacks. At the White Feathers in Aberystwyth, the laughter and exuberance of the two young men drew stern looks from a group of middle-aged drinkers, who happened to comprise the local Justice of the Peace, a doctor and a clergyman. Coleridge was expounding his idea that he and a group of friends should form a commune, which he called a Pantisocracy, where men and women could live together, without the marriage-tie, and have all their goods in common, as in the Acts of the Apostles. With their third or fourth glass of brandy, Tom was bold enough to propose a toast to General Washington, and this drew, from the red-faced doctor at the neighbouring booth, a toast of his own.

—I gives you a sentiment, Gemmen! May all Republicans be gull-otined!

—Then I toast the King! replied Coleridge.

—May he be the last, added Tom, with splutters of uncontrollable glee.

Youthful high spirits were stimulated by something Coleridge called Bhang, and which he had bought in Bristol. A gummy resinous substance, made from the leaves of the marijuana plant, it made a delicious odour in the bar saloon as they added it to their tobacco pipes. For some reason, when inhaled, it made their voices squeaky, and even quite ordinary remarks became hilarious.

When the effects of it died down, they ordered a bottle of claret, and fell to discussing the international situation.

—I never thought I'd agree with Mr Pitt, said Coleridge, but the peace must hold! We must not fight a war with France, while it leads us – the whole of Europe – towards its enlightened future.

—And if they imitate Oliver Cromwell? asked one of the stern old gentlemen in the fireside corner.

—Surely, said Tom, the French King has accepted the new constitution?

—Which constitution? asked the old Welsh Tory. They change it every few months.

—They won't cut off the head of the King! declared Coleridge.

—I'm glad to have your assurance, sir! said the red-faced old gentleman.

His irony was lost on the younger men, who burst into marijuana-infused merriment.

It was during that Welsh house party – when, at length, Tom and his talkative friend reached Pembrokeshire, and paced the springy turf on the clifftops at Whitesands Bay, and heard their new-found friend declaim in Greek from the *Dialogues* of Plato, and laughed with the girls over *A Sentimental Journey*, and picnicked in the Elizabethan ruins at Manorbier on cockles and mussels – that Tom and Jos, somewhat to their brother John's amazement, made their decision to combine their novel mania for Coleridge with the need to fulfil Pa's idea for the Portland Vase.

Old Josiah, whose health no longer permitted extended travel in Britain, let alone abroad, had formed the plan to take the finished Portland Vase on a tour of Europe. None of them were certain how feasible such a journey would be, given the present condition of things in France. But, they could visit Holland and the eastern borders of France. They had always done good trade in Strasbourg and in Germany. The Portland Vase was the apogee, the great signature, of Josiah Wedgwood's career. Just as the Israelites of old bore the Ark of the Covenant with them as a talisman of their success, the younger Wedgwoods might, in their father's judgement, make a considerable impression if they took the Vase on a European tour, and reminded them that, in spite of revolutions and wars, the great firm of Wedgwood was still in production. They could also collect the debts which had been accruing to the firm in Amsterdam and Berlin. The crowds who came to see the Vase, and to hear Cousin Byerley, with his actor's gifts, expound its story, would remain to place orders for dinner services and tea sets. Tom and Jos Junior loved the idea of a European jaunt.

Jos, in particular, however, grieved that their great wealth was, so much of it, being poured selfishly into the acquisition of lands and gentlemanly status for themselves, and that they were not putting their money to altruistic purposes. Somewhat to John's dismay, he and Tom proposed to give a proportion of their allowance – some hundreds of pounds each year – to Samuel Coleridge. They would finance this budding philosopher and poet to study German and to expound for English readers the contemporary metaphysics of Immanuel Kant and the genius of Lessing.

So, over the dinner table and on the lawns of Cresselly, as Coleridge talked and talked, and drank and smoked, the plans were formed. When the Vase went forth upon its European journey, the young philosopher would accompany them, at least as far as the German border, and the world would go their way, the way of peace, and science and enlightenment.

# 12

IT WAS JOSIAH'S LAST VISIT TO LONDON. HE WENT BY
coach, but Caleb brought the ten vases by barge. How the old potter,
with his trembling hand, had managed to accomplish them, was a
mystery to many, and not one about which Caleb chose to speak,
though he smiled darkly about it, and stroked the barrel which contained them as if it were the belly of a pregnant woman containing
precious young. Nine of the copies were kept in the showrooms in
Greek Street, and the best of them was displayed in the rooms of Sir
Joseph Banks, the President of the Royal Society, who resided round
the corner from the showrooms, in Soho Square. Caleb noted with a
smile that these vases were the only production of the Etruria factory
which were not stamped underneath with the name WEDGWOOD.

Sir Joseph held what the *Gazetteer and New Daily Advertiser*
termed a 'numerous conversazione' in honour of Josiah the Vase.
The *conversazione* was organized by Sir Joseph's sister, Sarah Banks,
herself an antiquarian and an inventive collector, who devised, drew
and painted comical invitation cards with anagrams of the family
name.

—Pa, do look. Sukey's card read 'Mr Wowedog'. Her brother
John's was to Mr Dogewow. Everyone affected amusement, but Josiah
could not find the cards funny. He felt that in some way the cards
were a joke at his expense, and he disliked the hint of impropriety

about them. In a couple of the cards, which each depicted the Vase, the seated figure of Life-in-Death had her finger on the genital regions of the man who reached towards her.

Josiah had invited Caleb – and Mrs Caleb – to accompany them to the *conversazione*, but Meribah did not go into society, and Caleb knew that he would have been out of place in such company. Josiah himself felt awestruck when Sir Joseph made a speech in his honour, praising his scientific acumen, his invention of the pyrometer, as well as his skills as a potter, and his contribution to the beautification of many an English and European household.

—Did he mention the air-closet? asked Heffie, when told of the event.

Reading aloud to his wife from the *Gazetteer* two weeks later, Caleb laughed.

—Sir Joseph did not mention our Jos's achievements in Ireland, either! He put his big wooden foot in it there, and all! No sooner had he opposed the extension of free trade into Ireland than the Irish closed down the Wedgwood salerooms in Dublin, and he hasn't sold one pot in the whole Emerald Isle – not one!

—No one will sell anything in Ireland now, thanks to Mr Tone, said Meribah. But as for Mr Jos, he deserves Sir Joseph's praise.

It was in part a tease between them, Caleb's continual belittling of Josiah and his achievements, but even though she caught its tone, Meribah would never allow such denigration.

—No one deserves praise more highly than Mr Jos.

—Ay? 'This Vase, which represents the apogee of the English ceramic craft', 'This Vase, made by the greatest Master Potter who ever . . .'

—And so he is, said Meribah, taking the paper from her husband's hands and kissing him fully on the lips. The rest of the article fell to the floor unread, with its text of Sir Joseph's speech. Thirty years since, said the newspaper, Mr Arkwright had set up the first water-propelled spinning frame. In those days, England exported twenty thousand pounds' worth of cotton goods. Now? Last year, it exported £1,662,369 worth! The North of England, with its rich seams of coal and its plentiful supplies of water, had been rediscovered as a source of abundant wealth. It was a discovery, said Sir Joseph, every bit as momentous as his own discovery, with Captain Cook, of New Zealand. Birmingham was a village no longer, thanks to the ingenuity of Messrs Boulton and Watt. And in all these changes, Mr Wedgwood had played his part, with the constructions of canals and roads. Mr Wedgwood was, however, a very different man from all these other industrialists, however ingenious they might be. For he combined their commercial skill with a keen scientific mind. Justly had he been made a Fellow of the Royal Society. And when the assembled gentlemen had inspected his Vase, and remembered the innumerable productions of his intelligent hand and eye, they would consider him an artist as well as . . .

But these words were not read by either Mr or Mrs Bowers, who had discarded not only the newspaper, but also their clothes.

Sir William Hamilton was there, at the Banks *conversazione*, with his lady. Sir William praised the way in which this copy had captured the 'sublime character of the original'. Mr Gibbon was there – he had by then completed his monumental study of the decline and fall of the Roman Empire. He was a cocksure, plump little man. Josiah was surprised by his appearance. For no logical reason, he had expected the chronicler of Roman history to be tall and thin.

—Curious man, Banks, Gibbon remarked, deflecting a compliment which Josiah was trying to bestow upon his *Decline and Fall of the Roman Empire*, only man I know who went to Eton *and* Harrow. Overdoing things a little, would you say?

Jos had laughed politely but, when he thought of his own

eighteen months struggling with Tooke at Mr Blunt's academy in Newcastle-under-Lyme, he wondered, as he did so often, that he could have journeyed so far, and could find himself mixing in such society. His jaw ached, oh how it ached and stiffened, in spite of the double dosage of laudanum to which he had applied himself before the party began.

The Prince of Wales came for ten minutes, and there was even talk, between Josiah the Younger (who was presented to His Royal Highness) and Cousin Byerley, about the likelihood of the Prince acquiring one of the copies.

—So, where will you take it? asked the Prince, when presented to the younger Josiah, and told of the scheme to conduct the Vase on a Grand Tour. Not the best of times for going through France, eh?

—Indeed not, sir. But there is Holland, and we have hopes for Germany.

But the Prince was not really listening.

# 13

## *SENTIMENTAL JOURNEY*
## *OF A VASE*

TIME AND DEATH. THEY ORDER, SAID I, THESE MATTERS better in France. Sickness in the packet. A crossing from Harwich which took all day and all night. Writhing. Groaning. Abominable, sharp pains in the gut. Esteesee talking, talking, talking, as Tom throws up – over the side, but the wind blows back the vomit on to his cheeks and clothes. The smell of vomit, his own, and that of twenty other passengers, is so powerful that he thinks it will never leave him. Is it the ship heaving, or is it his head?

—Immanuel Kant has effected a revolution in our thinking about Time which might, who knows, be as revolutionary in the sphere of metaphysics as . . .

Silent in their straw casing, the Vase-Goddesses sit – Death-in-Life, and Life-in-Death.

> The Night-Mare Life-in-Death was she
> Who thicks man's blood with cold.

Half-asleep on a bench indoors, young Josiah nursed the wooden case which cradled the Vase as if it were a delicate infant.

Pa's last baby.

Byerley is one of the few people on the packet who has not thrown up. He got sea-legs many years ago sailing the Atlantic, and, although it is rough, he finds the storm, and the rain and the sea on his cheeks suitable to his turbulent mood.

His nose is now a great beak, his bony cheeks are hollow, his youth has been swallowed by the great weight on his soul. He cannot get out of his head the absence of the word on the base of this Vase. Every other production of his uncle's genius had been stamped with his name – or, in days of yore, with the names of the winning partnership, WEDGWOOD AND BENTLEY.

Staying upright on deck through the night, managing to walk without a fall, leaning against the wind, he ignored his namesake Cousin Tom, and his friend Samuel, as they clutched one another, green-faced and agonized and dribbling. Byerley paced against the storm, with the tempest of the past blowing gales in his heart. He thought of Old Kowes, and the pottery. He saw her long, pale brown fingers fashioning the clay. He saw the hands, which he had so often caressed, mouthed, stroked, holding firm to the grey clay which would dry to purest white. He saw the Potter's Hand.

Through the howling wind on board ship, as he staggered, solitary, he could still hear his wife's tears in the darkness of the married chamber. A great sorrow gnawed at his consciousness, an intolerable burden which felt like guilt. He knew that he had been guilty of betraying a great love, but he did not know whether he had betrayed Blue Squirrel or Fan. The remembrance of Blue Squirrel – how could he ever have forgotten her? But for some years he had, he had – the remembrance had driven out his love for Frances and their shared gift of happiness.

Somehow, after the massacre at Old Kowes, he had been given the capacity to blot out the pain by the simple mechanism of forgetfulness. He had not needed to put it all behind him as an act of will; it had passed out of his mind automatically, as a dream dies at the opening day. Thereafter, had come Life – the return to England, the buckling down to work for Uncle Jos, the quest for a mate, the discovery of lovely Frances. Their early years together had been a perfection. He had greedily accepted that as his due. He knew that he was making her happy, and she had made him happier than he had imagined it was possible to be. And then – almost as if a curse had come upon him – there had been the recollection of Blue Squirrel.

Promiscuous from an early age, he had never subscribed to the notion that a man need only love once. Why, then, did the recollection of Blue Squirrel and all he had experienced with her, why did it invade his love for Frances – and why did it have this effect of desolation?

In his dejection, he felt a fool. He felt that at various stages he had taken wrong turnings, thrown away precious gifts – and one precious gift in particular. Seeing the way the Wedgwood boys doted upon Coleridge, the eager way in which they believed in his genius, awoke in Byerley a sense of his lost talent as a writer, as a would-be poet, as a dramatist, as an actor. He had been going to make something of life! And now, what was he? A salesman, and a damned bad one at that! If he had loved Blue Squirrel, it would not have mattered a jot whether he were a salesman, an actor, a butcher a baker a candlestick maker. It was his betrayal of a great love which now subsumed the whole of his life to a consciousness of its own triviality. He saw clearly enough why young layabouts like Tom Wedgwood and Coleridge blew their brains out with narcotics, for the bare consciousness of life, its pointlessness.

That Blue Squirrel should have come back into his life, and that she should have returned to the works, this was strange, and bad enough. But that she should be married to Caleb Bowers! He knew his Blue Squirrel. He knew that she had never told Caleb about her former loves, and he knew that she never would, and that imposed upon him the duty of absolute silence. Break, my heart, for I must hold my tongue. Break, my heart, as the wild wind howled, as the waves rose above the sides of the ship, as the packet heaved and tossed its way to Holland.

Poor Heffie Bowers was desolate, too. Byerley rather despised his cousins for mocking her, which they did so openly. After Caleb's wedding, it was not long before Heffie's son Ted started courting, and she was left alone. It was at this period that she had gone to a revivalist meeting, one of the last which old Mr Wesley brought to Stoke. The hymns, the collective hysteria of the massed crowd, worked their magic. Heffie did not say that she had been converted, or that she had given her heart to the Lord, but she had begun the habit of chapelgoing – she frequented the newly built Wesleyan conventicle in Etruria – and Sally Wedgwood, in particular, was beastly about it, with jests about the Road to Damascus. Poor Heffie smiled at the teasing, a Christian martyr. Her thick springy hair had turned white.

The storm ceased an hour before dawn, and the sky glimmered, then turned a brilliant orange as the sun rose behind the church towers of The Hague.

And so the Barberini Vase, as they still sometimes called it, began its European journey.

In The Hague, it was met by Pa's old friend William Eden, now Lord Auckland, Ambassador Extraordinary, who arranged for a reception, attended by the Princess of Orange.

*My dear Lord*, wrote Jos from Etruria, *You have made my sons and my nephew happy beyond their power of expression . . . Your patriotic motives for assembling such an illustrious group at Your Excellency's dejeune are far above my praise . . .*

But they were not especially happy as they traipsed about Europe. Josiah had laid a burden upon them, to tour Europe, to collect debts – in Cologne, in Göttingen, in Königsberg, in Strasbourg, if possible in Paris. As they went, they were to show the Vase, and to stimulate trade. But these were not times for trade. As the tiresome young whelp Coleridge intoned, when surfacing from one of his debauches,

> Amid this tumult, Kubla heard from far
> Ancestral voices prophesying war.

The Germans they met were all frightened by what was happening in France. Solid merchants in blue or grey woollen coats, with buff-coloured stockings covering their stout legs, these Lutheran men of business held no brief for King Louis and his Austrian wife; nor did they take much pleasure in the alliance between the Emperor Leopold and the King of Prussia. But, as they entertained Byerley and young Josiah, they did not like what they heard from their representatives in Paris.

Young Josiah had very basic German, Cousin Byerley much better. Tom Wedgwood had none, and Coleridge, who was coming in order to learn the language, did not stop talking English for long enough to master the German rudiments.

—Don't worry, Cousin Byerley, he is heading for Tübingen, we'll leave him in Cologne before we head east.

—You speak, interposed one of the smiling, gentle, solid Lutheran merchants, of your young friend? He is a very brilliant man – no?

—A genius, said Josiah with eyes aflame. My brother and I have this sense that, well, our father has made so much money, we want to put it to good use. Our father is a man of science, a philosopher, as well as a merchant. He would not want all his money to be spent merely making money. We thought – we have thought . . .

He smiled, wondering which was the more correct form of the past tense.

—Either, said the Frankfurt merchant, reading his dilemma. *Wir haben gedacht* is perfectly in order.

—We have thought that we our young friend to help should.

—Your German is very good, said the merchant politely.

—His will become perfect. He intends to go to Königsberg and hear Kant lecture. He is already reading Lessing, and he wishes to translate Schiller.

—And you have all been reading *The Sorrows of Young Goethe?*

—But it is the best book ever written! exclaimed Tom, picking up the name of the title, but not much else which was said.

—Mr Josiah Wedgwood, Byerley returned to the theme of their dinner, would be happy to deliver, say, twenty or thirty dinner sets per month to your emporium, if you think you were in a position to sell them.

—In times of peace, we were selling more than that. After the great Frog Service, said the businessman. But with the situation now in France, I cannot believe that the peace can hold.

—Mr Wedgwood is sure that the Revolution will settle down, that after the initial disquiet, the men of common sense will prevail over the hotheads. He is convinced that the Jacobins will eventually yield to the moderates, and that there will be no bloodshed.

Their host smiled genially.

—We must all hope for peace. And then his glistening features darkened into greater seriousness.

—We must pray for peace, he said.

The Vase which they carried, often at such inconvenience, in the various diligences which took them through the German towns became, for Byerley, a symbol of his burden. Young Josiah, quiet and serious, would do his duty by the father's inheritance, and, where necessary, do his bit for the firm. But it was clear that he would prefer to be absorbed in his own thoughts (whatever these were), to be reading philosophy or scientific books, and to be pursuing country pursuits in a gentleman's house miles from the manufactory. In his decent, gentle way, young Josiah cared no more for the works than did Tom, with his philosophical preoccupations and his belief that he would one day solve the question of how to fix photographic images on paper.

Byerley was left holding the Vase. Byerley, who felt less and less competent either in the sphere of commerce or in the skills of manufacture, was left with the future of Josiah Wedgwood and Sons as a business.

In town after town, he heard himself repeating mantras. It was almost like a return to his career on the stage. His own German was much more fluent than young Josiah's, so it was he who was their spokesman. If the peace held, twenty or thirty dinner sets a month. No future for the Jacobins. France gently evolving into a parliamentary democracy. Mr Paine to be preferred to Mr Burke. As to the Vase – on the one side, we saw Death-in-Life: we saw fearfulness of the human race in the face of its dying; we saw the turning away from mortality. But on the other side of the Vase, we saw hope, we saw the chance of Immortality.

Young Josiah might, just might, achieve immortality, through his quiet experiments. Tom, if he could wean himself from opium and alcohol, almost surely would turn out to be an inventor of the first rank, easily as famous as Dr Darwin or his friend Mr Humphry Davy. But it was an important conditional, and if he could not stop over-indulging in the mind-rotting poppy and the fermented grape, he would go the way of their dissolute young friend Samuel. Poor saps, Tom and Jos, they were bankrolling Coleridge. They hoped, by offering him a hundred and fifty pounds a year, that he would master the German philosophy, and write a long, serious poem about the meaning of existence. Instead, he had merely got drunk every night, and begun – or so the two brothers admitted, to their alarm – to compose some foolish little poem about an old sailor on a mysterious voyage.

Byerley wondered whether to caution his namesake Tom not merely that he was throwing away good money on this young trickster, but also that he was threatening to destroy his own life. But the truth was, as Byerley bitterly knew, Tom Wedgwood at least had the chance of Immortality – of a sort. It was he, Byerley, whose life had begun to be no more than a quotidian routine, a meaningless drawing in and letting out of breath. There was no side of the Vase which depicted the real truth about life, which was that it simply went: that great love could be forgotten in the routines of marriage and sex; that high ambitions for one's mental and spiritual development were deferred, because of the simple need to earn a living; that dreams died, and the humdrum filling in of account books, changing of stockings, nursing of minor illnesses . . . these everyday things ceased to be seen as interruptions of life: they were life. And if your wife cried in the darkness, and you felt that it had all swept past in a meaningless hurry, well – there were people worse off than yourself.

In Cologne, they said goodbye to Coleridge, and he went, his long locks greasy, his knapsack full of German metaphysical philosophy which he scarcely understood, his pocketbook full of Wedgwood money.

# I4

TIME AND DEATH. THE EUROPEANS HAD SEEN THEIR FIGURES on the Vase, but only one man had ordered a copy, a merchant in Frankfurt. Time and Death, and no more any hope in death. The Infamy had been expunged, and replaced by a new Infamy.

But it was impossible not to be hopeful in Paris. Tom Wedgwood achieved his ambition, and reached Paris by the beginning of July. Crossing the French countryside, at all-but breakneck speed in the diligence – never mind breakneck, said Cousin Byerley, what of break-Vase – they found churches turned into shops, they found refugees swarming the roads towards the German borders, just as, later in their journey home, they would find them crowding on to the Channel packets. They lodged with young Watt, son of the inventor, who was fuming for the Revolution. It had not gone far enough. He detested the moderation of Lafayette and Condorcet. They must get rid of the King! Did the French really wish to end up with their equivalents of Mr Pitt and George III? The Girondins were being thrown out, and people spoke of Civil War. Mr Watt knew which side he was on. Further the Revolution, *de l'audace, et de l'audace!*

George Leveson-Gower, the British Ambassador, had left the capital by the Anniversary, the fourteenth of July, of the Storming of the Bastille. There was a great fête in the Champs de Mars, a bright day, with a vivid blue sky and no clouds. Sun scorched upon the

Revolution. The three Englishmen, Tom, young Josiah and Byerley, stood in the crowd with Watt and some other likeminded young foreigners. Byerley had to translate the speeches for them, but they joined in the songs. The crowds and the banners seemed to the three very different. To Josiah, they signalled, that morning, the beginning of a wonderful dawn in the history of humanity. To Byerley, however, the momentous events of European history, being played out before his eyes, were no more than a background. He was tired. He had borne the burden of the Vase's journey, and he felt his eyelids heavy. He knew that he should have been attending more closely to the flag-waving and cheering; he knew that here was a case when he could tell his children in future years that he had witnessed some great thing. The truth was that it all made very little impression upon him. He longed to be home, and wondered, with a chill in his heart, whether Fan and he could ever recapture their early joys. He had so often expounded the allegory of Time and Death depicted upon the Barberini Vase, but each time that he had done so, in German or in French, the story had, in his imagination, become his story. He was the seated one, staring anxiously across at Fan, who had her back to him. And Blue Squirrel sat in the middle dividing them as she always would. He had shot the Albatross, and there was no going back, and no redemption. As the crowds, and the young Wedgwood boys, roared in the Champs de Mars about the Bright Dawn, Byerley felt only an Ending.

Later that day, the three went to the ruins of the Bastille, where souvenir-hunters were gathering bits of rubble, but it was not a good time to be in Paris, and that evening the boys accepted Byerley's urging to find a coach and head for home. A week after they left, the Prussians declared war, and German armies marched over the French border from the Netherlands. The following January, the King of France died on the guillotine. Next month, France was at war with

England. Famine spread throughout the French countryside. More violence, more bloodshed, urged Jean-Paul Marat. And like an avenging angel, the tall beautiful figure of Charlotte Corday arrived in Paris from Caen and lifted her dinner knife upon Citizen Marat while he was in his bath. But what is he among so many? Marie Antoinette and her children went to the guillotine in October, with the crowds singing the Marseillaise, and by November, the Terror had engulfed France. The Revolution was eating its children. Time and Death, Time and Death, Time and Death.

# 15

WHEN SHE WAS FIFTY, ONE MORNING IN 1816, SUKEY WAS sitting in the drawing-room of her substantial house in Shrewsbury. Her son, looking at least four years taller and more solid than his seven years, stood on the hearth-rug, leaning slightly backwards. Though he had both his legs, his posture so exactly recalled that of his grandfather, Josiah Wedgwood, that she longed to capture the image – as her brother Tom might have been able to do, had his photographic experiments come to anything. Charles Darwin, this large boy, always called Bobby in the family, had been birds'-nesting and held in his hand an extraordinary trophy. Easily the size of a duck's egg, it was brown as a nut, and mottled like a harvest moon.

—It's a falcon, Mama. A peregrine, I think.

—Where did you find it?

—I had been watching them for several days, down on the Welsh Bridge. A pair of them. They swoop over the river and in that meadow beyond.

—Oh, darling Bobby, is that a good idea? How can the mother have baby falcons if you steal her eggs?

—Mama, have you seen Bobby – oh, there you are!

The boy's elder sister, Caroline, came into the room.

—Bobby, if you won't stay in the schoolroom and read with me in the mornings, Papa is going to send you to Mr Case's school with Ras. Mama, it's hopeless if he won't concentrate!

—He's been birds'-nesting, naughty boy.

—And yesterday, he killed a hare on the lawn with a marble.

—With a marble? Sukey could not keep the indulgent amusement out of her voice.

—It was with a sling, Mama. Like David in the Bible.

—David killed a giant, said his mother, not a defenceless hare.

—What Papa would think if he knew that Bobby was running about like a wild thing and neglecting his studies!

But Caroline had no need to speculate about her father's view of the situation. At that moment, Dr Robert Darwin came into the drawing-room, mid-sentence.

—That brother of yours, he was addressing his wife, not his daughter, is going to be the ruin of all of us. They are both so USELESS.

Sukey could see that her husband was already in one of those humours, where seething could erupt into a Vesuvius of rage. His huge frame – Robert, at twenty stone, was even bigger than his man-mountain father, and temperamentally less good-humoured – was quivering, even before he took in the presence of the children.

—Sukey, what in the name of thunder are you doing, playing with the children? Bobby is supposed to be at his books. Caroline, you are meant to be in the schoolroom teaching him Latin, not playing games with your mother. By God! How can you be a doctor like me if you know NOTHING?

Sukey watched the veins in her husband's temple, as he bellowed. Would the throbbing blue worms on the side of his whiskered head one day actually burst?

—Have I fathered another of them?

This, as he furiously gestured towards Bobby.

—Oh, my dear, said Sukey quietly.

—Your brother John running into bankruptcy! A banker! He could not administer a tuppenny stall in Shrewsbury market. Your idle brother Jos, letting the business slide – no wonder they've closed the London offices! That cousin of yours, Byerley, bungling the Etruria Works – none of the three of them fit to run ANYTHING, and they come to me, they come to me . . . Oh get out, get OUT, he shouted uncontrollably at the children. You are lucky! – he yelled at the retreating form of Bobby – not to feel my cane upon your back. Am I to be the ONLY man in the family with any sense?

So the storm raged, ending, as it so often did, with a reproach to his wife, as if she were personally responsible for her youngest son's dreaminess, or his preference for natural history over Latin grammar; or as if her brothers' lack of commercial acumen were to be laid at her door.

Even before she married Robert Darwin, in the year after her father's death, she had known him to be a choleric man. She had seen the occasional explosion even in his youth, when he had lost at tennis or received some supposed slight from one of his siblings. She remembered Robert aged fourteen knocking over the chess-board when he was cornered by one of her brothers. As children, the Wedgwood boys had tormented Squirt, as they called him, enjoying the ease with which the overweight lad could be satisfyingly 'brought to the boil'.

Living with the rages, as a wife, was less easy. She soon taught herself a technique. Non-response was better than any response, and withdrawal from the scene as quickly as possible was the best remedy. He would shout after her as she swept from the room, but afterwards, when he was in a better humour, he would simmer down. Sometimes, embarrassingly to them both, he would attempt an apology.

It was better, she found, to undertake some task, even an unnecessary task, to drive away the feelings of hurt, the quivering of shock, the foolishly angry, though unspoken, ripostes which formed themselves in her head after one of his outbursts. That day, in 1816, the year before Sukey herself died of stomach cancer, she invented the task of tidying the books and papers which she kept in the wall-closet, in her own little boudoir next to the marital bedroom. There were letters here between her father and mother during their strange marriage; and letters she herself had written from London, that year she had spent living with the Bentleys. Her childish perceptions of London life – a glimpse of Dr Johnson on the pavement as they hurtled past in a chaise, the Greek Street salerooms full of aristocrats, dinners at the Bentleys' house in which Mr Griffiths spoke of his adventures among the Cherokee, all these had been recorded for her mother and father. What had never been written down, but now flooded back in a tide of memory, were all her thoughts and feelings. She remembered that this was the year in which it became clear that she would have an arranged marriage. At first, Cousin Byerley had been her appointed sire, until Dr Erasmus Darwin stepped in to rescue her. (To rescue her? Or merely to reserve her for his strange hulk of a son?)

Together with the letters of that vanished era, Sukey had placed a very small morocco-bound volume of Voltaire's *Candide*. On its flyleaf, in a tiny and very un-English version of copperplate script, were the words *A Mlle Wedgwood avec mes sentiments les plus respectueuses, Jean Potet, le 15ième avril, 1780*. Her birthday!

She held the little book in her long right hand and with the left, she held the window shutter, and looked down over the well-tended gardens of the Mount, past the shrubbery, and over the treetops to the Severn which swirled beyond in its foaming springtide energy.

Sukey was not given to self-pity, still less to regret. She had made what most women in England would regard as a 'good' marriage. Her husband was the best respected man in Shrewsbury. As a doctor and a banker, he knew the secrets, one way or another, of most of his fellow citizens. He was highly competent in both capacities. And, viewing the matter with detachment, as she was sometimes able to do, she could see that he had every reason to be impatient of Jos and John and Cousin Byerley. There was still enough Wedgwood money to keep them afloat, even though John had lost so much with his failed banking ventures, and Byerley was no businessman. She knew that her father had been a genius. There was no hope of Nature repeating the trick in each generation. As her eye took in the spring-time peace of Shrewsbury, the bursting of elm and ash buds, the floating of newly arrived swifts against the jasper blue of the sky, she became momentarily a timeless being; the whole of her existence upon earth, from dawning consciousness in childhood until now, was contained in this potent moment of meditation. She became aware of all her half-century of experience. Lifted from the wound of Robert Darwin's latest rage, she took in all of his childhood too. She remembered his father, with big sausage hands, feeling beneath her skirts, and breathing heavily as a thumb moved. She remembered her languid, melancholy mother, and Sally's father, the cheese merchant, with his cruel thin face, and she simultaneously was aware of her thin-faced, clever brother Tom, who, even before the opiates took their toll, had the look of death in his eyes.

If Sukey had run the business – as perhaps Mary Wollstonecraft would have imagined she should? But, even then, although she had a more practical turn than her brothers, and more money sense than Byerley (who had less?), could she have made trade pick up after the war? She thought of the rows and rows of Etruscan women in the decorating room, painting cups and plates and chattering as they did so. She thought of Mrs Willcox, in much earlier days, painting the

Frog Service. She thought of Caleb's wife, her strong brown hands submitting the grey moist clay to her skilled command. Why not a pottery run entirely by women? It was strange that, for all their progressive ideas, neither Pa nor Dr Erasmus had really much notion of the Rights of Women. And yet, both had made sure that she was a person of education. Like her mother, Sukey knew languages, and she was easily the best-read Wedgwood of her generation. How strange it was, in that almost extracorporeal awareness of the whole of her existence at once, to be aware of Mama and Pa, of all the Etruscan children, of the whole tribe of them, both as children and as grown-ups, and of their progeny, of Pa's energy and cleverness, of all the money he made, and of all the changes it wrought in their lives, of all the households of gentlefolk, dotted about southern England, which it had engendered, of the many children and the cousinage.

Standing beside the Shrewsbury window, the whole of her fifty years of life contained in this split second of awareness, Sukey watched her hulking husband stride across the lawn of the Mount and head for his greenhouses. It was there, surrounded by his tender shrubs, his azaleas, his potted orange trees and his ferns, that the poor man could cease to be the erupting Vesuvius and return to his decent, intelligent normality. Sukey was far too conscious of her good fortune, in material and personal terms, to regret her marriage. Marriage to Robert had been a continuation of her childhood, not a break from it. They shared a world of associations and value; they had read the same books, knew the same people, cherished the same hopes for themselves and for England. Poor M. Potet! He had long since faded. In her split-second mystic reverie, however, she had recalled her childish anguish, the tremor which the young man's mere presence in the room could cause her. Only in that moment, incidentally, did she know, for the first time, that this – but of course! – had been Mama's reason for sending her away from Etruria for a year, and lodging her with the Bentleys! What would have happened to her, had she married for love? The question suggested a condition of things which was in its way unimaginable. Presumably, those who marry for love either continue in a condition of happiness denied to almost every other person on this planet; or they endure disillusionment and loss of faith.

There had been no disappointment in Sukey's marriage because she had not entered into it with any very high hopes. Sukey and Robert accepted one another's faults from the beginning. And the passage of time, and the coming of their children, had brought with it a shared set of emotions which contained great fondness for one another. Sukey had learnt these lessons watching her mother and father in their struggles. She was schooled for such a life, and the story of Sally and Josiah, from the sawing off of his leg, to his death, had all been a preparation for her own journey through existence.

—Oh, Pa, she said aloud to the genius who, more than twenty years after his death, still haunted her. Oh, Pa.

# LAST

—AAW, AAW, AAAAW.

—I think not, sir.

—Aaw, aaw — ooth.

Mr James Bent, the surgeon who had removed Josiah's leg in 'sixty-eight was, nearly twenty-seven years later, peering into his patient's mouth, which he held open with one finger. The gesture of holding the flesh of his cheek with his thumb, and with one finger stuck inside the gob, recalled the digital motions necessary for throwing a pot. Josiah had the half-impression that the doctor was going to throw his head, lump of clay that it was, on a wheel and fashion it into a vase.

—There is some sign of decay, undoubtedly, said the medical gentleman, but I cannot ascribe the swelling of your face to a rotten tooth.

—Then to what? asked Josiah, when the man's finger was removed.

James Bent merely shook his head.

Wedgwood's face was a terrible colour, both florid and sickly. The tops of the cheekbones were almost scarlet, but the skin around the eyes was yellowy orange, and the eyes themselves were bloodshot. He wore no wig. The scrubs of hair on his big skull were wet with perspiration.

—I advise that we send for Dr Darwin.

—He'll be here next week anyway, said the patient. He said it from far away. Bent was there, and Josiah's head was there, a throbbing lump of pain. But where was he? Thoughts came and went, but it was as if he had to push them to the forefront. So Darwin would be here in a week.

In answer to the long silence of his physician,

—And yo' think I shan't be 'ere?

More silence. The pain danced and prodded, an appalling kind of music in his head, which tried to stop the words coming. But Bent's face was still there. Josiah could see the sawbone's face. Sawbones. Show a leg.

—Tell me, man. Should I send for the children? For Byerley?

Letters were dashed off, by Chisholm, to the boys. John and Josiah were spending Christmas at Cresselly, a two-day journey, if snow and ice permitted travel at all. Tom was with Coleridge in the North, where snow lay thick. Cousin Byerley could, however, be reached in London and sent word that he had begun his journey. Erasmus Darwin, to whom a rider had been dispatched as soon as Mr Bent's diagnosis was pronounced, came in the evening. He brought his son Robert, also a doctor, to Etruria.

Bent's wheels had skidded on the gravel drive. The world was coated with ice. The gentle slopes were white with frost and mist. Trees and bottle ovens were all smudged in whiteness, in a silver cold.

Bent's word for what he had seen in Wedgwood's mouth did not need to be uttered: mortification. The seemingly inexhaustible was about to be exhausted. The great Energy was spent. The women gathered.

—You're so hot, said Sally, and the house is so miserable, so miserably icy.

—Hot and shivering.

—

—He said something but you can't make out what it is.

—

—E isna rart sat int chayur. E'd be better off in bed.

He looked from one face to the other. The image of his own head as a lump of clay would not be dismissed. And he thought of the Cherokee lady, her long brown fingers working the old magic which he himself knew so well, pulling the clay into shape. He watched her fingers now, smoothing the wet top of the vase with her small sponge.

—

—I think he is saying something.

—And yer put water on 'is lips and he's sat that still yer doan't knaw lahk if it's what he wants.

—Oh, Pa.

—Is Pappy going to die?

—Just hold his hand, Kitty, don't try to talk to him.

—Kitty said Pappy was going to die, that wasn't very kind.

—It was only what Cook said, and Judy.

—But they didn't say it where he could hear it.

—Children, no more of this.

—Mother, it was Kitty, who—

—Oh, shut up, you two. Shall I put water on your brow, Pa?

—

The Cherokee woman had potter's hands. A potter's eye. Knew how to do it.

—We could try an' sing 'im an hymn, even if 'e disna jine in.

—I don't think so, Heffie.

A little later, however, there was a stirring. His own hands being held in Heffie's, as she sang, very softly, *Love Divine all Loves Excelling*. She punctuated the sung verses with the sort of expressions she had used for the children when they were fractious.

# The Potter's Hand

It was a comfort to feel Heffie's hands. All woman, our Heff. They's a good noss, our Heff. Bentley had said it once. Bentley knew about women. Should he have married our Heff?

> —Jaysu, Thar art a' compassion,
> Pewer unbinded luv Tharart
> Visit uz wi' tha compassion
> Enter every trembling Art . . .

She sang so soft, mother. Josiah could feel the rough ends of his mother's red fingers. The blackened cracks in the red finger ends made a marbled effect – dark red, pink, cream. What temp had they been fired at? Ten degrees otter un theyda cracked wide open. Mother.

—He's trying to talk?

—How long's he been like this?

—Yesterday he could talk. Now, it's this muttering.

—Pa, it's Jack and Jos, come from Cresselly.

—We came as fast as we could, sir.

—

—He seems to be in pain.

—M-m-more laudanum, sir, mix a few more grains of opium into the mixture.

—Is that safe?

They'd brought in Bentley. Good of him to come. My dear sir! Tell me about the London end. Trade in the saleroom. Where was Mother? Mother? Don't let Mother go!

—He's always gripping the sheet. He almost tears and twists it.

—

—Maybe if we give him a glass of wine?

The twisted sheets were riding too near the sun. The crumpled linen is the Stubbs bas-relief of Phaeton. Too close. Too hot. Too, too hot. The horses are galloping against the sky.

—Pa, you need covering up!

—Father, try to lie still.

—Lah dine, Jos, pet.

—Loh ans giower . . .

That was strange, the world had somehow moved. All the faces, some in terracotta, some in purest white biscuit, were frozen about him. But the walls, the pilasters, the swags and the paintings were performing a *danse macabre*. On his head was not a wig, not a pillow, it were a great saggar o' peen. At least e were still, even if rest ot cride, all arind couldna keep theysels still!

—Jos, are you sure?

Sally, who hardly ever touched Pa, had moved forward to take his elbow. Sukey took his other arm.

—He's saying he wants something.

—E nades tubby back in bed!

Heffie was right.

With two women holding each elbow, they staggered from the chair and towards the door.

—A l-l-little walk will not hurt him. H-h-he might need the stool.

—E wet issel, bless 'im.

—We'll get him t-t-tidied up, Heffie.

—We're all right, said Sally briskly. We can manage. I've had eight children.

—Get him into night clothes.

—He wanted to sit up, said Byerley to the Wedgwood young men, until you came.

They looked at one another – Tom, Cousin Byerley, Jos and Jack. The implication of what was happening had been hovering over them all since they came to manhood. But now it was really happening.

This. The works. The workforce. The practical day-to-day running of the business. The salerooms in Bath and London. The travelling salesmen. The seeing-off of industrial spies and commercial rivals. The answering of letters, the inspection of the machinery, the maintenance of discipline. The need for new designs, new technology. The drawing up of catalogues. The reading of balance sheets. The weight of its quotidian tedium, this great machine of Josiah's making, fell upon them all in the midst of the sickroom crisis.

When Mother and Sukey came back, one of them said,

— . . . with Dr Darwin.

Tom Wedgwood's face was the colour of a moist field mushroom. It looked as if it did not know the meaning of the phrase which one of his brothers was uttering –

—too much of that opium.

—One of us can go and sit with him, once he's settled, said Sally.

—We'll take it in turns, Mother. You need your rest.

—I'm all right.

In her bravery, half-scold, half-defiance of Fate, there returned a bit of the northernness – Ah'm all raht – which she had all but lost since association with the Bentleys and the Darwins, and which Jos never lost. Sukey retained touches of it – short 'a' for Bath and castle, 'appen for perhaps.

—He w-w-w-

The letter W was ever the worst with Dr Darwin. He was? He wished? He washed?

—wwwwww

—Shall I go to him? asked John.

Dr Darwin waved both hands across one another, a conjuror's gesture, while his words refused to come.

—alone. W-w-w- b-better alone.

—He wants to be alone? asked Sally. How do you know?

—Sally W-w- Sally, I've known you both thirty years, said Dr Darwin quietly.

The coming and going of the hours did not bring consolation exactly, but they brought an excuse to be doing particular things at particular times. Otherwise, there was nothing to do but wait. Dr Darwin told them that there might be days like this, or even weeks.

—He's a strong one.

So, they went through the formalities of dinner, walks in the mist, tea, cards, supper. Bed, even if no sleep came. Breakfast, walks in the mist, dinner.

It was after tea on the first day that Heffie came into the drawing-room and said,

—Eez locked and bolted izzel in t' room!

A little gaggle rushed across the hall and up the staircase. Everyone who made the journey had the same thought, but none expressed it – namely, that they would soon be carrying him, or rather it, down this staircase; and would it not have been easier to have made up a bed in one of the downstairs rooms?

—E musta summow got ite o' bed an locked issen in, cunning divil!

—D-d-do we have a ladder?

Cousin Byerley was the one who was sent to fetch the ladder and place it against the first-storey window. When the partly farcical pro-cedure had been undertaken, with one of the hands from the works needing to help him erect the double-ladder, and with the bottom of the thing slithering on the icy gravel, Byerley found his face peering into the room. Josiah sat upright, with a blanket round his shoulders. His eyes were open, and he had a glass in his hand. For a moment, Byerley felt reassured. The figure in the winged armchair could have been any old gentleman imbibing port after dinner. But although his eyes peered beyond the window, Josiah did not meet Byerley's anxious gaze.

—Uncle Jos? Uncle Jos!

Then, absurdly,

—Can you hear me? Are you all right, Uncle Jos?

—Luk after theysen, Mr Tom! called the hand from below. This ladder's a booger in t' frost.

A sacking offence in the days of Josiah's vigour, to call a ladder a booger. But now his authority was gone, and he was both there and not there.

—We can't leave our father up there, said John imperiously.

—My d-d-dear John, not for ever, no. But if w-w-w-w if he c-considers it right to be there, it is his choice.

—To lock us all out? There was terror in Sukey's voice as she said it.

—If th-that's what he w-w-w—

—No one could want that, said Sally petulantly.

—Animals go away alone to d-d-die, said Dr Darwin quietly. A d-d-death-bed is a th-th-theatre and our J-Jos w-w-w n-not a man of the theatre.

There were many expeditions to the landing over the next two days. Anxious straining of ears at the keyhole could make out groans, mutters, heavy breathing. A few more ascents of the ladder enabled them to see, through the windowpane, the great Master Potter slumped in the chair.

—Has he taken enough . . . enough to poison himself? asked Josiah the Younger.

—H-how much is that?

The faces at the windows and the noises at the door had become, for the patient in the chair, of no more interest than the stirring of mice behind a wainscot. Time had stopped at about the time he had last forgotten to wind his fob-watch. Night, day, dawn, dusk, were all one. Names had gone. Mother would be here soon. Until then, the battle was with the pain. In one fob-pocket, there was a twist of paper, with ten grains of opium left. The jaw throbbing, the head throbbing, the missing leg stabbing him with unbearable torture. Pain was all there was. Pain, and the destruction of pain. Had Time still been going on, he would have been able to observe that he spent about an hour and a half establishing the whereabouts of that twist of paper and pouring the remaining grains into the elegant little Madeira glass of laudanum.

There was some noise, at just the moment when the pain, blessedly and briefly, left him. Then there was a moment of terror that he might vomit out the palliative, and be faced with the pain and no opium. Someone was saying,

—Aasier to tak ite t' winder than bost open doer.

What was he doing? Phaeton, waving a screwdriver against the blazing glory of the Morning Sun? Behind him was Mr Bentley. Ahead was Mother. Beneath the bunch of elm branches sat that familiar figure from whom he had been limping as fast as his peg leg could carry him ever since the pox had tried to snatch him half a century before. Mother on the Portland Vase. Death, holding out her hand and welcoming him into the Underworld.

# AFTERWORD

*THE POTTER'S HAND* IS THE STORY OF A REAL FAMILY whose very name became synonymous with English pottery. The book, however, is a novel, which contains some characters who are real – Josiah Wedgwood and his family – and some, such as Caleb and Heffie Bowers, and Blue Squirrel, who are inventions. The broad outlines of the story, and most of the details, are true. Josiah Wedgwood did indeed buy his white clay from the Cherokee people; his nephew Tom Byerley, who eventually took over the running of the firm, was an actor in America at the time of the outbreak of the War of Independence. I found, however, in the course of composing and rewriting my story, that the demands of history and the demands of art are somewhat different. I have made the fictional Tom Byerley a little younger than he was in reality. I hope his many ancestors (he had eleven children) will forgive the liberty I have taken. Those who know the history of the real Josiah Wedgwood and his achievements will notice that I have altered dates and rearranged historical events. For example, he actually finished his famous Frog Service for the Empress of Russia a few years before the war with America, and the two events were unconnected in history. In my book, they became intertwined, and served as a prism through which to see Wedgwood's attitude to the convulsions in the world. Nearly all the letters in the book – from Wedgwood, from Voltaire, and from the Empress, for example – are invented. Only the letter from Flaxman to Wedgwood, telling him of the arrival in London of the Barberini, or so-called Portland, Vase quotes from an actual source. The book is meant to be read as fiction, even though it is intended, in part, as an act of homage to one of the great men of our history.

*A. N. W.*

# A NOTE ON THE AUTHOR

A. N. WILSON grew up in Staffordshire, where his father was Managing Director of Josiah Wedgwood & Sons. He was educated at Rugby and New College, Oxford. A Fellow of the Royal Society of Literature, he holds a prominent position in the world of literature and journalism. He is a prolific and award-winning biographer and celebrated novelist. His most recent novel, *Winnie and Wolf*, was longlisted for the 2007 Man Booker Prize. He lives in North London.